Doll Values:

Antique to Modern
13th Edition

Linda Edward

PAGE PUBLISHING, INC.
New York, NY

First originally published by Page Publishing, Inc. 2017

ISBN 978-1-64082-069-2 (Paperback)
ISBN 978-1-64082-070-8 (Digital)

Printed in the United States of America

ACKNOWLEDGMENTS

Thank you to the following collectors and auction houses for sharing their dolls and those of their friends' for this issue of Doll Values—Cathy Adams, Alderfer Auctions, Sara Bernstein, Joe Bucchi, Ben Cassara, Gloria Duddlesten, Kate Eaton, Joan Farrell, *Lynette Gross*, Jean Grout, Moira Hatton, Elaine Holda, Ladenburger Spielzeugauktion, Doreen Landess, Ann Lloyd, Tammy Loranger, McMasters-Harris Auctions, Sherry Minton, Morphy Auctions, Gary Passamonte, Susan Robison, Joyce Warnock Romer, Elizabeth Schmahl, Skinner Inc., Patricia Snyder, Nancy Stronczek, Sweetbriar Auctions, Carla Thompson, Domenic Vecchioli, *Terri Viola*, Suzanne Vlach, Helen Welsh, Philip Weiss Auctions, and Withington Auction Inc.

I would also like to thank every doll researcher and collector who has generously shared their dolls and knowledge through the many fine reference books, articles, seminars, special exhibits, and doll club programs. Without this constant exchange of information, we would all be searching in the dark for answers.

Finally, I must thank my husband, Al Edward, for his encouragement, support, and belief in me and the work I pursue.

INTRODUCTION

This book is a tool for the collector, a place to start on a journey of study that can enrich a lifetime. The best piece of advice this collector ever received was "buy every doll reference book you can find." Each volume, be it old or new, contains some piece of information that will be of aid to the collector. Building a reference library of your own will pay you back many times over in the knowledge it will bring you, knowledge that will ultimately allow you to make better decisions when purchasing a doll for your own collection. In addition to building a reference library, I would also suggest that you take every opportunity to look at dolls wherever you go. Nothing beats firsthand examination. Visit every doll museum and special display you can find. Go to shows and really look at the dolls that interest you most. Join a doll club to learn more and share your discoveries with others. All these experiences will put you in a better position to understand and evaluate a doll when you are considering a purchase.

The question of course is, how much is a doll worth? It is the question we contend with when buying our dolls, inheriting our dolls, insuring our dolls, and in deciding to sell our dolls. In the doll world, there are basically two types of value: historic value and monetary value. Historic value speaks to how important an item is to us and to the world in general. Does an item teach us something about the past, is it significant to some particular event or person, does an item have special sentimental value to us personally? This type of value, although important, is not always reflected in an item's monetary value. Monetary value or market value relates to how much it would cost to go out and purchase any particular item at the present time. Market value is collector driven. Demand for particular items, combined with the current economic climate, determine the market value of a doll. In other words, a perfectly wonderful example of any given doll will vary in market value during differing economic conditions. This makes certain times good selling times and other times good buying times. This book can be a guide to helping the collector make wise decisions in regard to their collecting actions.

The Current Marketplace

The world of doll value—that is, the marketplace dollar amount that a doll currently commands—is an ever-changing landscape. The dolls themselves remain what they are physically, historically, artfully, but collectors' attitudes do change. Economy and collector interests have major effects on a doll's market value. In compiling the information for this edition, some interesting trends have emerged. Antique dolls, both common and rare, have, for the most part, come down in value in recent years. Exceptional examples, particularly those in original clothing, continue to command higher prices, but the average example of most antiques dolls is still well below what it was fifteen years ago, although values are recovering from the recession values of five or six years ago. Numerous older and important collections have come to the marketplace in the past two years, and this has led to a new availability of older and rarer dolls that were less attainable in the past. This means collectors can be more choosy in deciding on their next purchase.

A new generation of collector has also entered the collecting area. Dolls of the 1960s–80s are rising in value as more collectors hunt for the dolls of their childhoods. Excellent condition examples of dolls of this period have risen in the past two-year period.

What does this mean to the buyer? It means pay accordingly. There is nothing wrong with buying a doll in less than perfect condition but do not pay a premium price for it, and by the same token do not expect to get a premium price when selling a doll in less than perfect condition. Buy the best example of a doll that your budget allows and enjoy having it in your collection!

Evaluating Dolls

When evaluating any doll, there are several questions to ask oneself. These relate to identification, quality, originality, condition, rarity, and value. Each component is important to the overall picture of any doll. All dolls should be thoroughly examined before making a purchase.

Identification, what is this doll? A doll is classified by the material from which its head is made; therefore, a doll with a composition head on a cloth body will be considered a composition doll, or a doll with a papier-mâché head on a leather body will be considered a papier-mâché doll, and so on. Look for and learn about maker's marks. These will be of invaluable aid in identifying the doll you are looking at. Many manufacturers marked their dolls on the back of the head or on the torso. An appendix of maker's initials and an appendix of known mold numbers are included in the back of this book to assist you.

Quality, as stated by Patsy Moyer in the first edition of this book, "All dolls are not created equal." Any model of doll made by any particular manufacturer can range vastly in quality depending on the conditions on the day it was made. Remember these dolls were produced in factories, which in many cases turned out thousands of dolls a year. How worn was the mold when this doll was poured, what weather conditions affected the materials it was made from, how tired was the worker who cleaned or painted a particular doll that day? If you line up 6:00 AM 390s, you will be looking at six different degrees of quality of finish. Therefore, when preparing to make a purchase, consider each example of doll carefully from a standpoint of quality. A sharply molded, evenly textured, well-painted doll will always be of more value than an example of the same doll with blurry molding, uneven texture, or poor quality painting.

Originality is another important component of a doll evaluation. Does the doll have the correct eyes, wig, body type, clothing? Each of these parts adds value to the doll, and dolls on incorrect bodies or with replaced clothing or wigs should not bring the same amount in the marketplace as examples in all original condition.

Condition, what is the overall condition of the doll? Check carefully to look for damage or repair to the doll. In most cases, a damaged or repaired doll will not be worth as much as a perfect example.

Rarity is perhaps one of the most important aspects of doll evaluation. How unusual is this doll? How many were made and have survived? How difficult would it be to find another example of this doll today? Sometimes rarity can cause us to forgive problems of originality or condition that would in a more common doll deter us from adding a particular example to our collection.

Value takes into account all the aforementioned qualifications we have discussed and combines them with somewhat more elusive components, such as collector demand and trends. At various points in time, collectors tend to favor certain dolls. A good example of this can be seen in the value of the Bye-Lo baby. Every generation of collectors tends to start out collecting the dolls they had or wanted as children. In the 1950s and 1960s, many adult collectors eagerly sought the Bye-Lo baby from the 1920s, and the dolls achieved comparatively high market price. In the past twenty years, the value of the Bye-Lo has changed very little compared to other antique dolls because collector demand for them has quieted down.

How to Use This Book

The goal of this book is to assist you in figuring out the current market value of a doll you are interested in buying or selling. Unless otherwise noted, the values stated in this volume represent dolls in good overall condition with original or appropriate clothing. When looking at the values presented here, gauge the particular doll you are considering accordingly. Allow a lower value for dolls that do not meet the standard for the values listed here. This is especially important in judging vintage collectible or modern dolls. These must be in perfect and completely original condition with appropriate hang tags to attain the values listed in this guide. For example, an all original #3 Barbie in good condition will bring approximately half the price of the same doll mint-in-box.

This book is laid out in alphabetical order. You will notice that it is not divided into "antique" and "modern" sections as some other books are. The reason for this choice is threefold. First, the line between antique and modern is not as clear-cut in doll collecting as it is in other areas. In furniture, for instance, a piece must be at least one hundred years old to be considered antique, whereas in car collecting a vehicle that is twenty-five years old is considered antique. In doll collecting, the line is blurry although it generally falls somewhere in the neighborhood of seventy-five years. Dolls thirty to seventy-five years old are most often referred to as "collectible vintage," and dolls thirty years old or less are usually referred to as modern. Second, many doll-making companies were in business for such long periods of time that they produced dolls that would now be considered antique as well as dolls that fall into the collectible vintage and modern categories. Third, it is the belief of this author that by not creating barriers between dolls of different ages we see a more complete picture of the doll world and promote a better understanding of the history of the dolls we love and of our fellow collectors.

As stated previously, this book is laid out in an alphabetical order by the manufacturer's name or by general type. Most dolls are marked in some way that indicates their maker. Wherever possible, those markings have been included for reference. The general-type headings include dolls made of like materials. Under these headings, you will find dolls made by small companies, or about which little is known as well as unmarked, and as yet unattributable dolls.

The values listed in this book are compiled from several sources including auction prices, online auction prices, dealer asking prices, dealer prices realized, as well as other sources. These values are then compiled, analyzed, and averaged. Although the collecting world is now much more global than it was even just a few years ago, there are still some regional differences in value that are generated by collector interest and doll availability in certain areas. This book is meant as a guide and is not the definitive word on doll value. Ultimately, a doll is worth whatever a particular collector wishes to pay for it. Neither this author nor the publisher of this book take any responsibility for any decision or action taken by an individual on the basis of the information presented here. As stated earlier, this book is one more tool for the collector to use in their decision-making process.

Finally, I will say that study, evaluation, and value, although important, are not the bottom line in doll collecting. Ultimately, we each need to "follow our bliss" as it were, and buy dolls that mean something to us and enrich our lives and collections.

Collectors seeking to learn more about dolls and exchange doll knowledge can turn to a national organization whose goals are education, research, preservation, and enjoyment of dolls. The United Federation of Doll Clubs can tell you if a doll club in your area is accepting members or tell you how to become a member-at-large. You may write for more information at:

United Federation of Doll Clubs, Inc.

10900 North Pomona Avenue

Kansas City, MO 64153

Phone: 816-891-7040

Fax: 816-891-8360

www.ufdc.org

CODES

GREEN UPPERCASE **Main Category/ Maker's Name or Doll Type**
For example: ADVERTISING DOLLS

Red   **First subcategory, usually a**
                        name of the doll, company,
                        or material
                        ex: Gerber Baby

Blue Italics   **Second subcategory**
                        ex: 1979–1985

Black   **Third subcategory**
                        ex: Talker

ADVERTISING DOLLS

19" Kleeko the Eskimo for Clicquot Club Soda, composition: $150. **Photo courtesy of Morphy Auctions.**

Dolls of various materials, made by a variety of manufacturers, to promote commercial brands or specific products. Doll in good condition with original clothing and accessories.

Aunt Jemima, **cloth (uncut panels will bring more), Aunt Jemima, Uncle Moses, Diana, and Wade Davis**

16"... $100.00–125.00

Blue Bonnet, 1986, for Nabisco, cloth doll by Dakin

10"... $8.00–12.00

Babbitt Cleanser Girl, **made for B. T. Babitt Co (Bab-O Cleanser) by Fortune Doll Co., hard plastic, wigged, sleep eyes, high heel feet**

10½"... $30.00–40.00

Bandy, **1929, made by Cameo, composition head, wood segmented body, marked on hat "General Electric Radio," designed by J. Kallus**

18½"... $1,100.00–1,200.00

Bonnie Breck, 1971, Hasbro, marked "Made in Hong Kong," vinyl head, plastic body

9"... $25.00–30.00

Campbell's Kids, **1910 on, based on Grace Drayton's drawings**

Composition–painted and molded hair, mark: "EIH © 1910"; cloth label on sleeve, "The Campbell Kids// Trademark by //Joseph Campbell// Mfg. by E.I. Horsman Co."
Composition on cloth body

10"–12".. $100.00–125.00

15"... $175.00–225.00

all Composition

8"–11".. $200.00–250.00

15"–16".. $300.00–350.00

16" Hotpoint for Hotpoint Electric Heating Company, made by Cameo, composition: $850. **Photo courtesy of Morphy Auctions.**

16" The Selling Fool for General Electric, made by Cameo, composition & wood: $1,000. **Photo courtesy of Philip Weiss Auctions.**

Vinyl–**Ideal, painted and molded hair, 1950s**

    8"...$25.00–30.00

Vinyl, 1970s–80s, maker unknown

    10"–11".. $20.00–25.00

Clicquot Club Eskimo, 1939, Reliable Doll Co, composition, painted eyes, plush snowsuit

    14–19"...$150.00–175.00

Colgate Fab Soap Princess Doll, **ca. 1951**

    5½" $12.00–18.00

Cream of Wheat, **Rastus, printed cloth doll, uncut panel will bring more**

    16"...$35.00–45.00

Gerber Baby, **1936 to present. An advertising and trademark doll for Gerber Products, a baby food manufacturer located in Fremont, Michigan. More for black or special sets with accessories.**

1936, **cloth one-piece doll, printed girl or boy, holds can**

    8"...$200.00–250.00

1955–1958, **Sun Rubber Company, designed by Bernard Lipfert, vinyl**

    12"–18".. $70.00–80.00

1965, **Arrow Rubber & Plastic Co., vinyl**

    14"...$125.00–150.00

1972–1973, **Amsco, Milton Bradley, vinyl**

    10"...$20.00–30.00

    14"–18".. $30.00–40.00

1979–1985, **Atlanta Novelty, vinyl, flirty eyes, cloth body**

    17"...$35.00–50.00

    black version.................................... $55.00–70.00

Talker

    17"...$80.00–100.00

Collector Doll, **christening gown, basket**

    12"...$75.00–90.00

Porcelain, **limited edition**

    17"...$275.00–325.00

1989–1992, **Lucky Ltd., vinyl**

    6"...$12.00–18.00

    11"...$35.00–40.00

    14–16"...$35.00–40.00

1994–1996, **Toy Biz, Inc., vinyl**

    8"...$15.00–20.00

    15"...$25.00–30.00

Battery operated

    12–13"...$25.00–30.00

Talker

    14"...$35.00–40.00

    17"...$45.00–50.00

Green Giant, **Sprout, 1973**

    10½" $18.00–25.00

Hotpoint Devil, **for GE Hotpoint, 1930s, made by Cameo, composition head, wooden segmented body**

    16"...$800.00–900.00

Kellogg's cereals

Goldilocks & Three Bears, **set of four, printed cloth**

    12"–15"...$120.00–150.00

Rice Crispies, Sanp, Crackle, Pop, **printed cloth**

    16"...$35.00–45.00

Little Debbie, **1972, made by Horsman, all vinyl with rooted hair**

    11"...$18.00–25.00

Miss Minute Maid, **1950s, hard plastic doll by Virga or Fortune Doll Co, wigged, sleep eyes**

    10"...$20.00–28.00

Mr. Peanut, 1940s, segmented wooden

    9"...$100.00–125.00

Prince Macaroni, **mail-in premium dolls, vinyl, dressed in costumes from the provinces of Italy**

    6¼" $15.00–20.00

Sunbeam Bread

Miss Sunbeam, **by Horsman, all vinyl, rooted hair**

　14"...$20.00–35.00

Swiss Miss Hot Chocolate, **1977, cloth doll, painted features, yarn hair**

　16"...$10.00–$15.00

"The Selling Fool," **1926, made by Cameo, wood segmented body, hat represents radio tube, composition advertising doll for RCA Radiotron**

　16"...$800.00–1,000.00

Uneeda Biscuit Boy, **1914, made by Ideal**

　15"...$350.00–425.00

ZuZu, **1916, composition doll made by Ideal to advertise ginger snaps made by the National Biscuit Co.**

　14"...$175.00–225.00

ALABAMA BABY

1900–1925, Roanoke, Alabama. Ella Gauntt Smith, cloth over plaster doll, stitched on skull cap, painted features. Tab jointed at shoulders and hips, painted feet may be bare with stitched toes or have shoes painted in pink, blue, black, brown, or yellow.

Earlier model with applied ears

　11"–14"..$1,500.00–2,200.00

　18"–24"..$1,800.00–2,400.00

Wigged

　24"...$1,800.00–2,400.00

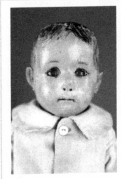

12" Alabama Baby, Ella Smith, cloth: $1,900. **Photo courtesy of McMasters Harris Apple Tree Doll Auctions.**

Black

14"–18" $4,800.00–5,500.00

18" in excellent conditon sold for $13,200 at auction

20"–22" $6,000.00–6,200.00

Later model with molded ears, bobbed hairstyle

14"–16" $1,800.00–1,900.00

18"–22" $1,900.00–2,100.00

Wigged

30".. $1,000.00

Black

14"–18" $2,800.00–3,000.00

20"–22" $3,800.00–5,800.00

MADAME ALEXANDER

16" David Copperfield, Alexander Doll Company, cloth: $550. **Photo courtesy of Morphy Auctions.**

16" Little Women, Alexander Doll Company, cloth: $2,200. **Photo courtesy of Sara Bernstein's Dolls.**

1912–present, New York City. In 1912 in New York City, Beatrice and Rose Alexander, known for making doll costumes, began the Alexander Doll Co. They began using the "Madame Alexander" trademark in 1928. Beatrice Alexander Behrman became a legend in the doll world with her long reign as head of the Alexander Doll Company. Alexander made cloth, composition, and wooden dolls, and eventually made the transition to hard plastic and vinyl.

Dolls are listed by subcategories of the material of which the head is made. With Madame Alexander dolls, especially those made from 1950 on, condition as it relates to value is extremely important. **For the values listed here the doll must be in perfect condition with complete original clothing and tags. Dolls with incomplete or soiled costumes will bring one-fourth to one-third of the value of perfect examples.** Unusual dolls with presentation cases, trousseaux, or rare costumes may bring much more.

Cloth, 1930–1950 on

18" Jane Withers, Alexander Doll Company, composition: $1,200. **Photo courtesy of Morphy Auctions.**

8" Dionne quintuplet, Alexander Doll Company, composition: $150. **Photo courtesy of McMasters Harris Apple Tree Doll Auctions.**

All-cloth head and body, mohair wig, flat or molded mask face, painted side-glancing eyes

Storybook characters **such as Little Women, Dickens characters, Edith, and others**

    16"..**$550.00–750.00**

Alice in Wonderland

    Flat face **$700.00–800.00**

Mask face,

    14"–16" **$450.00–600.00**

Animals, such as March Hare, Bunny Belle, etc.

    15"–16" **$300.00–600.00**

    Baby

    13"..**$475.00–525.00**

    17"..**$600.00–650.00**

    24"..**$675.00–725.00**

Bobby Q, **1940–1942**

    16"..**$375.00–450.00**

Funny, **1963–1977**

    18"..**$80.00–100.00**

Little Shaver, **1940–1944, yarn hair**

    7"..**$275.00–325.00**

    10"..**$325.00–450.00**

    15"..**$425.00–550.00**

    22"..**$500.00–650.00**

Muffin, **ca. 1963–1977**

    14"..**$65.00–75.00**

So Lite Baby or Toddler, **1930s–1940s**

    20"...$375.00–450.00

Suzie Q, **1940–1942**

    16"...$375.00–450.00

Teeny Twinkle, **1946, disc floating eyes**

    ....$475.00–550.00

Dionne Quintuplets, **various materials**

Cloth, **1935–1936**

    16"...$750.00–850.00

    24"...$1,200.00–1,400.00

Composition, **1935–1945, all-composition, swivel head, jointed toddler or baby body, molded and painted hair or wigged, sleep or painted eyes. Outfit colors: Annette, yellow; Cecile, green; Emilie, lavender; Marie, blue; Yvonne, pink. Add more for extra accessories or in layette.**

Baby

    8"...$150.00–160.00

    Complete set.....................................$700.00–800.00

Set of five with wooden nursery furniture

    8"...$800.00–900.00

Toddler

    8"...$200.00–250.00

    Complete set.....................................$1,100.00–1,200.00

    11"...$250.00–300.00

    Complete set.....................................$1,500.00–1,600.00

    14"...$325.00–375.00

    Complete set.....................................$1,800.00–2,000.00

    16"...$550.00–625.00

    Complte set $2,200.00–3,400.00

    20"...$575.00–625.00

    Complete set.....................................$3,500.00–3,800.00

On cloth body

    22"...$550.00–650.00

    Complete set.....................................$3,300.00–3,400.00

Dr. Dafoe, **1937–1939**

    14"...$700.00–800.00

15" McGuffy Anna & 11" Butch, Alexander Doll Company, composition: $600 McGuffy, $200 Butch. **Photo courtesy of Alderfer Auction Company, Inc.**

Nurse

    13"–15" $500.00–625.00

Vinyl, **1998 75ᵗʰ anniversary individually boxed**

    8" ....$300.00–350.00 **complete set**

Composition, **1930–1950**

Babies, **cloth body, sleep eyes, marked "Alexander," dolls such as Baby Genius, Butch, Baby McGuffy, Pinky, and others**

    10"–12" $150.00–225.00

    14"–16" $200.00–275.00

    18"–20" $250.00–300.00

Baby Jane, **1935**

    16" $600.00–700.00

Child

Alice in Wonderland, **1930s–1940s**

    7"–9" $175.00–250.00

    11"–14" $300.00–400.00

    18"–21" $500.00–600.00

swivel waist, 1930s

    13" $400.00–550.00

Babs Skater, **1948, marked "ALEX" on head, clover tag**

    18" $1,000.00–1,100.00

Carmen (Miranda), **1942, black hair**

    9"–11" $200.00–350.00

    14"–17" $400.00–475.00

    21" $600.00–700.00

7" Little Women, Alexander Doll Co., composition, Tiny Betty, circa 1935: $200 each **Photo courtesy of Alderfer Auction Company, Inc.**

18" Sonja Henie, Alexander Doll Company, composition: $800. **Photo courtesy of McMasters Harris Apple Tree Doll Auctions.**

Fairy Queen, **ca. 1939–1946, clover wrist tag, tagged gown**

 15–18"..$500.00–600.00

 21"–22"..$650.00–700.00

Flora McFlimsey, **1938, freckles, marked "Princess Elizabeth"**

 14"–17"..$500.00–650.00

 22"...$750.00–800.00

Jane Withers, 1937–1939, **green sleep eyes, open mouth, brown mohair wig**

 12"–13½".....................................$1,200.00–1,400.00

 15"–17"...$1,000.00–1,200.00

 18"–19"...$1,200.00–1,400.00

 20"–22"...$1,500.00–1,600.00

Jeannie Walker, **tagged dress, closed mouth, mohair wig**

 13"–14"..$600.00–725.00

 18"...$750.00–850.00

Karen Ballerina, **blue sleep eyes, closed mouth, "Alexander" on head**

 15"...$700.00–800.00

 18"...$750.00–850.00

Kate Greenaway, **yellow wig, marked "Princess Elizabeth"**

 13"–15"..$300.00–400.00

 18"...$500.00–700.00

 24"...$750.00–850.00

Little Betty, **1939–1943, side-glancing painted eyes**

 9"–11"..$200.00–250.00

Little Colonel

Closed mouth

 11"–15"..$350.00–500.00

 9" Wendy Ann, Alexander Doll Company, composition: $250. **Photo courtesy of McMasters Harris Apple Tree Doll Auctions.**

 8" Wendy Goes To A Garden Party, Alexander Doll Company, bkw, hard plastic, ca. 1956: sold at auction for $561. **Photo courtesy of McMasters Harris Apple Tree Doll Auctions.**

Open mouth

14"–17"...$450.00–550.00

23"–26"...$800.00–900.00

Little Genius, **blue sleep eyes, cloth body, closed mouth, clover tag**

12"–14"...$125.00–200.00

16"–20"...$225.00–300.00

24"–25"...$175.00–250.00

Little Women, **Meg, Jo, Amy, Beth**

7"...$150.00–225.00 each

9"...$250.00–300.00 each

13"–15"...$300.00–350.00 each

Madelaine DuBain, **1937–1944**

14"...$500.00–550.00

17"...$600.00–650.00

Marcella, **1936, open mouth, wig, sleep eyes**

17"–24"...$450.00–550.00

Margaret O'Brien, **1946–1948**

14"–17"...$550.00–750.00

19"–24"...$800.00–1,000.00

Margaret Rose (Princess) **1937–1938, sleep eyes, open mouth, tagged dress**

15"–18"...$600.00–700.00

McGuffey Ana, **1935–1937, sleep eyes, open mouth, tagged dress**

11"–13"...$425.00–500.00

14"–16"...$600.00–700.00

17"–20"...$600.00–750.00

15" Kathy Baby, Alexander Doll Company, vinyl, ca. 1954 - 1946: $110 MIB. **Photo courtesy of Alderfer Auction Company, Inc.**

20" Cissy, Alexander Doll Company, hard plastic: $500. **Photo courtesy of Charlotte's Web Vintage Dolls and Collectibles.**

21"–25" $800.00–900.00

28" $900.00–1,100.00

Painted eyes

9" $250.00–300.00

Marionettes **by Tony Sarg**

12" $250.00–350.00

Portraits, **1941–1947, Wendy Ann face**

20"–22" $2,000.00–5,000.00

Princess Elizabeth, **1937–1941**

Closed mouth

13" $450.00–500.00

Open mouth

13"–16" $450.00–500.00

18"–24" $500.00–650.00

28" $700.00–850.00

Scarlett, **1937–1946, add more for rare costume**

11" $300.00–500.00

14" $600.00–800.00

18" $600.00–750.00

21" $1,400.00–2,000.00

Snow White, **1939–1942, marked "Princess Elizabeth"**

13" $375.00–450.00

16"–18" $450.00–550.00

Sonja Henie, **1939–1942, open mouth, sleep eyes**

13"–15" $550.00–700.00

17"–18" $650.00–850.00

20"–23" $700.00–900.00

19" Bonnie, Alexander Doll Company, vinyl, circa 1954-1955: $140 MIB. **Photo courtesy of Alderfer Auction Company, Inc.**

Three Little Pigs, **1938–1939**

12"...$450.00–550.00 each

Set of 3...$1,800.00–2,500.00

Tiny Betty, **1934–1943, side-glancing painted eyes, elaborate or rare costumes bring high end of range**

7"...$175.00–275.00

W.A.A.C. (Army), W.A.A.F. (Air Force), W.A.V.E. (Navy), **ca. 1943–1944**

14"...$550.00–750.00

Wendy Ann, **1935–1948, more for special outfit**

11"–15"...$275.00–475.00

17"–21"...$550.00–675.00

Painted eyes

9"...$175.00–250.00

Swivel waist, molded hair or wig

14"...$400.00–600.00

Hard Plastic and Vinyl, **1948 on. MIB will bring double**

Alexander-kins, **1953 on**

1953, 7½"–8", **straight leg nonwalker**

Nude...$200.00–275.00

Dressed...$400.00–550.00

1954–1955, **straight leg walker**

Nude...$125.00–200.00

Dressed...$300.00–600.00

 10" Cissette, Alexander Doll Company, hard plastic, circa 1957: $600 MIB. **Photo courtesy Fourty Fifty Sixty.**

 13" Ballerina, Alexander Doll Company, hard plastic: $150. **Photo courtesy of Withington Auction Inc.**

1956–1965, **bent-knee walker, after 1963 marked "Alex"**

    Nude..$100.00–150.00

    Dressed..$300.00–550.00

1956

1965–1972, **bent-knee nonwalker, price depends on costume**

    Nude..$75.00–95.00

    Dressed..$200.00–450.00

1973–1976, **straight leg nonwalker, marked "Alex" on back of torso, price depends on costume**

    Dressed..$30.00–90.00

1976–1994, **straight leg nonwalker, marked "Alexander" on back of torso**

    Dressed..$15.00–35.00

Babies

Baby Brother or Sister, **1977–1979, vinyl & cloth**

    14"–20"..$30.00–45.00

Baby Ellen, **1965–1972, vinyl, rigid vinyl body, marked "Alexander 1965"**

    14"..$90.00–115.00

Baby Genius, **1956–1962, hard plastic and vinyl, price depends on costume**

    8"..$175.00–250.00

Baby McGuffy, **1974–1976, vinyl, cloth body**

    21"..$35.00–65.00

Bonnie, **1954–1955, vinyl**

    19"..$60.00–75.00

Fischer Quints, **1964, vinyl**

    8" set..$150.00–200.00

Happy, **1970 only, vinyl**

    20"..$65.00–100.00

25" Binnie Walker, Alexander Doll Company, hard plastic, 1954 -1955: $500. **Photo courtesy of Alderfer Auction Company, Inc.**

17" Bride, Alexander Doll Company, hard plastic, Margaret face, 1949 -1955: $450. **Photo courtesy of Alderfer Auction Company, Inc.**

Honeybun, **1951, vinyl**

    18"–19" **$125.00–175.00**

Huggums

Big, **1963–1979**

    25" **$50.00–70.00**

Little, **rooted hair, 1963–1988**

    12" **$40.00–50.00**

Kathy Baby, **1954–1956, vinyl**

    13"–15" .... **$ 45.00–55.00**

    20"–22" **$65.00–85.00**

Kathy Cry, **1957–1958, vinyl, nurser**

    11"–15" **$65.00–95.00**

    18"–25" **$120.00–140.00**

Kitten, **1962–1963, vinyl, cloth body**

    14"–18" **$65.00–75.00**

    24" ...., **ca. 1961 $80.00–90.00**

Little Angel, **1950–1957, vinyl head, latex body**

    9" **$100.00–125.00**

Little Bitsey, **1967–1968, all-vinyl**

    9" **$50.00–70.00**

Littlest Kitten, **vinyl**

    8" **$75.00–90.00**

Lively Kitten, **1962, vinyl, cloth body, knob makes head and limbs move**

    14" **$125.00–175.00**

Mary Cassatt, **1969–1970, vinyl**

    14" **$60.00–80.00**

    20" **$110.00–140.00**

12" Brenda Starr, Alexander Doll Company, vinyl: $185. **Photo courtesy Fourty Fifty Sixty.**

15" Caroline, Alexander Doll Company, vinyl, circa 1961, MIB: $200. **Photo courtesy of McMasters Harris Apple Tree Doll Auctions.**

Pussy Cat, **1965–1985, vinyl**

    14"...$75.00–90.00

    24"...$50.00–60.00

    18"...1989–1993 $35.00–55.00

Black, **1970–1976**

    14"...$60.00–90.00

Sweet Tears, **1965–1974**

    9"...$35.00–45.00

    14"...$50.00– 75.00

With layette

    1965–1973 ....$60.00–85.00

Victoria, **baby, 1967–1989**

    20"...$45.00–60.00

Cissette, **1957 on 10", hard plastic head, synthetic wig, pierced ears, closed mouth, seven-piece adult body, jointed elbows and knees, high-heeled feet, mold later used for other dolls. Marks: None on body, clothes tagged "Cissette." Dolls listed are in good condition with original clothing — value can be doubled for mint-in-box.**

Basic doll

    In undergarments $150.00–175.00

    In street dress....................................$350.00–450.00

    In formal wear...................................$450.00–1,000.00

Gibson Girl

    1962–1963 ....$350.00–450.00

Jacqueline, **rare costumes bring higher end of range**

    1961–1962 ....$350.00–600.00

Margot

    1961 ....$350.00–500.00

17" Cinderella, Alexander Doll Company, hard plastic: $500. **Photo courtesy of Morphy Auctions.**

16" Kelly, Alexander Doll Company, vinyl, ca. 1958-1959: $200. **Photo courtesy of McMasters Harris Apple Tree Doll Auctions.**

Portrette

    1968–1973 .... $250.00–350.00

Queen

    1957–1958 .... $200.00–300.00

Sleeping Beauty, **1959, authorized Disney, blue gown**

    .... $150.00–250.00

    Tinkerbelle, **1969**............................. $135.00–175.00

Cissy

1955–1959, **20", hard plastic, vinyl arms, jointed elbows and knees, high-heeled feet. Clothes are tagged "Cissy." MIB can bring double**

    Basic doll in undergarments................$400.00–500.00

    In street dress...................................... $400.00–700.00

    In formal wear....................................$700.00–1,800.00

Cissy Queen, ca. 1955, gown, MIB sold for $3,341.00 at online auction

1996 on, **21", vinyl**

    Yardley, **2001** $150.00–200.00

Other Hard Plastic & Vinyl, **MIB can bring double**

Alice in Wonderland, **1949–1952, hard plastic, Margaret and/or Maggie**

    14"... $350.00–400.00

    15", 18", 23" $400.00–600.00

1996, **vinyl**

    14"... $35.00–40.00

American Girl, **1962–1963, #388, seven-piece walker body, became McGuffey Ana in 1964–1965**

    8"... $130.00–160.00

14" Amy (Little Women), Alexander Doll Company, hard plastic, circa 1947-1956: $250. **Photo courtesy of Morphy Auctions.**

Annabelle, **1951–1952, Maggie head**

    14"... $600.00–700.00

    20"–23".. $800.00–1,000.00

Anne of Green Gables, **1993, in Concert dress**

    8"... $65.00–80.00

Babs Skater, **1948–1950, hard plastic, Margaret**

    15"... $500.00–800.00

    17"–18".. $700.00–1,000.00

Betty, **1959, vinyl, flirty eyes, rooted hair**

    31"... $375.00–475.00

Bible Character Dolls, **1954 only, hard plastic, original box made like Bible**

    8"... $8,500.00+

1990s, various

    8"... $15.00–20.00

Bill/Billy, **1960, seven-piece walker body**

    8"... $125.00–175.00

Binnie Walker, **1954–1955, Cissy face, elaborate costumes bring higher end of range**

    15"... $200.00–300.00

    18"... $300.00–575.00

    25"... $350.00–575.00

Brenda Starr, **1964 only, 12" hard plastic, vinyl arms, red wig**

    In street dress...................................... $90.00–195.00

    In formal wear..................................... $125.00–275.00

Bunny, **1962 only**

    18"... $100.00–150.00

18" Madeline, Alexander Doll Company, vinyl, ca. 1961: $250. **Photo courtesy of Withington Auction Inc.**

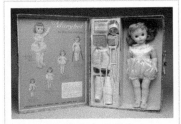

14" Marybel, Alexander Doll Company, vinyl, circa 1959 - 65: $175. **Photo courtesy of Morphy Auctions.**

Caroline, **1961, #131, vinyl**

    15"...**$160.00–225.00**

Chatterbox, **1961, vinyl & plastic, talker**

    24"...**$60.00–80.00**

Cinderella,

1950–1951, **MaryAnn face, 14", hard plastic**

Ballgown

    14"...**$425.00–525.00**

    18"...**$450.00–550.00**

Poor Cinderella, gray dress, original broom

    14"...**$325.00–400.00**

1967–1992, **Mary Ann face, plastic and vinyl**

    14"...**$20.00–30.00**

Cowgirl & Cowboy, **1967–1970, hard plastic, jointed knees**

    8"...**$125.00–175.00**

Cynthia, **1952 only, hard plastic**

    15"...**$375.00–475.00**

    18"...**$600.00–750.00**

    23"...**$900.00–$1,000.00**

Easter Doll, **1968, vinyl**

    14"...**$200.00–300.00**

Edith, The Lonely Doll, **1958–1959, vinyl head, hard plastic body**

    8"...**$300.00–350.00**

    16"...**$100.00–175.00**

    22"...**$125.00–200.00**

2004, **wooden, limited edition 750, with 3" Mr. Bear**

    8"..$75.00–80.00

Elise

1957–1964, **16½", hard plastic, vinyl arms, jointed ankles and knees**

    Street dress......................................$200.00–450.00

    Ballerina $200.00–300.00

    Formal wear....................................$400.00–800.00

1963 only, **18", hard plastic, vinyl arms, jointed ankles and knees,**

    Bouffant hairstyle............................$150.00–225.00

1966–1972, **17", hard plastic, one piece vinyl arms, jointed ankles and knees**

    Street dress......................................$150.00–175.00

1966–1991

    Ballerina $45.00–55.00

1997, **vinyl**

    16"..$25.00–45.00

Fairy Queen, **1948–1950, Margaret face**

    14½" $300.00–375.00

1949–1950

    21"..$500.00–650.00

Fashions of a Century, **1954–1955, Margaret face, hard plastic**

    14"–18"..$1,200.00–1,600.00

First Ladies, **14", 1976–1990**

Set 1

    1976–1978 ....$40.00–50.00 ea.

Set 2

    1979–1981 ....$25.00–35.00 ea.

Set 3

    1982–1984 ....$20.00–30.00 ea.

Set 4

    1985–1987 ....$20.00–30.00 ea.

Set 5,

    1988 ....$15.00–20.00 ea.

Set 6

    1989–1990 ....$15.00–20.00 ea.

Flower Girl, **1954, hard plastic, Cissy**

    15"–18"..$450.00–500.00

Glamour Girl Series, **1953 only, hard plastic, Margaret head, auburn wig, straight leg walker**

    18".. $750.00–900.00

example sold for $3,342.00 at auction

Godey Bride, **1950–1951, Margaret, hard plastic**

    14".. $1,200.00–2,0000.00

    18".. $1,300.00–1,500.00

Godey Lady, **1950–1951, Margaret, hard plastic**

    14".. $1,400.00–1,600.00

Godey Groom, **1950–1951, Margaret, hard plastic**

    14".. $600.00–700.00

    18".. $700.00–800.00

Gold Rush, **1963 only, hard plastic, Cissette**

    10".. $250.00–350.00

Grandma Jane, **1970–1972, #1420, Mary Ann, vinyl body**

    14".. $15.00–25.00

Groom,

1949–1951, **Margaret, hard plastic**

    14"–16".. $300.00–450.00

1953–1955, **Wendy Ann, hard plastic**

    7½" $27.00–375.00

Jacqueline, **1961–1962, 21", hard plastic, vinyl arms**

    Street dress $700.00–900.00 225

    Formal wear $750.00–950.00 350

1962 Marshal Fields Trunk Set, **sold online for $3,156.00**

Janie, **1964–1966, #1156, toddler, vinyl head, hard plastic body, rooted hair**

    12".. $60.00–125.00

Jenny Lind and Listening Cat, **1970–1971,**

    14".. $230.00–260.00

Joanie Nurse, **1960–1961,**

    36".. $350.00–475.00

    Nurse, 1960 .... $200.00–275.00

Kathryn Grayson, **early 1950s, hard plastic**

21" sold for $5,350.00 at online auction

Kelly

1959 only, **hard plastic, Lissy face**

    12".. $200.00–300.00

1958–1959, **hard plastic, Marybel** face

    15"–16"..$125.00–200.00

1958

    18"...................................$350.00–375.00

1958–1959

    22"...................................$300.00–400.00

Leslie **(black Polly), 1965–1971, 17", vinyl head, hard plastic body, vinyl limbs, rooted hair**

    Street dress or ballerina $150.00–250.00

    In formal $250.00–350.00

Lissy, **hard plastic, wigged**

1956–1958, **12", elbow and knee joints**

    In Undies $175.00–200.00

    Street dress......................................$250.00–400.00

    Formal $450.00–700.00

1959–1967, **as above but no elbow and knee joints**

    Street dress......................................$150.00–225.00

2006, **vinyl**

    12"...................................$35.00–75.00

Little Shaver, **1963–1965, painted eyes, vinyl body**

    12"...................................$100.00–175.00

Little Women,

1947–1956, **Meg, Jo, Amy, Beth, plus Marme, Margaret and Maggie faces**

    14"–15"..$200.00–350.00 **each**

1955, **Meg, Jo, Amy, Beth, plus Marme, Wendy Ann, straight-leg walker**

    8"....................................$75.00–125.00 **each**

1956–1959, **Wendy Ann, bent-knee walker**

    8"....................................$65.00–85.00 **each**

1974–1992, **straight leg, #411–#415**

    8"....................................$40.00–55.00 **each**

1957–1958, **Lissy, jointed elbows and knees**

    12"...................................$250.00–300.00

1959–1968, **Lissy, one-piece arms and legs**

    12"...................................$100.00–175.00

1983–1989, **Nancy Drew face**

    12"...................................$35.00–45.00 **each**

Madeline, **1961, vinyl, multiple joints**

    18"...**$175.00–250.00**

Maggie Mixup, **1960–1961, hard plastic, freckles, price depends on outfit**

    8"...**$200.00–400.00**

1961 only

    17"...**$175.00–225.00**

Maggie Teenager, **1951–1953, hard plastic, price depends on outfit**

    15"–18"...**$350.00–400.00**

Maggie, **hard plastic**

1948–1954

    20"–21"...**$450.00–600.00**

1949–1952

    22"–23"...**$500.00–650.00**

1949–1953

    17"–18"...**$400.00–550.00**

1949–1953, **walker**

    15"–18"...**$125.00–200.00**

Margaret O'Brien, **1949–1951, hard plastic**

    14"...**$600.00–850.00**

    18"–21"...**$400.00–900.00**

Margot Ballerina, **1951–1953, Margaret and Maggie, dressed in various colored outfits**

    15"–18"...**$550.00–750.00**

Marlo Thomas as "That Girl," **1967 only, Polly face, vinyl**

    17"...**$200.00–300.00**

Mary Ellen, **1954 only, rigid vinyl walker**

    31"...**$450.00–525.00**

Mary Ellen Playmate, **1965 only, bendable vinyl body**

    17"...**$250.00–300.00**

Mary Martin, **1948–1952, South Pacific character Nell, two-piece sailor outfit, hard plastic**

    14"–17"...**$800.00–1,000.00**

Marybel, "The Doll That Gets Well," **1959–1965, rigid vinyl, in case with accessories**

    16"...**$150.00–175.00**

1998

75th anniversary, MIB

    reissue...**$65.00–85.00**

McGuffey Ana

1948–1950, **hard plastic, Margaret**

    14"...$1,000.00–1,200.00

    18"..$950.00–1,050.00

    21"...$1,200.00–1,400.00

1956 only, **hard plastic, #616, Wendy Ann face**

    8"...$675.00–750.00

1963 only, **hard plastic, rare doll, Lissyface**

1977–1986, **vinyl, Mary Ann face**

    14"...$35.00–45.00

Melanie, **1979–1980, dotted swiss gown pink trim**

    21"...$60.00–80.00

Melinda, **1962–1963, plastic/vinyl, cotton dress**

    14"–22"...$150.00–225.00

Muffin, **1989–1990, Janie face, vinyl**

    12"...$25.00–45.00

Nancy Drew, **1967 only, vinyl body, Literature Series**

    12"...$250.00–325.00

Nina Ballerina, **1949–1951, Margaret head, clover wrist tag**

    15"...$300.00–400.00

    19"...$450.00–700.00

    21"–23"...700.00–900.00

Pamela,–**1962–1963, Lissy face, changeable wigs**

    12" In box with wardrobe $500.00–700.00

Peter Pan, **1953–1954, Margaret**

    15"...$400.00–500.00

1969, **14" Wendy (Mary Ann head),**

12" Peter, Michael (Jamie head), 10"

Tinkerbelle (Cissette head)

    Peter, Wendy $125.00–175.00

    Michael..$100.00–150.00

    Tinkerbelle $100.00–150.00

Polly, **1965 only, vinyl & plastic, elaborate costume brings high end of range**

    17"...$125.00–275.00

Polly Pigtails, **1949–1951, hard plastic**

    17"...$ 450.00–500.00

Pollyanna

1960–1961, **vinyl, Marybel face**

    16"..$275.00–325.00

1987–1988, **Mary Ann face**

    14"..$45.00–55.00

2000–2001, **Wendy face**

    8"..$25.00–35.00

Portraits, **1960 on, marked "1961," Jacqueline face, 21", early dolls have jointed elbows, later one piece. For models made over long periods the older dolls bring the higher end of the values listed, later dolls the lower end. MIB can bring double.**

Agatha, **1967–1980**

    #2171 ....$160.00–225.00

Coco, **1966**

    ....$250.00–$300.00

Cornelia, **1972**

    #2191 ....$125.00–200.00

Gainsborough, **1968–1978**

    #2184 ....$125.00–200.00

Godey, **1977, in ecru & red**

    #2298 ....$225.00–325.00

Goya, **1968**

    #2183 ....$125.00–150.00

Jenny Lind, **1969–1970**

    #2193 ....$550.00–650.00

Lady Hamilton, **1968**

    #2182 ....$200.00–225.00

Madame Alexander, **1988–1990**

    ....$60.00–75.00

Marie Antionette, **1987–1988**

    ....$150.00–175.00

Manet, **1982–1983**

    #2225 ....$135.00–165.00

Melanie, **1971**

    #2162 ....$100.00–200.00

Renoir, **1965**

    #2154 ....$650.00–700.00

Scarlett, **1979–1985, green velvet gown**

    #2240 .... $100.00–150.00

Southern Belle, **1965**

    #2155 .... $575.00–675.00

Prince Charming, 1948–1950, hard plastic, Margaret face, brocade jacket, white tights

    14"... $350.00–425.00

    18"... $325.00–400.00

Princess Margaret Rose

1949–1953, **hard plastic, Margaret face**

    14"... $350.00–450.00

    18"... $450.00–525.00

1953 only, **#2020B, hard plastic,**

Queen, **1965, Elise face**

    18"... $300.00–375.00

Quiz-Kin, **1953, hard plastic, back buttons, nods yes or no**

    8"... $125.00–175.00

Renoir Girl, 1972–1986, vinyl body, pink multi-teired dress

    14"... $25.00–35.00

Scarlett O'Hara

1950 on, **hard plastic, Margaret face**

    14"–16"... $800.00–900.00

1966–1972, **jointed knees, Wendy Ann face**

    8"... $200.00–250.00

1969–1986, **vinyl, Mary Ann face, white gown**

    14"... $40.00–50.00

1994, **#50001 floral picnic gown, straw hat, Jacqueline face**

    21"... $125.00–200.00

Shari Lewis, **1958–1959**

    14"... $400.00–500.00

21"700.00–850.00

Sleeping Beauty, **1959, Disneyland Special**

    10"... $190.00–260.00

    16"... $200.00–300.00

    21"... $550.00–600.00

Smarty, **1962–1963, vinyl body**

    12"... $35.00–55.00

Snow White

1970–1985, **Mary Ann face, Classic series, vinyl**

14"25.00–35.00

1990–1992, **Wendy face, vinyl**

    8"...**$40.00–50.00**

2002–2004, **Cissette face, came with 5" dwarves**

    10", complete set **$130.00–160.00**

Sonja Henie, **1951 only, Madeline face, vinyl head**

    15"...**$300.00–400.00**

Sound of Music, **1965–1970 (large), 1971–1973 (small), vinyl**

Brigitta

    10"..**$35.00–45.00**

    14"..**$50.00–80.00**

Friedrich

    8"..**$35.00–50.00**

    10"..**$20.00–30.00**

Gretl

    8"..**$30.00–40.00**

10"45.00–60.00

Liesl

    10"..**$45.00–65.00**

    14"..**$25.00–35.00**

Louisa

    10"..**$30.00–45.00**

    14"..**$25.00–35.00**

Maria

    12"..**$40.00–65.00**

    17"..**$65.00–80.00**

Marta

    8"..**$35.00–55.00**

    10"..**$75.00–125.00**

Suzy, **1970 only, vinyl head, Janie face**

    12"..**$70.00–80.00**

Timmy Toddler, **1960–1961, vinyl head, hard plastic body**

    23"..**$100.00–125.00**

1960 only

30".. $150.00–200.00

Tommy Bangs, **1952 only, hard plastic, Little Men Series**

11"... $300.00–400.00

Victoria, **1954 only, Me & My Shadow Series**

21" sold for $1,440.00 at auction

Wendy, Wendy Ann, Wendy-kin: See Alexander-kins section.

Special Event dolls, limited edition

Collector's United

Sailing With Sally, 1995,

8"... $30.00–40.00

Le Petite Boudoir, **1993**

10"... $45.00–65.00

Disney

Mousketeer, **1991, Disney theme parks only**

8"... $30.00–50.00

Snow White, **WDWC 1990, limit 750**

12"... $50.00–75.00

Madame Alexander Doll Club Convention

Lissy Party Dress, **2007**

12"... $200.00–225.00

Miss Liberty, **1991**

10"... $35.00–50.00

U.F.D.C

Susan, **2000, Wendy**

8"... $55.00–65.00

Music, **2007, convention souvenir in wardrobe trunk**

10"... $100.00–125.00

HENRI ALEXANDRE

1888–1891, Paris. Succeeded by Tourrel in 1892 and in 1895 merged with Jules Steiner.

Incised HA model, **bisque socket head, paperweight eyes, closed mouth with space between lips, straight wrist body**

17"–20" $5,500.00–6,900.00

Bébé Phénix, **trademarked in 1895, bisque socket head, paperweight eyes, pierced ears, composition body**

Child, closed mouth

10"–14"...$2,200.00–3,200.00

16"–18"...$4,000.00–4,500.00

20"–24"...$5,000.00–6,000.00

Child, open mouth

16"–18"...$1,800.00–2,100.00

20"–24"...$2,200.00–2,400.00

ALL-BISQUE FRENCH

3.75" all bisque, Simon Halbig for the French market, swivel neck: $1,800. **Photo courtesy of Morphy Auctions.**

1880 on, made by various French and German doll companies. Sold as French products. Most are unmarked. Some have numbers only. Allow more for original clothes and tags, less for chips or repairs.

Glass eyes, **swivel head, molded shoes or boots**

4"–5"...$1,800.00–2,500.00

6"–7"...$3,500.00–5,000.00

10"...$5,500.00–6,000.00

Jointed elbows

5"–6"...$2,800.00–3,000.00

Five-strap boots, **glass eyes, swivel neck**

5"–6"...$2,000.00–2,800.00

Painted eyes

2½"–3½"...$600.00–700.00

4"...$900.00–1,000.00

Bare feet

5"–7" $2,500.00–4,000.00

Later style, 1910–1920, glass eyes, molded shoes, swivel neck, long stockings

2½" $325.00–375.00

5"–6" $625.00–675.00

7" $725.00–750.00

ALL-BISQUE GERMAN

12.5" all bisque, swivel neck: $1,600. **Photo courtesy of Withington Auction Inc.**

11.5" all bisque, Kestner, mold 155: $800. **Photo courtesy of McMasters Harris Apple Tree Doll Auctions.**

1880s onward, made by various German doll companies including Alt, Beck & Gottschalk; Bähr & Pröschild; Hertel Schwab & Co.; Kämmer & Reinhardt; Kestner; Kling; Limbach; Bruno Schmidt; Simon & Halbig. Some incised "Germany" with or without numbers. Others have paper labels glued onto their torsos. More for labels, less for chips and repairs. **WARNING: Numerous reproductions of German all-bisque dolls are currently coming out of Europe and being sold as originals.**

All-Bisque, Black or Brown: See Black or Brown Section.

Painted eyes, 1880–1910, stationary neck, molded painted Mary Janes or boots, dressed or undressed, all in good condition

2"–3" $100.00–125.00

4"–5" $125.00–200.00

6"–8" $250.00–300.00

Black or brown stockings, **tan slippers**

4"–5" $350.00–400.00

6" $425.00–475.00

Ribbed hose or blue or yellow shoes

4"–5" $275.00–325.00

6" $425.00–475.00

8" $825.00–875.00

Molded hair

4½" $125.00–200.00

6" $125.00–175.00

Early very round face

7" $2,100.00–2,300.00

Molded clothing, 1890–1910, jointed at shoulders only or at shoulders and hips, painted eyes, molded hair, molded shoes or bare feet, excellent workmanship, no breaks, chips, or rubs

3½"–4" $85.00–100.00

5"–6" $120.00–160.00

7" $160.00–170.00

Lesser quality

3" $65.00–75.00

4" $75.00–85.00

6" $90.00–110.00

Molded on hat or bonnet

5–6½" $365.00–395.00

8–9" $500.00–550.00

Stone bisque (porous)

4–5" $50.00–65.00

6–7" $75.00–85.00

Glass eyes, 1890–1910, stationary neck, molded painted footwear, excellent bisque, open or closed mouth, sleep or set eyes, good wig, nicely dressed, molded one-strap shoes. Includes doll with sticker reading Prize Baby.

3"–4" $130.00–180.00

5" $180.00–200.00

6"–7" $250.00–300.00

8"–9" $350.00–400.00

Elaborate footwear or stockings

3" $375.00–400.00

4½" $450.00–500.00

6"–7" $600.00–700.00

8"–8½" $800.00–900.00

Mold 100, 125, 130, 150, 225 (preceded by 83/), **rigid neck, fat tummy, jointed shoulders and hips, glass sleep eyes, open mouth, molded black one-strap shoes with tan soles, white molded stockings with blue band. Similarly molded dolls, imported in 1950s by Kimport, have synthetic hair, lesser-quality bisque. Add more for original clothing.**

9" 2 of the dolls called Our Golden Three, all bisque, Ernst Heubach: $2,200 each. **Photo courtesy of Sweetbriar Auctions.**

5" Bonnie Babe, $1,275. **Photo courtesy of Sara Bernstein's Dolls.**

Mold number appears as a fraction with the following size numbers under 83; Mold "83/100," "83/125," "83/150," or "83/225." One marked "83/100" has a green label on torso reading, "Princess//Made in Germany."

4½"–6½" $300.00–400.00

7½"–8½" $500.00–650.00

10"–12" $900.00–1,000.00

Swivel neck and glass eyes, **1880–1910, molded painted footwear, pegged or wired joints, open or closed mouth. Allow more for unusual footwear such as yellow or multi-strap boots or flirty eyes.**

3"–4" $500.00–600.00

5"–6" $700.00–800.00

7"–8" $900.00–1,000.00

9"–10" $1,100.00–1,500.00

Simon & Halbig or Kestner types, **closed mouth, excellent quality. Molds 130, 150, 160, 184, 208, 602, 881, 886, 890, and others**

4"–5" $600.00–900.00

6"–7" $800.00–2,000.00

8" $1,200.00–2,000.00

10" $2,500.00–3,000.00

Jointed knees

5½"– 8½" $5,500.00–6,000.00

10" $6,000.00– $7,000.00

Bare feet

5"–6" $2,800.00–3,000.00

8"–10" $3,400.00–3,700.00

Praying, **molded bent kness & bent elbows, hands in praying position**

7½" $10,000.00–12,000.00

6" Mildred the Prize Baby, all bisque, character baby: $4,000. **Photo courtesy of Morphy Auctions.**

5.5" all bisque, Kestner, jointed knees: $5,500. **Photo courtesy of Morphy Auctions.**

Early round face

6"... $1,600.00–1,800.00

8"... $2,200.00–2,300.00

Mold 102, Wrestler (**so called), fat thighs, arm bent at elbow, open mouth (can have two rows of teeth) or closed mouth, stocky body, glass eyes, socket head, individual fingers or molded fist**

3½"–5"... $2,000.00–2,500.00

8"–9"... $ 3,000.00–4,000.00

Slender dolls, **1900 on, stationary neck, slender arms and legs, glass eyes, molded footwear, usual wire or peg-jointed shoulders and hips. Allow much more for original clothes. May be in regional costumes. Add more for unusual color boots, such as gold, yellow, or orange, all in good condition.**

3"–4"... $200.00–250.00

5"–6"... $275.00–325.00

Swivel neck, **closed mouth**

4"... $275.00–300.00

5"–6"... $450.00–500.00

8½"... $800.00–900.00

10".. $1,000.00–1,100.00

Jointed knees and/or elbows with swivel waist

6"... $1,950.00–2,050.00

8"... $3,000.00–3,200.00

Swivel waist only

6"... $2,000.00–2,200.00

Baby, **1900 on, jointed at hips and shoulders, bent limbs, molded hair, painted features**

2½"–3½"....................................... $80.00–90.00

5"–6"... $175.00–225.00

Character Baby, **1910 on, jointed at hips and shoulders, bent limbs, molded hair, painted features**

Glass eyes, molds 391, 830, 833, and others

4"–5" $325.00–425.00

6"–7" $425.00–500.00

8" $600.00–625.00

11" $750.00–850.00

Painted eyes

3½" $95.00–125.00

4"–5" $150.00–200.00

7" $250.00–300.00

8" $350.00–400.00

Swivel neck, **glass eyes**

5"–6" $500.00–800.00

8"–10" $1,000.00–1,200.00

Swivel neck, **painted eyes**

5"–6" $325.00–350.00

7"–8" $550.00–600.00

16" .... $1,150.00 at auction

Baby Bo Kaye, **mold 1394, designed by Kallus, distributed by Borgfeldt**

5" $1,700.00–2,000.00

7"–8" $2,100.00–2,200.00

Baby Darling, **mold 497, Kestner, one-piece body, painted eyes**

6" $850.00–950.00

8" $950.00–1,000.00

10" $1,100.00–1,200.00

Baby Peggy Montgomery **made by Louis Amberg, paper label, pink bisque with molded hair, painted brown eyes, closed mouth, jointed at shoulders and hips, molded and painted shoes/socks**

3½" $325.00–375.00

5½" $525.00–575.00

Bonnie Babe, **1926 on, designed by Georgene Averill, glass eyes, swivel neck, wig, jointed arms and legs**

4¾–6" $1,200.00–1,350.00

7"–8" $1,350.00–1,450.00

Bye-Lo: See Bye-Lo section.

Mildred The Prize Baby,(NOT to be confused with all bisque child dolls bearing the label Prize Baby)* **mold 880, 1914 on, made for Borgfeldt; molded, short painted hair; glass**

eyes; closed mouth; jointed at neck, shoulders, and hips; round paper label on chest; molded and painted footwear

5"–7" $3,900.00–4,500.00

Our Darling, open mouth with teeth, glass eyes

5½" $160.00–200.00

Tynie Baby, made for E. I. Horsman, wigged or painted hair, glass eyes

6" $1,900.00–2,100.00

8"–10" $2,700.00–3,000.00

Mold 231 (A.M.), toddler, swivel neck, with glass eyes

9" $1,300.00–1,400.00

Mold 369, 372

7" $650.00–725.00

9" $1,000.00–1,100.00

11" $1,400.00–1,500.00

Mold 151, by Hertel & Schwab

10" $350.00–450.00

Character Doll, 1910

Molds 155, 156, glass eyes

4"–5" $400.00–450.00

6"–7" $525.00–625.00

Heubach, Ernst, 1913–1920s, jointed at shoulders and hips, molded painted hair, some with ribbons etc., intaglio eyes, Our Golden Three, molds such as 9557, 9558, 10134, 10490, 10499, 10511, others

8"–9" $1,500.00–2,200.00

Orsini, 1919 on, designed by Jeanne Orsini for Borgfeldt, produced by Alt, Beck & Gottschalk, Chi Chi, Didi, Fifi, Mimi, Vivi

Glass eyes

5" $2,000.00–2,600.00

7" $3,300.00–3,700.00

Painted eyes

5" $900.00–1,100.00

Our Fairy, mold 222, wigged, glass eyes

4½"–5" $800.00–1,000.00

6"–7" $1,300.00–1,500.00

11" $1,800.00–2,000.00

5" Orsini, all bisque: $2,300. **Photo courtesy of McMasters Harris Apple Tree Doll Auctions.**

5" Max & Moritz, Kestner, all bisque: $5,000 pair. **Photo courtesy of Morphy Auctions.**

Painted eyes, **molded hair**

> 5"..$450.00–550.00
>
> 8"..$750.00–850.00
>
> 12"..$950.00–1,500.00

Jointed animals, **1910 on, wire jointed shoulders and hips, crocheted clothing, makers such as Kestner, others.**

2"–3½"

> *Rabbit*..$500.00–600.00
>
> *Bear*..$450.00–550.00
>
> *Frog, Monkey, Pig, Mouse*......................$600.00–900.00

Miniature dolls, **painted eyes, crocheted clothing, various makers**

> 1"–1¾"..$90.00–110.00

Character Dolls, **painted eyes, 1913 on**

Campbell Kid, **molded clothes, Dutch bob**

> 4"–6"..$150.00–200.00

No molded clothing, **molded footwear only**

> 4½"–5½" $500.00–600.00

Chin-chin, **Gebruder Heubach, 1919, jointed arms only, triangular label on chest**

> 4"–5"..$175.00–200.00

Happifats, **designed by Kate Jordan for Borgfeldt, ca. 1913–1921**

> 4"..$225.00–300.00

HEbee, SHEbee

> 4"–5"..$600.00–700.00
>
> 7"..$700.00–800.00

Max, Moritz, **Kestner1914, jointed at the neck, shoulders, and hips, many companies produced these characters from the Wilhelm Busch children's story**

> 4½"–6"...$2,000.00–3,000.00 each

 3.5" So-called Flapper children, all bisque: $200 pair. **Photo courtesy of The Museum Doll Shop.**

 3.5" Knotters, All bisque: $100 pair. **Photo courtesy of Morphy Auctions.**

Mibs, **Amberg, 1921, molded blond hair, molded and painted socks and shoes, pink bisque, jointed at shoulders, legs molded to body, marked "C.//L.A.&S.192// GERMANY"**

3"..$150.00–200.00

5"–6"...$325.00–400.00

8"...$400.00–475.00

Peterkin, **1912, one-piece baby, side-glancing googly eyes, molded and painted hair, molded blue pajamas on chubby torso, arms molded to body with hands clasping stomach**

5"–6"...$200.00–250.00

September Morn, **jointed at shoulders and hips, Grace Drayton design, George Borgfeldt**

4"–5"...$1,400.00–1,700.00

6"–8"...$1,900.00–2,200.00

Later issue with painted eyes, **1920 on, painted hair or wigged, molded painted single strap shoes, white stockings, makers such as Limbach, Hertwig & Co, others**

3½" $80.00–90.00

4"–5"...$100.00–115.00

6"–7"...$135.00–150.00

Molded "paper hat" and dagger in belt

4.5"–5.5"...$150.00–200.00

Infant, **1920 on, so-called candy babies**

3"–4"...$50.00–65.00

So-called Flapper, **1920, tinted bisque, molded bobbed hairstyle, painted features, molded single strap shoes**

Child

2½"–3½" $95.00–115.00

Adult

5½" $175.00–225.00

Molded loop for bow

2½" $150.00–200.00

5"...$275.00–350.00

6"–7"...$400.00–450.00

Molded hat

3½"–4"...$200.00–250.00

Aviatrix

5"...$325.00–375.00

Swivel waist

4½"..$375.00–400.00

Wigged

3½"..$95.00–125.00

Knotters, 1920 on, immobile body, head attached with elastic, makers such as Hertwig & Co., others, molded clothes, Knotters heads do not bobble but are strung with knotted cord through top of head

Animals, cat, dog, rabbit

3"–5"..$80.00–120.00

Child/adult

3"–4"..$45.00–55.00

Comic characters

3"–5"..$120.00–135.00

Santa Claus or Indian

3"–4"..$140.00–150.00

Teddy Bear...$180.00–200.00

Immobiles, 1920, one-piece doll with molded clothing, top layer of paint not fired on and the color can be washed off, some have molded hats

Baby

3½"..$30.00–40.00

5"...$40.00–50.00

Adults and Children

3"...$30.00–40.00

5"...$55.00–65.00

Child with pet on leash, **Hertwig & Co**

3"–4"..$150.00–170.00

Bathing Beauties, 1910–1930s, various German porcelain factories made these bisque figures, painted features

Average Quality

3"...$100.00–300.00

6"...$400.00–500.00

High Quality, **makers such as Galluba & Hoffman**

    4½"–6"... $2,000.00–2,500.00

8"–10" 3,000.00–4,000.00

Reclining woman, **lying on stomach**

    2½" $135.00–165.00

    4"... $375.00–425.00

High Quality, **makers such as Galluba & Hoffman**

    8"... $900.00–1,000.00

Mermaid tail

    4"... $300.00–325.00

Two figures molded together

    4½"–5½" $1,500.00–1,700.00

Wigged

    5"... $900.00–1,100.00

Too few in database for a reliable range.

Painted bisque child, **1920–1930s, all in original clothing**

    3"–4"... $35.00–60.00

ALL-BISQUE JAPANESE

5" all bisque, fired decoration, molded hat, marked "Nippon": $150. **Photo courtesy of The Museum Doll Shop.**

1915 onward, made by a variety of Japanese companies. Quality varies widely, stationary dolls or jointed at shoulders and/or hips. Marked "Made in Japan" or "Nippon."

Fired bisque, **fired on color, some jointed at shoulders, some immobile**

Characters **such as Que San Baby, Cho Cho San, etc.**

    4"–4½"... $125.00–175.00

Painted bisque, top layer of paint not fired on and the color can be washed off, usually one-piece figurines with molded hair, painted features, including clothes, shoes, and socks, some have molded hats

Baby

3"–5"...	$15.00–25.00
5"–7"..	$30.00–40.00

Black baby, **with pigtails**

4"–5"...	$40.00–55.00

Bye-Lo Baby-type, **fine quality**

3½"..	$60.00–75.00
5"...	$100.00–120.00

Child

3"–5" 15.00–35.00

Child with molded clothes

4½"..	$30.00–45.00
6"...	$50.00–60.00

Child, 1920s–1930s, **pink or painted bisque with painted features, jointed at shoulders and hips, has molded hair or wig, excellent condition**

3"–4"...	$25.00–35.00
4"–6"...	$45.00–55.00

Betty Boop, **bobbed hair style, large eyes painted to side, head molded to torso**

4"...	$18.00–25.00
6"...	$30.00–40.00

Bride & Groom, **all original costume**

3"–4"...	$40.00–60.00

Happifats, **pair**

3½"..	$100.00–125.00

Hebee, Shebee

4½"..	$70.00–90.00

Immobile characters, **Indian, Pirate, etc.**

5"...	$15.00–35.00

Skippy

6"...	$110.00–120.00

Snow White

5"...	$50.00–60.00

Boxed with Dwarfs

....	$250.00–300.00

Three Bears/Goldilocks

Boxed set $300.00–350.00

Occupied Japan mark

Betty Boop look

4"– 5" $25.00–35.00

Black baby with 3 pigtails

3"–5" .... $40.00 –60.00

Child, **jointed shoulders, may have molded features suxch as hairbows, etc.**

5"–7" $40.00–60.00

ALT, BECK & GOTTSCHALCK

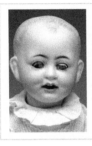

13" mold 1322, ABG, bisque, character baby: $300. **Photo courtesy of Morphy Auctions.**

32" mold 1362, ABG, bisque: $650. **Photo courtesy of Oldeclectics.**

1854, Nauendorf, Thüringia, Germany. Produced bisque and china headed dolls for a variety of companies including Bergmann and Borgfeldt.

Shoulder Heads, china, 1880 on. Mold 639, 698, 784, 870, 890, 912, 974, 990, 1000, 1008, 1028, 1032, 1044, 1046, 1064, 1112, 1123, 1127, 1142, 1210, 1222, 1234, 1235, 1254, 1304, cloth or kid body, bisque lower limbs, molded hair or wig, no damage and nicely dressed. Allow more for molded hat or fancy hairdo.

10"–13" $100.00–200.00

15"–22" $300.00–400.00

23"–26" $450.00–550.00

Shoulder Heads, bisque, **1880. Cloth or kid body, bisque lower arms, closed mouth, molded hair or wig.** Molds such as 784, 911, 912, 916, 990, 1000, 1008, 1028, 1044, 1046, 1064, 1127, 1142, 1210, 1234, 1254, 1304 and so-called Schoolboy style. Allow more for molded hat or fancy hairdo.

Glass eyes, **closed mouth**

9"–11" $325.00–375.00

15"–17" $400.00–500.00

20"–24" $600.00–700.00

Painted eyes, **closed mouth**

14"–18" $275.00–300.00

21"–23" $350.00–400.00

Turned Bisque Shoulder Heads, **1885, solid dome head or plaster pate, kid body, bisque lower arms, glass eyes, wigged, all in good condition, nicely dressed. Dolls marked 639, 698, 870, 1032, 1123, 1235, "DEP" or "Germany" after 1888. Some have "Wagner & Zetzsche" marked on head, paper label inside top of body. Allow more for molded bonnet or elaborate hairdo.**

Closed mouth, **glass eyes**

15"–18" $450.00–600.00

20"–22" $550.00–700.00

24"– 26" $800.00–1,000.00

Open mouth

16"–18" $300.00–375.00

20"–22" $475.00–550.00

Character Baby, **1910s on, open mouth, sleep eyes, bent limb body. Allow more for flirty eyes or toddler body. Molds such as 1322, 1342, 1346, 1352, 1361.**

10"–12" $250.00–300.00

16"–19" $300.00–425.00

22"–24" $325.00–450.00

Mold 1407, **Baby Bo-Kaye**

8"–9" $2,300.00–2,400.00

15"–19" $1,600.00–2,000.00

Child, All-Bisque: See All-Bisque Section.

Child, **1880 onward, bisque socket head, ball-jointed composition body, glass eyes, wig, closed mouth**

Mold 630, **glass eyes, closed mouth, ca. 1880**

20"–22" $1,200.00–1,500.00

Mold 911, 915, 916, **swivel head, closed mouth, ca. 1890, more for lady body**

16"–18" $1,500.00–1,700.00

20"–22" $1,900.00–2,100.00

Mold 938, **swivel head, closed mouth, ca. 1890**

22"–24" 2,500.00–3,100.00

Mold 1362, **ca. 1912, Sweet Nell,**

14"–16" $350.00–450.00

18"–20" $300.00–375.00

22"–24" $400.00–500.00

26"–28" $500.00–600.00

29"–32" $550.00–650.00

Character Child, ca. 1910 onward, bisque socket head, composition ball-jointed body

Mold 1357, ca. 1912, solid dome or wigged, painted eyes, open mouth; mold 1358, ca. 1910, molded hair, ribbon, flowers, painted eyes, open mouth

15"–20" $975.00–1,700.00

Mold 1322, 1342, 1352, 1361, glass eyes

14"–16" $425.00–500.00

18"–20" $550.00–650.00

28"–30" $650.00–750.00

Mold 1367, 1368, ca. 1914, less for baby body

15" $450.00–475.00

LOUIS AMBERG & SONS

1878–1930, Cincinnati, Ohio, and New York City. Importer, wholesaler, and manufacturer. First company to manufacture all American-made composition dolls.

Newborn Babe, Bottle Babe, 1914 on, bisque head on cloth body, hands of celluloid, bisque, or rubber, sleep eyes, painted hair, closed or open mouth, molds such as 886, 371

Closed mouth

8"–10" $100.00–150.00

12"–14" $175.00–250.00

16"–18" $200.00–275.00

Charlie Chaplin, 1915, composition head with molded moustache, cloth body, composition hands, cloth label on sleeve

12"–14" $400.00–500.00

31" $600.00–650.00

AmKid, 1918, composition shoulder head, kidolene body, composition arms, sleep eyes, wig

22" $100.00–150.00

Happinus, 1918, all-composition with head and torso molded in one piece, coquette-style, brown painted hair molded with hair ribbon

10" $275.00–325.00

Baby Peggy, portrait of child-actress Peggy Montgomery

Composition, 1923, composition head, arms, and legs, cloth body, molded bobbed hair painted brown, painted eyes

18"–20" $600.00–800.00

20" Baby Peggy, Amberg, mold 983, bisque shoulderhead: $1300. **Photo courtesy of Sara Bernstein's Dolls.**

Bisque, **1924, bisque socket head or shoulder head, composition or kid body, sleep eyes, brown mohair wig**

Molds 972, 973, **socket head**

18"–22"... $2,300.00–2,500.00

Molds 982, 983, **shoulder head**

18"–22"... $1,200.00–1,500.00

Baby Peggy, All-Bisque: See All-Bisque, German Section.

Composition Toddler, **1928, composition head and body, molded hair, painted eyes**

13"–15".. $225.00–275.00

Little Phyllis May, 1921, **composition shoulder head, and lower arms, cloth body, molded hair**

14"... $175.00–225.00

Mibs, **1921, composition turned shoulder head, designed by Hazel Drukker, cloth body with composition arms and legs, painted eyes, molded painted hair, molded painted shoes and socks or barefoot mama-style leg**

16"... $900.00–1,100.00

Mibs, All-Bisque: See All-Bisque, German Section.

Miss Victory, **composition dolly faced doll, ball jointed composition body, wig, sleep eyes**

16"–20".. $150.00–200.00

Sunny Orange Maid, 1924, **composition shoulder head, cloth body with composition arms and legs, head has molded "orange" bonnet**

14"... $650.00–800.00

Vanta Baby, **1927 on, sold through Sears, advertising for Vanta baby clothes, bent-limb composition body, sleep eyes, open mouth with two teeth, painted hair**

Bisque head

14"–18".. $500.00–700.00

22"–27".. $850.00–1,100.00

Composition head

> 10"–14"..$150.00–175.00
>
> 18"–23"..$225.00–250.00

Edwina, Sue, or It, **1928, all-composition, painted features, molded side-part hair with swirl on forehead, body twist construction**

> 12"–14"..$275.00–425.00

Tiny Tots, Body Twists, **1929, all-composition, swivel waist ball attached to torso with a ball, molded hair, painted features, boy or girl**

> 7½"–8½" $70.00–100.00

Peter Pan, **1928, all-composition, round joint at waist, wearing original Peter Pan fashion dress**

> 14"..$325.00–425.00

AMERICAN CHARACTER
DOLL COMPANY

12" Puggy, American Character, composition: $300. **Photo courtesy of Morphy Auctions.**

16" Tiny Tears w/Rock-a-Bye eyes, American Character, vinyl: $375. **Photo courtesy of Charlotte's Web Vintage Dolls and Collectibles.**

1919–1963, New York City. Made composition dolls, in 1923 registered the trademark "Petite" for mama and character dolls, later made cloth, rubber, hard plastic, and vinyl dolls. In 1960 the company name was changed to American Character Doll & Toy Co.

"A.C." or "Petite" marked composition doll, **1923, composition heads and limbs, cloth body**

Baby

> 11"–14"..$80.00–125.00
>
> 16"–20"..$150.00–200.00

Mama doll, **sleep eyes, human hair wig**

> 16"–18"..$125.00–175.00
>
> 24"..$175.00–225.00

Petite girls, **1930s, all-composition**

16"–18" $175.00–225.00

24" $275.00–300.00

Toddler

13" $175.00–200.00

Bottletot, **1926, composition head and bent limbs, cloth body, painted hair, open mouth, one arm molded to hold molded celluloid bottle**

13" $200.00–225.00

18" $300.00–325.00

All-rubber, **drink and wet, painted eye doll in layette case, labeled Bottletot, A Petite Baby, doll marked on back with Horsman horseshoe with "petite Dolls // Pt. Pending"**

9½" $100.00–150.00

Puggy, **1928, all-composition, character face with frown and side-glancing painted eyes, molded painted hair, jointed at neck, shoulders, and hips, original outfits included baseball player, boy scout, cowboy, and newsboy. Mark: "A // Petite // Doll," clothes tagged "Puggy // A Petite Doll"**

13" $275.00–325.00

Sally, **1930, Patsy-type, all-composition, molded hair or wig, marks: "Petite" or "American Char. Doll Co.," painted or sleep eyes**

12" $75.00–100.00

14"–16" $150.00–175.00

18"–22" $150.00–200.00

Sally, **Shirley-type wig**

24" $300.00–325.00

Sally-Joy, **composition head on cloth body**

13"–16" $80.00–150.00

18"–24" $150.00–225.00

Carol Ann Beery, **1935, portrait doll of child-actor, daughter of Wallace Beery, all-composition, mohair wig with two braids drawn up across top of head, marks: "Petite Sally" or "Petite"**

13" $300.00–400.00

16" $500.00–600.00

20" $625.00–700.00

Little Love **(also called Newborn Babe), 1942, composition flange neck head and hands, cloth body, molded hair, sleep eyes, a Bye-Lo type doll**

16"–20" $160.00–200.00

Vinyl, **sleep eyes, molded hair**

16" $100.00–120.00

18" Annie Oakley, American Character, hard plastic: $200. **Photo courtesy of McMasters Harris Apple Tree Doll Auctions.**

18" Sweet Sue, American Character, walker, hard plastic: $125. **Photo courtesy of McMasters Harris Apple Tree Doll Auctions.**

Tiny Tears, **1950s, hard plastic head with tear ducts, drink and wet doll. More for Rock-A-Bye eyes. Doll in excellent condition with layette can bring double value listed or more.**

Rubber body

11½"	**$250.00–350.00**
13½"	**$350.00–450.00**
16"	**$375.00–475.00**
18"	**$450.00–500.00**

Clothing and accessories

Bottle	**$35.00**
Bubble pipe	**$25.00**
Bracelet	**$30.00**
Plastic cradle	**$200.00**
Romper	**$35.00**

All-vinyl, **1963**

11½"	**$100.00–150.00**
13½"	**$200.00–225.00**
16"	**$200.00–275.00**
20"	**$275.00–300.00**

Danbury Mint, **2000, reissue, porcelain, with layette, <u>complete and perfect</u>**

10"	**$100.00–175.00**

Sweet Sue, 1953–1961, all-hard plastic or hard plastic and vinyl, saran wig, some on walker bodies others fully jointed including elbows, knees, and ankles, marks: "A.C." "Amer. Char. Doll" or "American Character" in a circle. Elaborate costumes bring higher end of range.

15"	**$100.00–150.00**
18"–20"	**$125.00–200.00**
22"–25"	**$175.00–275.00**
31"	**$300.00–400.00**

30" Little Miss Echo, American Character, vinyl, MIB: $300. **Photo courtesy of Charlotte's Web Vintage Dolls and Collectibles.**

11" Ben Cartwright, vinyl, MIB: $200. **Photo courtesy of Morphy Auctions.**

Sweet Sue Sophisticate, **vinyl head, earrings**

    20"... $150.00–375.00

Annie Oakley, 1953, hard plastic walker

    14".. $200.00–250.00

18"–20" 175.00–225.00

I Love Lucy Baby, 1952, girl doll dressed in pink, made for 1 year only as the birth of the baby was awaited on "I Love Lucy" television show

    14".. $550.00–600.00

Ricky Jr., 1954–1956, personality doll based on character from "I Love Lucy" television show, baby

Hard plastic with rubber body, **1952**

    14"–16"... $200.00–400.00

All-vinyl, **1953–1956**

    13"... $150.00–175.00

    18"–21"... $175.00–200.00

Toodles, 1956, hard rubber drink and wet doll

Teeny Toodles

    11"... $100.00–150.00

    18"–21"... $175.00–200.00

    29"... $225.00–300.00

Toodles Toddler, **1960, vinyl and hard plastic, "Peek-a-Boo" eyes**

    24"... $200.00–250.00

    30"... $275.00–300.00

Eloise, 1955, cloth with molded mask face, yarn hair

    22"... $225.00–175.00

Toni, 1958, vinyl head with rooted hair

    14"... $175.00–250.00

20"..$200.00–300.00

25"..$300.00–400.00

Little Miss Toni

10½"..$90.00–175.00

Little Miss Echo, **1964, vinyl, recorder mechanism in torso**

30"..$125.00–175.00

Miss America, **1963** $50.00–65.00

Tressy, **1963–1965, vinyl, grow hair doll, marks: "American Doll & Toy Corp. // 19C.63" in a circle. MIB dolls will bring double the values here.**

11"..$50.00–65.00

Black $150.00–200.00

Pre-teen Tressy, **1963**

15"..$75.00–100.00

Tressy family and friends

Cricket

9"..$40.00–50.00

Mary Make-Up, **non-grow hair**

11½"..$50.00–80.00

Chuckles, **1969, vinyl, rooted hair, sleep eyes**

16"..$65.00–85.00

22"..$125.00–200.00

Whimsies, **1960, all-vinyl characters**

Dixie the Pixie, Hedda Get Bedda (three face), Miss Take, Tiller the Talker, Wheeler the Dealer, and others

19"–20"..$100.00–225.00

Whimettes, **1963 smaller doll modeled after the whimsies**

7½"..$100.00–175.00

Cartwrights, Ben, Hoss, Little Joe, **1966, personality dolls based on characters from the "Bonanza" television show. MIB dolls will bring double the values here.**

9"..$85.00–100.00

Bonanza Outlaw

9"..$200.00–225.00

ANNALEE MOBILITEE DOLL CO.

1934 to present, Meredith, New Hampshire. Dolls originally designed by Annalee Thorndike, cloth with wire armature "mobilitee" body, painted features.

Early dolls, **1934–1960**

9"–10½"... $300.00–500.00

Later dolls, **must be in excellent condition with tags**

10" Folk Hero dolls

Robin Hood & Johnny Appleseed

1983–1984 .... $25.00–45.00

Annie Oakley,

1985 .... $80.00–125.00

Mark Twain,

1986 .... $65.00–80.00

7" 1991 Logo Kid, Annalee, felt: $25. **Courtesy of private collection.**

Ben Franklin,

1987 .... $60.00–75.00

Sherlock Holmes,

1988 .... $45.00–50.00

Abraham Lincoln,

1989 .... $45.00–50.00

Betsy Ross,

1990 .... $45.00–50.00

Christopher Columbus,

1991 .... $45.00–50.00

Uncle Sam,

   1992 .... **$55.00–65.00**

Pony Express,

   1993 .... **$55.00–75.00**

"50's Style" Bean Nose Santa,

   1994 .... **$40.00–65.00**

Pocahontas,

   1995 .... **$30.00–45.00**

   Logo Kid dolls .... **$15.00–$25.00**

Milk & Cookies, **1985** Sweetheart, **1986**
Naughty, **1987**
Raincoat, **1988**
Christmas Morning, **1989**
Clown, **1990**
Reading, **1991**
Back to School, **1992**
Ice Cream, **1993**
Dress-Up Santa, **1994**
Goin' Fishin', **1995**
Little Mae Flowers, **1996**
Tea for Two?, **1997**
15th Anniversary Kid, **1998**
Mending My Teddy, **1999**
Precious Cargo, **2000**
Mother's Little Helper, **2001**
Sand Castle Susie, **2002**

Museum Collection Dolls

   1997 Skier **$25.00–40.00**

MAX OSCAR ARNOLD

1877–1930, Neustadt, Thüringia, Germany. Made dressed dolls and mechanical dolls including phonograph dolls.

Baby, *bisque socket head,* **composition body**

   12" **$100.00–125.00**

   16" **$225.00–250.00**

   19" **$350.00–400.00**

18" mold 201, Max Oscar Arnold, bisque: $250. **Photo courtesy of The Museum Doll Shop.**

Child

Shoulder head, **kid body, open mouth, glass sleep eyes, wigged**

12"–19" $200.00–300.00

Bisque socket head, **composition body, glass sleep eyes, wigged, molds such as 200, 201, 250, or MOA**

High-quality bisque

6½" on flapper body $300.00–325.00

12" $175.00–200.00

15"–18" $200.00–250.00

21"–24" $300.00–350.00

32"–35" $425.00–500.00

Low-quality bisque

15" $100.00–125.00

18"–20" $175.00–225.00

24" $225.00–275.00

ARRANBEE DOLL CO.

1922–1958, New York City. Sold to the Vogue Doll Company who continued to use their molds until 1961. Some bisque heads used by Arranbee were made by Armand Marseille and Simon & Halbig. The company also produced composition, rubber, hard plastic, and vinyl dolls.

My Dream Baby, **1924+**

Bisque Head, **head made by Armand Marseille, marked Germany, cloth body with rubber hands**

14"–16" $200.00–275.00

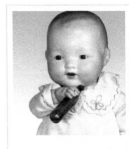

15" Bottletot, Arranbee, bisque head, detail shot of molded bottle in doll's hand: $225. **Photo courtesy of Memories of Things Past.**

21" Debuteen, Arranbee, composition: $375. **Photo courtesy of Phillip Weiss Auctions.**

Composition head, **1927, composition, lower arms and legs, cloth body, metal sleep eyes**

8"–10" $120.00–150.00

17"–23" $200.00–250.00

Composition

Baby

8" $125.00–175.00

12"–14" $200.00–225.00

23" $240.00–260.00

Bottletot, **1926, all-composition, molded bottle in hand**

13" $200.00–225.00

16" $325.00–350.00

Bisque head, **molded bottle in hand**

12"–14" $225.00–250.00

Child, **1930s and 1940s, all-composition, mohair wig, marks: "Arranbee" or "R & B"**

9" $110.00–130.00

14"–15" $160.00–200.00

Debu 'Teen, **1938 on, all-composition, elaborate costume brings higher end of price range**

11" $175.00–275.00

14" $200.00–400.00

17" $275.00–450.00

21" $325.00–450.00

Skating costume

14" $225.00–250.00

17" $250.00–275.00

21" $350.00–375.00

13" Nancy with trunk set, Arranbee, composition: $275. **Photo courtesy of Alderfer Auction Company, Inc.**

21" Nancy Lee, Arranbee, composition: $300. **Photo courtesy of Alderfer Auction Company, Inc.**

WAC

18"..$500.00–525.00

Kewty, **1934–1936, all-composition, mohair wig, marks: "Kewty"**

14"..$250.00–300.00

Little Angel Baby, **1940s, composition head, cloth body, molded painted hair**

11"..$120.00–140.00

16"..$150.00–170.00

18"..$170.00–200.00

Hard Plastic

18"..$150.00–225.00

Mama doll, **1920s on, composition and cloth**

20"–24"..$190.00–225.00

Nancy, **1930s, Patsy-type, all-composition, marks: "Arranbee" or "Nancy"**

Molded hair, painted eyes

12"..$200.00–250.00

17"–21"..$250.00–350.00

Nancy Lee, **all-composition, mohair wig, sleep eyes**

12"–14"..$175.00–225.00

17"–19"..$200.00–250.00

Storybook dolls, **1935, composition dolls dressed as storybook charactors**

8½"–10"..$100.00–130.00

Hard Plastic & Vinyl

Cinderella, **1952, hard plastic**

14"..$175.00–225.00

20"..$325.00–375.00

Coty Girl, **1958, vinyl, high heel fashion doll, allow more for rare outfits**

10½"..$125.00–175.00

9" Little Bo Peep, Storybook Series, Arranbee, composition, MIB. $110. **Photo courtesy of Minton's Doll and Curiosity Shop.**

11" Littlest Angel, Arranbee, hard plastic, MIB: $135. **Photo courtesy of Charlotte's Web Vintage Dolls and Collectibles.**

Lil Imp, **1960, vinyl with red hair and freckles**

    10".. $75.00–100.00

Littlest Angel, **1956, hard plastic, bent knee walker, mark: "R & B"**

    11".. $90.00–110.00

My Angel, **1961, hard plastic and vinyl**

    17".. $45.00–55.00

    22".. $75.00–100.00

    36".. $155.00–165.00

Walker, **1957–1959**

    30".. $130.00–150.00

Vinyl head on oilcloth body, **1959**

    22".. $50.00–60.00

Nanette, **1949–1959, hard plastic, synthetic wig, sleep eyes, closed mouth**

    14".. $100.00–125.00

    17".. $125.00–175.00

Nanette Walker, **1957–1959, vinyl head with hard plastic body, wigged**

    15".. $90.00–120.00

    17".. $120.00–160.00

    20".. $225.00–275.00

17" in black cocktail outfit, mint condition sold for $972.00 in online auction

Nancy, **1951–1952, vinyl head with hard plastic body, wigged**

    14".. $125.00–150.00

    18".. $170.00–190.00

Nancy Lee, **1950–1959, hard plastic**

    14".. $225.00–275.00

    17".. $300.00–375.00

    20".. $450.00–500.00

17" Nanette, Arranbee hard plastic, MIB: $135. **Photo courtesy of Phillip Weiss Auctions.**

Nancy Lee Baby, **1952, painted eyes, crying face**

    15"...$95.00–115.00

Sweet Pea, **1956, vinyl drink and wet baby, rooted hair, sleep eyes**

    12"...$45.00–55.00

Taffy, **1956, Cissy-type**

    18"–23"...$95.00–115.00

ARTIST DOLLS

Original artist dolls may be one-of-a-kind pieces or limited edition pieces made by the designing artist. Production artist dolls are artist series produced in workshop or factory settings, worked on by people other than the designing artist, often limited edition. Values listed reflect secondary market prices. Retail from the artist will differ.

Original Artist Dolls

Martha Armstrong-Hand, **porcelain**

    Babies...$1,600.00–1,800.00

Children

    Brandon, Elizabeth...........................$450.00–500.00

Bob and June Beckett, **wood**

    Baby...$100.00–125.00

    Children $200.00–250.00

Floyd Bell, **wood, historic figures**

    13"–16"...$150.00–300.00

Jane Bradbury, **cernit**

    14"–15"...$600.00–750.00

 11" Baby Alex Paul, Martha Armstrong-Hand, 1978 LE of 25, bisque: $1,800. **Photo courtesy of Morphy Auctions.**

 11" Betty Curtis, molded cloth: $200. **Photo courtesy of Morphy Auctions.**

Resin

23"–24" $120–150.00

Frances Bringloe, **wood**

Pioneer Children or Parents

6¼" $300.00–400.00

Muriel Bruyere, **low-fire porcelain**

Children

8" $200.00–225.00

Helen Bullard, **wood**

Original artist dolls

12"–24" $700.00–1,000.00

Production artist dolls

Holly, Barbry Allen

10"–11" $200.00–250.00

Tennessee Mountain Kids

.... $40.00–50.00

Hedy Cayton, **cloth over solid form**

Children

18" $250.00–300.00

Emma Clear, **porcelain**

China or bisque ladies

10"–24" $250.00–600.00

George & Martha Washington

Painted eyes .... $800.00–1,200.00 **pair**

Glass eyes .... $900.00–1,300.00 **pair**

 14" Edith and Little Bear, Haut Melton, felt, ca. 1997: $1,200 **Photo courtesy of Alderfer Auction Company, Inc.**

 18" Sandreuter, all wooden, ca 1993: $2,200. **Photo courtesy of Alderfer Auction Company, Inc.**

Dewees Cochran, **various media: latex composition**

Grow Up Series

    13"–18"..$1,200.00–1,800.00

Look Alikes, portrait children

    15"–16"...$800.00–1,500.00

    18"–20"..$2,000.00–3,000.00

Production doll, **Cindy**

    15"..$500.00–900.00

Betty Curtis, **molded cloth**

    11"– 13"...$200.00–300.00

Dianne Dengel, **cloth**

    3½" $100.00–125.00

    15"–21"...$200.00–300.00

Gertrude Florian, **ceramic, composition**

Ladies

    15"–17"...$150.00–225.00

Patti Hale, **wood**

    9"–15" $175.00–300.00

Cathy Hansen, **porcelain**

    All bisque child $200.00–400.00

Haut Melton, **molded felt**

Edith the Lonely Doll

    14"..$650.00–1,200.00

Dorothy Heizer, **cloth**

20th Century Fashion Ladies

    ....$1,600.00–2,000.00

26" Ellen, Barefoot Children Series, Annette Himstedt, vinyl: $200. **Photo courtesy of Morphy Auctions.**

12" Goldilocks with 8" crying Baby Bear, R. John Wright Dolls, Inc., felt: $850. **Photo courtesy of Withington Auction Inc.**

Historic Figures, **10"–11"**

Men and more simple costumes

.... $2,600.00–3,200.00

More elaborate costume (**queens, etc.**)

.... $3,500.00–5,000.00

Maggie Head Kane, **porcelain**

19"–25" $100.00–130.00

Avis Lee, **wood**

Americanettes

11" $500.00–800.00

Tykes, cloth body

11" $375.00–425.00

Maryanne Oldenburg, **porcelain**

Children $100.00–150.00

Irma Park, **wax**

Wax over porcelain miniatures

2"–3" $50.00–125.00

Ann Parker, **resin**

12" $100.00–300.00

Frances & Bernard Ravca, **various media**

Crepe paper

6"–7" $110.00–160.00

Cloth, **needlesculpted**

Peasants

10"–14" $150.00–200.00

Other figures

10"–14" $250.00–400.00

Composition, cloth and paper

Celebrities, such as Sinatra, Lena Horne, Veronica Lake, etc.

10"–14" $500.00–1,000.00

Kathy Redmond, **porcelain**

Ladies

13"–14" $300.00–450.00

Regina Sandreuter, **wood**

17"–18" $2,000.00–2,200.00

Madeline Saucier, **cloth**

15"–19" $225.00–300.00

Sherman Smith, **wood, 5"–6"**

Simple style...................................... $250.00–325.00

More elaborate $450.00–550.00

Bisque head on wooden body

.... $200.00–450.00

Lewis Sorenson, **wax**

Kewpie type

15"... $100.00–150.00

Ladies

14"–25" $450.00–600.00

Peddler

18"–25" $450.00–500.00

Martha Thompson, **porcelain**

Early reproductions of antique dolls

13"–18" $350.00–450.00

19th Century Fashion Ladies

10"–14" $700.00–1,200.00

Betsy $400.00–500.00

Prince Dharles and Princess Anne

10"– 11" .... $1,000.00–1,200.00 ea.

Fashion plate ladies

8"–14"... $800.00–2,000.00

Little Women.................................... $350.00–400.00 each

Ellery Thorpe, **porcelain**

Children $400.00–500.00

Vargas, **wax**

Ethnic figures

 10"–11" $600.00–700.00

Clara Wade **porcelain, marked Clarmaid**

Buster Brown, glass eyes

 18".. $350.00–450.00

Faith Wick, **porcelain, Mother Goose, Lindberg, etc.**

 18"–21" $100.00–180.00

Fawn Zeller, **porcelain**

 One-of-a-Kind $1,000.00–2,000.00

US Historical Society

 Holly... $200.00–300.00

 Polly II $175.00–225.00

Production Artist Dolls

Sabine Esche, **vinyl by Sigikid**

 22"... $200.00–300.00

Julie Good Kruger, **vinyl**

 16"–22" $75.00–125.00

Hildegard Gunzel, **various media**

Porcelain for Seymour Mann, **limited 1,200**

 26"... $100.00–140.00

Vinyl

Children

 24"–30" $125.00–300.00

Sonja Hartmann, **various media**

Porcelain

 20"... $200.00–250.00

Vinyl

 18"–23" $50.00–100.00

Philip Heath, **vinyl**

World of Children Collection

 23"–32" $400.00–700.00

Karin Heller, **cloth**

 Children $100.00–200.00

Annette Himstedt, **1986 on. Distributed by Timeless Creations, a division of Mattel, Inc. Swivel rigid vinyl head with shoulder plate, cloth body, vinyl limbs, inset eyes, real lashes, molded eyelids, holes in nostrils, human hair wig, bare feet, original in box.**

Barefoot Children, **1986, Bastian, Beckus, Ellen, Fatou, Kathe, Lisa, Paaula**

    26"..**$175.00–250.00**

The World Children, **1988, 31"**

      Friederike **$325.00–400.00**

      Kasimir..**$325.00–400.00**

      Makimura..**$250.00–300.00**

      Malin **$375.00–400.00**

      Michiko...**$175.00–225.00**

Reflections of Youth, **1989–1990, Adrienne, Ayoka, Kai, Mia Yin, Neblina, Tarea**

    26"..**$150.00–225.00**

World Children's Summit,

    35"..**$500.00–1,000.00**

Maggie Iacono, **cloth**

Children

    11"–16"..**$300.00–800.00**

Helen Kish **vinyl**

Children

    7"..**$150.00–200.00**

    10"–12"..**$300.00–400.00**

Lee Middleton, **vinyl**

    Babies & toddlers.............................**$75.00–85.00**

Bubba Chubbs

    22"..**$65.00–75.00**

Harold Nabor **resin**

Children

    14"–15"..**$85.00–100.00**

Lynn & Michael Roche, **porcelain**

Children

wood body

    17"–22"..**$1,000.00–1,800.00**

cloth body

    17"–22"..**$500.00–1,000.00**

Robert Tonner, **vinyl**

Fashion Models

19"..$175.00–225.00

Robin Woods, **1980s on. Creative designer for various companies, including Le Petit Ami, Robin Woods Company, Madame Alexander (Alice Darling), Horsman, and Playtime Productions.**

Cloth

1985, **clowns** $25.00–35.00

Vinyl

2000, **Halle Angel, for Home Shopping Network**

14"..$20.00–25.00

R. John Wright, **cloth**

Early Adult Peasant characters

....$600.00–900.00

Children $450.00–900.00

Gepetto & Pinocchio

18"..$1,800.00–2,000.00

Scootles $300.00–400.00

Raggedy Ann $550.00–600.00

U.F.D.C. Souvenir dolls, **various artists for special events**

Wendy Lawton, **2002, Katrena**

9"..$90.00–110.00

Kathy Redmond, **Alice Roosevelt, 1990, porcelain**

9"..$60.00–75.00

MaggieIacono, **Dolly's Dream, 2015 event**

11"..$250.00–300.00

Fawn Zeller, **porcelain, 1991, Janette**

13"..$100.00–125.00

ASHTON-DRAKE

Located in Niles, Illinois, Ashton-Drake is a division of Bradford Industries. Manufactures dolls designed by a number of well-known artists. Sells its doll lines through distributors or via direct mail-order sales to the public. Doll in perfect condition with original clothing and tags.

34" Patti Playpal, Ashton Drake, vinyl reissue: $150. **Photo courtesy of McMasters Harris Apple Tree Doll Auctions.**

Yolanda Bello

Picture Perfect Babies

Jason, **1985**.....................................$80.00–100.00

Heather, **1986**

Jennifer, **1987**

Matthew, **1987**

Amanda, **1988**

Sarah, **1989**

Jessica, **1989**

Michael, **1990**

Lisa, **1990**

Emily, **1991**

Danielle, **1991**

....$15.00–25.00 each

Playtime Babies, 1994

Lindsey, Shawna, Todd

....$25.00–35.00 each

Lullaby Babies...............................$20.00–25.00

Blythe, 2005, vinyl, reissue of Hasbro doll

11½" ....$150.00–225.00 each

Diana Effner

Heroines of Fairy Tale series,

Cinderella, Snow White, Goldilocks, Red Ridinghood, Rapunzel

16"..$40.00–50.00

Mother Goose series, Mary Mary, Curl with a Curl, Curly Locks, Snips & Snails

14"..$40.00–55.00

Julie Good-Krueger

Amish Blessings series

Rebeccah, Rachel, Adam

....$25.00–35.00

Joan Ibarolle

Little House on the Prairie series, **1992–1995**

Laura, Mary, Carrie, Ma & Pa

....$35.00–65.00

Baby Grace $55.00–75.00

Nellie, Almanzo

....$30.00–40.00

Wendy Lawton

Little Women, **set of 5,**

16"...$75.00–100.00

Mary Had a Little Lamb, Little Bo Peep, Little Miss Muffet

....$18.00–25.00

Others

Glamor of the Gibson Girl, **1987, porcelain, designed by Arlene Siegel**

18"...$25.00–30.00

Patty Playpal Reissues

35"–37"...$150.00–200.00 MIB

Princess Diana, **porcelain**

19"...$45.00–55.00

Mel Odom

GENE

1995, **designed by Mel Odom marketed through Ashton Drake**

Premier, **1**st

1995 ....$60.00–70.00

Monaco, **2**nd

1995 ....$35.00–45.00

Red Venus, **3**rd

1995 ....$30.00–40.00

Other Genes

Bird of Paradise

1997 ....$35.00–35.00

Blue Goddess....................................$45.00–55.00

Breathless

    1999 .... $45.00–550.00

    Iced Coffee $35.00–45.00

Midnight Romance

    1997 .... $55.00–75.00

Song of Spain

    1999 .... $35.00–40.00

White Hyacinth

    1997 .... $30.00–40.00

Gene Specials

An American Countess, **NALED**

    1999 .... $45.00–55.00

Covent Garden, **NALED**

    1998 .... $30.00–35.00

Heart of Hollywood

    2000 .... $45.00–65.00

King's Daughter, **NALED**

    1997 .... $35.00–45.00

Moments to Remember, **MDCC, limited edition 250**

    2000 .... $130.00–150.00

My Favorite Witch, **MDCC, limited edition 350**

    1997 .... $260.00–270.00

Night at Versailles, **FAO Schwarz**

    1997 .... $70.00–80.00

On the Avenue, **FAO Schwarz**

    1998 .... $45.00–55.00

Priceless, **FAO Schwarz exclusive**

    1999 .... $55.00–65.00

Sparkling Seduction, **NALED**

    1997 .... $35.00–45.00

Titus Tomescu

From This Day Forward bridal series,

    1994 .... $40.00–50.00

Barely Yours Series, **babies**

.... $40.00–75.00 each

I Am the Way, the Truth, and the Life Collection

.... $50.00–60.00

ASIAN DOLLS

20" Bru Jne, bisque: sold at auction for $54,900. **Photo courtesy of Morphy Auctions.**

16" mold 1169, Simon Halbig, bisque: $2,100. **Photo courtesy of Sweetbriar Auctions.**

1850 to present. Dolls depicting Asian peoples. Made by companies in Germany, America, Japan, and others.

All-Bisque

Heubach, Gebrüder, **Chin-Chin**

4"–4½ " $150.00–200.00

Kestner

6"... $1,200.00–1,300.00

7½ " $1,400.00–1,500.00

8".. $1,700.00–1,900.00

Simon & Halbig, **mold 852, ca. 1880, all-bisque, Asian, swivel head, yellow tint bisque, glass eyes, closed mouth, wig, painted socks and curled pointed toe shoes**

4½" 5½ " $950.00–1,100.00

6½"–7"... $1,050.00–1,300.00

Unmarked or unknown maker, **presumed German or French**

4"–6"... $200.00–500.00

European Bisque

Bisque head, **jointed body**

Bähr & Pröschild, **mold 220, socket head, closed mouth, glass eyes, wigged**

11"–14" $1,800.00–2,800.00

75

Belton-type, **mold 193, 206**

    10"..$1,900.00–2,075.00

    14"..$2,500.00–2,700.00

Bru, **pressed bisque swivel head, glass eyes, closed mouth**

    20" Bru Jne sold for.........................$54,900.00 at auction

Kestner, J. D., **1899–1930+, mold 243, bisque socket head, open mouth, wig, bent-leg baby body, add more for original clothing**

    13"–14"...$1,600.00–2,200.00

    16"–18"...$3,000.00–3,500.00

Solid dome, **painted hair**

    15"...$4,500.00–5,000.00

Konig Wericke, **mold 155, glass eyes, open mouth**

    18"...$1,700.00–1,800.00

Armand Marseille, **1925, mold 353, solid-dome bisque socket head, glass eyes, closed mouth**

Baby body

    7½"..$400.00–500.00

    9"–12"...$600.00–700.00

    14"–16"...$900.00–1,000.00

Toddler

    16"...$1,200.00–1,500.00

Painted bisque

    7"...$350.00–400.00

Schmidt, Bruno, **marked "BSW," mold 500, ca. 1905, glass eyes, open mouth**

    11"–14"...$900.00–1,200.00

    18"...$1,500.00–1,900.00

Schoenau & Hoffmeister, **mold 4900, bisque socket head, glass eyes, open mouth, tinted composition wood jointed body**

    8"–10"...$600.00–750.00

    18"...$950.00–1,000.00

Simon & Halbig, **mold 1079, 1099, 1129, 1159, 1199,1329, bisque socket head, glass eyes, open mouth, pierced ears, composition wood jointed body**

    8"–10"...$1,200.00–1,300.00

    12"–14"...$1,500.00–2,000.00

    16"–18"...$2,100.00–2,500.00

    20"–24"...$3,000.00–4,500.00

Unknown maker, **socket head, jointed body, closed mouth, glass eyes**

　　4½" $550.00–650.00

　　8"–10" $700.00–900.00

　　12"–14" $1,000.00–1,200.00

　　20" $2,600.00–2,800.00

Cloth

Ada Lum dolls, **1940s on, Shanghai, cloth dolls depicting Chinese people, embroidered features, black yarn hair**

　　8"–14" $100.00–150.00

　　18"–24" $125.00–200.00

Shaohsing Industrial Mission, **Chekang Province, China, cloth dolls depicting Chinese people, painted features**

Miniature doll, **flat silk faces**

　　1½"–3" $30.00–40.00

5 Finger Ching (so-called), **molded cloth head**

　　9"–11" $200.00–250.00

　　15"–19" $300.00–450.00

Amusco, **1925, composition**

　　17" $800.00–1,000.00

Effanbee

Butin-nose, **in basket with wardrobe, painted Asian features including black bobbed hair, bangs, side-glancing eyes, excellent color and condition**

　　8" $400.00–500.00

Patsy, **painted Asian features, including black bangs, straight across the forehead, brown side-glancing eyes, dressed in silk Chinese pajamas and matching shoes, excellent condition**

　　14" .... $ 700.00–800.00

Horsman

Molded Turban head child, **1910 on, composition head and lower arms, cloth body, molded turban on head, painted eyes**

　　11" .... $ 375.00–425.00

Jap Rose Kids, **1911 on, composition head, arms, cloth body, molded painted hair, painted eyes, made as an advertising tie-in to Jap Rose soap**

13" boy or 14" girl

　　.. $ 350.00–375.00

Baby Butterfly, **1914+, composition head, hands, cloth body, painted hair, features**

　　13" .... $ 250.00–300.00

　　15" .... $ 350.00–400.00

Quan-Quan Co., **California, Ming Ming Baby, all-composition jointed baby, painted features, original costume, yarn queue, painted shoes**

> 9"–11" .... $ 75.00–100.00

Traditional Chinese

Man or woman, **composition type head, cloth-wound bodies, may have carved arms and feet, in traditional costume**

> 11" .... $ 75.00–125.00

> 14" .... $ 150.00–225.00

Traditional Japanese

Ichimatsu, **1870s on, a play doll made of papier-mâché-type material with gofun finish of crushed oyster shells, swivel head, shoulder plate, cloth midsection, upper arms, and legs, limbs and torso are papier-mâché, glass eyes, pierced nostrils. Early dolls may have jointed wrists and ankles, in original dress. Later 1950s+ dolls imported by Kimport**

Meiji era, **ca. 1870s–1912**

> 10"–12" .... $ 600.00–750.00

> 16"–18" .... $ 850.00–950.00

> 22"–24" .... $ 1,400.00–1,800.00

Child or Baby

Painted hair, **1920s**

> 12"–15" .... $ 450.00–550.00

> 17"–18" .... $ 575.00–625.00

> 24" .... $ 825.00–875.00

1930s

> 12"–15" .... $ 350.00–425.00

> 17"–18" .... $ 550.00–600.00

1940s on

> 10"–12" .... $ 125.00–150.00

> 14"–16" .... $ 175.00–225.00

Lady

1920s–1930s

> 12"–14" .... $ 200.00–250.00

> 16" .... $ 250.00–275.00

1940s–1950s

> 12"–14" .... $ 70.00–95.00

> 16" .... $ 100.00–135.00

Hina Matsuri, Emperor or Empress, **seated,**

Ca. 1890s

  8"...$ 500.00–575.00

Ca. 1920s

  4"–6"..$ 150.00–175.00

  10"–12".......................................$ 250.00–300.00

Warrior

1880–1890s

  16"...$ 650.00–850.00

Too few in database for reliable range.

On horse

  15"...$ 900.00–1,100.00

Too few in database for reliable range.

1920s

  15"...$ 350.00–400.00

Too few in database for reliable range.

On horse

  13"...$ 800.00–850.00

Wooden dolls

Door of Hope: See Door of Hope section.

AUTOMATONS

25" Edison Phonograph doll, Jumeau head, bisque: $8,000. **Photo courtesy of McMasters Harris Apple Tree Doll Auctions.**

18" Marquis with Butterfly and Flowers, automaton, Lambert, Jumeau head: $6,500. **Photo courtesy of Ann Lloyd Antique Dolls.**

Various manufacturers used many different mediums including bisque, wood, wax, cloth, and others to make dolls that performed some action. More complicated models performing more or complex actions bring higher prices. The unusual one-of-a-kind dolls in this category make it difficult to provide a good range. All these auction prices are for mechanicals in good working order.

Autoperipatetikos, 1860–1870s

Bisque, china, or papier-mâché by American Enoch Rice Morrison, key wound mechanism

    12".. $ 800.00–1,000.00

    With more elaborate, head $1,500.00–2,000.00

Ballerina

Bisque Jumeau head, key rotates head and arms lower, on velvet-covered box

    24".. $ 2,400.00–2,800.00

Edison Phonograph Doll

Simon Halbig or Jumeau **bisque head doll with mechanism in torso of composition body**

Jumeau head

    25".. $ 8,000.00–8,000.00

Simon Halbig **head mold 719**

    23".. $ 3,500.00–4,500.00

Girl Puppeteer

Bisque head Jumeau Triste mold, toy theater in one hand puppy in basket in other hand, when wound girl turns, curtain riseson theater, acrobats perform, puppy peeks out of backet and barks, GustavVichy, ca. 1885

30" sold at auction for $45,200.00

Marquis with Butterfly

French bisque head Jumeau, key wound, raises Butterfly in one hand; flowers in other hand, Leopold Lambert

    18".. $ 6,000.00–7,000.00

Spanish Mandolin Player

Jumeau head, when wound plays mandolin, turns head and leg moves in time to music, Leopold Lambert

23" sold at auction for $ $20,340.00

Troubador

Bisque head, Jumeau, plays mandolin, turns head, Roullet et Descamps

    17".. $ 9,000.00–11,000.00

Piano Player, **bisque head Gaultier, GustavVichy, ca. 1878**

    18".. $ 11,000.00–13,000.00

Riding Toy, **key wind, fur covered horse with doll, metal with German bisque head, when wound the horse gallops across the floor, heads such as Cowboys, Indians, George Washington**

    6".. $ 700.00–900.00

Waltzing Couple, **by Vichy, french poupee heads**

13".. $ 10,000.00–11,000.00

Waltzing Lady, **by Steiner**

16".. $ 6,000.00–7,000.00

Walking doll

Toddling baby, **Heubach baby head, key wound**

13".. 9,000.00–1,100.00

SFBJ head, **simple hand-operated walker mechanism**

14".. $ 750.00–900.00

Roullet et Descamps. **Simon Halbig 1078 head, key wound**

17"–23" .... $ 1,000.00–2,000.00

Steiner

15".. $ 6,000.00–8,000.00

GEORGENE AVERILL

19" Bonnie Babe, Georgene Averill, bisque: $650. **Photo courtesy of McMasters Harris Apple Tree Doll Auctions.**

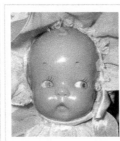

17" Little Cherub, Georgene Averill, composition, Mint condition: $1,000. **Photo courtesy of Dollyology Vintage Dolls.**

1913–1960s, New York City. Georgene and James Averill began their doll business dressing dolls. Georgene was the designer, James the businessman. They began as Averill Manufacturing Company. In 1915 they trademarked the name "Madame Hendron" for doll designs. In 1923 the Averills ended their association with Averill Manufacturing, which continued to make dolls designed by other artists. The Averills also continued to manufacture their own dolls under the name Georgene Novelties.

All-bisque Bonnie Babe: See All-bisque, German section.

Bisque

Allie Kat, **bisque head by Alt, Beck & Gottschalk, glass eyes, open mouth with wobble tongue and teeth, plush Puss in Boots style body with composition boots**

15".. $ 10,000.00–12,000.00

28" Dolly Rekord, composition, phonograph mechanism: $900. **Photo courtesy of Morphy Auctions.**

Allie Dog, **bisque head by Alt, Beck & Gottschalk, glass eyes, open mouth with tongue and teeth, mold 1405**

> 12"–15" .... $ 4500.00–5,5000.00

Bonnie Babe, **1926–1930s, bisque heads made in Germany by Alt, Beck and Gottschalk, cloth bodies made in the USA by K&K toys.**

Bisque head, **open mouth with two lower teeth, composition or celluloid lower arms and legs, cloth body, molds 1368, 1402**

> 10"–12" .... $ 450.00–550.00
>
> 15" .... $ 500.00–600.00
>
> 18"–24" .... $ 600.00–700.00

Celluloid

> 10" .... $ 350.00–400.00
>
> 16" .... $ 525.00–575.00

Composition

Baby Georgene or Baby Hendron, **composition head, arms, and legs, cloth body, marked with name on head**

> 13"–16" .... $ 100.00–175.00
>
> 18"–22" .... $ 200.00–250.00
>
> 24"–26" .... $ 225.00–275.00

Body Twists, **1927, composition with bale swivel joint in torso**

Dimmie & Jimmie

> 14½" .... $ 450.00–500.00

Character or ethnic doll, **1915 on, composition head, cloth or composition body, character faces, painted features**

Indian, Sailor, Dutch Boy, etc.

> 12" .... $ 125.00–175.00
>
> 16" .... $ 200.00–250.00

Black

> 14" .... $ 300.00–350.00

Dolly Reckord, **1922–1928, composition head, arms, and legs, cloth body with record player inside, human hair wig, sleep eyes, open mouth with teeth**

    26"... $ 750.00–900.00

Little Cherub, **designed by Harriet Flanders, composition with painted eyes**

    12"... $ 700.00–800.00

    16"... $ 800.00–900.00

Lullabye Baby, **1920–1925, composition head and hands, cloth body**

    15"–19"... $ 175.00–250.00

Mama doll, **1918 on, composition head, arms and swing style legs, cloth body, voice box in torso, molded hair or mohair wig, painted or sleep eyes**

    15"–18"... $ 150.00–200.00

    20"–22"... $ 300.00–350.00

    28"... $ 400.00–450.00

Peaches, **1928 on, Patsyall-composition, jointed at hips and shoulders, molded hair or wigged, painted eyes or glass, open mouth or closed**

    14"... $ 275.00–325.00

    17"... $ 350.00–400.00

Snookums, **1927, child actor at Universal Stern Brothers studio, composition, laughing mouth with two rows of teeth**

    14"... $ 500.00–600.00

Whistling doll, **1925–1929, doll made a whistling noise when its head was pushed down** Whistling Dan, etc.

    14"–15"... $ 350.00–450.00

Celluloid

Sunny Girl or Sunny Boy, **1927, celluloid head, cloth body, turtle mark**

    15"... $ 275.00–325.00

Cloth

Brownies, Girl Scouts: See Girl Scout section.

Character animals **such as Uncle Wiggley, Nurse Jane, Krazy Kat, and others**

    18"... $ 200.00–250.00

Mask face, **1920s on, molded cloth mask face, painted features, sometimes inset hair eyelashes, yarn hair, cloth body, many dressed in international costumes**

    12"–15"... $ 75.00–110.00

    18"... $ 120.00–150.00

    24"... $ 200.00–250.00

Comic Characters, **1944–1965, cloth, molded mask face, cloth body, appropriate character clothing**

Alvin, Nancy, Sluggo, Little Lulu, etc.

14"...$ 375.00–450.00

Becassine, **1950s, French character doll**

13"...$ 650.00–700.00

Kris Kringle, **cloth mask face**

14"...$ 100.00–150.00

Grace Drayton designs, **1923, flat faced cloth dolls with painted features, some with yarn hair**

Chocolate Drop

10"...$ 300.00–350.00

14"...$ 400.00–450.00

Dolly Dingle

11"...$ 300.00–350.00

15"...$ 425.00–475.00

Maude Tausey Fangel designs, **1938, flat-faced cloth dolls with painted features**

Sweets, Snooks, etc.

12"–14"...$ 275.00–325.00

15"–17"...$ 450.00–525.00

21"...$ 625.00–750.00

Tear Drop Baby, **designed by Dianne Dengel, cloth mask face, molded tear on cheek**

16"...$200.00–250.00

BABYLAND RAG DOLL

Babyland Rag dolls were a line of dolls sold by Horsman from 1893 to 1928. The actual manufacturer of these dolls is still unknown. The dolls were originally marked with paper tags which read "Genuine//Babyland//Trade//Mark." Dolls had flat cloth faces, cloth body, some with mohair wigs. Dolls listed are in good, clean condition with original clothing. Faded, stained or worn examples can bring half the values listed.

Painted face

12"–15"...$ 450.00–550.00

18"–22"...$ 900.00–1,100.00

30"...$ 1,300.00–1,800.00

Black

15"–17"...$ 900.00–1,200.00

20"–22"...$ 1,200.00–1,500.00

17" Babyland Rag, painted face, cloth: $750. **Photo courtesy of Sara Bernstein's Dolls.**

Topsy-Turvy

    13"–15"...**$ 750.00–850.00**

Lithographed face, 1907 on

    12"–15"...**$ 350.00–450.00**

    24"–30"...**$ 550.00–850.00**

Topsy-Turvy

    14"...**$ 450.00–600.00**

BADEKINDER

1860–1940. Most porcelain factories made china and bisque dolls in one-piece molds with molded or painted black or blond hair, and usually undressed. Sometimes called Bathing Dolls, they were dubbed "Frozen Charlotte" from a song about a girl who went dancing dressed lightly and froze in the snow. They range in size from under 1" to over 19". Some were reproduced in Germany in the 1970s to the present. Allow more for pink tint, extra decoration, or hairdo.

All china

Low quality

2"–3" 20.00–35.00

    4"–5"...**$35.00–50.00**

Good quality

    2"–3"...**$65.00–95.00**

    4"–5"...**$120.00–155.00**

    6"–7"...**$180.00–220.00**

    9"–10"...**$230.00–300.00**

    14"–15"...**$450.00–525.00**

4.5" parian-type, Badekinder, "Alice" hair, lustre boots: $450. **Photo courtesy of Oldeclectics.**

Black china

    5"–6".. $190.00–250.00

Blond hair, flesh tones head and neck

    9"–12".. $300.00–425.00

    14"–15".. $400.00–600.00

Molded boots

    4"–5".. $150.00–225.00

    8"... $250.00–300.00

Molded clothes or hats

    1½"–3".. $200.00–275.00

    5"–6".. $300.00–375.00

    8"... $350.00–425.00

Pink tint, hairdo

    3".. $250.00–350.00

    5"–8".. $350.00–450.00

    13"–14".. $550.00–700.00

Pink tint, bonnet-head

    3".. $450.00–475.00

    5".. $550.00–575.00

Bisque

Good quality

    5".. $125.00–175.00

Fancy hair, molded boots

    4"–5".. $225.00–275.00

Stone bisque, molded hair, one piece

3".. $18.00–25.00

6".. $25.00–35.00

Parian-type, **1860**

Simple hairstyle

3"–5".. $125.00–200.00

7".. $250.00–275.00

Molded boots or fancy hair

3"–5".. $350.00–450.00

BÄHR & PRÖSCHILD

18" mold 678, Bähr & Pröschild, bisque: $300. **Photo courtesy of Philip Weiss Auctions.**

11" mold 604, Bähr & Pröschild, bisque, character baby: $135. **Photo courtesy of McMasters Harris Apple Tree Doll Auctions.**

1871–1930s, Orhdruf, Thüringia, Germany. Porcelain factory that made its own dolls as well as providing heads for companies such as Kley & Hahn, Bruno Schmidt, Heinrich Stier, and others.

Belton-type, **1880 on. Solid dome head with flat crown with small stringing holes in it, closed mouth, paperweight eyes, pierced ears, straight wrists, composition or kid body, molds in the 200 series**

12".. $1,300.00–1,600.00

14"–16"... $1,400.00–1,800.00

18"–20"... $2,000.00–2,400.00

Child, **1888, dolly-face bisque head, open or closed mouth, human hair or mohair wig, composition body in German or French style or kid body, molds 213, 224 239, 246, 252, 273, 275, 277, 286, 289, 293, 297, 309, 325, 332, 340, 343, 379, 394**

11"–14"... $200.00–350.00

16"–18"... $400.00–550.00

22"–24"... $600.00–750.00

Kid body

    13"–16"...$225.00–275.00

    22"–24"...$275.00–325.00

Mold 224, **with dimples**

    14"–16"...$800.00–900.00

    22"–24"...$1,000.00–1,200.00

Character Child

Mold 247, **open/closed mouth**

    26"...$2,600.00–2,900.00

Mold 531

    15"–19"...$800.00–1,200.00

Mold 536

    18"–20"...$3,750.00–3,800.00

Mold 604, **open/closed mouth**

    11"–14"...$750.00–850.00

    18"–22"...$950.00–1,050.00

Mold 624, **open mouth**

    12"–17"...$900.00–2,000.00

*Too few in database for a reliable range.

Character Baby, 1909 on, bisque socket head, solid dome or wigged, sleep eyes, open mouth, bent limb body, molds:535, 585, 586, 587, 602, 604, 619, 620, 624, 630, 641, 678

    9"–10"..$100.00–125.00

    12"–14"...$150.00–300.00

    17"–19"...$250.00–350.00

    22"–24"...$400.00–450.00

Toddler body

    10"–12"...$250.00–1350.00

    18"–20"...$350.00–450.00

BARBIE®

Barbie', 1959 to present, Hawthorne, California, 11½" fashion doll manufactured by Mattel Inc. Values listed are for perfect condition dolls in original clothing and bearing all appropriate tags. Played with and undressed dolls should be valued at one-fourth to one-third the value of perfect. Mint-in-box examples will bring double to triple the values listed here.

11.5"Barbie®, # 2, Mattel, vinyl: $6,000. **Photo courtesy of McMasters Harris Apple Tree Doll Auctions.**

11.5"Barbie®, swirl ponytail, Mattel, vinyl: $400. **Photo courtesy of McMasters Harris Apple Tree Doll Auctions.**

Lilli, 1955–1964, a German cartoon character, created by Reinhard Beuthien for the tabloid *Bild-Zeitung* in Hamburg, Germany, inspiration for Barbie design

7½" $2,000.00–3,000.00

12" $4,000.00–5,000.00

Hong Kong copies of Lilli see Vinyl section

#1 Barbie®, 1959, heavy, solid vinyl torso, faded to pale white color, white irises, pointed arch eyebrows, soft texture ponytail hairstyle, black and white swimsuit, gold hoop earrings, metal lined holes in bottom of feet and shoes to accept doll stand

Blond $6,500.00–8,000.00

Brunette $7,000.00–9,500.00

#2 Barbie®, 1959, doll same as previous doll, but with no holes in feet, some wore pearl earrings

Blond $4,000.00–6,000.00

Brunette $4,000.00–5,000.00

#3 Barbie®, 1960, same as previous doll, but now has blue irises and curved eyebrows

Blond $600.00–800.00

Brunette $800.00–900.00

#4 Barbie®, 1960, same as previous doll, but torso now has a flesh-tone color

Blond or brunette $300.00–400.00

#5 Barbie®, 1961, same as previous, but now has a hollow, hard plastic torso, hair is now firmer texture saran

Blond, titian or brunette $275.00–325.00

#6 Barbie®, 1962, same as previous, but now the doll is available in many more hair and lipstick colors and wears a red swimsuit

.... $200.00–250.00

Swirl Ponytail, 1964, smooth bangs swirled across forehead and to the side instead of the curly bangs of the previous ponytail dolls

.... $400.00–600.00

11.5"Barbie®, fashion queen, Mattel, vinyl, MIB: $500. **Photo courtesy of McMasters Harris Apple Tree Doll Auctions.**

11.5" Barbie®, bubble cut, Mattel, vinyl, MIB: $650. **Photo courtesy of Morphy Auctions.**

Bubblecut Barbie®, 1961, same doll as others of this year but with new bubble cut hairstyle

Brown $400.00–450.00

White Ginger $350.00–400.00

Others $150.00–200.00

Side-part bubblecut $300.00–350.00

Barbie® Fashion Queen, 1963, doll has molded hair with a hair band and three interchangeable wigs, gold and white striped swimsuit and turban

.... $200.00–250.00

Miss Barbie®, 1964, doll has molded bendable legs, hair with a hair band and three interchangeable wigs, sleep eyes

.... $200.00–250.00

American GirlBarbie®, 1965, bobbed hairstyle with bangs, bendable legs

.... $400.00–500.00

Side-part American girl

.... $1,800.00–2,200.00

Color Magic Barbie®, 1966, dolls hair can change color

Blond $500.00–600.00

Midnight to ruby red $575.00–750.00

Twist N' Turn Barbie®, 1967, swivel jointed at waist

.... $250.00–350.00

Talking Barbie®, 1968, doll now has pull-string talker

200.00–250.00

Living Barbie®, 1970, joints at neck, shoulder, elbow, wrist, hip, knee, and ankle

.... $100.00–160.00

Other Barbie® dolls. **Dolls listed are in excellent condition, wearing original clothing, Mint-in-box can bring double the values listed.**

Angel Face

    1983 .... $10.00–15.00

Ballerina

    1976 .... $20.00–30.00

Beautiful Bride

    1976 .... $95.00–110.00

Beauty Secrets

    1980 .... $30.00–40.00

Bicyclin'

    1994 .... $10.00–15.00

Busy Barbie

    1972 .... $125.00–150.00

Dance Club

    1989 .... $10.00–15.00

Day-To-Night

    1985 .... $20.00–25.00

Doctor

    1988 .... $12.00–15.00

Fashion Jeans

    1982 .... $10.00–15.00

Fashion Photo

    1978 .... $30.00–40.00

Free Moving

    1975 .... $50.00–70.00

Gold Medal Skater

    1975 .... $45.00–60.00

Golden Dream

    1980 .... $35.00–55.00

Growin' Pretty Hair

    1971 .... $100.00–200.00

Hair Fair

    1967 .... $125.00–150.00

Hair Happenin's

    1971 .... $225.00–300.00

Ice Capades, 50th

    1990 .... $8.00–10.00

11.5" Barbie®, American Girl, Mattel, vinyl: $400. **Photo courtesy Fourty Fifty Sixty.**

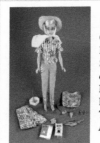

11.5" Barbie®, Color Magic, Mattel, vinyl: $500. **Photo courtesy of McMasters Harris Apple Tree Doll Auctions.**

Kissing

1979 .... $25.00–35.00

Live Action on Stage

1971 .... $100.00–125.00

Loving You

1983 .... $25.00–35.00

Magic Curl

1982 .... $18.00–25.00

Magic Moves

1986 .... $18.00–22.00

Malibu (Sunset)

1971 .... $20.00–30.00

Miss America Walk Lively

1972 .... $55.00–70.00

Movin Groovin Barbie

1997 .... $12.00–18.00

My First Barbie

1981 .... $8.00–12.00

My Size

1993 .... $100.00–150.00

Newport the Sport's Set

1973 .... $25.00–40.00

Peaches 'n Cream

1985 .... $80.00–100.00

Pink & Pretty

1982 .... $25.00–35.00

11.5" Barbie®, Twist N'Turn, Mattel, vinyl: $350. **Photo courtesy of McMasters Harris Apple Tree Doll Auctions.**

11.5" Barbie®, Silkstone in Trace of Lace, Mattel, vinyl, MIB: $100. **Photo courtesy of Charlotte's Web Vintage Dolls and Collectibles.**

Porcelain, **Faberge Imperial Elegance 1997, Faberge Imperial Splendor 2000, Faberge Imperial Grace 2001**

.... $250.00–350.00

Rappin' Rockin'

1992 .... $12.00–15.00

Rocker

1986 .... $15.00–20.00

Roller Skating

1980 .... $30.00–45.00

Secret Hearts

1993 .... $10.00–12.00

Sensations

1988 .... $10.00–12.00

Silkstone Barbie, varuious from 2000–2016

.... $60.00–100.00

Sun Lovin' Malibu

1979 .... $12.00–16.00

Sun Valley, The Sports Set

1973 .... $40.00–50.00

Super Size, 18"

1977 .... $25.00–40.00

Superstar Promotional

1978 .... $70.00–80.00

Talking Busy

1972 .... $150.00–200.00

Twinkle Lights

1993 .... $10.00–15.00

Walk Lively

1972 .... $80.00–100.00

Western (3 hairstyles)

1981 .... $18.00–25.00

Gift Sets

complete set prices; add more for NRFB (never removed from box), less for worn or faded.

Barbie Hostess

1966 .... $450.00–500.00

Beautiful Blues, **Sears**

1967 .... $400. 00–450.00

Color Magic Gift Set, **Sears**

1965 .... $250.00–300.00

On Parade

1960 .... $450.00–500.00

Pink Premier

1969 .... $300.00–350.00

Round the Clock

1964 .... $800.00–900.00

Skipper Party Set

1960 .... $300.00–400.00

Sparkling Pink

1964 .... $300.00–400.00

Travel in Style, **Sears**

1964 .... $150.00–225.00

Wedding Party

1964 .... $300.00–400.00

Store Specials or Special Editions, mint-in-box

American Stories Series

1990s $15.00–20.00

Avon Mrs PFE Albee

1997 .... $25.00

Billy Boy Feelin' Groovy

1986 .... $50.00

Bloomingdales

Savvy Shopper 1994, Donna Karan 1995, Ralph Lauren 1996,

11.5" Barbie®, Goddess of Africa, Mackie, Mattel, vinyl, 1999: $125. **Photo courtesy of The Museum Doll Shop.**

11.5" Christie, Twist n' Turn Mattel, vinyl: $125. **Photo courtesy of McMasters Harris Apple Tree Doll Auctions.**

Calvin Klein Jeans 1996

.... **$25.00**

Bob Mackie –**values are for mint-in-box**

Gold

1990 .... **$150.00**

Platinum

1991 .... **$175.00**

Starlight Splendor, black

1992 .... **$100.00**

Empress

1992 .... **$400.00**

Neptune Fantasy

1992 .... **$90.00**

Masquerade Ball

1993 .... **$40.00**

Queen of Hearts

1994 .... **$75.00**

Goddess of the Sun

1995 .... **$45.00**

Moon Goddess

1996 .... **$40.00**

Madame du Barbie®

1997 .... **$300.00**

Goddess of the Africa

1999 .... **$250.00**

Goddess of the Americas

2000 .... **$200.00**

Goddess of the Asia

1998 ....**$150.00**

Goddess of the Arcitic

2001 ....**$250.00**

Sterling Silver Rose

2002 ....**$30.00**

The Tango

1999 ....**$250.00**

Classique Series

Benefit Ball

1992 ....**$20.00**

City Style

1993 ....**$20.00**

Opening Night

1994 ....**$30.00**

Evening Extravaganza

1994 ....**$20.00**

Uptown Chic

1994 ....**$25.00**

Midnight Gala

1995 ....**$20.00**

Disney

Euro Disney

1992 ....**$15.00**

Disney Fun

1993 ....**$15.00**

Disney World, **25th anniversary**

1996 ....**$15.00**

FAO Schwarz

Golden Greetings

1989 ....**$40.00**

Winter Fantasy

1990 ....**$90.00**

Night Sensation

1991 ....**$40.00**

11.5" Barbie®, Classique Series, Midnight Gala, Mattel, vinyl, 1995: $20. **Photo courtesy of The Museum Doll Shop.**

11.5" Alan, Mattel, straight leg, molded hair, vinyl, MIB: $200. **Photo courtesy Fourty Fifty Sixty.**

Madison Avenue

　　1991 .... $30.00

Rockette

　　1993 .... $35.00

Silver Screen

　　1994 .... $30.00

Lilly

　　1997 .... $25.00

Summer in San Francisco

　　1998 .... $30.00

La Papplion, Bob Mackie

　　1999 .... $50.00

Great Eras, **Gibson Girl & Flapper 1993, Southern Belle & Egytian Queen 1994, Elizabethian & Medieval Lady 1995, Grecian Goddess & Victorian Lady 1996, Chianese Empress & French Lady 1997**

Gibson Girl

　　.. $25.00

Hills

Party Lace 1989, Evening Sparkle 1990, Moonlight Rose 1991, Hula Hoop 1997

　　.. **$12.00–20.00**

Holiday Barbie®, **values are for mint-in-box**

　　1988, **red gown** $350.00

　　1989, **white gown** $100.00

1990 through 2010

　　.. $20.00–$25.00

Hollywood Legends

Scarlett O'Hara, **white gown**

　　1994 .... $30.00

11.5" Francie,
Twist n' Turn,
Mattel, vinyl, :
$210. **Photo
courtesy of
The Museum
Doll Shop.**

Dorothy, *Wizard of Oz*

    1994 .... **$40.00**

Maria, *Sound of Music*

    1995 .... **$35.00**

Marilyn Monroe, *Seven Year Itch*

    1997 .... **$30.00**

Home Shopping Club

Evening Flame

    1991 .... **$15.00**

J.C. Penney

Evening Elegance

    1990 .... **$15.00**

Enchanted Evening

    1991 .... **$15.00**

Golden Winter

    1993 .... **$18.00**

Royal Enchantment, **blond**

    1995 .... **$10.00**

K-Mart

Peach Pretty

    1989 .... **$15.00**

Root 66 University

    2003 .... **$12.00**

Little Debbie

    1993 .... **$15.00**

Nostalgia Series

35th Anniversary

    1994 .... **$20.00**

Solo in the Spotlight

1994 .... **$15.00**

Busy Gal

1995 .... **$18.00**

Enchanted Evening

1996 .... **$20.00**

Poodle Parade

1996 .... **$20.00**

Commuter Set

1998 .... **$60.00**

Sears

Celebration, **100ᵗʰ Anniversary**

1986 .... **$15.00**

Lilac & lovely

1987 .... **$18.00**

Star Dream

1987 .... **$15.00**

Blossom Beautiful

1992 .... **$25.00**

Ribbons & Roses

1995 .... **$15.00**

Service Merchandise

Blue Rhapsody

1991 .... **$15.00**

Satin Nights

1992 .... **$15.00**

Sparkling Splendor

1993 .... **$12.00**

Sea Princess

1996 .... **$25.00**

Spiegel

Sterling Wishes

1991 .... **$30.00**

Regal Reflections

1992 .... **$25.00**

11.5" Ken, Mattel, straight leg, molded hair, vinyl, MIB: $130. **Photo courtesy of McMasters Harris Apple Tree Doll Auctions.**

11.5" Talking Ken, Mattel, vinyl, MIB: $140. **Photo courtesy of McMasters Harris Apple Tree Doll Auctions.**

Royal Invitation

    1993 ....**$15.00**

Theater Elegance

    1994 ....**$20.00**

Shopping Chic

    1995 ....**$25.00**

Winner's Circle

    1996 ....**$22.00**

Target

Gold 'n Lace

    1989 ....**$20.00**

Party Pretty

    1990 ....**$15.00**

Golden Evening

    1991 ....**$25.00**

35th Anniversary Barbie

    1997 ....**$20.00**

Barbie & Kelly Easter Egg Hunt Set

    1997 ....**$18.00**

Stars & Stripes Collection

Air Force

    1990 ....**$25.00**

Navy

    1991 ....**$25.00**

Marine

    1992 ....**$30.00**

Army Gift Set

    1993 ....**$30.00**

11.5" Midge, bendable leg, Mattel, vinyl, MIB: $260. **Photo courtesy of Morphy Auctions.**

Air Force Gift Set

1994 .... **$30.00**

Toys R Us

Dance Sensation

1985 .... **$50.00**

Pepsi Spirit

1989 .... **$30.00**

Vacation Sensation

1989 .... **$25.00**

Radiant in Red

1992 .... **$24.00**

Very Violet

1992 .... **$28.00**

Moonlight Magic

1993 .... **$22.00**

Harley-Davidson, **#1**

1997 .... **$75.00**

Firefighter

1995 .... **$45.00**

WalMart

Pink Jubilee, **25th Anniversary**

1987 .... **$30.00**

Frills & Fantasy

1988 .... **$20.00**

Tooth Fairy

1994 .... **$25.00**

Skating Star

1995 .... **$18.00**

Wholesale Clubs

Party Sensation

1990 .... **$18.00**

Fantastica

1992 .... **$25.00**

Royal Romance

1992 .... **$35.00**

Winter Royale

1994 .... **$20.00**

After the Walk, **Sam's Club**

1997 .... **$30.00**

Country Rose, **Sam's Club**

1997 .... **$22.00**

Woolworths

Special Expressions, **white**

1989 .... **$15.00**

Sweet Lavender

1992 .... **$22.00**

Family and other related dolls. **Dolls listed are in excellent condition, wearing original clothing. Mint-in-box can bring double the values listed.**

Alan, **1964–1967**

Straight leg....................................... **$75.00–100.00**

Bendable leg **$80.00–110.00**

Brad, **Talking, 1970, African-American, bendable leg**

.... **$65.00–80.00**

Buffy & Mrs. Beasley **$55.00–65.00**

Cara, Quick Curl, **1974, African-American**

.... **$65.00–75.00**

Casey, Twist N' Turn

1967 .... **$90.00–150.00**

Non-twist n'turn **$75.00–90.00**

Chris, **brunette, bendable leg**

1967 .... **$45.00–55.00**

9" Living Skipper, Mattel, vinyl: $80. **Photo courtesy of Doll Hugs Shop.**

11.5" Talking Stacey, Mattel, vinyl: $175. **Photo courtesy of The Museum Doll Shop.**

Christie, **African-American**

    Talking 1968–1972 .... $175.00–225.00

    Twist n'turn 1970–1972 .... $75.00–125.00

    Live action 1971-1972 .... $150.00–200.00

Francie

Bendable leg

    1966 .... $150.00–185.00

Straight leg

    1966 .... $100.00–140.00

Twist 'N Turn

    1967 .... $180.00–210.00

Black

    1967 .... $850.00–950.00

Malibu

    1971 .... $20.00–25.00

Growin' Pretty Hair

    1971 .... $45.00–65.00

Jamie, **Walking**

    1970 .... $100.00–150.00

Sears Exclusives, Furry Friends 1970–1971 & Strollin in style 1972

    .... $150.00–200.00

Julia, Twist 'N Turn

    1969 .... $120.00–140.00

Talking

    1969 .... $90.00–120.00

Kelly

Quick Curl

    1973 .... $90.00–110.00

Yellowstone

1974 .... **$120.00–150.00**

Ken, **#1, straight leg, blue eyes, hard plastic hollow body, flocked hair, 12", mark: "Ken˚ MCMLX//by//Mattel//Inc."**

1961 .... **$70.00–80.00**

Molded hair

1962 .... **$60.00–70.00**

Bendable legs

1965 .... **$100.00–130.00**

Talking

1968 .... **$50.00–70.00**

Mod Hair

1968 .... **$40.00–50.00**

New Good Lookin

1970 .... **$60.00–80.00**

Busy Talking

1971 .... **$35.00–45.00**

Walk Lively

1971 .... **$25.00–35.00**

Live Action

1971–1972 .... **$65.00–80.00**

Living Fluff

1971–1972 .... **$50.00–70.00**

Midge

Straight leg

1963 .... **$65.00–100.00**

No freckles

1963 .... **$175.00–250.00**

Bendable legs

1965 .... **$110.00–130.00**

Wig wardrobe

1965 .... **$125.00–175.00**

P.J. Talking

1970 .... **$55.00–175.00**

Twist 'N Turn

1970 90.00–110.00

6" Todd, Mattel, vinyl: $45.
Photo courtesy of The Museum Doll Shop.

Live Action/Stage

1971 .... **$65.00–80.00**

Sears Gift Set, Swingin Silver, 1970

sold for $1,140.00 at online auction

Ricky, straight legs

1965 .... **$45.00–60.00**

Skipper

Straight leg

1964 .... **$45.00–60.00**

Bendable leg

1965 .... **$90.00–110.00**

Twist 'N Turn

1968 .... **$100.00–120.00**

Living

1969 .... **$65.00–90.00**

Growing Up

1975 .... **$35.00–45.00**

Skooter

Straight leg

1965 .... **$30.00–40.00**

Bendable leg

1966 .... **$40.00–55.00**

Stacey

Talking

1968 .... **$150.00–175.00**

Twist 'N Turn

1968 .... **$165.00–200.00**

Steffie, **Walk Lively**

    1972 .... $125.00–175.00

Todd, **bendable, posable**

    1966 .... $40.00–55.00

Tutti, **bendable, posable**

    1967 .... $45.00–55.00

Pairs in sets

    Tutti & Todd, Sundae Treat $80.00–100.00

    Angie & Tangie $100.00–150.00

    Lori & Rorie $80.00–100.00

Twiggy, Twist 'N Turn

    1967 .... $200.00–250.00

Barbie Accessories

Animals, **price for mint in package, much less for loose.**

All American (horse)

    1991 .... $45.00

Blinking Beauty (horse)

    1988 .... $35.00

Champion (horse)

    1991 .... $40.00

Dancer (horse)

    1971 .... $45.00

Midnight (horse)

    1980 .... $25.00

Fluff (kitten)

    1983 .... $25.00

Prancer (horse)

    1984 .... $70.00

Prince (poodle)

    1985 .... $50.00

Snowball (dog)

    1990 .... $25.00

Cases

Fashion Queen, **black, zippered**

    1964 .... $100.00

Barbie & Ken, **black patent**

1965 .... **$35.00**

Miss Barbie, **zippered**

1964 .... **$60.00**

Skipper & Skooter, **pink**

1965 .... **$50.00**

Clothing

Name of outfit, stock number; price for mint in package, much less for loose.

Aboard Ship, #1631

sold for $475.00 at online auction

Arabian Knights, Ken #0774

sold for $110.00 at online auction

Beautiful Bride #1698

sold for $110.00 at online auction

Black Magic Ensemble #1609

sold for $512.00 at online auction

Enchanted Evening #983

sold for $212.00 at online auction

Guinevere, Little Theater #0873

sold for $195.00 at online auction

Golden Evening # 1610

sold for $184.00 at online auction

London Tour #1661

sold for $345.00 at online auction

Mood For Music #940

sold for $208.00 at online auction

Pony coat, #1240

sold for $106.00 at online auction

Swingin Easy #955

sold for $341.00 at online auction

Twigster, #1727

sold for $294.00 at online auction

Furniture, **Suzy Goose, good conditon, MIB brings double or more**

Canopy Bed,

1960s **$250.00**

Chifferobe,

1960s **$65.00**

Queen Size Bed, **pink**

> **1960s**.................................**$60.00**

> Vanity, **pink**...................................**$80.00**

Vehicles, **good conditon, MIB brings double or more**

Austin Healy, **orange & aqua**

> **1964** **$100.00**

Beach Bus

> **1974** **$25.00**

Mercedes, **blue-green**

> **1968** **$75.00**

Speedboat, **blue-green**

> **1964** **$85.00**

Sun 'n Fun Buggy

> **1971** **$30.00**

United Airlines Plane

> **1973** **$65.00**

E. BARROIS

10" Barrois, bisque, painted eyes: $1,500. **Photo courtesy of Morphy Auctions.**

1846–1877, Paris, France. Assembled, sold, and distributed lady-type dolls with bisque heads, closed mouths, on kid and cloth bodies. It is still largely unknown which French and German porcelain factories made heads for Barrois, although it is known that the heads Barrois supplied to Steiner and Blampoix were made by Frayon.

Mark: EB

Poupée (Fashion-type), **kid bodies bring lower end of range, articulated or kid-over-wood the higher end of range**

108

Painted eye

    10"–13" $1,500.00–1,800.00

    14"–16" $1,600.00–1,900.00

    19"–21" $2,200.00–2,600.00

man, molded painted hair

    12"–17" $500.00–3,500.00

Glass eye

    10"–12" $2,200.00–3,000.00

    14"–16" $4,000.00–6,500.00

    19"–21" $4,000.00–8,000.00

    23"–24" $5,000.00–9,000.00

BELTON-TYPE

24" French Look Belton, bisque, Germany: $4,000. **Photo courtesy of Morphy Auctions.**

1875 on, made by various German manufacturers including Bähr & Pröschild, Kestner, Simon & Halbig, and others. Solid dome bisque socket head doll with small holes in crown for stringing and/or wig application. Paperweight eyes, straight wristed wood and composition body, closed mouth, pierced ears. Belton-type is a name applied to this type of doll by modern doll collectors and is not a reference to a specific maker. Mark: none or mold numbers only.

Bru-look face

    12"–14" $2,000.00–2,600.00

French-Look, **dolls with a French look that were manufactured for the French market, molds 137, 138, or unmarked**

    10"–16" $1,000.00–2,000.00

    18"–24" $2,400.00–4,000.00

German look dolls

12"–15" $700.00–1,000.00

18"–20" $1,000.00–1,200.00

Mold 200: See Bähr & Pröschild listing.

C.M. BERGMANN

32", C M Bergmann, bisque: $625. **Photo courtesy of Alderfer Auction Company, Inc.**

1888–1931, Walterhausen, Thuringia, Germany. Doll factory that distributed in the United States through L. Wolfe & Co. Bergmann had bisque doll heads made for them by Alt, Beck & Gottschalk, Armand Marseille, Simon & Halbig, and others. Registered trademarks: Cinderella 1897, Columbia 1904, My Gold Star 1926. Dolls listed are in good condition, appropriately dressed.

Character Babies, **bisque socket head on bent-limb composition body**

Open mouth

12"–14" $250.00–300.00

15"–18" $400.00–5000.00

Mold 612, **character**

15"–18" $700.00–900.00

Mold 134, **character toddler**

12" $950.00–1,000.00

Child, **bisque socket head, open mouth, wigged, sleep or set eyes, ball-jointed composition body, mold 1916 or others, some marked with Simon Halbig/Bergman mark**

14"–18" $300.00–400.00

20"–24" $350.00–450.00

26"–28" $500.00–575.00

30"–32" $550.00–625.00

37" $600.00–650.00

Flapper-type body

12"..	$425.00–475.00
16"..	$450.00–500.00

Eleonore

18"..	$475.00–525.00
25"..	$550.00–600.00

BETSY MCCALL

20" Betsy McCall, Ideal, flirty eyes, vinyl: $375. **Photo courtesy of Alderfer Auction Company, Inc.**

30" Betsy McCall, American Character, vinyl: $300. **Photo courtesy of Charlotte's Web Vintage Dolls and Collectibles.**

Dolls based on *McCall's Magazines* paper doll Betsy McCall. Dolls listed are in excellent condition wearing original clothing, mint-in-box can bring double the values listed.

Ideal Toy Corp., 1952–1953

Doll with vinyl head, on a hard plastic Toni body, saran wig

14".. $125.00–175.00

1958, **vinyl, four hair colors, rooted hair, flat feet, slim body, round sleep eyes, may have swivel waist or one-piece torso, mark: "McCall 19©58 Corp." in circle**

14".. $100.00–200.00

1959, **vinyl, rooted hair, slender limbs, some with flirty eyes, one-piece torso, mark: "McCall 19©58 Corp." in a circle**

19"–20".. $325.00–375.00

1961, **vinyl, five colors of rooted hair, jointed wrists, ankles, waist, blue or brown sleep eyes, four to six outfits available, mark: "McCall 19©61 Corp." in a circle**

22".. $125.00–175.00

29".. $200.00–250.00

American Character Doll Co., 1957 to 1963, 8" hard plastic doll with jointed knees, sleep eyes, molded eyelashes, metal barrettes in hair. First year these dolls had mesh cap saran wigs and plastic pin joints in knees. Second year they had vinyl skull-caps on their wigs and metal knee pins.

In undies $100.00–125.00

In street dress $125.00–200.00

In formal wear................................$200.00–375.00

8" doll clothing

Dresses $45.00–85.00

Shoes and socks................................$20.00–25.00

Complete outfit $60.00–75.00

Vinyl doll, **1958 on, jointed at shoulder, neck & hip, sleep eyes, allow more for elaborate costumes**

14"..$125.00–175.00

20"..$150.00–250.00

30"..$300.00–350.00

36"..$350.00–450.00

Additional joints at wrists, waist, knees, and ankles

22"..$250.00–300.00

29"..$225.00–275.00

Companion-size Betsy McCall, **1959, vinyl, rooted hair, mark: "McCall Corp//1959" on head**

34"..$400.00–500.00

Linda McCall **(Betsy's cousin), 1959, vinyl, Betsy face, rooted hair, mark: "McCall Corp//1959" on head**

34"..$300.00–400.00

Sandy McCall **(Betsy's brother), 1959, vinyl, molded hair, sleep eyes, red blazer, navy shorts, mark: "McCall 1959 Corp."; tag reads "I am Your Life Size Sandy McCall"**

35"..$250.00–350.00

Uneeda

1964, vinyl, rooted hair, rigid vinyl body, brown or blue sleep eyes, slim pre-teen body, wore mod outfits, some mini-skirts, competitor of Ideal's Tammy, mark: none

11½" $200.00–275.00

Horsman

1974, vinyl with rigid plastic body, **sleep eyes, came in Betsy McCall Beauty Box with extra hair piece, brush, bobby pins on card, eye pencil, blush, lipstick, two sponges, mirror, and other accessories, mark: "Horsman Doll Inc.//19©67" on head; "Horsman Dolls Inc." on torso**

12½" $35.00–55.00

1974, vinyl with rigid plastic teen type body, **jointed wrists, sleep eyes, lashes, rooted hair with side part (some blond with ponytails), closed mouth, original clothing marked "BMc" in two-tone blue box marked "©1974//Betsy McCall — she WALKS with you," marks: "Horsman Dolls 1974"**

29"..$150.00–175.00

Tomy

1984, porcelain head, arms, legs, cloth bodies, stationary eyes, wigged

16"... $10.00–15.00

Rothchild

1986, 35th anniversary Betsy, hard plastic, sleep eyes, painted lashes below eyes, single stroke eyebrows, tied ribbon emblem on back, marks: hang tag reads "35th Anniversary// BetsyMcCall//by Rothschild (number) 'Betsy Goes to a Tea Party,' or 'Betsy Goes to the Fair,'" box marked "Rothchild Doll Company//Southboro, MA 01722"

8"... $18.00–24.00

Robert Tonner

1996 to present, vinyl (some porcelain), rooted hair, rigid vinyl body, glass eyes, closed smiling mouth, mark: "Betsy McCall//by//Robert Tonner//©Gruner & Jahr USA PUB." Values below are secondary market prices, dolls still available at retail as well.

8"

In undies... $20.00–30.00

Dressed $35.00–50.00

14"... $40.00–70.00

29"... $70.00–85.00

BING ART DOLLS

10.5" Bing, cloth: $400. **Photo courtesy of Withington Auction Inc.**

Germany, 1921–1932. Gebrüder Bing was founded in 1882. In 1921 it became a part of a conglomerate called the Bing Werke Corporation. This is when they began making their cloth "art dolls." Molded cloth face, sometimes with a heavy coating of gesso giving a composition appearance, cloth head and body, oil-painted features, wigged or painted hair, pin-jointed at neck, shoulders, and hips, seams down front of legs, mitt hands.

Painted hair or wigged, **cloth, unmarked or "Bing" on bottom of foot**

8"–10" $300.00–400.00

13"...$350.00–450.00

15"...$450.00–550.00

Felt head, **cloth body**

12"...$250.00–350.00

BISQUE, UNKNOWN OR LITTLE-KNOWN MAKERS

Various manufacturers of bisque-headed child dolls working from 1870 on. No separate listing for these makers. No damage, appropriately dressed.

French

Unknown Maker

Early desirable very French-style face, **marks such as "J. D.," "J. M. Paris," and "H. G." (possibly Henri & Granfe-Guimonneau)**

12"...$8,000.00–10,000.00

17"...$15,000.00–16,000.00

21"...$17,000.00–19,000.00

27"...$22,000.00–25,000.00

Jumeau or Bru style face, **may be marked "W. D." (Wilhalm Dehler, German doll for French trade) or "R. R."**

13"–14"...$1,800.00–2,000.00

19"–21"...$2,000.00–2,100.00

24"...$2,400.00–2,700.00

26"–27"...$3,000.00–3,200.00

Closed mouth, **marks: "J," "137," "136," or others**

Excellent quality, **unusual face**

10"–12"...$3,400.00–3,700.00

15"–17"...$4,000.00–5,000.00

23"–25"...$6,000.00–7,500.00

Standard quality, **excellent bisque**

13"...$2,200.00–2,450.00

18"–19"...$2,800.00–3,000.00

22"– 23"...$3,200.00–3,500.00

 16.5" WD, bisque head: $2,100. **Photo courtesy of Alderfer Auction Company, Inc.**

 22" M Bebe, bisque: $4,800. **Photo courtesy of Withington Auction Inc.**

Lesser quality, **may have poor painting and/or blotches on cheeks**

15"	$800.00–900.00
21"	$1,100.00–1,400.00
26"	$1,600.00–2,000.00

Open mouth

Excellent quality, **ca. 1890 on, French body**

15"	$1,100.00–1,300.00
18"	$1,700.00–1,900.00
21"	$2,100.00–2,200.00
24"	$2,400.00–2,700.00

High cheek color, **ca. 1920s, may have five-piece papier-mâché body**

15"	$525.00–575.00
19"	$650.00–700.00
23"	$800.00–875.00

Known Makers

Danel et Cie., 1889–1895, Paris, France. Bisque socket head on composition body, paperweight eyes, wigged, pierced ears

Paris Bébé

11"–15"	$3,200.00–4,000.00
18"	$5,000.00–5,500.00
22"	$6,000.00–6,500.00
24"	$7,500.00–8,000.00
28"	$9,000.00–9,5000.00

Bébé Francaise

14"	$2,800.00–3,000.00
20"	$3,500.00–4,000.00

9"dolly face, Verlingue, bisque: $200. **Photo courtesy of Sweetbriar Auctions.**

15" dolly face, mold 129, Carl Muller, bisque socket, German,: $300. **Photo courtesy of McMasters Harris Apple Tree Doll Auctions.**

Delcroix, Henri, **1887, Paris and Montreuil sous Bois. Pressed bisque socket head, closed mouth, paperweight eyes, marked Pan Bébé**

8"–9" $4,000.00–5,000.00

19"–25" $8,000.00–10,000.00

Falck & Roussel, **1880s, socket head, closed mouth, paperweight eyes, wood and composition body, marked: F.R.**

15"–16" $13,000.00–15,000.00

18" $16,000.00–17,000.00

Halopeau, A., **1881–1889, Paris, pressed bisque socket head, closed mouth, paperweight eyes, cork pate, French wood and composition body, marked: H**

13" $36,000.00–50,000.00

16"–18" $50,000.00–54,000.00

21"–24" $56,000.00–62,000.00

Lefebvre et Cie., Alexander, **1975, pressed bisque socket head, closed mouth, paperweight eyes, French wood and composition body, marked: A.L.**

22" $35,000.00

Too few in database for a reliable range.

Joanny, Joseph Louis, **1888, pressed bisque socket head, closed mouth, paperweight eyes, French wood and composition body, marked: J.**

8"–12" $4,500.00–6,00.00

17"–18" $8,000.00–10,000.00

22"–23" $12,000.00–14,000.00

26"–28" 15,000.00–18,000.00

J. M. Bébé 0, **1880s, pressed bisque socket head, closed mouth, paperweight eyes, French wood and composition body, marked: J.M.**

19"–26" $9,000.00–14,000.00

Too few in database for a reliable range.

M. Bebe, **1890s, pressed bisque socket head, closed mouth, paperweight eyes, pierced ears, French wood and composition body, marked: M with size number**

12"–14" $3,000.00–4,000.00

19"–23" $4,500.00–5,000.00

Marque, Albert, **1914, fewer than 100 dolls are believed to have been made**

21"–22" .... $122,000.00 at auction

May Frères Cie, **1890–1897, later Steiner (1898 on), closed mouth paperweight eyes, pierced ears, composition body, marked: Bébé Mascotte**

18"–23" $4,800.00–5,500.00

Mothereau, Alexandre, **1880–1895, pressed bisque socket head, closed mouth, paperweight eyes, French wood and composition body, marked: B.M.**

12"–15" $14,000.00–16,000.00

22"–24" $22,000.00–24,000.00

28"–29" $25,000.00–27,000.00

Pannier, **1875, pressed bisque socket head, closed mouth, paperweight eyes, French wood and composition body, marked: C.P.**

16" $3,500–4,000.00

Too few in database for a reliable range.

Petite et Dumontier, **1878–1890, Paris. Pressed bisque socket head, closed mouth, paperweight eyes, French wood and composition body, some with metal hands, marked: P. D. with size number**

16" $10,000.00–11,000.00

18"–19" $12,000.00–14,000.00

23" $15,000.00–16,000.00

Pintel et Godchaux, **1880–1889, Montreuil, France, pressed bisque socket head, closed mouth, paperweight eyes, French wood and composition body, trademark: Bébé Charmant**

10" $1,800.00–2,000.00

20"–22" $5,000.00–6,000.00

Open mouth

18"–23" $1,800.00–2,000.00

Van Rozen, **1912–1914, Paris, France, bisque character socket head, open mouth, glass eyes, composition body**

16"–17" $16,000.00–24,000.00

Verlingue, **1915–1921, Montreuil & Boulogne, France, bisque socket head, open mouth, glass eyes, composition body, trademark: J V with anchor**

9"–15" $200.00–400.00

18"–22" $500.00–800.00

German

Various German manufacturers of bisque-headed dolls working from 1870 on. No separate listing for these makers. Marks: May be unmarked or only a mold or size number or Germany.

Baby

Character Baby, **1910 on, solid dome or wigged, open mouth, glass eyes, bent-limb composition body, marks: G.B., P.M. (Porzellanfabrik Mengersgereuth), F.B., or unmarked**

9"–12"	$125.00–200.00
14"–16"	$250.00–350.00
19"–21"	$400.00–450.00

Toddler

18"–23" toddler	$550.00–600.00

Newborn Baby, **1924, bisque head on cloth body, bisque or celluloid hands, marks: Baby Weygh, IV, others.**

10"–12"	$140.00–170.00
14"–17"	$200.00–250.00

Gerling Baby

17"	$275.00–325.00

Dolly face child, **1880 on, bisque socket-head, wigged, glass eyes, open mouth, ball-jointed composition body, mark: G.B., K inside H, L.H.K., P.Sch, D.& K., and or unmarked**

8"–10"	$200.00–225.00
12"–15"	$250.00–300.00
18"–20"	$325.00–400.00
23"–25"	$400.00–425.00
30"	$475.00–550.00

Mold 50, 51, **square teeth**

14"–16"	$900.00–1,000.00

Mold 422, 444, 457, 478

17"	$600.00–650.00
23"	$800.00–825.00

My Girlie, My Dearie, Olimpia, Pansy, Princess, Special, Sweetheart, Viola, **G.&S., MOA, A.W.**

13"	$150.00–200.00
18"–20"	$225.00–275.00
22"–24"	$300.00–350.00
26"–28"	$400.00–450.00
32"–35"	$450.00–500.00

Shoulder head, wigged, **1880–1890, glass eyes, open mouth, kid or cloth body, special and other molds or no mold mark**

    10"–12" $125.00–200.00

    15"–17" $250.00–325.00

    20"–23" $300.00–400.00

Closed mouth

Unmarked, **composition body**

    11"–13" $1,200.00–1,300.00

    16"–18" $1,600.00–1,800.00

Mold 50, **shoulder head**

    14"–16" $450.00–650.00

    22"–24" $1,200.00–1,275.00

Mold 120, 126, 132, **Bru-look**

    13" $2,500.00–2,600.00

    19"–21" $3,800.00–4,000.00

Mold 51, **swivel neck shoulder head**

    17" $950.00–1,100.00

E.G., **maker Ernst Grossman**

    16" $2,500.00–2,600.00

Shoulder head with molded hair, **1880 on**

American Schoolboy-type

    12"–14" $250.00–325.00

    18"–20" $400.00–450.00

Small Child, **1890 to mid 1910s, bisque socket head, open mouth, set or sleep eyes, five-piece composition body**

High quality bisque, flapper style body

    5"–6" $325.00–350.00

    8"–10" $350.00–400.00

Crude 5 piece body

    7"–8" $125.00–175.00

Fully jointed body

    7"–8" $325.00–425.00

Closed mouth

    4"–5" $475.00–500.00

    8" $550.00–600.00

23" dolly face, bisque, incised "Pansy": $325.
Photo courtesy of Alderfer Auction Company, Inc.

Character, **1910 on, glass eyes, open or open/closed mouth, solid dome or wigged, composition body**

Mold 125, smiling, attributed to Adolf Wislizenus

18" sold for $32,000.00 at auction

Mold 159

    23"...$1,100.00–1,200.00

Mold 213, 214, **maker Bawo & Dotter**

    18"...$12,100.00–12,200.00

Mold 221, **toddler**

    16"...$2,500.00–2,600.00

Mold 411, **shoulder head lady**

    13"–14"...$2,000.00–2,200.00

Mold 838, **P.M. Coquette (Porzellanfabrik Mengersgereuth) mark for Fleischmann & Craemer**

    11"...$550.00–575.00

K&K Mama doll, **1924, German bisque shoulder head, American made cloth Mama style body with composition limbs, glass eyes, made for George Borgfeldt**

    15"–23"...$300.00–375.00

Wolfe, Louis & Co., **1870–1930 on, Sonneberg, Germany, Boston, and New York City. Made and distributed dolls, also distributed dolls made for them by other companies such as Hertel Schwab & Co. and Armand Marseille. They made composition as well as bisque dolls and specialized in babies and Red Cross nurses before World War I. May be marked "L.W. & C."**

Baby, **open or closed mouth, sleep eyes**

    10"–14"...$250.00–300.00

    17"...$300.00–400.00

    26"...$500.00–575.00

28" toddler body

    ....$800.00–900.00

13" mold 411, shoulder head lady, bisque: $ 2,200. **Photo courtesy of Sara Bernstein's Dolls.**

18" child, Morimura Brothers, bisque, Japan: $200. **Photo courtesy of Morphy Auctions.**

Sunshine Baby, **solid dome, cloth body, glass eyes, closed mouth**

 15"–22".. $1,000.00–2,000.00

Japanese

1915 on, Japan. Bisque head dolls often in imitation of the German bisque dolls. Distributed in the United States by companies such as Morimura Brothers, Yamato Importing Co., and others, marks: 1915 to 1921 marked Nippon, after 1921 marked Japan.

Character baby, **bisque socket head, solid dome or wigged, open mouth with teeth, bent limb composition body**

 11"–12".. $100.00–125.00

 13"–15".. $125.00–150.00

 19"–21".. $175.00–200.00

Hilda look-alike

 13"... $450.00–500.00

 18"–19".. $650.00–700.00

Heubach pouty look-alike, **300 series**

 17"... $800.00–900.00

Child, **bisque head, mohair wig, glass sleep eyes, open mouth, composition or kid body**

 9"–11".. $100.00–125.00

 13"–15".. $150.00–200.00

 19"–21".. $200.00–350.00

 25"–28".. $250.00–300.00

Shoulderhead dolly

 12"–15".. $70.00–90.00

 19"–22".. $100.00–150.00

England

Nottingham Toy Industries, **bisque head, mohair wig, glass eyes, closed mouth, composition or kid body, marked N.T. I.**

 12"–17".. $300.00–400.00

BLACK OR BROWN DOLLS

Dolls both homemade and made by various European and American manufacturers. Shades range from black to tan. Sometimes Caucasian mold in dark color, other times ethnic sculpted mold was used. Dolls listed are in good condition, appropriately dressed.

All-bisque

Glass eyes, **wigged**

    4"–5" $375.00–475.00

Hertwig, **character**

    2½" $85.00–100.00

Gebruder Kuhnlenz

    3½"–4" $550.00–650.00

    5"–6" $1,100.00–1,200.00

Kestner, **swivel neck**

    5"–6" $1,300.00–1,500.00

    7"–8" $1,800.00–2,000.00

18" Tête Jumeau, open mouth, bisque, socket head: $4,100. **Photo courtesy of McMasters Harris Apple Tree Doll Auctions.**

13" Ernst Heubach, mold 399, bisque, socket head: $750. **Photo courtesy of Alderfer Auction Company, Inc.**

Stiff neck

    4"–6" $550.00–600.00

Simon & Halbig, **886**

    5"–7" $1,200.00–1,700.00

Japanese, **paonted bisque, 3 pigtails, painted eyes**

    5"–7" $35.00–40.00

Bisque, 1880 on, French and German makers. Bisque socket head, painted black or black color in slip, brown composition or kid body

French

Poupée (**Fashion-type**), kid body

Unmarked

14"–15" $3,000.00–3,400.00

FG

14" $3,200.00–3,400.00

Bru

14" $10,000.00–11,000.00

17" $12,000.00–13,000.00

Jumeau

15" $8,500.00–9,000.00

Bébé

Bru

Circle Dot

13" 28,000.00–30,000.00

17"–19" $32,000.00–42,000.00

Bru Jne

10"–17" $18,000.00–25,000.00

E.D., **open mouth**

13"–16" $2,500.00–2,900.00

22" $3,100.00–3,300.00

Eden Bebe, **open mouth**

15" $2,300.00–2,500.00

Gaultier, Francois, **closed mouth**

12" $5,000.00–6,000.00

Jumeau

E.J., closed mouth

10" $6,500.00–7,500.00

15"–17" $8,200.00–9,300.00

Tété, open mouth

10" $2,800.00–3,200.00

15" $3,500.00–3,900.00

20"–24" $4,500.00–5,000.00

Tété, closed mouth

15"–16" $4,800.00–4,900.00

16" Kämmer & Reinhardt, mold 122, bisque, bent limb baby body: $1,100. **Photo courtesy of Morphy Auctions.**

16" mold 739, Simon & Halbig, bisque: $1,500. **Photo courtesy of McMasters Harris Apple Tree Doll Auctions.**

18"...$5,000.00–5,200.00

22"–24"..$5,400.00–6,500.00

DEP, open mouth

16"..$2,400.00–2,600.00

Lanternier

18"–20"...$1,000.00–1,300.00

Mothereau

15"–16"...$16,500.00–18,000.00

Paris Bebe, **closed mouth**

13"..$3,900.00–4,300.00

16"..$4,500.00–4,600.00

19"..$5,300.00–5,500.00

S.F.B.J.

Molds 226, 235

14"–17"...$2,800.00–3,200.00

Molds 301, 60 (Unis France mark also), jointed composition body, open mouth

8"–10"...$300.00–400.00

14"–18"...$650.00–900.00

Steiner

Figure A series, closed mouth

10"–11"...$5,000.00–5,500.00

14"–16"...$5,000.00–6,000.00

18"–22"...$6,500.00–7,000.00

Open mouth

8"..$2,700.00–3,500.00

13"..$3,800.00–4,000.00

16"...$4,200.00–4,500.00

23"...$6,000.00–6,500.00

Series C

18"...$6,000.00–6,200.00

21"...$6,400.00–6,600.00

Van Rozen, 1912–1914, Paris, France, bisque character socket head, open mouth, glass eyes, composition body

16"–17"...$20,000.00–30,000.00

German

Unmarked

Closed mouth

10–11"...$350.00–400.00

14"...$450.00–500.00

17"...$600.00–675.00

21"...$825.00–875.00

Open mouth

5"...$450.00–500.00

9"–10"..$600.00–700.00

11"–13"...$800.00–900.00

15"...$900.00–950.00

Painted bisque

Closed mouth

16"...$400.00–450.00

19"...$550.00–600.00

23"...$900.00–1,000.00

Open mouth

7"...$125.00–175.00

12"...$175.00–225.00

14"...$275.00–325.00

18"...$475.00–525.00

Ethnic features

15"...$3,000.00–3,200.00

18"...$3,800.00–4,000.00

Indian, open mouth, often scowling expression, glass eyes, wigged

10"–15"..$200.00–300.00

9.5" mold 1079, Simon & Halbig, bisque: $1,000. **Photo courtesy of Withington Auction Inc.**

Bähr & Pröschild, **open mouth, mold 277, ca. 1891**

10"–12" $600.00–800.00

Mold 244, Indian or native

11" $550.00–625.00

14"–16" $800.00–1,000.00

Bye-Lo Baby

9" $900.00–1,200.00

16" $3,200.00–3,000.00

Goebel, **open mouth, dolly face**

10" $175–200.00

Handwerck, Heinrich, **mold 79, 119**

Open mouth

12"–16" $800.00–1,000.00

18"–21" $1,300.00–1,500.00

Heubach, Ernst (Koppelsdorf)

Mold 145, **dolly faced, socket head, glass eyes, open mouth, 5 piece composition body**

10" $275.00–325.00

Mold 271, **1914, shoulder head, painted eyes, closed mouth**

10" $425.00–475.00

Mold 320, 339, 350

10" $375.00–425.00

13" $500.00–525.00

18" $650.00–700.00

Mold 399, **allow more for toddler**

10"–14" $575.00–650.00

17"–22" $750.00–850.00

18.5" cloth, *Stockinette Baby* (often mis-called Black Beecher): $3,500. **Photo courtesy of Alderfer Auction Company, Inc.**

16" Islander, Norah Wellings, cloth: $250. **Photo courtesy of McMasters Harris Apple Tree Doll Auctions.**

Mold 414

9"–11"..................................$6750.00–750.00

17"..................................$775.00–950.00

Mold 418 (**grin**)

9"..................................$675.00–725.00

14"..................................$850.00–900.00

Mold 444, 451

9"..................................$250.00–300.00

14"..................................$550.00–600.00

Mold 452, **brown**

7½"..................................$425.00–475.00

10"..................................$525.00–600.00

15"..................................$675.00–700.00

Mold 458

10"–12"..................................$200.00–250.00

15"..................................$300.00–375.00

Mold 463

12"–13"..................................$450.00–550.00

16"..................................$950.00–1,050.00

Mold 473

13"..................................$425.00–475.00

Mold 1900

14"..................................$500.00–600.00

17"..................................$675.00–775.00

Heubach, Gebruder, **Sunburst mark**

Mold 7657, 7658, 7668, 7671

9"–10"..................................$2,000.00–2,300.00

12"–13"..................................$2,400.00–2,500.00

Mold 7620, 7661, 7686

> 10".....................................$1,800.00–2,100.00
>
> 14".....................................$3,500.00–4,000.00
>
> 17".....................................$4,100.00–4,200.00

Molds 8457, 9467, **Indians**

> 14".....................................$2,400.00–2,500.00

Mold 9457, **ca. 1914, square mark, dome, intaglio eyes, Princess Angeline, Native American woman, wrinkled face, downcast eyes, wigged believed to be a portrait of the daughter of Chief Seattle**

> 13"–15".....................................$2,000.00–2,700.00
>
> 18".....................................$3,800.00–4,000.00

Kämmer & Reinhardt (**K * R**)

Child, **no mold number**

> 8"– 14".....................................$400.00–800.00
>
> 17"–19".....................................$1,000.00–1,800.00

Mold 100

> 10"–11".....................................$850.00–950.00
>
> 17"–20".....................................$1,600.00–1,900.00

Mold 101, **painted eyes**

> 15"–18".....................................$4,000.00–4,900.00

Mold 101, **glass eyes**

> 15"–17".....................................$4,300.00–4,800.00

Mold 114

> 13".....................................$5,000.00–5,500.00

Mold 116, 116a

> 15".....................................$4,000.00–4,500.00
>
> 19".....................................$5,900.00–6,200.00

Mold 122, 126, **baby body**

> 7".....................................$400.00–500.00
>
> 10"– 12".....................................$700.00–750.00
>
> 16"–18".....................................$1,100.00–1,200.00

Mold 126, **toddler**

> 18".....................................$1,400.00–1,600.00

Mold 192, **open mouth child**

> 12".....................................$900.00–1,100.00

Kestner, J. D.

Baby, **no mold number, open mouth, teeth**

    10"...$1,500.00

Too few in database for a reliable range.

Hilda, **mold 245**

    12"–14"..$2,800.00–3,100.00

    16"– 18"..$4,000.00–4,500.00

Child, **no mold number**

Closed mouth

    14"...$900.00–1,100.00

    17"...$1,500.00–1,700.00

Open mouth

    12"–13"..$750.00–800.00

    16"–18"..$900.00–1,100.00

Five-piece body

    9"...$285.00–300.00

    12"...$350.00–400.00

AT-look, closed mouth

    15"...$6,000.00–6,500.00

Kley & Hahn, **Walkure composition body**

    12"–14"..$550.00–650.00

Knoch, Gebruder, **mold 201 child, composition body**

    8"–10"..$350.00–400.00

Koenig & Wernicke (**KW/G**)

    10"–14"..$350.00–$400.00

    18"–20"..$450.00–550.00

Ethnic features

    17"...$1,000.00–1,100.00

Kuhnlenz, Gebruder

Closed mouth

    15"...$675.00–900.00

    18"...$1,350.00–1,800.00

Open mouth, **mold 34.14, 34.16, 34.24, etc.**

    7"–9"..$500.00–700.00

    12"...$1,000.00–1,100.00

Ethnic features

    16"..$3,800.00–4,000.00

Marseille, Armand

Mold 370, **shoulder head**

    10"– 11" $300.00–350.00

Too few in database for a reliable range.

Mold 341, 351, 352, 362

    8"–10" $275.00–400.00

    14"–16" $500.00–550.00

    18"–20" $600.00–700.00

Mold 390, 390n

    14"–16" $350.00–400.00

    19"–23" $575.00–650.00

Mold 966, 970, 971, 992, 995 **(some in composition)**

    9"..$265.00–290.00

    14"..$550.00–600.00

    18"..$875.00–900.00

Mold 1894, 1897, 1902, 1912, 1914

    10"–12" $350.00–450.00

    14"..$500.00–600.00

    18"..$700.00–800.00

Recknagel, **marked "R.A.," mold 126, 138**

    9"–10" $550.00–600.00

    16"..$800.00–950.00

Schmidt, Franz

Mold 1255, **baby**

    14"–15" $400.00–450.00

    21"..$600.00–650.00

Closed mouth child, **glass eyes, wig**

    15"..$2,300.00–3,000.00

Schoenau Hoffmeister **(S PB H)**

Hanna

    7"–8" $150.00–175.00

    10–12" $200.00–275.00

    15"..$350.00–400.00

    18"..$550.00–600.00

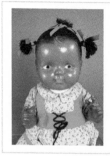

18" composition, unmarked: $120. **Photo courtesy of McMasters Harris Apple Tree Doll Auctions.**

16" Patsy Joan, Effanbee, composition: $950. **Photo courtesy of Morphy Auctions.**

Painted bisque Hanna, **glass eyes, wig**

    9"...$100.00–150.00

Mold 1909

    16"..$575.00–625.00

    19"..$750.00–850.00

Simon & Halbig

Mold 126

    8" toddler body $875.00–925.00

Mold 639

    14"..$6,400.00–6,800.00

    18"..$9,000.00–10,000.00

Mold 739, **open mouth**

    10"..$1,000.00–1,200.00

    16"..$1,500.00–1,800.00

    22"..$2,80.00–3,000.00

Closed mouth

    13"..$1,500.00

Too few in database for reliable range.

    17"..$2,400.00–2,600.00

Mold 939

Closed mouth

    18"..$3,000.00–3,300.00

    21"..$4,300.00–4,500.00

Open mouth

    13"..$2,300.00 **original outfit**

Too few in database for reliable range.

Mold 949

Closed mouth

18".. $3,200.00–3,400.00

21".. $3,750.00–3,950.00

Open mouth

15".. $2,600.00–2,800.00

Mold 1009, 1039, 1078, 1079, 1248, **open mouth**

11"–12".. $1,200.00–1,400.00

15"–16".. $1,600.00–1,800.00

18"–19".. $1,900.00–2,100.00

34".. $1,900.00–2,000.00

Pull-string sleep eyes

19".. $2,200.00–2,300.00

Mold 1248, **open mouth**

15".. $1,400.00–1,500.00

18".. $1,600.00–1,800.00

Mold 1272

20".. $1,800.00–2,000.00

Mold 1302, **closed mouth, glass eyes, character face**

18".. $9,000.00–10,000.00

Indian, sad expression, brown face

18".. $7,000.00–7,400.00

Mold 1303, **Indian, thin face, man or woman**

15"–16".. $6,000.00–6,500.00

21".. $7,800.00–8,000.00

Mold 1339, 1368

16".. $5,700.00–5,900.00

Mold 1348

15".. $5,000.00–6,000.00

Mold 1358

12"–13".. $5,000.00–6,500.00

19"–24".. $8,000.00–12,000.00

28".. $16,000.00–18,000.00

13" Cotton Joe, Horsman, and 14.5" Aunt Dinah, Effanbee, composition: Cotton Joe $350, Aunt Dinah $325. **Photo courtesy of Sweetbriar Auctions.**

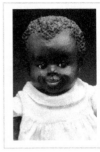

16" Leo Moss-type, composition: $5,800. **Photo courtesy of Morphy Auctions.**

Herm Steiner, *Mold 128*

    11"–13" $150.00–200.00

Living Eye Googly

    10" sold at auction...........................$570.00

Papier-mâché, **shoulder head on cloth or leather body**

    10"–13" $425.00–525.00

Squeeze toy, **molded head, glass eyes**

    10"–13" $200.00–300.00

Wood

Cooperative Manufacturing Co., **1873–1874, Joel Ellis manufactured wooden dolls with pressed heads and mortise and double tennon joints, with metal hands, black dolls were painted to order**

    12"..$2,500.00–3,000.00

China

Frozen Charlie/Charlotte

    3"..$100.00–135.00

    6"..$225.00–250.00

    8–9"..$300.00–350.00

Shoulder-head doll

    9"–11" $400.00–1,000.00

Celluloid

All-celluloid, **German or American**

    10"..$150.00–200.00

    15"..$275.00–350.00

    18"..$500.00–600.00

Celluloid shoulder head, **kid body, add more for glass eyes**

    17"..$275.00–350.00

    21"..$375.00–450.00

8" Angela, Vogue, hard plastic, ca. 1953: $1,100. **Photo courtesy of McMasters Harris Apple Tree Doll Auctions.**

17" Sara Lee, Ideal, vinyl: $450. **Photo courtesy of Dollyology Vintage Dolls**

French-type, **marked "SNF"**

14".. $300.00–350.00

16"–18".. $400.00–500.00

Kämmer & Reinhardt, **mold 728, 775, 778**

11".. $200.00–250.00

16"–18".. $375.00–450.00

Cloth

Alabama Baby: See Alabama section.

Babyland Rag Doll: See Babyland section.

Brazilian, **embroidered features, shell fingernails**

17"–21".. $500.00–600.00

Bruckner: See Bruckner section.

Homemade, **painted, embroidered, or appliquéd features, values vary according to the skill of the maker and the charm of the doll**

Mid nineteenth century–early twentieth century

8"–12".. $900.00–1,000.00

15"–20"...................................... $1,000.00–1,200.00

1900–1920

15"–18".. $375.00–500.00

1920–1940

15"–18".. $275.00–400.00

1930s Mammy-type

14".. $400.00–500.00

18".. $500.00–600.00

Chase: See Chase section.

Golliwog, **1895 to present. Character from 1895 book** *The Adventures of Two Dutch Dolls and a Golliwogg,* **all-cloth, various English makers. See also Deans Rag.**

1895–1920

    13"...$750.00–800.00

1930–1950

    11"...$300.00–400.00

    15"...$450.00–500.00

    18"...$600.00–700.00

1950–1970s

    13"–18"...$150.00–225.00

Steiff, **1996**

    Molly Golli & Peg............................$450.00

Mask face, **1920–1930s, American**

    13"–18"...$65.00–100.00

Stockinette Baby **(often mis-called Black Beecher), embroidered features, glass eyes**

    20"–22"...$3,500.00–4,500.00

Wellings, Norah, **1926 to 1960, Wellington, Shropshire, England, The Victoria Toy Works molded heads and bodies of velvet, velveteen, plush, and felt**

Black Islander, **glass eyes**

    13"–14"...$140.00–220.00

    16"...$250.00–300.00

    28"...$400.00–450.00

Composition, **doll in good condition with original clothing**

Unkown Marker

Baby with three pigtails, **painted eyes**

    8"–10"...$45.00–60.00

Arranbee Doll Co.

Dream Baby, **1927, composition, lower arms and legs, cloth body, metal sleep eyes**

    8"–10"...$150.00–200.00

Averill

Madame Hendron, **designed by Grace Drayton**

    13"...$400.00–500.00

Cameo

Kewpie, **All-composition, jointed body, blue wings**

    8"...$150.00–175.00

    11"–13"...$200.00–250.00

Scootles, **1925 on, Rose O'Neill design, all-composition, no marks, painted side-glancing eyes, paper wrist tag**

    12"...$350.00–425.00

Effanbee

Baby Grumpy

> 12"–16"...$200.00–400.00

Grumpy Aunt Dinah, **black, cloth body, striped stocking legs**

> 14½"...$200.00–325.00

Bubbles

> 17"–22"...$650.00–750.00

Candy Kid, **original shorts, robe, and gloves**

> 12"..$350.00–400.00

Patsy Joan

> 16"..$900.00–1,000.00

Skippy, **with original outfit**

> 14"..$900.00

Too few in database for reliable range.

Horsman

Baby bumps

> 10"–12"...$225.00–300.00

Campbell Kid, **1910 on, designed by Helen Trowbridge, based on Grace Drayton's drawings, composition head, painted and molded hair, side-glancing painted eyes, closed smiling mouth**

> 10"–11"..$250.00–300.00

Cotton Joe, **black**

> 13"..$300.00–375.00

Ideal

Marama, **Shirley Temple body, from the movie *Hurricane***

> 13"..$450.00–500.00
>
> 18"..$850.00–900.00

Koenig & Wernicke, **mold 134**

> 14"..$450.00–500.00

Leo Moss type

> 16"..$5,300.00–6,000.00

Patsy-type

> 13"–14"...$200.00–300.00

Skookum Apple, **character head**

> 10"–14"...$150.00–200.00

Tony Sarg **Mammy with baby**

> 18"..$800.00–900.00

Topsy-type, **cotton pigtails**

    10"–12" $150.00–200.00

Rubber

Amosandra, **from Amos & Andy radio show, 1949**

    10" $225.00–275.00

Sun Rubber So-Wee,

    10" $150.00–200.00

Hard Plastic

Pedigree

Mandy Lou, **Ashtrakan wig, flirty eyes**

    16" $125.00–150.00

    Walker 21" $175.00–200.00

Terri Lee

Benji, **painted plastic, 1946–1962, black lamb's wool wig**

    16" $900.00–1,100.00

Patty Jo, **1947–1949**

    16" $700.00–1,000.00

Bonnie Lou,

    16" $600.00–900.00

Vogue

Strung Ginny, **1950–1953, hard plastic, sleep eyes, strung joints, marked "Vogue" on head, "Vogue Doll" on body, painted eyes, molded hair with mohair wig, clothing tagged "Vogue Dolls" or "Vogue Dolls, Inc. Medford Mass.," inkspot tag on white with blue letters**

    8" $1,000.00–1,300.00

Vinyl

Baby Crissy, **1973–1976, all-vinyl, jointed body, legs and arms foam filled, rooted auburn grow hair, two painted teeth, brown sleep eyes, mark: "©1972//IDEAL TOY COPR.//2M 5511//B OR GHB-H-225" on back**

    24" $150.00–200.00

Beautiful Crissy, **1969–1974, all-vinyl, dark brown eyes, long hair, turn knob in back to make hair grow, some with swivel waist (1971), pull string to turn head (1972), pull string to talk (1971), reissued ca. 1982–1983, first year hair grew to floor length**

    17½" $100.00–200.00

Drowsy, **Mattel, 1965–1974, vinyl head, stuffed body, sleepers, pull-string talker**

    15½" $150.00–200.00

Dee & Cee, **1960– 1970s, Canada, vinyl head and body, rooted hair. See also Vinyl.**

    12"–15" $50.00–60.00

Effanbee Fluffy, **1957 on**

    8"...**$30.00–40.00**

FloJo, **Florence Griffin Joyner, made by LJN**

    11½" **$15.00–20.00**

Gotz

World of Children Series

    23"..**$150.00–180.00**

Mindy, **1957, Earl Pullan Co. Canada, vinyl head with molded braids, stuffed vinyl body**

    15"..**$200.00–250.00**

Miss Peep, **Cameo**

    18"..**$100.00–125.00**

Sara Lee, **Ideal, 1950, vinyl head and limbs, cloth body, sleep eyes**

    17"..**$400.00–500.00**

BLEUETTE

10 5/8" Bleuette, Premiere, bisque: $5,200. **Photo courtesy of McMasters Harris Apple Tree Doll Auctions.**

1905–1960, France. This premium doll was first made in bisque and later in composition for a weekly children's periodical, *La Semanine De Suzette* (The Week of Suzette), that also produced patterns for Bleuette. Premiere Bleuette was a bisque socket head, Tété Jumeau, marked only with a "1" superimposed on a "2," and 10⅝" tall. She had set blue or brown glass eyes, open mouth with four teeth, wig, an d pierced ears. The composition jointed body was marked "2" on back and "1" on the sole of each foot. This mold was made only in 1905. S.F.B.J., a bisque socket head, began production in 1905, using a Fleischmann and Bloedel mold marked "6/0," blue or brown glass eyes, wig, open mouth, and teeth. S.F.B.J. mold marked "SFBJ 60" or "SFBJ 301 1" was a bisque socket head, open mouth with teeth, wig, and blue or brown glass eyes. All Bleuettes were 10⅝" tall prior to 1933, after that all Bleuettes were 11⅜".

Bisque

Premiere, **1905, Jumeau head**

    10⅝" $5,000.00–5,800.00

SFJB 6/0, **1905–1915, head made in Germany by Fleischman**

    10⅝" $2,200.00–3,000.00

SFBJ 60 8/0, **1916–1933**

    10⅝" $1,500.00–2,000.00

SFBJ 301 1

    10⅝" $1,800.00–2,200.00

71 Unis France 149 60 8/0

    10⅝" $1,000.00–1,500.00

71 Unis France 149, **1933 on**

    11⅜" $1,400.00–1,600.00

Composition, **1930–1933**

SFBJ 301 or 71 Unis France 149 251, **1930–1933**

    10⅝" $800.00–1,000.00

SFBJ or 71 Unis France 149 251, **1933 on**

    11⅜" $500.00–700.00

BONNET HEAD

11" bonnet head, Hertwig, bisque: $190. **Photo courtesy of Joan & Lynette Antique Dolls and Accessories.**

14" bonnet head, wax-over: $525. **Photo courtesy of Oldeclectics.**

1860s–1940s on, dolls made of a variety of materials by numerous manufacturers, all with molded bonnets or hats. More elaborate hat brings higher end of range.

All-bisque, **German immobiles, painted eyes**

    5" $125.00–175.00

    7"–8" $275.00–325.00

Stone bisque immobile

    3½"–5" $25.00–35.00

Wire Jointed

    4½"–5½" $85.00–125.00

Bisque, socket or shoulder head, five-piece composition body, kid body or cloth body. Elaborate headwear brings higher end of range

Painted eyes

    5"–8" $100.00–250.00

    11"–14" $150.00–500.00

    18"–20" $200.00–500.00

Glass eyes

    7"–9" $250.00–350.00

    12"–15" $500.00–750.00

Alt, Beck & Gottschalk, **Elaborate headwear brings higher end of range**

Painted eye

    13"–16" $500.00–2,000.00

Glass eye

    18" $1,530.00

Too few in database for a reliable range.

Handwerck, Max, **painted eyes, mark: Elite**

Marked "Elite," **Molded Military helmet, bisque socket head, glass eyes, closed mouth**

    10"–14" $1,800.00–2,500.00

Marked "Elite," **Bellhop style molded hat**

    11"–12" $2,000.00–2200.00

Marked "Elite," **two faced**

    12" $3,000.00–3,200.00

Heubach, Gebruder

Molds 7877, 7977, **"Baby Stuart," ca. 1912, socket head, molded bonnet, closed mouth, painted eyes**

    6"–9" $650.00–800.00

    11"–13" $1,300.00–1,600.00

    15" $1,700.00–2,000.00

Mold 7975, **"Baby Stuart," ca. 1912, socket head, glass eyes, removable molded bisque bonnet**

    9"–13" $2,200.00–2,400.00

Molds 8326, **"Baby Stuart," shoulder head, molded bonnet, closed mouth, painted eyes**

    11"–13" $500.00–600.00

19" bonnet head, untinted bisque (so-called Parian), German: $1,000. **Photo courtesy of Joan & Lynette Antique Dolls and Accessories.**

Hertwig, **molded bonnet, jointed shoulders**

6"–10" $100.00–175.00

14"–16" $200.00–350.00

Japan

8"–9" $85.00–95.00

12" $125.00–145.00

Molded shirt or top

15" $750.00–850.00

21" $1,200.00–1,305.00

Recknagel, **Bonnet head baby, painted eyes, open-closed mouth, teeth. Molds 22, 28, 44, molded white boy's cap, bent-leg baby body**

8"–9" $300.00–350.00

10"–12" $450.00–500.00

Stone bisque

8"–9" $100.00–150.00

12"–15" $175.00–225.00

China, **blond or black hair, painted eyes**

Common style and quality

10"–13" $250.00–300.00

High quality

8" -10½" $5,000.00–7,000.00

12"–14" $6,000.00–8,000.00

Paper-mache, **leather body, wood lower limbs**

Painted eyes

12"–18" $1,500.00–1,800.00

Man, **molded military hat, 1840s–1850s**

16" $4,500.00–5,500.00

Glass eyes

13" $5,000.00–6,000.00

Untinted Bisque (so-called Parian-type), **cloth body with composition or wood lower limbs. Elaborate headwear brings higher end of range**

Painted eyes

    4"–6"...$400.00–900.00

    10"–17"......................................$1,000.00–1,600.00

Glass eyes

    10"–14"......................................$2,500.00–5,000.00

Wax-over composition, **cloth body with composition or wood lower limbs, glass eyes**

    7"–13"...$250.00–500.00

    19"–23"...$600.00–900.00

BOUDOIR DOLLS

31" boudoir, cloth head: $400. **Photo courtesy of Alderfer Auction Company, Inc.**

1915–1940s, made in France, Italy, and United States usually. Long-limbed dolls of a variety of materials, used primarily as decorative items, fancy costumes, usually 28"–30".

Cloth mask face, **1920s, French-made, Blossom(USA), others**

High quality with silk floss hair

    ....$500.00–650.00

    Average quality...................................$160.00–250.00

Composition or Paper-mâché head, **1920–1940s**

    Smoker..$700.00–900.00

    High quality $200.00–450.00

    Average quality.....................................$75.00–125.00

Suede, **1920–1930s**

    High quality $700.00–900.00

Hard plastic, **1940s**

    ....$60.00–125.00

BRU

17.5" Bru Smiler Poupée, bisque, kid body: $5,500. **Photo courtesy of Gloria's Antique Dolls.**

10" Bru Breveté, bisque: $14,000. **Photo courtesy of Withington Auction Inc.**

1866–1899, Bru Jne. & Cie, Paris and Montreuil-sous-Bois, France. Bru eventually became one of the members of the S.F.B.J. syndicate (1899–1953). Bébés Bru with kid bodies are some of the most collectible dolls, highly sought after because of the fine quality of bisque, delicate coloring, and fine workmanship. Brus are made of pressed bisque and have a metal spring stringing mechanism in the neck. Add more for original clothes and rare body styles.

Poupée (Fashion-type lady), **1866–1877, pressed bisque socket head attached to bisque shoulder plate with metal spring stringing, painted or glass eyes, pierced ears, cork pate, mohair wig, kid body, mark: numbers only, some marked B. Jne et Cie on shoulder plate**

> 12"–13" $3,900.00–4,200.00
>
> 15"–17" $4,200.00–5,500.00
>
> 20"–21" $4,200.00–4,800.00

Wooden lower arms

> 16"–19" $5,700.00–6,000.00

Wooden body

> 15"–16" $8,900.00–9,500.00
>
> 26" $12,000.00–14,000.00

Smiler, **1873 on, closed smiling mouth, mark: size letters A through O**

Kid body with kid or bisque lower arms

> 11" $3,600.00–3,800.00
>
> 13"–15" $4,000.00–5,000.00
>
> 20"–21" $7,500.00–8,500.00

Wooden lower arms

> 16"–19" $5,500.00–7,500.00

17" Bru Bébé Teteur, bisque: $12,000. **Photo courtesy of Terri's Treasures From Above.**

19" Bru Jne, size6, bisque: $27,000. **Photo courtesy of Joan & Lynette Antique Dolls and Accessories.**

Wooden body

15"–16"...$8,000.00–9,500.00

18"–21"...$11,000.00–15,000.00

Bru Breveté, 1879–1880, pressed bisque socket head on bisque shoulder plate, paperweight eyes, multi-stroked eyebrows, closed mouth with space between the lips, full cheeks, pierced ears, cork pate, skin wig, kid or wood articulated body, mark: size number only on head

10"–12"...$14,000.00–20,000.00

14"–16"...$17,000.00–22,000.00

19"–22"...$24,000.00–28,000.00

Circle Dot or Crescent mark Bru, 1879–1884, pressed bisque socket head on bisque shoulder plate, paperweight eyes, multi-stroked eyebrows, open/closed mouth with molded, painted teeth, full cheeks, pierced ears, cork pate, mohair or human hair wig, gusseted kid body with bisque lower arms

12" size 1 ....$16,000.00–20,000.00

13"–14"...$15,000.00–22,000.00

18"–19"...$19,000.00–24,000.00

22"–24"...$20,000.00–26,000.00

31"...$32,000.00–35,000.00

BruJne, 1880–1891, pressed bisque socket head on bisque shoulder plate with deeply molded shoulders, paperweight eyes, multi-stroked eyebrows, open/closed mouth with molded, painted teeth, pierced ears, cork pate, mohair or human hair wig, gusseted kid body with wood upper arms, bisque lower arms and kid or wood lower legs

12"–14"...$19,000.00–26,000.00

15"–17"...$20,000.00–28,000.00

20"–24"...$26,000.00–30,000.00

30"–35" 32,000.00–38,000.00

Bru JneR, 1891–1899, pressed bisque socket head on bisque shoulder plate with deeply molded shoulders, paperweight eyes, multi-stroked eyebrows, open/closed mouth with four to six teeth, pierced ears, cork pate, mohair or human hair wig, articulated wood and composition body

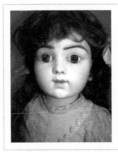

22" Bru Jne R., size 9, bisque, closed mouth: $8,000. **Photo courtesy of Gloria's Antique Dolls.**

Open mouth

12"..$3,000.00–3,500.00

18"–21"...$5,500.00–7,000.00

Closed mouth

10½"..$4,500.00–5,000.00

12"–13"...$5,500.00–7,000.00

15"–16"...$9,500.00–10,000.00

19"–21"...$7,500.00–8,500.00

27"–29"...$8,500.00–9,500.00

Mechanical Specialty Dolls

Bébé Teteur (nursing), **1879–1898, open mouth for insertion of bottle, screw key at back of head allowed doll to drink**

13"..$7,500.00–8,500.00

15"–17"...10,000.00–12,000.00

19"–24"...$12,000.00–13,000.00

Bébé Gourmand **(eating), 1880 on, open mouth with tongue, bisque lower legs, when fed food pellets went in through mouth and out through holes on the bottom of the feet, special shoes with a flap opening on the bottom allowed for food removal**

16"–18"...$40,000.00–50,000.00

Bébé Modele, **1880 on, Breveté face, carved wood body**

16"–19"...$28,000.00–32,000.00

Bébé Musique (musical), **1892 on, cirle dot head on wooden body with Swiss music box inside**

17" sold for $44,000.00 at auction

Bébé Baiser (kiss throwing), **1892 on, pull string mechanism raises dolls arm and simulates throwing a kiss**

11"..$4,100.00–4,200.00

15"..$4,300.00–4,400.00

22"..$5,500.00–6,000.00

Bébé Respirant (breathing), **1892 on, key or lever in torso activates mechanism to simulate chest movement**

20"–24" $12,000.00–15,000.00

Surprise Doll, **poupée or bébé with two faces**

13"–21" $11,000.00–18,000.00

Bru shoes

.. $800.00–1,200.00

ALBERT BRUCKNER

13.5" Bruckner, cloth: $245. **Photo courtesy of McMasters Harris Apple Tree Doll Auctions.**

1901–1930 on, Jersey City, New Jersey. Made some dolls for the Horsman Babyland line. These dolls had molded cloth mask faces, cloth bodies, and printed features. Later made flat-faced cloth dolls.

Molded cloth, mask faces

12"–14" $185.00–245.00

Black $300.00–400.00

Topsy-Turvy $350.00–450.00

Flat faced, **printed, 1925 on, such as Dollypop, Pancake Baby, others**

12"–13" $175.00–250.00

BUCHERER

1921–1930s, Armisil, Switzerland. Metal bodies with metal ball joints, composition head, hands and feet, mark: "MADE IN SWITZERLAND PATENTS APPLIED FOR"

6½"–7" $250.00–300.00

7" Bucherer,
metal: $350.
**Photo courtesy of
Morphy Auctions.**

Regional and characters **such as baseball player, fireman, military, Pinocchio, others**

.... **$400.00–600.00**

Comic characters **such as Charlie Chaplin, Happy Hooligan, Katzenjammers, Maggie & JiggsMutt & Jeff, others**

.... **$350.00–700.00**

BUDDY LEE

12.5" Buddy Lee,
hard plastic: $400.
**Photo courtesy of
Morphy Auctions.**

1920–1962, United States. Made by the H.D. Lee Co., Inc. as an advertising doll to spotlight their overalls and work gear. Doll with molded hair, painted side-glancing eyes, jointed shoulders, legs molded apart, all original clothing, mark: embossed Buddy Lee.

Composition, **1920–1948, 13"**

Engineer, Cowboy, Phillips 66

.... **$375.00–500.00**

Football uniform, Gulf Oil, Minneapolis Moline uniform

.... **$800.00–2,000.00**

Too few in database for reliable range.

Hard Plastic, **1949–1962, 13"**

Engineer, Phillips 66, others

....$300.00–400.00

John Deere

....$450.00–550.00

Vinyl Reissue, **1997**

13"...$65.00–100.00

BURGARELLA

16" Burgarella, composition: $4,000. **Photo courtesy of Sweetbriar Auctions.**

1925 to WWII, Rome, Italy. Made by Gaspare Burgarella, designed by Ferdinando Stracuzzi. Mark: cloth label sewn into outfit BURGARELLA Made in Italy.

Child, **high-quality composition, expressively painted eyes with heavy shading, high-quality human hair or mohair wig, jointed at neck, shoulders, hips, and knees.**

16"–18"...$3,500.00–4,500.00

22"...$4,500.00–5,500.00

BYE-LO BABY

1922–1952. Baby doll designed by Grace Storey Putnam to represent a three-day-old infant. Distributed by George Borgfeldt & Co. Bisque heads made by German makers such as Hertel & Schwab, Kestner, Kling, others. Cloth bodies made by K&K in the United States. Composition bodies made by Koenig & Wernicke in Germany. Composition head made by Cameo Doll Co.

16" Bye-Lo baby, composition, American: $350. **Photo courtesy of Alderfer Auction Company, Inc.**

All-bisque, 1925 on, made by Kestner, some with pink or blue booties, mark: G. S. Putnam on back, paper sticker on chest reads Bye-Lo Baby

Painted eye

4"–5" $275.00–375.00

6" $400.00–450.00

8" $450.00–500.00

Glass eye, **wigged**

4"–6" $550.00–700.00

8" $800.00–900.00

Swivel neck, **glass eyes**

5"–6" $800.00–1,000.00

8" $1,100.00–1,300.00

Bisque head, flange neck head on cloth body with "frog" style legs or straight legs, closed mouth, molded, painted hair, blue sleep eyes, celluloid or composition hands, mark: head incised, some bodies stamped Bye-Lo Baby

8"–9" $250.00–3000.00

10"–12" $175.00–225.00

14"–16" $250.00–350.00

18"–22" $375.00–450.00

Socket head on composition body

11"–15" $900.00–1,200.00

Composition head, 1924 on, molded painted hair, sleep or painted eyes, closed mouth, cloth body

12"–13" $200.00–300.00

16" $350.00–400.00

Celluloid, made by Karl Standfuss, Saxony, Germany

All-celluloid

    4"..$125.00–175.00

    6"..$200.00–250.00

Celluloid head on cloth body

    10"..$200.00–225.00

    12"..$275.00–325.00

Wax, **1925, sold in New York boutiques**

    18"–20"..$1,500.00–2,000.00

Wood, **1925, made by Schoenhut**

    ....$2,300.00–2,500.00

Vinyl, **Horsman, 1972, mark: Grace Storey Putnam on head**

    14"...$35.00–40.00

Other Putnam dolls

Fly-Lo, **1926–1930. Bisque, ceramic, or composition head, glass or metal sleep eyes, molded painted hair, flange neck on cloth body, celluloid hands, satin wings in pink, green, or gold, mark: "Corp. by //Grace S. Putnam" on head**

Bisque, **less for ceramic**

    9"–11"...$3,000.00–4,000.00

Composition

    12"–14"..$450.00–650.00

CABBAGE PATCH KIDS

1978 to present, initially designed by Xavier Roberts as an all-cloth needle-sculpted doll. The dolls were made in varying skin tone and hair and eye color combinations giving them each a unique look and "personality." Kids were 22", Newborns 17", and Preemies 15". Later licensing agreement led to vinyl-headed dolls made by Coleco. In 1988 rights for the vinyl-headed dolls went to Hasbro and in 1994 to Mattel. In 2004 rights for vinyl production were sold Play Along Toys and 4Kids Entertainment. Dolls listed are in perfect condition with original clothing and tags or paperwork.

1978 on, Babyland General Hospital, Cleveland, GA, **cloth, needle sculpture, signature color changes year to year. All in excellent conditon with paperwork.**

"A" blue edition

    1978 ....$650.00–750.00

"B" red edition

    1978 ....$550.00–650.00

16" Mai Ling, Cabbage Patch Kid, Shader, porcelain head, circa 1985, MIB: $60. **Doll courtesy of private collection.**

"C" burgundy edition

1979t **$675.00–850.00**

"D" purple edition

1979 .... **$350.00–450.00**

black **$600.00**

"E" bronze edition

1980 .... **$200.00–250.00**

Preemie edition

1980 .... **$120.00–170.00**

New Ears edition

1981 .... **$75.00–125.00**

Ears edition

1982 .... **$75.00–125.00**

Green edition

1983 .... **$100.00–150.00**

"KP" dark green edition

1983 .... **$100.00–150.00**

"KPR" red edition

1983 .... **$100.00–150.00**

"KPB" burgundy edition

1983 .... **$100.00–150.00**

"KPZ" edition

1983–1984 .... **$70.00–90.00**

Champagne edition

1983–1984 .... **$45.00–60.00**

"KPP" purple edition

1984 .... **$40.00–100.00**

"KPF," "KPG," "KPH," "KPI," "KPJ" editions

1984–1985 .... $75.00–90.00

Emerald edition

1985 .... $50.00–75.00

Aquamarine

1988 .... $80.00–150.00

Jade or Ruby

1989 .... $50.00–70.00

Garnet

1991 .... $40.00–100.00

1989 through 1990s

Kid, Newborn, or Preemie

.... $90.00–120.00

2004 on

Kid $150.00–400.00

Coleco Cabbage Patch Kids, 1983 on, vinyl head, cloth body, black signature stamp. All in excellent conditon with paperwork.

Kid, Newborn, or Preemie

.... $40.00–50.00

Popcorn hairdos, **rare**

.... $75.00–115.00

Cornsilk Kid $40.00–60.00

Porcelain, 1985, made by Shaders

Kid $30.00–50.00

CAMEO DOLL CO.

1922–1930 on, New York City, Port Allegheny, Pennsylvania. Joseph L. Kallus's company made composition dolls, some with wood segmented bodies and cloth bodies. All dolls listed are in good condition with original clothing, allow less for crazed or undressed dolls.

Bisque

Baby Bo Kaye

Bisque head, **made in Germany, molded hair, open mouth, glass eyes, cloth body, composition limbs, good condition, mark: "J.L. Kallus: Corp. Germany//1394/30"**

7"–12" $1,000.00–1,100.00

17"–20" $1,700.00–2,500.00

12" Betty Boop, Cameo, composition: $850. **Photo courtesy of Morphy Auctions.**

12" Giggles, Cameo, composition: $250. **Photo courtesy of Morphy Auctions.**

All-bisque, **molded hair, glass sleep eyes, open mouth, two teeth, swivel neck, jointed arms and legs, molded pink or blue shoes, socks, unmarked, some may retain original round sticker on body**

5"... $1,700.00–2,000.00

7"–8" $2,100.00–2,200.00

Celluloid

Baby Bo Kaye

Celluloid head, **made in Germany, molded hair, open mouth, glass eyes, cloth body**

12"–16" $750.00–950.00

Composition

Annie Rooney, 1926, Jack Collins, designer, all-composition, yarn wig, legs painted black, molded shoes

13"... $475.00–500.00

17"... $850.00–900.00

Excellent condition 17" sold at auction for $1,243.00

Baby Blossom, 1927, "DES, J.L.Kallus," composition upper torso, cloth lower body and legs, molded hair, open mouth

19"–20" $300.00–350.00

Baby Bo Kaye

Composition head, **molded hair, open mouth, glass eyes, light crazing**

14"... $650.00–675.00

Bandy, 1929, composition head, wood segmented body, marked on hat "General Electric Radio," designed by J. Kallus

18½" $1,100.00–1,200.00

Betty Boop, 1932, composition head character, wood segmented body, molded hair, painted features, label on torso

12"... $850.00–950.00

20"... $1,050.00–1,150.00

Champ, **1942, composition with freckles**

16"..$575.00–600.00

Eugene the Jeep, **composition and wood segmented doll from Popeye comics**

12"–17"..$900.00–1,100.00

Felix the Cat, **composition and wood segmented doll**

9"–13"...$350.00–400.00

Giggles, **1946, "Giggles Doll, A Cameo Doll," composition with molded loop for ribbon**

12"–14"..$250.00–300.00

Ho-Ho **1940, painted plaster, laughing mouth**

5½" $125.00–150.00

Joy, **1932, composition head character, wood segmented body, molded hair, painted features, label on torso**

10"...$200.00–250.00

15"...$225.00–300.00

Margie, **1929, composition head character, wood segmented body, molded hair, painted features, label on torso**

10"...$100.00–160.00

15"...$200.00–275.00

17"...$300.00–350.00

Pete the Pup, **1930–1935, composition head character, wood segmented body, molded hair, painted features, label on torso**

9"–12"...$275.00–375.00

Pinkie **1930–1935, composition head character, wood segmented body, molded hair, painted features, label on torso**

7"–10"..$200.00–250.00

Popeye, **1935, composition head character, wood segmented body, molded hair, painted features, label on torso**

14"...$450.00–600.00

Pretty Bettsie, **composition head, molded hair, painted side-glancing eyes, open/closed mouth, composition one-piece body and limbs, wooden neck joint, molded and painted dress with ruffles, shoes, and socks, triangular red tag on chest marked "Pretty Bettsie//Copyright J. Kallus"**

18"...$400.00–450.00

Scootles, **1925 on, Rose O'Neill design, all-composition, no marks, painted side-glancing eyes, paper wrist tag**

7"–8"...$225.00–275.00

12"...$300.00–400.00

15"...$500.00–600.00

16" Scootles, Cameo, vinyl, MIB: $175. **Photo courtesy of Alderfer Auction Company, Inc.**

22" $700.00–800.00

26" $950.00–1,150.00

Composition, **sleep eyes**

15" $575.00–650.00

Black composition

12" $350.00–425.00

Hard Plastic and Vinyl, **dolls listed here are in good condition wearing original clothing, allow double for mint-in-box.**

Baby Mine, **1962–1964, vinyl and cloth, sleep eyes**

16" $60.00–75.00

19" $75.00–100.00

Ho Ho, **"Rose O'Neill," laughing mouth, squeaker, tag**

White

7" $45.00–60.00

Black

7" $80.00–105.00

Miss Peep, **1957–1970s, pin-jointed shoulders and hips, vinyl**

15" $70.00–85.00

18" $90.00–100.00

Black

18" $100.00–125.00

1984, Jesco reissue, all vinyl

16" $25.00–30.00

Miss Peep, Newborn, **1962, vinyl head and rigid plastic body**

14"–18" $70.00–120.00

Pinkie, **1950s**

10"–11" $125.00–150.00

Scootles, **1964, vinyl**

    14"–16" $70.00–100.00

    20" $125.00–175.00

1980s, **Jesco**

    12" $25.00–30.00

    16" $35.00–40.00

    19" $50.00–60.00

CATTERFELDER PUPPENFABRIK

17" mold 207, Catterfelder Puppenfabrik, bisque: $3,700. **Photo courtesy of Morphy Auctions.**

1906 on, Catterfeld, Thuringia, Germany. Had heads made by Kestner. Trademark: My Sunshine

C.P. Child, 1902 on, dolly face, bisque socket head, glass sleep eyes, wigged, open mouth with teeth, ball-jointed composition body

Mold 264 and others

    9" $300.00–350.00

    14"–16" $400.00–500.00

    25"–28" $600.00–80.00

Shoulder head, **mold 505, dolly face, kid body**

    27" $200.00–225.00

C.P. Character child, 1910 on, bisque socket head, painted eyes, wigged, open mouth with teeth, ball-jointed composition body

Mold: 207, 210, 215, 219, 217, others

    10"–12" $2,000.00–3,000.00

    15"–16" $2,500.00–3,500.00

Mold 220, **glass eyes**

    14" $6,000.00–6,500.00

Character Baby, 1910 on, bisque socket head, molded hair or wig, painted or glass sleep eyes, composition baby body, solid dome with painted eyes bring higher end of range

Mold: 200, 201, 207, 208, others

8"–10" $275.00–450.00

14"–16" $300.00–500.00

19"–21" $575.00–700.00

Toddler

8"–11" $800.00–1,100.00

Mold 262, 263, 268

15"–17" $450.00–500.00

20"–22" $550.00–600.00

Toddler

28" $1,200.00–1,400.00

CELLULOID

8", French, all celluloid: each $45 each. **Photo courtesy of Alderfer Auction Company, Inc.**

Early form of plastic made from nitrocellulose and a plasticizer such as camphor. Came into use in 1869 and an improved version became popular about 1905.

Made in numerous countries:

England — Wilson Doll co., Cascelliod Ltd. (Palitoy)

France — Petitcollin (profile of eagle head), Widow Chalory, Convert Cie, Parisienn Cellulosine, Neuman & Marx (dragon), Société Industrielle de Celluloid (SIC), Société Nobel Francaise (SNF in diamond), Sicoine, Urika others.

Germany — Bähr & Pröschild, Buschow & Beck (helmet Minerva), Catterfelder Puppenfibrik Co., Cuno & Otto Dressel, E. Maar & Sohn (3M), Emasco, Kämmer

& Reinhardt, Kestner, Koenig & Wernicke, A. Hagendorn & Co., Hermsdorfer Celluloidwarenfabrik (lady bug), Dr. Paul Hunaeus, Kohn & Wengenroth, Rheinsche Gummi und Celluloid Fabrik Co. later known as Schildkröte (turtle mark), Max Rudolph, Bruno Schmidt, Franz Schmidt & Co., Schoberl & Becker (mermaid) who used Cellba as a trade name, Karl Standfuss, Albert Wacker, others.

USA — Averill, Bo-Peep (H.J. Brown), DuPont Viscaloid Co., Horsman, Irwin, Marks Bros., Parsons-Jackson (stork mark), Celluloid Novelty Co., others.

All Celluloid

Baby, **1910 on, painted eyes**

4"–8"	$65.00–80.00
12"–15"	$140.00–160.00
19"–21"	$190.00–215.00

Marked France

3"	$95.00–115.00
5"–9"	$120.00–200.00
16"–18"	$325.00–425.00

Marked German character baby

12" 325.00–400.00

Marked Japan

4"–5"	$18.00–22.00
8"–10"	$45.00–55.00
13"–15"	$125.00–150.00

Occupied Japan

24"	$150.00–175.00

Child, **painted eyes, jointed at shoulder and hips**

3"–7"	$35.00–75.00
11"–14"	$125.00–175.00
18"–20"	$225.00–275.00

Glass eyes

12"–13"	$200.00–250.00
15"–16"	$250.00–300.00
24"	$350.00–375.00

Marked France

7"–9"	$150.00–175.00
14"–18"	$250.00–275.00
22"–24"	$325.00–375.00

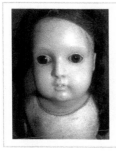

16" celluloid, Kestner mold 201, German: $300. **Photo courtesy of Gloria's Antique Dolls.**

12" mold 717, Kammer & Reinhardt, celluloid, flirty eyes: $650. **Photo courtesy of Morphy Auctions.**

Marked Japan

With molded clothing

   3"–4"...$40.00–60.00

   8"–9"...$115.00–130.00

Jointed shoulders only

   3"–4"...$18.00–22.00

   8"–10"...$30.00–40.00

Occupied Japan

   6"–8"...$90.00–100.00

In regional costume, **tagged LeMinor, Poupée Magali, others**

   8"...$40.00–55.00

   12"–15"..$75.00–95.00

   19"...$125.00–150.00

Carnival-type, **may have feathers glued on head or body**

   8"–12"...$30.00–45.00

Kewpie: **See Kewpie listing.**

Shoulder head child, **1900 on, German, molded hair or wig, open or open/closed mouth, kid or cloth body, sometimes arms of other materials**

Painted eye

   11"–14"..$100.00–160.00

   16"–18"..$200.00–225.00

Glass eye

   16"–18"..$200.00–250.00

   22"–24"..$250.00–300.00

Kestner, **mold 201**

   16"..$300.00–350.00

Bye-Lo Baby: **See Bye-Lo listing.**

Socket-head child, 1910 on, open mouth, glass sleep eyes, wig, composition body

French, such as Petitcolin, others, glass eyes, wigged

 18"–19" $350.00–400.00

Jumeau

 13" $450.00–500.00

 16" $575.00–600.00

Urika, celluloid called Rhodoid, 1947–1957, character dolls with celluloid heads and hands, cloth bodies

 13" $300.00–400.00

German, various makers

Molded hair, painted eyes

 11"–13" $200.00–300.00

 16"–19" $225.00–325.00

Glass eyes

 14"–17" $200.00–400.00

Heubach Koppelsdorf, mold 399

 11" $75.00–100.00

Kämmer & Reinhardt

Shoulderhead child, mold 255, 405, 406, others

 21"–23" $150.00–225.00

Baby, mold 721, 727, 728

 10"–15" $225.00–275.00

 17"–21" $300.00–400.00

Toddler, flirty eyes

 17" $400.00–450.00

Child, socket head, mold 701, 717

 12"–14" $650.00–750.00

 21"–28" $1,000.00–1,500.00

Kestner, mold 203 character baby

 12" $425.00–450.00

Koenig & Wernicke (K & W)

Toddler

 15"–19" $375.00–500.00

Max & Moritz

 7" ....$300.00–350.00 each

American

Parsons-Jackson (**stork mark**)

Baby

     9"–12" **$110.00–160.00**

     14" **$175.00–225.00**

Toddler

     12"–15" **$150.00–200.00**

CENTURY DOLL CO.

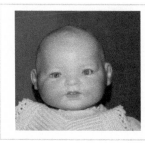

18" century baby, Century Doll Co., bisque: $850. **Photo courtesy of** The Museum Doll Shop

1909–1930, New York City. Founded by Max Scheuer and sons, used bisque heads on many later dolls. In about 1929, Century merged with Domec to become the Doll Corporation of America. Some heads were made by Kestner Herm Steinerand other firms for Century. Dolls listed here are in good condition, with original clothes or appropriately dressed. More for boxed, tagged, or labeled exceptional doll.

Bisque

Baby, **1926, by Kestner bisque head, molded and painted hair, sleep eyes, open-closed mouth, cloth body**

     13" **$325.00–375.00**

     16"–18" **$425.00–525.00**

Mold 275, **solid dome, glass eyes, closed mouth, cloth body, composition limbs**

     14" **$800.00–850.00**

Child

Molds 285, 287, **by Kestner bisque socket head, glass eyes, wig, ball-jointed body**

     14" **$600.00–625.00**

     19"–24" **$625.00–650.00**

Molds 279, **by Kestner, bisque socket head, molded bobed hair, glass eyes, wig, ball-jointed body–looks like Patsy**

     15" **$425.00–475.00**

Composition

Child, **composition shoulder head, cloth body, composition arms and legs, molded hair, painted eyes**

13"–17"...$150.00–225.00

Century Baby, **1920s, composition flange head and hands, open mouth, cloth baby body, resembles Marseilles's Dream Baby**

15"–18"...$200.00–300.00

Chuckles, **1927–1929, composition shoulder head, arms, and legs, cloth body with crier, open mouth, molded short hair, painted or sleep eyes, two upper teeth, dimples in cheeks, came as a bent-leg baby or toddler**

14"–16"...$125.00–200.00

18"–22"...$200.00–300.00

Mama dolls, **1922 on, composition head, tin sleep eyes, cloth body, with crier, swing legs and arms of composition**

16"..$175.00–200.00

23"–24"...$250.00–275.00

Bisque shoulder head, mold 281

15"..$300.00–350.00

CHAD VALLEY

917–1930s, Harbonne, England. Founded by Johnson Bros. in 1897, in 1917 began making all types of cloth dolls, early ones had stockinette faces, later felt, with velvet body, jointed neck, shoulders, hips, glass or painted eyes, mohair wig, used designers such as Mabel Lucie Atwell and Norah Wellings.

Animals

Cat

12"..$215.00–230.00

Bonzo, **cloth dog with painted eyes, almost closed and smile**

7"...$250.00–275.00

12"..$5000.00–600.00

Bonzo, **eyes open**

5½" $375.00–450.00

14"..$575.00–600.00

Dog, **plush**

12"..$260.00–280.00

18" Bambino, Chad Valley, designed by Mabel Lucy Atwell, felt: $850. **Photo courtesy of Joan & Lynette Antique Dolls and Accessories.**

Characters

Captain Blye, Fisherman, Long John Silver, Pirate, Policeman, Train Conductor, Africans and Islanders, etc.

Glass eyes

10"–12"..$150.00–200.00

18"–20"..$750.00–850.00

Painted eyes

13"–15"..$275.00–325.00

18"–20"..$575.00–625.00

Ghandi/India

13"..$625.00–675.00

Snow White & Dwarfs

Dwarf, 6½"......................................$175.00–225.00

Set 10" dwarves, **16" Snow White**

....$1,700.00–2,000.00

Red Riding Hood

14"–19"..$350.00–450.00

Golliwog

14"–16"..$150.00–300.00

Child

Glass eyes

12"–16"..$300.00–475.00

18"–21"..$450.00–550.00

Painted eyes

9"–10"..$125.00–200.00

12"–15"..$250.00–350.00

18"..$350.00–400.00

Mabel Lucy Atwell design, **wide impish face, glass eyes**

    14"... $650.00–750.00

    18"... $800.00–950.00

Royal Family, **all with glass eyes, 16"–18"**

Princess Alexandra

    .... $1,300.00–1,400.00

Prince Edward, **Duke of Windsor**

    .... $1,000.00–1,200.00

Princess Elizabeth

    .... $1,300.00–1,900.00

Princess Margaret Rose

    .... $1,000.00–1,800.00

CHASE DOLL COMPANY

1889 to 1981, Pawtucket, Rhode Island. Founded by Martha Chase, earlier dolls had heads of molded stockinette with heavily painted features including thick lashes, closed mouth, painted textured hair, jointed shoulder, elbows, knees, and hips, later dolls jointed only at shoulders and hips, later dolls had latex heads on vinyl coated bodies, all in good condition with original or appropriate clothing.

Baby or child, **short hair with curls around face**

    12"–16" $750.00–900.00

    17"–20" 700.00–950.00

    22"–24" 800.00–1,050.00

    26"–30" $900.00–1,100.00

12" Black child sold for $5,985.00

Hospital-type, **weighted doll with pierced nostrils and ear canals**

    20"–23" $500.00–600.00

    26"–29" $700.00–800.00

Child

Molded bobbed hair

    12"–15" $2,000.00–2,500.00

    20"–22" $2,100.00–2,600.00

16" brown haired sold at auction for $4,104.00

Side-part painted hair

15"–16" $1,600.00–2,000.00

Characters, 1905 to 1920s, produced characters based on Alice in Wonderland, Dickens, Joel Chandler Harris books, and George Washington

Dickens Characters, **needlesculpted hairstyles including buns, curls, etc.**

15"

Lady or man $2,500.00–5,000.00

Young man sold at auction for $7,125.00

Little Nell, **braids**............................ $1,800.00–2,100.00

George Washington

15" –25" $4,100.00–4,900.00

Mammy

26"... $9,000.00–11,000.00

Later Dolls, latex heads

20" Chase, cloth: $850. **Photo courtesy of McMasters Harris Apple Tree Doll Auctions.**

Hospital Baby

14"–15" $200.00–250.00

19"... $250.00–300.00

Baby

12"... $75.00–150.00

Black

12"... $175.00–200.00

Child

15"... $90.00–160.00

Black

15"... $125.00–200.00

CHINA OR GLAZED PORCELAIN HEAD

22" china, pink tint, "Covered Wagon" style: $1,100. **Photo courtesy of Withington Auction Inc.**

19" china, Bald head: $1,100. **Photo courtesy of Withington Auction Inc.**

1840 on. Most china shoulder head dolls were made in Germany by various firms. Prior to 1880, most china heads were pressed into the mold; later ones poured. Pre-1880, most china heads were sold separately with purchaser buying commercial body or making one at home. Original commercial costumes are rare; most clothing was homemade. Early unusual features are glass eyes or eyes painted brown. After 1870, pierced ears and blond hair were found, and after 1880, more child chinas with shorter hair and shorter necks were popular. Most common in this period were flat tops and low brows, and the latter were made until the mid-1900s. Later innovations were china arms and legs with molded boots. Most heads are unmarked or with size or mold number only, usually on the back shoulder plate. Identification tips: hair styles, color, complexion tint, and body help date the doll. Dolls listed are in good condition with original or appropriate clothes. More for exceptional quality.

1840 Styles

China shoulder head with long neck, painted features, black or brown molded hair, may have exposed ears and pink complexion, with red-orange facial detail, may have bust modeling, cloth, leather, or wood body, nicely dressed, good condition.

Early marked china (**Nuremberg, Rudolstadt, Schlaggenwald**)

12"–14"..$1,800.00–2,800.00

17"–24"..$3,500.00–5,000.00

Pink complexion, **bun or coronet**

13"–15"..$6,000.00–8,000.00

18"–21"..$10,000.00–12,000.00

Wooden body, with china lower arms, 1840s on

5"–8"..$3,000.00–4,500.00

12"..$4,000.00–5,000.00

19" china, "Greiner" style, glass eyes: $3,600. **Photo courtesy of Joan & Lynette Antique Dolls and Accessories.**

16" china, "Sophia Smith" style, circa 1850s: $3,500. **Photo courtesy of Joan & Lynette Antique Dolls and Accessories.**

Covered Wagon

Center part, **combed back to form sausage curls, pink tint complexion**

7"–10"...$550.00–700.00

14"–17"..$900.00–1,000.00

20"–25".....................................$1,000.00–1,200.00

28"–31".....................................$1,700.00–1,800.00

Kinderkopf (child-head)

Pink tint child head doll, **brush strokes around face**

12"–16".....................................$2,100.00–3,500.00

20"–21".....................................$4,000.00–4,200.00

K.PM (**KPM–Königliche Porzellanmanufaktur, Berlin**) -1840s–1850s on, marked **KPM inside shoulder plate**

Brown hair man

16"–18".....................................$6,500.00–9,000.00

22"–23"..................................$10,000.00–12,000.00

Lady, brown hair in bun

14"–18".....................................$5,000.00–6,000.00

20"–24".....................................$7,000.00–9,000.00

1850 Styles

China shoulder head, painted features, bald with black spot or molded black hair, may have pink complexion, cloth, leather, or wood body, china arms and legs, nicely dressed, good condition.

Various unmnamed styles, **variations of buns and side waves**

12"–16".....................................$2,000.00–3,000.00

24"–26".....................................$4,000.00–6,000.00

Alice in Wonderland, **snood, headband**

12"–14" 650.00–800.00

16"–18".....................................$1,100.00–1,400.00

17" china, "Nymphenburg",: *$ 3,500.* **Photo courtesy of Gloria's Antique Dolls.**

20"–22".......................................$1,300.00–1,600.00

On Taufling style body

11"–14" 5,500.00–9,000.00

Bald head **(so-called Biedermeier style), glazed china with black spot, painted eyes, human hair or mohair wig. Higher quality brings higher end of range.**

7"–12".......................................$300.00–1,000.00

14"–16".......................................$750.00–1,200.00

20"–24".......................................$1,000.00–1,200.00

Baderkinder (Frozen Charlies or Charlottes): See that section.

Greiner-type **with painted black eyelashes**

Painted eyes

14"–15".......................................$850.00–900.00

18"–24".......................................$1,000.00–1,200.00

Glass eyes

13"–15".......................................$2,900.00–3,200.00

18"–22".......................................$3,200.00–4,000.00

French, **1850s on, some heads may have been made in Germany for the French makers.**

Morning Glory, **brown hair with molded morning glories**

21"–24".......................................$5,500.00–8,000.00

Nymphenburg, **downward glacing eyes**

16"–17".......................................$3,000.00–4,000.00

Poupée-type, **glass or painted eyes, open crown, cork pate, wig, kid body, china arms**

12"–14".......................................$2,500.00–3,500.00

17"–21".......................................$5,500.00–7,000.00

Slit head, **molde slot on top of head to receive human hair**

17".......................................$3,000.00–4,500.00

18" china, "Curly Top" style: $800. **Photo courtesy of Withington Auction Inc.**

15" china, "Currier & Ives" style: $800. **Photo courtesy of Withington Auction Inc.**

Sophia Smith, **straight sausage curls ending in a ridge around head, rather than curved to head shape**

17"–24" $4,000.00–6,000.00

Young Queen Victoria, **molded braids looped around ears, bun in back**

16"–18" $3,100.00–4,100.00

22"–24" $4,100.00–4,900.00

1860 Styles

China shoulder head, center part, smooth black curls, painted features, seldom brush marks or pink tones, all-cloth bodies or cloth with china arms and legs, may have leather arms. Decorated chinas with fancy hair styles embellished with flowers, ornaments, snoods, bands, ribbons, may have earrings.

Flat top Civil War

Black hair, **center part, with flat top, curls on sides and back**

5"–7" $200.00–250.00

10"–14" 300.00–350.00

18"–22" $350.00–400.00

24"–26" $450.00–500.00

34" $550.00–600.00

Swivel neck

15" $1,000.00–1,200.00

Molded necklace

21"–24" $500.00–600.00

Highbrow, **curls, high forehead, round face**

3½"–5" $200.00–275.00

9"–10" $100.00–200.00

12"–13" $300.00–400.00

15"–18" $500.00–600.00

19"–22" $650.00–700.00

25"–32" $750.00–800.00

Conta & Boehme, **pierced ears**

9"–10" $650.00–750.00

14"–16" $725.00–775.00

18"–20" $750.00–850.00

Curly Top

11"–12" $600.00–700.00

18"–19" $800.00–900.00

Currier & Ives, **long hair lying on shoulders**

15"–17" $800.00–900.00

Dagmar, **curls on forehead, curls gathered at nape with barrette**

13"–18" $600.00–1,000.00

22"–25" $1,200.00–1,400.00

Dolley Madison, **with molded bow**

9" $300.00–325.00

14"–16" $350.00–400.00

20"–24" $450.00–550.00

Man or boy with curls

17"–19" $1,100.00–1,400.00

Grape Lady, **with cluster of grape leaves and blue grapes**

15"–20" $1,400.00–1,900.00

Mary Todd Lincoln, **black hair, gold snood, gold luster bows at ears**

14"–15" $800.00–900.00

18"–21" $1,100.00–1,300.00

Blond **with snood**

12"–16" $800.00–900.00

18"–21" $1,000.00–1,300.00

Spill Curls, **with or without headband, a lot of single curls across forehead, around back to ringlets in back**

13"–15" $700.00–900.00

18"–20" $1,000.00–1,100.00

24"–26" $1,200.00–1,400.00

23" china, "Jenny Lind" style: $2,400. **Photo courtesy of Withington Auction Inc.**

25" china, Bawo & Dotter: $375. **Photo courtesy of Minton's Doll and Curiosity Shop.**

1870 Styles

China shoulder head, poured, finely painted, well molded, black or blond hair, cloth or cloth and leather bodies, now with pink facial details instead of earlier red-orange.

    14"–16"... $350.00–400.00

    18"–24"... $425.00–475.00

Adelina Patti, **hair pulled up and away, center part, brush-stroked at temples, partly exposed ears, ringlets across back of head**

    13"–15".. $650.00–750.00

    18"–22".. $850.00–950.00

    26".. $1,000.00–1,100.00

Bangs, **full cut across forehead, sometimes called Highland Mary**

    14"–16".. $350.00–400.00

    19"–21".. $425.00–4505.00

Jenny Lind, **black hair pulled back into a bun or coronet**

    12"–15".. $1,300.00–1,700.00

    20"–24".. $2,200.00–2,500.00

1880 Styles

Now may also have many blond as well as black hair examples, more curls, and overall curls, narrower shoulders, fatter cheeks, irises outlined with black paint, may have bangs, china legs have fat calves and molded boots

Child, **short black or blond curly hairdo with exposed ears, makers such as Alt, Beck & Gottschalk, Kling, and others.**

    14"–18"... 225.00–275.00

    20"–24".. $300.00–400.00

    27"–30".. $500.00–600.00

Bawo & Dotter, **patented 1880**

    13"–14".. $200.00–225.00

    18"–20".. $275.00–325.00

    24"–27".. $350.00–400.00

24" china, "High Brow", circa 1860s:
$700. **Photo courtesy of Joan & Lynette Antique Dolls and Accessories.**

1890 Styles

Shorter fatter arms and legs, may have printed body with alphabet, emblems, flags

Common or low brow, **black or blond center part wavy hairdo that comes down low on forehead**

4"–8"	$75.00–125.00
10"–14"	$125.00–150.00
16"–17"	$175.00–200.00
19"–23"	$200.00–225.00
27"–28"	$250.00–275.00

With jewel necklace

8"	$135.00–150.00
17"	$200.00–225.00
20"–22"	$325.00–425.00

Pet Names, 1899–1930 on

Agnes, Bertha, Daisy, Dorothy, Edith, Esther, Ethel, Florence, Helen, Mabel, Marion, Pauline, and Ruth, made for Butler Brothers by various German firms, china head and limbs on cloth body, molded blouse marked in front with name in gold lettering, molded blond or black allover curls

9"	$100.00–145.00
12"–14"	$150.00–175.00
17"–21"	$200.00–250.00

Japanese, 1910–1920, marked or unmarked, black or blond hair

10"	$100.00–125.00
15"	$160.00–190.00

Reissue Royal Copenhagen, 1978–1981, head only in 3 1840s styles

4½–5"	$250.00–400.00

CLOTH

22" Eloise,
Hol-Le Toy,
cloth: $175.
**Photo courtesy
of Alderfer
Auction
Company, Inc.**

17" Maggie
Bessie., cloth:
$15,000.
**Photo
courtesy
of Morphy
Auctions.**

Various American and European manufacturers of cloth-headed dolls working from 1850 on. No separate listing for these makers. Marks: Many are unmarked or carried paper hang tags.

Becassine, French comic character, originally drawn by Emile Joseph Porphyre Pinchon for La Semaine de Suzette. Made in doll form by various makers, needle-sculpted nose, painted features.

Reine Dégrais, **1947–1972,**

8"–14"...$200.00–250.00

Minerve, **1972 on**

12"–16"...$140.00–160.00

See Averill section for additional listing.

Homemade, nineteenth and early twentieth centuries. Makers unknown, many one-of-a- kind type dolls. Embroidered or painted features. Dolls vary greatly according to the skill of the maker. Values may differ substantially for individual examples.

Mid nineteenth century–1900

8"–12"...$300.00–900.00

15"–20".......................................$900.00–1,600.00

28"–31".....................................$1,700.00–2,100.00

1900–1930

15"–18".......................................$250.00–600.00

16"–24".....................................$700.00–1,200.00

Known Makers

Baps, **1946 on, Burgkunstadt, Germany. Made by Edith von Arps. Felt doll with felt over wire armature body, yarn hair, metal feat, painted features. Many represent storybook characters. Allow more for sets**

2½"–6"

Single figures....................................$40.00–150.00

24" Wellington baby, cloth: $8,000. **Photo courtesy of Sweetbriar Auctions.**

Blossom, **1920s on, New York, NY. Made cloth, mask faced dolls depicting children as well as long-limbed lady dolls (See Boudoir dolls section.)**

    11".. $45.00–60.00

Hol-Le Toy, **1950s, New York, NY.**

Eloise, cloth mask face based on the fictional character created by Kay Thompson

    21".. $190.00–210.00

Junel Novelties, **1930s on, cloth doll with mask face, painted features, yarn hair**

    18".. $50.00–70.00

Maggie Bessie dolls, **1890s on, Salem, NC. Margaret and Elizabeth Pfohl made cloth dolls with oil painted faces in three sizes, 13/14", 17/18", and 20/22"**

    13"–18".. $10,000.00–15,000.00

Molded cloth shoulder head dolls, **So-called Linen Head dolls. Mid nineteenth century on. Dolls resemble the china and papier-mâché dolls of the era.**

    19"–24".. $3,000.00–4,500.00

Nelke, **1917 to 1930, Philadelphia, Pennsylvania. Harry Nelke founded the Elke Knitting Mills Co. in 1901 and began making stockinette crib dolls in 1917. The dolls were made of a silky stockinette fabric with painted features. Clothing integral to body, added band of stockinette around neck, and/or added collars, hats, etc. Doll in clean, unfaded condition.**

    8"–10".. $30.00–45.00

    13"–15".. $60.00–75.00

Tebbetts Sisters, **1922 on, Pittsburg, Pennsylvania, Mary, Elizabeth, Marion, and Ruth Tebbetts patented and made cloth dolls**

Petiekins, **cloth mask face, crepe or flannel body**

    6½".. $400.00–475.00

Baby Sister, **needle-sculpted stockinette doll with painted features, wigged**

    18".. $2,200.00–2,800.00

Tiny Town, **1949 into the 1950s, San Francisco, California. Alma LeBlanc took out a patent under the business name of Lenna Lee's Tiny Town Dolls for these dolls. The dolls have felt faces with painted features, mohair wigs, and wrapped wire armature bodies with metal feet**

    4"–7"... $85.00–100.00

(double for MIB)

Wellington, Martha, **1883 on, Brookline, Massachusetts, needlesculpteed, painted stockinette with wire frame under facial features**

20"–22" $6,500.00–8,000.00

Worsted dolls, **1878–1900s, Emil Wittzack of Gotha, Thuringia, Germany. Woolen crib dolls with needle-sculpted features, bead eyes, chenille embroidered designs on bodies, some had bells sewn on them**

7"–10" $45.00–65.00

15"–18" $115.00–125.00

CLOTH, PRINTED

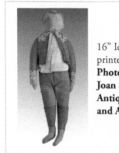

16" Ida Gutsell, printed cloth: $375. **Photo courtesy of Joan & Lynette Antique Dolls and Accessories.**

1876 on. Made by various American, British, and German firms including Arnold Print Works, North Adams, MA, Cocheco Manufacturing Co., Art Fabric Mills, and other lesser or unknown firms who printed fabric for making cutout dolls to be sewn together and stuffed. Dolls listed are in good, clean condition, uncut sheets bring double the values listed here.

Improved Life Size Doll, **with printed underwear**

16"–18" $100.00–150.00

20"–24" $175.00–225.00
26"–30" 250.00–300.00

Punch and Judy, **pair**

6" $75.00–100.00

Brownies, **1892–1907, produced by Aronld Printworks. Printed cloth dolls based on copyrighted figures of Palmer Cox; 12 different figures, including Canadian, Chinaman, Dude, German, Highlander, Indian, Irishman, John Bull, Policeman, Sailor, Soldier, and Uncle Sam**

Single Doll

7½" $90.00–175.00

Printed underwear, **Dolly Dear, Flaked Rice, Merry Marie, etc.**

    7"–9" $75.00–100.00

    16"–18" $125.00–150.00

    20"–24" $175.00–200.00

Child with printed clothing, **1903**

    12"–14" $100.00–175.00

    17"–19" $200.00–250.00

Columbian Sailor, **Arnold Printworks, 1892**

    10" $150.00–175.00

    16" $175.00–225.00

Foxy Grandpa

    18" $150.00–1725.00

Gutsell, Ida, **1893 on, made by Cocheco Manufacturing. Designed and patented by Ida Gutsell of Ithaca, New York. Printed boy doll with a center-seam face, removable clothing with printed detail**

    16" $350.00–400.00

Mother's Congress, **1900 on, Philadelphia, PA. Designed and patented by Madge L. Meade. The uniquely styled pattern piece used for the head included a round section to produce the crown and several darts in the neck area. Unbleached muslin doll with lithographed facial features, blond hair with a blue bow and black Mary Jane style shoes, marked with a stamp: "Mother's Congress Doll//Baby Stuart//Children's Favorite//Philadelphia, Pa.//Pat. Nov. 6, 1900"**

    17"–24" $550.00–700.00

Our Soldier Boys

    15" $125.00–150.00

Red Riding Hood

    16" $150.00–175.00

Peck, **1886 Santa Claus/St. Nicholas**

    15" $300.00–350.00

COLUMBIAN

1891 on, Oswego, NY. Emma E. Adams designed and made rag dolls, sold directly or through stores such as Marshall Field & Co. Won awards at the 1893 Chicago World Fair. Succeeded by her sister, Marietta Adams Ruttan. Cloth dolls had hand–painted features, stitched fingers and toes. Values are for dolls in good condition wearing appropriate clothing, **exceptional condition examples will sell for more.**

23" Columbian,
cloth: $4,100.
**Photo courtesy
of Joan &
Lynette Antique
Dolls and
Accessories.**

14"–15" $6,000.00–8,000.00

19"–23" $7,000.00–9,000.00

28"–30" $8,000.00–10,000.00

COMPOSITION

Dolls listed are in good condition with original or appropriate dress. Allow more for exceptional dolls with elaborate costume or accessories.

American

Animal head doll, **1930s, all-composition on Patsy-type five-piece body, could be wolf, rabbit, cat, monkey**

   10" $230.00–260.00

Baby, **1910 on, wigged or molded hair, painted or sleep eyes, composition or cloth body with bent legs**

   12"–14" $125.00–150.00

   18"–20" $225.00–275.00

Bester Doll Company, **1918–1921, Bloomfield and Newark, New Jersey. Composition doll in the style of German dolly faced dolls, ball-jointed body, sleep eyes, wigged**

   18"–22" $300.00–350.00

Character Baby

   18" $350.00–400.00

Child, **costumed in ethnic or theme outfit, all-composition, sleep or painted eyes, mohair wig, closed mouth, original costume**

Lesser quality

   9"–11" $35.00–55.00

17" Cowgirl, unmarked, composition, circa 1940s: $. **Photo courtesy of Alderfer Auction Company, Inc.**

11" Denny Dimwitt, Toycraft Inc., composition: $400. **Photo courtesy of Morphy Auctions.**

Better quality

9"–11" $80.00–100.00

16" $150.00–200.00

Coleman Walker

24"–28" $175.00–200.00

Denny Dimwitt, **Toycraft Inc, 1948, all-composition, nodder, painted clothing**

11½" $300.00–350.00

Early child, **1910–1920, all-composition, unmarked, painted features, may have molded hair**

12" $145.00–165.00

18"–19" $200.00–250.00

Elektra Toy & Novelty Co, New York,

Rosie Posie, Stationary legs, Kewpie-type, Black

11" $325.00–350.00

Character Baby

22"–23" $250.00–300.00

Character face, **1910–1920, unmarked, cork-stuffed cloth body, painted features, may have molded hair**

12"–15" $175.00–225.00

18"–20" $275.00–325.00

23"–24" $375.00–425.00

Jackie Robinson, **complete in box**

13" $1,000.00–1,200.00

Little Annie Rooney, **Colonial Toy Co, painted eyes, yarn hair**

15" $175.00–225.00

Lone Ranger (or Tonto), **"TLR Co, Inc.//Doll Craft Novelty Co. NYC," cloth body, hat marked**

20" $450.00–600.00

Maiden America, "1915, Kate Silverman," all-composition, patriotic ribbon

   8½" $165.00–185.00

Mama doll, 1922 on, wigged or painted hair, sleep or painted eyes, cloth body, with crier and swing legs, lower composition legs and arms

   16"–18" $200.00–225.00

   20"–22" $275.00–325.00

   24"–27" $350.00–400.00

Miss Curity, composition, eye shadow, nurse's uniform

   18"–21" $175.00–225.00

Patsy-type girl, 1928 on, molded and painted bobbed hair, sleep or painted eyes, closed pouty mouth, composition or hard stuffed cloth body

   9"–10" $45.00–65.00

   14"–16" $75.00–150.00

   19"–20" $200.00–250.00

With molded hair loop

   12"–15" $90.00–110.00

Pinocchio, composition and wood character

   16½" $150.00–225.00

Puzzy, 1948, "H of P"

   15" $325.00–400.00

Quintuplets, 1934 on, all-composition, jointed five-piece baby or toddler body, molded hair or wig, with painted or sleep eyes, closed or open mouth

   7"–8" .... $140.00–160.00 each

   13" .... $175.00–200.00 each

Santa Claus, composition molded head, based on character from movie *Miracle on 34ᵗʰ St.*, composition body, original suit, sack

   19" $400.00–450.00

Shimmy Doll, 1920s, key wind shimmy dancer

   12"–18" $150.00–300.00

Shirley Temple-type girl, 1934 on, all-composition, five-piece jointed body, blond curly wig, sleep eyes, open mouth, teeth, dimples

   16"–19" $250.00–300.00

Sizzy, 1948, "H of P"

   14" $250.00–300.00

Thumbs-Up, to raise money for ambulances during WWII,

   8" $150.00–175.00

20.25" Lone Ranger & Tonto, composition: sold for $1,200 at auction. **Photo courtesy of Morphy Auctions.**

20" Miss Curity, composition: $250. **Photo courtesy of Morphy Auctions.**

Whistler, **composition head, cotton body, composition arms, open mouth**

    14½" $200.00–225.00

Canadian

Kewty, **1930, made by Domec of Canada, all-composition Patsy-type, molded bobbed hair, closed mouth, sleep eyes, bent left arm**

    14" $300.00–350.00

Eskimo, **Pullan, all composition**

    13" $45.00–60.00

Little Lulu, **Pullan**

    14" $300.00–400.00

German, **composition head, composition or cloth body, wig or molded and painted hair, closed or open mouth with teeth, dressed, may be Amusco, Sonneberger Porzellanfabrik, Winkler, or others**

Character Baby

Cloth body

    18"–25" $175.00–225.00

Composition baby body, **bent limbs**

    16" $250.00–275.00

Child

Composition shoulder head, **cloth body, composition arms**

    20" $225.00–250.00

Socket head, **all-composition body**

    12"–14" $200.00–250.00

    19"–21" $325.00–375.00

Japanese

Quintuplets

    7"–9" .... $75.00–100.00 each

COSMOPOLITAN DOLL & TOY CORP.

8" Ginger, Cosmopolitan Doll & Toy corp., hard plastic, painted lashes: $50. **Photo courtesy of McMasters Harris Apple Tree Doll Auctions.**

1950s on, Jackson Heights, New York. Dolls listed are in perfect condition with original clothing. **Mint-in-box can be double or more the values listed here, naked dolls bring one-third the values listed here.**

Ginger, 1955 on, 7½", hard plastic

Painted lash straight leg walker

....$40.00–55.00

Molded lash straight leg walker

....$30.00–45.00

Bent knee walker..............................$30.00–40.00

Vinyl head..$30.00–40.00

Boxed outfit......................................$50.00–100.00

Cardboard house and furniture

....$130.00–150.00

Miss Ginger, 1957 on, vinyl, rooted hair, sleep eyes, teen doll, tagged clothes

10½"..$55.00–90.00

Boxed outfit......................................$50.00–90.00

Little Miss Ginger, 1958 on, vinyl, rooted hair, sleep eyes, teen doll, tagged clothes

8"..$50.00–70.00

CRÈCHE

12"crèche figure, terra cotta: $1,200. **Photo courtesy of Morphy Auctions.**

Figures of various materials made especially for religious scenes such as the Christmas manger scene. Usually not jointed, some with elaborate costumes. Some early created figures were gesso over wood head and limbs, fabric covered bodies with wire frames, later figures made of terracotta or other materials, some with inset eyes.

Wood, carved, 18ᵗʰ or 19ᵗʰ century, vlaues vary widely dependant on age and elaboratness of costume

Man or woman, **shoulder head, glass eyes, wire body**

8".. $400.00–500.00

10"–14".. $500.00–2,200.00

17"–23".. $2,0000.00–4,000.00

15" 18ᵗʰ century woman in elborate costume sold for

.... $4,407.00 at auction

Terra Cotta, **mid-19ᵗʰ century on, shoulder head, wire frame**

Man or woman

7"–10".. $400.00–900.00

12" -15"... $1,200.00–1,800.00

17"–22".. $2000.00–2,500.00

Elaborate figure such as King, Angel, other

15" -19"... $4,500.00–7,000.00

DE FUISSEAUX

1909–1912, Baudour, Belgium. Porcelain heads, often highly colored. Marked with D.F.B, or F1 (and other #s), D1 (and other numbers).

Open mouth dolly face, **sleep eyes, wig, cardboard and composition ball-jointed body**

18"–22" $275.00–325.00

9" De Fuisseaux, bisque, Kämmer Reinhardt style: $425. **Photo courtesy of Morphy Auctions.**

Character doll

Painted eyes,

Child, resembles Kämmer & Reinhardt 101, various body types

8" $450.00–500.00

Man, closed mouth, painted beard or without, various body types

11"–12" $700.00–750.00

Child, resembles Gebrusder Heubach, ball-jointed composition body

18" $1,000.00–1,200.00

Glass eyes, **resembles Heubach, ball-jointed composition body**

12"–18" $1,200.00–1,600.00

Portrait style girl or lady, **cloth body**

14"–19" $1,100.00–1,800.00

DEANS RAG BOOK CO.

18" and under Alice in Wonderland dolls, Deans Rag Book Co., mask face cloth: sold at auction for $4,270. **Photo courtesy of Morphy Auctions.**

1905 on, London. Subsidiary of Dean & Son, Ltd., a printing and publishing firm, used "A1" to signify quality, made Knockabout Toys, Tru-to-Life, Evripoze, and others. An early designer was Hilda Cowham.

Child, **painted eyes**

 10"–13" $225.00–450.00

 16"–17" $550.00–600.00

 24" $650.00–700.00

Printed cloth, **cut and sew type**

 10"–16" $80.00–125.00

 24" $175.00–250.00

Mask face, **velvet, with cloth body and limbs**

 12"–15" $100.00–150.00

 18"–24" $200.00–275.00

 30"–34" $325.00–400.00

 40" $500.00–600.00

Dancing Dolls, **cloth dolls sewn together at hands to look like a dancing couple, on a string.**

 12"–14" $75.00–100.00

Lupino Lane

 12" $100.00–150.00

Mickey Mouse

 6"–10" $600.00–700.00

Golliwogs **(English black character doll)**

11"...$325.00–400.00

15"...$425.00–525.00

18"...$575.00–625.00

Ronnie**, 1950s, molded rubber head, plush body**

15"...$150.00–175.00

DELUXE READING

21" Candy Fashion, Deluxe Reading, vinyl, MIB: $150. **Photo courtesy of Morphy Auctions.**

6" Angie from Dawn Series, Deluxe Reading, vinyl: $25. **Doll from Private Collection.**

1955–1972, Elizabeth, NJ. Also used the names Deluxe Toy Creations, Deluxe Premium Corp., Deluxe Topper, Topper Toys, and Topper Corp. Dolls listed are complete, all original, in good condition, wearing original clothes, with original accessories if applicable, hard plastic or vinyl. Allow double for mint-in-box.

Baby

Baby Boo, **1965, battery operated**

21"...$90.00–110.00

Baby Brite, **1963, raises arms when button is pushed**

13½"...$45.00–55.00

Baby Catch A Ball, **1969 (Topper Toys), battery operated**

18"...$45.00–55.00

Baby Magic, **1966, blue sleep eyes, rooted saran hair, magic wand has magnet that opens/closes eyes**

18"...$55.00–75.00

Baby Party, **1968, blows horns baloons, etc.**

18"...$35.00–45.00

Baby Peek 'N Play, **1969, battery operated**

18"...$20.00–25.00

Baby Tickle Tears

14" $20.00–30.00

Nancy Nurse, **1963, battery operated, with bed**

21" $150.00–200.00

Suzy Cute, **move arm and face changes expressions**

7" $20.00–30.00

Tickles, **1963, battery operated, talks and laughs**

20" $75.00–95.00

Child or Adult

Betty Bride, **1957, also called Sweet Rosemary, Sweet Judy, Sweet Amy, one-piece vinyl body and limbs, more if many accessories**

30" $75.00–85.00

Bonnie Bride, **1964, battery operated, walks and throws bouquet**

21" $75.00–95.00

Candy Fashion, **1958, made by Deluxe Premium, a division of Deluxe Reading, sold in grocery stores, came with three dress forms, extra outfits**

21" $75.00–85.00

Dawn Series, **circa 1969–1970s, all-vinyl doll with additional friends, Angie, Daphne, Denise, Glori, Jessica, Kip, Long Locks, Majorette, Maureen, black versions of Van and Dale, accessories available, included Apartment, Fashion Show, outfits**

Dawn and friends

6" $20.00–25.00

Dancing Dawn and friends

6" $35.00–50.00

Dawn & other outfits

Loose, **but complete** .... $10.00+

NRFP $35.00–45.00

Go Gos, **1965, soft vinyl bendable body. Cool Cat, Private Ida, Tom Boy, values listed for dolls in the original clear plastic box**

6" $20.00–30.00

Little Miss Fussy, **battery operated**

18" $55.00–60.00

Nancy the Nurse, **hard plastic and vinyl**

24" $50.00–60.00

Penny Brite, **1963 on, all-vinyl, rooted blond hair, painted eyes, bendable and straight legs, extra outfits, case, furniture available, marks: "A–9/B150 (or B65) DELUXE READING CORP.//c. 1963"**

8" $20.00–30.00

Outfit, **NRFP** $35.00–45.00

Snow White & f 7 Dwarfs, **1958, hard plastic and vinyl, for Walt Disney**

    Snow White 21"............................$55.00–65.00

    full set with 8" Dwarfs...................$175.00–$200.00

Suzy Homemaker, **1964, hard plastic and vinyl, jointed knees, mark: "Deluxe Reading Co."**

    21"..$40.00–45.00

Suzy Smart, **ca. 1962, vinyl, sleep eyes, closed mouth, rooted blond ponytail, hard plastic body, The Talking School Doll, desk, chair, easel**

    25"..$175.00–200.00

Sweet Ann, **vinyl head, soft vinyl body, high-heel foot**

    30"..$75.00–85.00

Sweet Rosemary, **vinyl head, soft vinyl body, high-heel foot**

    28"..$55.00–75.00

DEP

16.5" DEP, bisque: $900. **Photo courtesy of Gloria's Antique Dolls.**

The "DEP" mark on the back of bisque heads stands for the French "Depose" or the German "Deponirt," which means registered claim. Some dolls made by Simon & Halbig have the "S&H" mark hidden above the "DEP" under the wig. Bisque head, swivel neck, appropriate wig, paperweight eyes, open or closed mouth, good condition, nicely dressed on French-style wood and composition body. Dolls listed are in good condition with original or appropriate clothing.

Closed mouth

    15"..$1,800.00–2000.00

18"–20" $2,000.00–2,500.00

23"–25" $3,000.00–3,300.00

Open mouth, **including those marked Jumeau**

13"–15" $700.00–900.00

18"–20" $800.00–1,000.00

23"–25" $1,400.00–1,700.00

28"–30" $2,000.00–2,200.00

DOLLHOUSE DOLLS

6" dollhouse nurse, bisque: $300. **Photo courtesy of Sara Bernstein's Dolls.**

Small German dolls generally under 8" usually dressed as member of a family or in household-related occupations, often sold as a group. Made of any material, but usually bisque head by 1880. Dolls listed are in good condition with original clothes.

Bisque

Adult, **man or woman,**

Painted eyes, **molded hair or wig**

4"–5" $100.00–225.00

6"–7" $200.00–400.00

Glass eyes

Molded hair

6" $150.00–250.00

Wigged

4"–6" $150.00–300.00

Black man or woman, **molded hair, original clothes**

6" $400.00–650.00

Molded headwear, **Chauffeur, Aviator, Top hat**

> 6".. $200.00–285.00

More Uncommon hat

> 6".. $400.00–500.00

5"Golfer with molded cap and knee socks, with bag of golf clubs sold for $4,030.00 at auction

Grandparents, **or with molded on hats**

> 6".. $175.00–225.00

Military man, **mustache, original clothes**

> 6".. $625.00–750.00

With molded-on helmet

> 6".. $600.00–900.00

Children, **all-bisque**

> 4".. $100.00–150.00

China

With early hairdo

> 4".. $300.00–600.00

With low brow or common hairdo, **1900 on**

> 4".. $75.00–125.00

Composition, **papier-mâché, plaster, etc.**

> 5".. $150.00–200.00

DOOR OF HOPE

1901–1950, Shanghai, China. Cornelia Bonnell started the Door of Hope Mission in Shanghai to help poor girls sold by their families. As a means to learn sewing skills, the girls dressed carved pear wood heads from Ning-Po. The heads and hands were natural finish; stuffed cloth bodies were then dressed in correct representation for 26 different Chinese classes. Carved wooden head with cloth or wooden arms, original handmade costumes, in very good condition. Dolls listed are in good condition with clean bright clothing. Exceptional dolls could be higher. Values are lower for dolls in faded costumes.

Adult, **man or woman**

> 11"–13"... $900.00–1,500.00

Amah with Baby

> 11" (amah) $2,800.00–3,000.00

11" Door of Hope, wood, Amah with child; $2,800. **Photo courtesy of Withington Auction Inc.**

Baby in bunting

7" at auction $5,085.00

Boy or girl in silk

6"–9" $1,100.00–1,500.00

Boy with western hairstyle

8"–9" $650.00–750.00

Bride & Groom

12" $1,600.00–2,800.00

Farmer in bamboo raincoat

12" $1,200.00–1,500.00

Kindergarten child

6" $1,200.00–1,600.00

Male Mourner

12" $700.00–1,000.00

Policeman

11½" $1,600.00–2,000.00

Preist

11½" $4,000.00–4,500.00

CUNO & OTTO DRESSEL

1857–1943, Sonneberg, Thüringia, Germany. The Dressel family began its business in the early 1700s and was dealing in toys from a very early date. Cunno & Otto became involved in the 1880s. The Dressels made wood, wax, wax-over-composition, papier-mâché, composition, china, and bisque heads for their dolls which they produced, distributed, and exported. Their bisque heads were made by Simon & Halbig, Armand Marseille, Ernst

Heubach, Schoenau & Hoffmeister, and others. Dolls listed are in good condition with appropriate clothing.

Bisque

Baby, **1910 on, character face, marked "C.O.D.," more for toddler body**

    12"–14"..$225.00–275.00

    15"–17"..$225.00–300.00

    19"–23"..$300.00–400.00

Child, mold 1912, **others, open mouth, jointed composition body**

    14"–16"..$350.00–400.00

    18"–24"..$400.00–500.00

Shoulder head child

Molds 93, 1896, or no mold #, **bisque, wigged, open mouth, kid or cloth body, glass eyes**

    13"–15"..$150.00–200.00

    18"–24"..$225.00–275.00

Bisque, **closed mouth, molded hair, kid or cloth body, glass eyes**

    14"..$300.00–325.00

Child, character face, **closed mouth, jointed child or toddler body**

Painted eyes

    14"–16"..$1,200.00–1,300.00

    18"–20"..$1,500.00–1,700.00

Glass eyes

    12"–15"..$1,400.00–1,800.00

    18"–20"..$2,800.00–2,000.00

Flapper, **molds 14 68, 1469, lady doll, closed mouth, five-piece composition body with thin legs and high heel feet, painted on hose up entire leg, mold 1469**

    12"–15"..$3,000.00–4,000.00

Composition

Holz-Masse, **1875 on, shoulder head, wigged or molded hair, painted or glass eyes, cloth body, composition limbs, molded on boots**

    13"–15"..$300.00–350.00

    18"–20"..$400.00–475.00

    24"–29"..$525.00–600.00

Glass eyes

    12"..$400.00–450.00

    16"–18"..$500.00–600.00

20" mold 1349, Cuno & Otto Dressel, character, bisque: $700. **Photo courtesy of Joan & Lynette Antique Dolls and Accessories.**

14" Uncle Sam, Cuno & Otto Dressel, bisque: $1,700. **Photo courtesy of Morphy Auctions.**

Wigged

    18"... $650.00–750.00

Jutta

Baby, **open mouth, bent-leg body**

    16"–18"... $325.00–375.00

    20"–24"... 400.00–550.00

Child, **1906–1921, open mouth, marked with "Jutta" or "S&H" mold 1914, 1348, 1349, etc.**

    14"–16"... $325.00–375.00

    17"–19"... $350.00–400.00

    21"–24"... $400.00–450.00

    25"–29"... $500.00–600.00

Toddler

    8".. $575.00–650.00

    14"–16"... $675.00–725.00

    17"–19"... $800.00–850.00

Portrait dolls, 1896 on, bisque head, glass eyes, composition body

Admiral Dewey, Admiral Byrd, other military

8" 950.00–1,000.00

    12"–14"... $1,500.00–2,500.00

Buffalo Bill

    8"–10"... $2,000.00–2,500.00

Farmer, Old Rip, Witch

8" 1,000.00–1,200.00

    12".. $2,000.00–2,500.00

Father Christmas

    11".. $2,200.00–2,400.00

Uncle Sam

    16".. $2,200.00–2,400.00

E.D.

22" ED, bisque, closed mouth: $. **Photo courtesy of Withington Auction Inc.**

15" bébé, bisque, closed mouth, French, marked "ED": $4,800. **Photo courtesy of McMasters Harris Apple Tree Doll Auctions.**

1857–1899, Paris. E.D. Bébés marked with "E.D." and a size number and the word "Depose" were made by Etienne Denamur. It is important to note that other dolls marked E.D. with no Depose mark were made when Emile Douillet was director of Jumeau and should be priced as Jumeau Tété face dolls. Denamur had no relationship with the Jumeau firm, and his dolls do not have the spiral spring used to attach heads used by Jumeau. Denamur bébés have straighter eyebrows, the eyes slightly more recessed, large lips, and lesser quality bisque. Smaller sizes of Denamure E.D. bébés may not have the Depose mark. Dolls listed are in good condition, appropriately dressed. Allow more for exceptional clothing.

Closed mouth

    11"–15"...................................... $3,800.00–4,800.00

    18"–22"...................................... $4,800.00–5,400.00

    25"–30"...................................... $6,000.00–7,000.00

Open mouth

    14"–16"...................................... $1,800.00–2,000.00

    18"–21"...................................... $2,200.00–2,600.00

    25"–27"...................................... $2,800.00–3,000.00

EDEN BÉBÉ

17" bébé, Eden, bisque, open mouth,
5 pc. body: $1,800. **Photo courtesy
of Oldeclectics.**

1890–1899, made by Fleischmann & Bloedel; 1899–1953, made by Société Francaise de
Fabrication de Bébés & Jouet (S.F.B.J). Dolls had bisque heads, jointed composition bodies.
Dolls listed are in good condition, appropriately dressed.

Closed mouth, **pale bisque**

    14"–16" $2,500.00–3,000.00

    18"–24" $3,000.00–4,600.00

    14"–16" on 5 pc body $1,800.00–2,100.00

Open mouth

    15"–18" $2,000.00–2,500.00

    20"–26" $2,500.00–2,700.00

High color, **five-piece body**

    13" $800.00–1,200.00

    19" $1,300.00–1,500.00

    22" $1,900.00–2,100.00

EEGEE

1917 on, Brooklyn, NY. Owned by E. G. Golderberger, assembled and made dolls, some
of their dolls had bisque heads imported from Armand Marseille. Eegee also made their
own heads and complete dolls of composition, hard plastic, and vinyl. Dolls listed are in all
original, good condition. Add more for exceptional doll, tagged, extra outfits, or accessories.

11.5" Annette, Eegee, vinyl, MIB: $140. **Photo courtesy Fourty Fifty Sixty.**

22" Puppetrina, Eegee, vinyl, MIB: $200. **Photo courtesy of Morphy Auctions.**

Composition

Baby, **cloth body, bent limbs**

16"...$75.00–125.00

Child, **open mouth, sleep eyes**

14"...$135.00–150.00

18"...$175.00–200.00

MaMa Doll, **1920s–1930s, composition head, sleep or painted eyes, wigged or molded hair, cloth body with crier, swing legs, composition lower arms and legs**

16"...$200.00–225.00

20"...$300.00–325.00

Miss Charming or Little Miss Movie, **1936, all-composition, Shirley Temple look-alike**

19"–22"...$250.00–450.00

Pin-back button $50.00

Hard Plastic and Vinyl

Andy, **1963, vinyl, teen-type, molded and painted hair, painted eyes, closed mouth**

12"...$30.00–40.00

Annette or Babette, **1963, vinyl, teen-type fashion, rooted hair, painted eyes**

11½" $55.00–70.00

Annette, **1961 on, PlayPal type**

17"–19"...$40.00–50.00

32"–35"...$100.00–140.00

Walker, all-vinyl rooted long blond hair or short curly wig, blue sleep eyes, closed mouth

25"–28"...$60.00–85.00

30"- 36"...$95.00–115.00

Babette, **1970, vinyl head, stuffed limbs, cloth body, painted or sleep eyes, rooted hair**

15"...$40.00–50.00

20"– 25"...$85.00–95.00

Baby Care, **1969, vinyl, molded or rooted hair, sleep or set glassine eyes, drink and wet doll, with complete nursery set**

    18"...$75.00–95.00

Baby Carrie, **1970, rooted or molded hair, sleep or set glassine eyes with plastic carriage or carry seat**

    24"...$100.00–175.00

Baby Luv, **1973, vinyl head, rooted hair, painted eyes, open/closed mouth, marked "B.T. Eegee," cloth body, pants are part of body**

    14"...$30.00–40.00

Baby Susan, **1958, marked "Baby Susan" on head**

    8"...$30.00–40.00

Baby Tandy Talks, **1963, pull string activates talking mechanism, vinyl head, rooted hair, sleep eyes, cotton and foam-stuffed body and limbs**

    14"...$25.00–35.00

    20"–24"...$55.00–65.00

Ballerina

1964, **vinyl head and hard plastic body**

    31"...$75.00–100.00

1967, **vinyl head, foam-filled body**

    18"...$30.00–40.00

Barbara Cartland, **painted features, adult**

    15"...$45.00–52.00

Beverly Hillbillies, **Clampett family from 1960s TV sitcom**

Granny Clampett, **gray rooted hair**

    14"...$55.00–65.00

Bundle of Joy, **1964, vinyl head, arms, legs, cloth body, rooted hair, sleep eyes**

    19"...$30.00–40.00

Fields, W. C., **1980, vinyl ventriloquist doll by Juro, division of Goldberger**

    30"...$65.00–75.00

Flowerkins, **1963, marked "F–2" on head; seven dolls in series**

    16"...$45.00–45.00

Gemmette, **1963, rooted hair, sleep eyes, jointed vinyl, dressed in gem colored dress, includes child's jeweled ring**

Misses Amethyst, Diamond, Emerald, Ruby, Sapphire, and Topaz

    15½"...$30.00–40.00

Georgie, Georgette, **1971, vinyl head, cloth bodies, redheaded twins**

    22"...$75.00–85.00 each

Gigi Perreau, **1951, early vinyl head, hard plastic body, open/closed smiling mouth**

    17"..$550.00–700.00

Honey, **1949, hard plastic**

    12"..$45.00–55.00

Karena Ballerina, **1958, vinyl head, rooted hair, sleep eyes, closed mouth, hard plastic body, jointed knees, ankles, neck, shoulders, and hips, head turns when walks**

    21"..$45.00–55.00

Lil' Sister, **vinyl head, rooted hair, painted eyes, looks like Mattel's Skipper®**

    9"..$20.00–25.00

Little Debutantes, **1957, vinyl head, rooted hair, sleep eyes, closed mouth, hard plastic body, swivel waist, high-heeled feet**

    15"..$30.00–70.00

    17"..$60.00–100.00

Debutante, **1958**

    28"..$75.00–100.00

Little Miss Debutante, **1958**

    10½"..$40.00–60.00

Miss Debby, **all-vinyl, high-heel fashion type, swivel waist, fully jointed**

    20"..$65.00–75.00

My Fair Lady, **1958, all-vinyl, fashion type, stufed vinyl body**

    15"..$60.00–75.00

Parton, Dolly, **1978**

    11½"..$20.00–30.00

    18"..$35.00–50.00

Posi Playmate, **1969, vinyl head, foam-filled vinyl body, bendable arms and legs, painted or rooted hair, sleep or painted eyes**

    12"..$15.00–20.00

Puppetrina, **1963 on, vinyl head, cloth body, rooted hair, sleep eyes, pocket in back for child to insert hand to manipulate doll's head and arms**

    22"..$80.00–100.00

Shelly, **1964, Tammy-type, grow hair**

    12"..$22.00–30.00

Sniffles, **1963, vinyl head, rooted hair, sleep eyes, open/closed mouth, marked "13/14 AA–EEGEE"**

    12"..$30.00–40.00

Susan Stroller, **1955, vinyl head, hard plastic walker body, rooted hair, closed mouth**

    17"– 20"..$55.00–70.00

    23"–26"..80.00–100.00

Tandy Talks, **1963, vinyl head, hard plastic body, freckles, pull string talker**

    21"...$55.00–75.00

    36"...$175.00–200.00

Ventriloquist dolls, **1960s, Bozo, Lester, Charlie McCarthy, Groucho, Howdy Doody, Suzie Sez, vinyl and cloth**

    14"–31"...$35.00–75.00

EFFANBEE

1910 to present, New York City. Founded by Bernard Fleischaker and Hugo Baum. This company began selling composition-headed dolls. These heads were made for them by Otto Ernst Denivelle (marked Deco). Effanbee eventually did their own manufacturing. By the late 1920s they were one of the leading manufacturers of American composition dolls. They went on to make dolls of hard plastic and vinyl. In 2002 the company was purchased by Robert Tonner. The new management of the company is currently reissuing many of the designs from the past as well as new pieces. Values shown are for early dolls in good condition with original clothing, dolls from 1950 on in perfect condition with appropriate tags. More for exceptional doll with wardrobe or accessories.

Bisque/ Composition

Mary Jane, 1920, **dolly-faced doll to compete with German bisque. Some with bisque heads, others composition; bisque head, manufactured by Lenox Potteries, NJ, for Effanbee, sleep eyes, composition body, wooden arms and legs, also kid body with wood and composition limbs**

Composition shoulder head **marked Effanbee on kid body (marked with Effanbee sticker), wooden ball-jointed arms and legs, composition hands, wigged, sleep eyes**

    24"...$350.00–425.00

Early Composition

Babies

Baby Bud, **1918 on, all-composition, painted features, molded hair, open/closed mouth, jointed arms, legs molded to body, one finger goes into mouth**

    6"...$175.00–195.00

    Black $200.00–225.00

Baby Dainty, **1912 on, name given to a variety of dolls, with composition heads, cloth bodies, some toddler types, some mama-types with crier**

    12"–14"...$125.00–175.00

    15"...$130.00–200.00

Vinyl

    10"...$30.00–40.00

Baby Effanbee, **1925, composition head, cloth body**

  12"–13" $165.00–185.00

Baby Evelyn, **1925, composition head, cloth body**

  17" $275.00–300.00

Baby Grumpy, **1915 on, also later variations, composition character, heavily molded and painted hair, frowning eyebrows, painted intaglio eyes, pin-jointed limbs, cork-stuffed cloth body, gauntlet arms, pouty mouth**

Mold #172, 174, 176

  12"–16" $500.00–600.00

  Black $550.00–650.00

12" Grumpykins Pennsylvania Dutch, Effanbee, composition: $675. **Photo courtesy of Joan & Lynette Antique Dolls and Accessories.**

19" Charlie McCarthy, Effanbee, composition: $400. **Photo courtesy of Alderfer Auction Company, Inc.**

Baby Grumpy Gladys, **1923, composition shoulder head, cloth body, marked in oval, "Effanbee//Baby Grumpy// corp. 1923"**

  15" $375.00–450.00

Grumpy Aunt Dinah, **black, cloth body, striped stocking legs**

  14½" $275.00–325.00

Grumpykins, **1927, composition head, cloth body, composition arms, some with cloth legs, others with composition legs**

  12" $175.00–225.00

  Black $250.00–275.00

Grumpykins, Pennsylvania Dutch Dolls, **1936, dressed by Marie Polack in Mennonite, River Brethren, and Amish costumes**

  12" $325.00–375.00

Bubbles, **1924 on, composition shoulder head, open/closed mouth, painted teeth, molded and painted hair, sleep eyes, cloth body, bent-cloth legs, some with composition toddler legs, composition arms, finger of left hand fits into mouth, wore heart necklace, various marks including "Effanbee//Bubbles//Copr. 1924//Made in U.S.A."**

  16"–18" $200.00–250.00

  20"–22" $325.00–375.00

  24"–29" $425.00–500.00

19" American Child, Effanbee, closed mouth, painted eyes, composition, designed by Dewees Cochran: $900. **Photo courtesy of Alderfer Auction Company, Inc.**

14" Skippy Aviator, Effanbee, composition, mint: $650. **Photo courtesy of Gandtiques.**

Lamkin, **1930 on, composition molded head, sleep eyes, open mouth, cloth body, crier, chubby composition legs, with feet turned in, fingers curled, molded gold ring on middle finger**

16".. $325.00–375.00

Lovums, **1928 on, child doll, composition swivel head, shoulder plate, and limbs, cloth body, sleep eyes, molded and painted hair or wigged, can have bent baby legs or toddler legs**

16"–18" $300.00–375.00

20"–22" $400.00–450.00

24"–28" $500.00–600.00

Pat-o-Pat, **1925 on, composition head, painted eyes, cloth body with mechanism which, when pressed causes hands to clap**

13".. $200.00–250.00

15".. $250.00–275.00

Cloth mask faced

15".. $575.00–600.00

Sugar Baby, **1936 on, composition molded head, sleep eyes, cloth body, composition legs & hands**

22"–28" $350.00–550.00

Character Children, **1912 on, composition, heavily molded hair, painted eyes, pin-jointed cloth body, composition arms, cloth or composition legs, some marked "Deco"**

Betty Bounce, **1915, composition girl, molded hair with stapled on hairbow, painted eyes, cloth body**

13".. $350.00–400.00

Cliquot Eskimo, **1920, painted eyes, molded hair, felt hands, mohair suit**

18".. $450.00–525.00

Coquette, Naughty Marietta, **1915, composition girl, molded bow in hair, side-glancing eyes, cloth body**

12"–14" $375.00–600.00

Harmonica Joe, **1923, cloth body, with rubber ball, when squeezed provides air to open mouth with harmonica**

15"... $425.00–450.00

Irish Mail Kid, **1915, or Dixie Flyer, composition head, cloth body, arms sewn to steering handle of wooden wagon**

10"... $300.00–325.00

Johnny Tu-face, **1912, composition head with face on front and back, painted features, open/closed crying mouth, closed smiling mouth, molded and painted hair, cloth body, red striped legs, cloth feet, dressed in knitted romper and hat**

16"... $275.00–325.00

Pouting Bess, **1915, composition head with heavily molded curls, painted eyes, closed mouth, clothcork stuffed body, pin jointed, mark: "162" or "166" on back of head**

15"... $275.00–300.00

Whistling Jim, **1916, composition head, with heavily molded hair, painted intaglio eyes, perforated mouth, cork stuffed cloth body, black sewn-on cloth shoes, wears red striped shirt, blue overalls, mark, label: "Effanbee//Whistling Jim//Trade Mark"**

15"... $350.00–400.00

MaMa Dolls, **1921 on, including Rosemary and Marilee, composition shoulder head, painted or sleep eyes, molded hair or wigged, cloth body, swing legs, crier, with composition arms and lower legs**

14"... $175.00–200.00

17"–19" $150.00–225.00

24"–27" $275.00–400.00

Later Composition

American Children, **1936–1939 on, all-composition, designed by Dewees Cochran, open mouth, separated fingers can wear gloves, marks: heads may be unmarked, "Effanbee//Anne Shirley" on body**

Barbara Joan, Barbara Ann

14"–17" $400.00–650.00

Barbara Lou

21"... $800.00–850.00

Closed mouth, **separated fingers, sleep or painted eyes, marks: "Effanbee//American// Children" on head; "Effanbee//Anne Shirley" on body**

Painted eye **such as Peggy Lou and others**

14"–17" $750.00–850.00

19"–21" $1,100.00–1,400.00

Sleep eye **such as Gloria Ann and others**

17"–21" $1,000.00–1,600.00

Anne Shirley, **1936–1940, never advertised as such, same mold used for Little Lady, all-composition, more grown-up body style, mark: "EFFANBEE//ANNE SHIRLEY"**

    10"..$300.00–350.00

    14"–15"...$400.00–450.00

    17"–18"...$500.00–550.00

    21"..$500.00–550.00

    27"..$550.00–600.00

Movie Anne Shirley, **1935–1940. 1934 RKO movie character, Anne Shirley from Anne of Green Gables movie, all-composition, marked "Patsy" or other Effanbee doll, red braids, wearing Anne Shirley movie costume and gold paper hang tag stating "I am Anne Shirley." The Anne Shirley costume changes the identity of these dolls.**

Mary Lee/Anne Shirley, **open mouth, head marked "©Mary Lee," on marked "Patsy Joan" body**

    16"..$300.00–400.00

Patsyette/Anne Shirley, **body marked "Effanbee// Patsyette// Doll"**

    9½" $325.00–375.00

Patricia/Anne Shirley, **body marked "Patricia"**

    15"..$500.00–550.00

Patricia-kin/Anne Shirley, **head marked "Patricia-kin," body marked "Effanbee//Patsy Jr.," hang tag reads "Anne Shirley"**

    11½" $325.00–375.00

Babyette, **1943, eyes molded closed, composition head, hands, legs, cloth body**

    13"..$150.00–200.00

Bright Eyes, **1940, composition head, hands, legs, cloth body, molded hair**

    14"–16"...$275.00–350.00

Brother or Sister, **1943, composition head, hands, cloth body, legs, yarn hair, painted eyes**

    12"–16" $125.00–275.00

Butin-nose: See Patsy family, and vinyl.

Candy Kid, **1946 on, all-composition, sleep eyes, toddler body, molded and painted hair, closed mouth**

    13"..$250.00–300.00

    in boxing outfit.............................$400.00–450.00

Charlie McCarthy, **1937, composition head, hands, feet, painted features, mouth opens, cloth body, legs, marked: "Edgar Bergen's Charlie McCarthy//An Effanbee Product"**

    15"–20"...$250.00–400.00

Happy Birthday Doll, **1940, music box in body, heart bracelet**

    17"..$450.00–550.00

25" Sweetie Pie, Effanbee, composition: $450. **Photo courtesy of Minton's Doll and Curiosity Shop.**

Historical Dolls, **1939 on, all-composition, jointed body, human hair wigs, painted eyes, made only three sets of 30 dolls depicting history of apparel, 1492–1939, very fancy original costumes, metal heart bracelet, head marked "Effanbee//American// Children," on body, "Effanbee//Anne Shirley"**

21"... $2,250.00–2,500.00

Historical Replicas, **1939 on, all-composition, jointed body, copies of sets above, but smaller, human hair wigs, painted eyes, original costumes**

14".. $450.00–550.00

Honey, **1947–1948, all-composition jointed body, human hair wig, sleep eyes, closed mouth**

18"–21"... $200.00–275.00

All hard plastic, ca. 1949–1955, see Vinyl and Hard Plastic later in this category.

Ice Queen, **1937 on, composition, open mouth, skater outfit**

17"... $625.00–750.00

Little Girl, **1933 on, all-composition, painted side-glancing eyes, molded hair.**

9½" 150.00–175.00

Little Lady, **1939 on, used Anne Shirley mold, all-composition, wigged, sleep eyes, more grown-up body, separated fingers, gold paper hang tag, many in formals, as brides, or fancy gowns with matching parasol, during war years yarn hair was used, may have gold hang tag with name, like Gaye or Carole**

15"... $200.00–250.00

18"... $225.00–300.00

21"... $350.00–400.00

27"... $375.00–450.00

Mae Starr, **1928, talking doll, composition shoulder head, cloth body, open mouth, four teeth, with cylinder records, marked: "Mae//Starr// Doll"**

29"... $500.00–600.00

Marionettes, **1937 on, puppets designed by Virginia Austin, composition, painted eyes**

Clippo, **clown**

15"... $75.00–115.00

Emily Ann

14"... $85.00–150.00

Kilroy Cop

15"... $80.00–100.00

Portrait Dolls, 1940 on, all-composition, Bo-Peep, Ballerina, Bride, Groom, Gibson Girl, Colonial Maid, etc.

12"... $275.00–350.00

Suzanne, 1940, all-composition, jointed body, sleep eyes, wigged, closed mouth, may have magnets in hands to hold accessories, more for additional accessories or wardrobe

14"... $150.00–200.00

Suzette, 1939, all-composition, fully jointed, painted side-glancing eyes, closed mouth, wigged

12"... $250.00–275.00

Sweetie Pie, 1939 on, also called Baby Bright Eyes, Tommy Tucker, Mickey, composition bent limbs, sleep eyes, caracul wig, cloth body, crier, issued again in 1952+ in hard plastic, cloth body, and vinyl limbs, painted hair or synthetic wigs, wore same pink rayon taffeta dress with black and white trim as Noma doll

16"–18"... $275.00–300.00

20"–24"... $450.00–525.00

W. C. Fields, 1929 on, composition shoulder head, painted features, hinged mouth, painted teeth

17½"... $900.00–950.00

Patsy Family, 1928 on, composition through 1947, later issued in vinyl and porcelain, many had gold paper hang tag and metal bracelet that read "Effanbee Durable Dolls," more for black, special editions, costumes, or with added accessories

Babies

Patsy Baby, 1931, painted or sleep eyes, wigged or molded hair, composition baby body, advertised as Babykin, came also with cloth body, in pair, layettes, trunks, marks: on head, "Effanbee//Patsy Baby"; on body, "Effanbee //Patsy// Baby"

10"–13"... $350.00–450.00

Patsy Babyette, 1932, sleep eyes, marked on head "Effanbee," on body "Effanbee//Patsy //Babyette"

9"... $175.00–225.00

Patsy Baby Tinyette, 1934, painted eyes, bent-leg composition body, marked on head "Effanbee," on body "Effan-bee//Baby//Tinyette"

7"... $175.00–225.00

Quints, 1935, set of five Patsy Baby Tinyettes in original box, from FAO Schwarz, organdy christening gowns and milk glass bottles, excellent condition

Set of five

7"... $1,700.00–2,100.00

11" Patsy Jr., Effanbee, composition, wigged: $500. **Photo courtesy of McMasters Harris Apple Tree Doll Auctions.**

10" Patsy Babykin, Effanbee, composition, mint condition: sold for $1,600.00 online. **Photo courtesy of Dollyology Vintage Dolls.**

Children

Patsy

1924, cloth body, composition legs,   open mouth, upper teeth, sleep eyes, painted or human hair wig, with composition legs to hips, marked in half oval on back shoulder plate: "Effanbee//Patsy"

   15"... $300.00–350.00

1928, all-composition jointed body, painted or sleep eyes, molded headband on red molded bobbed hair, or wigged, bent right arm, with gold paper hang tag, metal heart bracelet, marked on body: "Effanbee//Patsy// Pat. Pend.//Doll"

   14"... $375.00–425.00

Asian with black painted hair, painted eyes, in fancy silk pajamas and matching shoes

   14"... $750.00–800.00

1946, all-composition jointed body, right facial coloring, painted or sleep eyes, wears pink or blue checked pinafore

   14"... $300.00–350.00

Patsy Ann, **1929,** all-composition, closed mouth, sleep eyes, molded hair, or wigged, marked on body: "Effanbee//'Patsy-Ann'//©//Pat. #1283558"

   19"... $250.00–325.00

1959, limited edition, vinyl, sleep eyes, white organdy dress, with pink hair ribbon, marked "Effanbee//Patsy Ann//©1959" on head, "Effanbee" on body

   15"... $225.00–275.00

Patsyette, **1931, composition**

   9"... $250.00–300.00

Black, Dutch, George & Martha
Washington

   9"... $250.00–300.00 each

Patsy Fluff, **1932, all-cloth, with painted features, pink checked rompers and bonnet**

    16"... $900.00–1,000.00

Patsy Joan, **1931, composition**

    16"... $225.00–300.00

1946, **marked "Effanbee" on body, with extra "d" added**

    17"... $325.00–375.00

Patsy Jr., **1931, all-composition, advertised as Patsykins, marks: "Effanbee//Patsy Jr.// Doll"**

    11½" $450.00–550.00

Patsy Lou, **1930, all-composition, molded red hair or wigged, marks: "Effanbee//Patsy Lou" on body**

    22"... $450.00–525.00

Patsy Mae, **1934, shoulder head, sleep eyes, cloth body, crier, swing legs, marks: "Effanbee//Patsy Mae" on head, "Effanbee// Lovums//c//Pat. No. 1283558" on shoulder plate**

    29"... $1,500.00–1,600.00

Patsy Ruth, **1934, shoulder head, sleep eyes, cloth body, crier, swing legs, marks: "Effanbee//Patsy Ruth" on head, "Effanbee//Lovums//©//Pat. No. 1283558" on shoulder plate**

    26"... $1,400.00–1,700.00

Patsy Tinyette Toddler, **1935, painted eyes, marks: "Effanbee" on head, "Effanbee// Baby//Tinyette" on body**

    7¾" $325.00–375.00

Tinyette Toddler, **tagged "Kit & Kat"**

    In Dutch costume .... $800.00 for pair

Wee Patsy, **1935, head molded to body, molded and painted shoes and socks, jointed arms and hips, advertised only as "Fairy Princess," pin back button, marks on body: "Effanbee//Wee Patsy"**

    5¾" $350.00–450.00

Related items

Metal heart bracelet, **reads "Effanbee Durable Dolls"**

    .... $25.00

Metal personalized name bracelet for Patsy family

    .... $65.00

Patsy Ann, Her Happy Times, **ca. 1935, book by Mona Reed King**

    .... $75.00

Patsy For Keeps, **c 1932, book by Ester Marian Ames**

    .... $125.00

8" Butin-nose, Effanbee, composition: $225. **Photo courtesy of McMasters Harris Apple Tree Doll Auctions.**

19" Honey, Effanbee, hard plastic, walker: $225. **Photo courtesy of McMasters Harris Apple Tree Doll Auctions.**

Patricia Series, **1935, all sizes advertised in Patsytown News, all-composition slimmer bodies, sleep eyes, wigged, later WWII-era Patricia dolls had yarn hair and cloth bodies**

Patricia, **wig, sleep eyes, marked, "Effanbee Patricia" body**

    15"... $200.00–250.00

Patricia Ann, **wig, marks unknown**

    19"... $500.00–550.00

Patricia Joan, **wig, marks unknown, slimmer legs**

    16"... $400.00–450.00

Patricia-Kin, **wig, mark: "Patricia-Kin" head; "Effanbee//Patsy Jr." body**

    11½"... $350.00–300.00

Patricia Lou, **wig, marks unknown**

    22"... $375.00–425.00

Patricia Ruth, **head marked: "Effanbee//Patsy Ruth," no marks on slimmer composition body**

    27"... $1,100.00–1,250.00

Patsy Related Dolls and Variants

Betty Bee, **1932, all-composition, short tousle wig, sleep eyes, marked on body: "Effanbee//Patsy Lou"**

    22"... $325.00–375.00

Betty Bounce, **tousle head, 1932 on, all-composition, sleep eyes, used Lovums head on body, marked: "Effanbee//'Patsy Ann'/ /©//Pat. #1283558"**

    19"... $300.00–350.00

Betty Brite, **1932, all-composition, short tousle wig, sleep eyes, some marked: "Effanbee//Betty Brite" on body and others marked on head "© Mary-Lee," on body "Effanbee Patsy Joan," gold hang tag reads "This is Betty Brite, The lovable Imp with tiltable head and movable limb, an Effanbee doll."**

    16"... $250.00–300.00

Butin-nose, **1936 on, all-composition, molded and painted hair, features, distinct feature is small nose, usually has regional or special costume**

    8"... $175.00–225.00

Asian, **with layette**

8"...$400.00–500.00

Mary Ann, 1932 on, composition, sleep eyes, wigged, open mouth, marked: "Mary Ann" on head, "Effanbee//'Patsy Ann'//©//Pat. #1283558" on body

19"...$350.00–375.00

Mary Lee, 1932, composition, sleep eyes, wigged, open mouth, marked: "©//Mary Lee" on head, "Effanbee//Patsy Joan" on body

16½" $300.00–350.00

Patsy/Patricia, 1940, used a marked Patsy head on a marked Patricia body, all-composition, painted eyes, molded hair, may have magnets in hands to hold accessories, marked on body: "Effanbee//'Patricia'"

15"...$400.00–450.00

Skippy, 1929, advertised as Patsy's boyfriend, composition head, painted eyes, molded and painted blond hair, composition or cloth body, with composition molded shoes and legs, marked on head: "Effanbee//Skippy//©//P. L. Crosby," on body "Effanbee//Patsy//Pat. Pend// Doll"

14"

Military or aviator outfit

....$400.00–600.00

Cowboy outfit sold online for   **$1,020.00**

Boy's outfit.....................................$150.00–225.00

Rubber

Dy-Dee, 1934 on, hard rubber head, sleep eyes, jointed rubber bent-leg body, drink/wet mechanism, molded and painted hair. Early dolls had molded ears, after 1940 had applied rubber ears, nostrils, and tear ducts, later made in hard plastic and vinyl, marked: "Effanbee//Dy-Dee Baby" with four patent numbers, allow double or more for mint ocondition or layette packaging

Dy-Dee-Wee

9"...$375.00–400.00

Dy-Dee-Ette

11"...$450.00–550.00

Dy-Dee-Kin

13"...$650.00–750.00

Other Dy-Dee dolls

15"...$225.00–375.00

20"...$425.00–475.00

Dy-Dee in Layette Trunk, **with accessories**

11"–13"...$900.00–1,500.00

15" Prince Charming, Effanbee, hard plastic: $400. **Photo courtesy of Gandtiques.**

16" Tintair, Effanbee, hard plastic, mint: $275. **Photo courtesy of American Beauty Dolls.**

Vinyl Reissue, 1984 **molded hair or curly rooted hair**

14"...$55.00–65.00

Hard Plastic and Vinyl, **dolls listed are all in good condition wearing original clothing, allow more for MIB**

Alyssa, **1960–1961, vinyl head, hard plastic jointed body, walker, including elbows, rooted saran hair, sleep eyes**

23"...$200.00–225.00

Baby Lisa, **1980, vinyl, designed by Astri Campbell, represents a three-month-old baby**

11"...$11.00–18.00

with layette $35.00–45.00

Baby Lisa Grows Up, **1983, vinyl, toddler body, in trunk with wardrobe**

11"...$30.00–40.00

Brenda Starr, **2002–2007, designed and produced under Robert Tonner**

16"...$65.00–100.00

Butterball, **1969, all vinyl, molded hair or rooted, sleep eyes**

12"...$25.00–35.00

1989 version, **molded hair**

12"...$15.00–20.00

Button Nose, **1968–1971, vinyl head, cloth body**

18"...$25.00–35.00

2004 version, **produced under Robert Tonner**

18"...$45.00–60.00

Champagne Lady, **1959, vinyl head and arms, rooted hair, blue sleep eyes, lashes, hard plastic body, from Lawrence Welk's TV show, Miss Revlon-type**

21"...$175.00–225.00

23"...$250.00–300.00

Currier & Ives, **vinyl and hard plastic**

12"...$15.00–25.00

Disney dolls, **1977–1978, Snow White, Cinderella, Alice in Wonderland, and Sleeping Beauty**

    14"...$15.00–22.00

    16½" $70.00–125.00

Fluffy, **1954+, all-vinyl**

Molded hair

    8"...$35.00–40.00

Rooted hair

    8"...$30.00–35.00

    11"...$40.00–45.00

Grand Dames,   **1970 on, vinyl, sleep eyes, rooted hair elaborate costumes**

    11"...$12.00–18.00

    15"...$20.00–25.00

    18"...$18.00–22.00

Gumdrop, **1962 on, vinyl, jointed toddler, sleep eyes, rooted hair**

    16"...$25.00–30.00

Hagara, Jan, **designer, all-vinyl, jointed, rooted hair, painted eyes, Christina 1984, Larry 1985, Laurel 1984, Lesley 1985**

    15"...$20.00–25.00

Half Pint, **1966–1983, all-vinyl, rooted hair, sleep eyes, lashes**

    11"...$40.00–60.00

Happy Boy, **1960, vinyl, molded hair, tooth, freckles, painted eyes**

    11"...$55.00–70.00

Hibel, Edna, **designer, 1984 only, all-vinyl**

Flower Girl

    12½" $14.00–20.00

Contessa

    11"...$16.00–22.00

Honey, **1949–1958, hard plastic (see also composition), saran wig, sleep eyes, closed mouth, marked on head and back, "Effanbee," had gold paper hang tag that read: "I am//Honey//An//Effanbee//Sweet/ /Child"**

Honey, 1949–1955, **all hard plastic, closed mouth, sleep eyes**

    14"...$150.00–200.00

    18"...$200.00–300.00

    24"...$400.00–500.00

Honey Walker, **1952 on, all hard plastic with walking mechanism, Honey Walker Junior Miss, 1956–1957, hard plastic, extra joints at knees and ankles permit her to wear flat or high-heeled shoes, add $50.00 for jointed knees, ankles**

    14"...$125.00–175.00

    19"...$175.00–225.00

    Humpty Dumpty, **1985 ....$15.00–25.00**

Katie, **1957, molded hair**

    8½" $35.00–40.00

Legend Series, **vinyl, 15½", allow double for MIB**

    1980, **W.C. Fields............................$20.00–25.00**

1981, **John Wayne, cowboy**

    ...$20.00–25.00

1982, **John Wayne, cavalry**

    ...$22.00–27.00

    1982, **Mae West...............................$10.00–1500**

    1983, **Groucho Marx.......................$20.00–25.00**

1984, **Judy Garland, Dorothy**

    ...$20.00–25.00

    1985, **Lucille Ball............................$20.00–25.00**

    1986, **Liberace $45.00–50.00**

    1987, **James Cagney $15.00–20.00**

    1988, **Humphrey Bogart.................$15.00–20.00**

Lil Sweetie, **1967, nurser with no lashes or brow**

    16"...$25.00–30.00

Limited Edition Club, **vinyl**

    1975, **Precious Baby.........................$ 40.00–55.00**

    1976, **Patsy Ann ....$ 35.00–45.00**

    1977, **Dewees Cochran ....$ 25.00–35.00**

    1978, **Crowning Glory....................$ 15.00–25.00**

    1979, **Skippy....................................$ 35.00–50.00**

1980, **Susan B. Anthony 15.00–20.00**

1981, **Girl with Watering Can**

    ...$ 30.00–40.00

    1982, **Princess Diana ....$ 50.00–65.00**

    1983, **Sherlock Holmes...................$ 15.00–25.00**

1984, **Bubbles** .... $ 15.00–25.00

1985, **Red Boy** .... $ 12.00–18.00

1986, **China head**............................. $ 12.00–18.00

1987–1988, **Porcelain Grumpy (2,500)** $ 30.00–50.00

Vinyl Grumpy .... $ 18.00–25.00

Martha and George Washington, **1976–1977, all-vinyl, fully jointed, rooted hair, blue eyes, molded lashes**

11" pair .... $ 25.00–30.00

Mary Jane, **1959, all-vinyl, walker, rooted hair, flirty eyes, Companion doll**

30"... $ 150.00–200.00

Mickey, **1956–1972, all-vinyl, fully jointed, some with molded hat, painted eyes**

10".. $ 20.00– 30.00

Miss Chips, **1966–1981, all-vinyl, fully jointed, side-glancing sleep eyes, rooted hair**

17".. $ 20.00–30.00

example in original mod style rain outfit sold online for $ 293.00

Black

17".. $ 25.00–35.00

Most Happy Family, **1958, vinyl, 21" mother, 10" brother and sister, 8" baby**

Set.. $ 475.00–500.00

Noma, The Electronic Doll, **1950, hard plastic, cloth body, vinyl limbs, battery-operated talking doll, wore pink rayon taffeta dress with black and white check trim**

27".. $ 250.00–300.00

Polka Dottie, **1954, vinyl head, with molded pigtails on fabric body, or with hard plastic body**

21".. $ 65.00–85.00

Latex body

11".. $ 50.00–60.00

Personality Series, **allow double for MIB**

1984, **Sir Winston Churchill**.............................$ 10.00–15.00

1984, **Louis Armstrong** ....$ 15.00–20.00

1984, **Mark Twain**...$ 15.00–20.00

1985, **Eleanor Roosevelt**....................................$ 10.00–15.00

Presidents, **1984 on, allow double for MIB**

Abraham Lincoln

18".. $ 15.00–20.00

George Washington

16".. $ 12.00–18.00

Teddy Roosevelt

    17".. $ 10.00–15.00

Franklin D. Roosevelt

    1985 .... $ 10.00–15.00

Andrew Jackson

    1989 .... $ 15.00–20.00

Princess Diana, **1982, vinyl**

    18".. $ 15.00–20.00

Pun'kin, **1966–1983, all-vinyl, fully jointed toddler, sleep eyes, rooted hair**

    11".. $ 35.00–40.00

Regal Heirloom Collection, **1965, vinyl, rooted hair, sleep eyes**

    18".. $ 80.00–12.00

Rootie Kazootie, **1954, vinyl head, cloth or hard plastic body, smaller size has latex body**

    11".. $ 80.00–100.00

    21".. $ 85.00–100.00

Santa Claus, **1982 on, designed by Faith Wick, "Old Fashioned Nast Santa," No. 7201, vinyl head, hands, stuffed cloth body, molded and painted features, marked "Effanbee**

    18".. $ 10.00–15.00

Sugar Pie, **1960, vinyl nurser, rooted or molded hair, sleep eyes**

    14"–16"... $ 30.00–40.00

Storybook Series, **1976, Hiedi, Red Ridinghood, Alice In Wonderland, others**

    11".. $ 10.00–15.00

Suzie Sunshine, **1961–1979, designed by Eugenia Dukas, all-vinyl, fully jointed, rooted hair, sleep eyes, lashes, freckles on nose, add $25.00 more for black**

    18".. $ 20.00–30.00

Sweetie Pie, **1952, hard plastic**

    27".. $ 200.00–250.00

Tintair, **1951, hard plastic, hair color set, to compete with Ideal's Toni**

    14"–16"... $ 125.00–225.00

    20".. $ 180.00–275.00

Wicket Witch, **1981–1982, designed by Faith Wick. No. 7110, vinyl head, blond rooted hair, painted features, cloth stuffed body, dressed in black, with apple and basket, head marked: "Effanbee//Faith Wick//7110 19cc81"**

    18".. $ 20.00–25.00

FARNELL-ALPHA TOYS

16" George VI, Farnell, cloth: $400. **Photo courtesy of Hatton's Gallery of Dolls.**

1915–1930s, Acton, London. Cloth dolls with molded felt or velvet heads, cloth bodies, painted features, mohair wigs.

Baby

    15"...$ 300.00–350.00

    18"...$ 400.00–500.00

Child

    10"...$ 275.00–300.00

    14"–15"...$ 350.00–400.00

    20"...$ 425.00–475.00

Black

    13"–15"...$ 400.00–550.00

Characters **such as Islanders, pirates etc.**

    15"...$ 100.00–175.00

Long Limbed Lady doll

    26"...$ 700.00–750.00

King George VI, **"H.M. The King"**

    15"...$ 400.00–500.00

Palace Guard, "Beefeater"

    15"...$ 150.00–200.00

FISHER PRICE

18" My Baby Beth, Fisher Price, vinyl, MIB: $140. **Photo courtesy of The Museum Doll Shop.**

Fisher-Price, 1931 on, New York. Began to make infant's and child's toys. Eventually, the product line was expanded to include the dolls. Values are for secondary market dolls in perfect condition wearing original clothing, many are still available retail.

My Friend Mandy Series, **1977 on, vinyl head and limbs, cloth body, rooted hair, painted eyes**

 16"..$ 35.00–45.00

My Baby Beth, **1978, vinyl head and limbs, cloth body, rooted hair, painted eyes**

 18"..$ 50.00–70.00

FRANKLIN MINT

The Franklin Mint, 1964 on, began to make legal tender coins for foreign countries, as well as commemorative medallions, casino tokens, and precious metal ingots. Eventually, the product line was expanded to include the sculptures, deluxe games, precision die-cast models, and collector dolls. Since 2003 the doll lines have been reduced in production, some phased out completely. Values are for secondary market dolls in perfect condition wearing original clothing. Many are still available retail. Allow double for MIB.

Vinyl

Jackie Kennedy

 14½"..$ 40.00–60.00

Marilyn Monroe

 16"..$ 50.00–100.00

18.5" Princess Diana, Franklin Mint, porcelain, MIB: $80. **Photo courtesy of Phillip Weiss Auctions.**

Princess Diana

15½" .... $ 60.00–75.00

Twiggy

16" .... $ 6500–75.00

Porcelain

Arwen Evenstar

22" .... $ 75.00–120.00

Country Store Advertising Logo Dolls, **1986 on**

13" .... $ 15.00–20.00

Gibson girl

21" .... $ 55.00–90.00

Jackie Kennedy

15" .... $ 40.00–70.00

With trunk and wardrobe

.... $ 200.00–300.00

Wedding Portrait

16" .... $ 60.00–75.00

Marilyn Monroe

19" .... $ 50.00–140.00

Scarlett O'Hara, **in wedding gown**

19" .... $ 75.00–125.00

Princess Diana

18½" .... $ 35.00–45.00

FRENCH POUPÉE

17" Poupée bois, bisque, unmarked: $10,000. **Photo courtesy of Morphy Auctions. Auctions.**

13.75" Blampoix, bisque, wooden upper arms, bisque lower arms: $3,500. **Photo courtesy of Gloria's Antique Dolls.**

1869 on. Glass eyes, doll modeled as an adult lady, with bisque shoulder head, stationary or swivel neck, closed mouth, earrings, kid or kid and cloth body, nicely dressed, good condition. Add more for original clothing, special body such as Gesland, Kintzbach, Terrenne, black, or exceptional doll.

Poupée Peau (kid body), unmarked or with size number only

Glass eyes

10"–14"..	$ 2,000.00–4,000.00
16"–18"..	$ 4,000.00–7,000.00
21"..	$ 6,000.00–9,000.00
27"..	$ 10,000.00–12,000.00

Painted eyes, kid body

14"–16"..	$ 1,600.00–1,900.00

Blown kid body

14"–17"..	$ 11,000.00–19,000.00

Too few in database for a reliable range.

Poupée Bois (wood body), unmarked or with size number only, articulated body, glass eyes

13"..	$ 7,500.00–9,000.00
15"..	$ 7,000.00–9,500.00
18"..	$ 7,500.00–9,000.00

Kid-over wood body

15"–18"..	$ 5,000.00–7,000.00

Barrois: See Barrios section.

B.S., Blampoix, **allow more for wood over kid or wood body.**

12"–14" .... $ 2,600.00–3,400.00

16"–17" .... $ 4,000.00–7,000.00

A. Dehors, **1860, swivel neck, bisque lower arms**

Generic face, kid body

14"–15" .... $ 6,000.00–7,000.00

17"–20" .... $ 7,000.00–10,000.00

Portrait face

17"–18" .... $ 16,000.00–20,000.00

L.D., **Louis Doleac, kid body**

17"–20" .... $ 8,000.00–10,000.00

Wood body

18" .... $ 14,000.00–16,000.00

Too few in database for a reliable range.

Simonne

Kid body

12"–14" .... $ 4,000.00–5,000.00

16"–18" .... $ 6,000.00–10,000.00

Wood body

14" .... $ 7,500.00–8,500.00

18" .... $ 10,500.00–12,000.00

Fortune Teller Dolls, **fashion-type head with swivel neck, glass or painted eyes, kid body, skirt made to hold many paper "fortunes," exceptional doll may be more**

Closed mouth

15"–18" .... $ 4,100.00–7,000.00

Open mouth

18" .... $ 3,100.00+

China, **glazed finish, 1870–1880 hairstyle**

14"–15" .... $ 5,000.00–5,500.00

18" .... $ 8,500.00–9,000.00

Accessories

Dress .... $ 600.00+

Shoes **marked by maker** .... $ 500.00+

Unmarked .... $ 250.00

Trunk .... $ 250.00+

Wig .... $ 250.00+

RALPH A. FREUNDLICH

15" WWII Soldier, Freundlich, composition: $175. **Photo courtesy of Alderfer Auction Company, Inc.**

1924–1945, New York City, later Clinton, Massachusetts. Ralph Freundlich worked for Jeanette Doll Co. then opened Silver Doll & Toy Manufacturing Co. in 1923. In 1924 became Ralph Freundlich Inc. and made composition dolls. Dolls listed are in good condition wearing original clothing.

Baby Sandy, **1939–1942, all-composition, jointed toddler body, molded hair, painted or sleep eyes, smiling mouth**

> 8".. $ 150.00–200.00

> 12".. $ 225.00–300.00

> 15".. $ 325.00–325.00

> 20".. $ 350.00–375.00

Dummy Dan, **ventriloquist doll, Charlie McCarthy look-alike**

> 15".. $ 50.00–75.00

> 21".. $ 100.00–125.00

General Douglas MacArthur, **1942, all-composition, jointed body, bent arm salutes, painted features, molded hat, jointed, in khaki uniform, with paper tag**

> 18".. $ 200.00–275.00

Military dolls, **1942+, all-composition, molded hats, painted features, original clothes, with paper tag Soldier, Sailor, WAAC, or WAVE**

> 15".. $ 150.00–200.00

Orphan Annie **and her dog, Sandy**

> 12".. $ 400.00–450.00

Pig Baby, **1930s, composition pig head, with painted features on unmarked five-piece body, freundlich presumed maker of similar composition cat, rabbit, and monkey dolls**

> 9".. $ 350.00–400.00

Pinocchio, composition and cloth, with molded hair, painted features, brightly colored cheeks, **large eyes, open/closed mouth, tagged: "Original as portrayed by C. Collodi"**

16"... $ 350.00–400.00

Red Riding Hood, Wolf, Grandma, **1934, composition, set of three, in schoolhouse box, original clothes**

Set of three

9".. $ 450.00–600.00

Three Little Pigs, Wolf, **1934, composition, set of four, original clothes**

Set of four

10"... $ 575.00–675.00

Trixbe **(Patsy-type), all-composition girl, painted features, molded painted hair with bow pined into head**

11"... $ 100.00–125.00

FULPER POTTERY CO.

17" shoulder head child, Fulper, bisque: $90.
Photo courtesy of Alderfer Auction Company, Inc.

1918–1921, Flemington, New Jersey. Made dolls with bisque heads and all-bisque dolls. Sold dolls to Amberg, Colonial Toy Mfg. Co., and Horsman. "M.S." monogram stood for Martin Stangl, in charge of production. Dolls listed are in good condition wit h original or appropriate clothes.

Baby, bisque socket head, glass eyes, open mouth, teeth, mohair wig, bent-leg body

14"–16"... $ 175.00–225.00

22".. $ 275.00–325.00

Toddler

16"–18"... $ 300.00–350.00

Child, **socket-head, glass eyes, open mouth**

Shoulderhead, **Kid body**

18"–22".. $ 100.00–150.00

Socket head, **Open mouth, composition body**

16"–18".. $ 200.00–250.00

22"–24".. $ 300.00–350.00

Closed mouth, **composition body**

15"–17".. $ 300.00–400.00

GABRIEL

The Lone Ranger Series, **1970s, vinyl action figures with horses, separate accessory sets available. Doll in very good condition with original clothing and accessories. Mint-in-box can bring double values listed.**

Dan Reed on Banjo, **blond hair, figure on palomino horse**

9".. $ 70.00–80.00

Butch Cavendish on Smoke, **black hair, mustache, on black horse**

9".. $ 70.00–80.00

Hopi medicine man

9".. $ 110.00–120.00

Lone Ranger on Silver, **masked figure on white horse**

9".. $ 130.00–155.00

Lone Ranger, no horse

9".. $ 65.00–85.00

Mysterious Prospector set, Mule and mining items

.... $ 50.00–60.00

Tonto on Scout, **Indian on brown and white horse**

9".. $ 80.00–90.00

Tonto, no horse

9".. $ 55.00–65.00

GANS & SEYFARTH PUPPENBABRIK

33" child, Gans & Seyfarth, bisque: $550. **Photo courtesy of Morphy Auctions. Auctions.**

1908–1922, Waltershausen, Thüringia. Made bisque dolls; had a patent for flirty and googly eyes. Partners separated in 1922, Otto Gans opened his own factory.

Baby, **bent-leg baby, original clothes or appropriately dressed, allow more for toddler**

10"–14" .... $ 275.00–300.00

16"–20" .... $ 325.00–400.00

25" .... $ 500.00–600.00

Child, **open mouth, composition body, original clothes, or appropriately dressed, no mold number or molds 120, 6589**

13"–15" .... $ 225.00–275.00

21"–24" .... $ 300.00–400.00

28" .... $ 450.00–500.00

FRANCOIS GAULTIER

1860–1899. After 1899, became part of S.F.B.J, located near Paris. They made bisque doll heads and parts for lady dolls and for bébés and sold to many French makers of dolls including Gesland, Jullien, Petite et Dumontier, Rabery et Delphieu, and Thuillier. Also made all-bisque dolls marked "F.G." Dolls listed are in good condition, appropriately dressed.

Poupée **(fashion-type), 1860 on, F.G., marked swivel head on bisque shoulder plate, kid body, may have bisque lower arms, higher quality or elaborate original costume brings higher end of range**

16" Bébé, Gaultier, bisque, scroll mark: $4,000. **Photo courtesy of Withington Auction Inc.**

Glass eyes

> 10"–11"..............................$ 1,000.00–3,000.00
>
> 12"–13"..............................$ 2,000.00–4,500.00
>
> 15"–17"..............................$ 3,200.00–4,500.00
>
> 18"–20"..............................$ 4,000.00–5,000.00
>
> 23"–24"..............................$ 6,000.00–6,200.00
>
> 30"–32"..............................$ 4,000.00–5,000.00

Painted eyes

> 16"–17"..............................$ 1,800.00–2,000.00

Wood body

> 16"–18"..............................$ 8,000.00–9,000.00

Later one-piece shoulder head, **kid body, often in regional dress**

Painted eyes

> 12"–15"..............................$ 600.00–800.00

Glass eyes

> 18".....................................$ 800.00–1,000.00

Bébé (child), "F.G." in block letters, **1879–1887, closed mouth, excellent quality bisque socket head, glass eyes, pierced ears, cork pate**

Composition and wood body with straight wrists

> 10"–11"..............................$ 3,500.00–4,500.00
>
> 13"–16"..............................$ 3,800.00–5,000.00
>
> 18"–22"..............................$ 5,500.00–6,500.00
>
> 27"–29"..............................$ 7,000.00–8,000.00

Kid body, may have bisque forearms

> 10"–12"..............................$ 4,000.00–4,500.00
>
> 13"–15"..............................$ 4,500.00–5,000.00
>
> 17"–19"..............................$ 5,500.00–6,000.00

Bébé (child), "F.G." inside scroll, **1887–1900, composition body, closed mouth**

    12"–13" .... $ 3,800.00–4,500.00

    15"–17" .... $ 3,500.00–4,200.00

    22"–24" .... $ 4,400.00–5,000.00

    28" .... $ 5,200.00–5,300.00

Composition body, open mouth

    14"–16" .... $ 1,700.00–2,000.00

    20"–24" .... $ 2,800.00–3,500.00

    27" .... $ 4,000.00–4,200.00

GESLAND

1860–1928, Paris. Made, repaired, exported, and distributed dolls, patented a doll body, used heads from Francois Gaultier with "F.G." block or scroll mark. In 1926 became part of the Société Industrielle de France. Gesland's doll's body had metal articulated armature covered with padding and stockinette, with bisque or wood/composition hands and legs. Dolls listed are in good condition, appropriately dressed. Allow more for exceptional original clothing.

Poupée (fashion-type) Gesland, **stockinette covered metal articulated fashion-type body, bisque lower arms and legs**

    14"–15" .... $ 4,500.00–5,000.00

    16"–17" .... $ 5,000.00–6,000.00

    23"–24" .... $ 6,000.00–7,000.00

Bébé **(child) on marked Gesland body, closed mouth**

    12"–15" .... $ 3,800.00–4,000.00

    17"–20" .... $ 5,000.00–6,000.00

    22"–24" .... $ 6,500.00–7,500.00

    28"–30" .... $ 7,500.00–8,000.00

RUTH GIBBS

1946 on, Flemington, New Jersey. Made dolls with china heads and limbs on cloth bodies. The dolls were designed by Herbert Johnson. Dolls listed are in good condition wearing original clothing, in original box can bring double the values listed.

7" Godey lady, Ruth Gibbs, china: $95. **Doll courtesy of The Museum Doll Shop.**

Godey's Lady Book Dolls, pink-tint or white shoulder head, cloth body

7"..$ 70.00–95.00

9"..$ 80.00–90.00

12"..$ 125.00–150.00

Blond special for G Fox 100th anniversary CT,

12"..$ 150.00– $ 180.00MIB

With molded necklace

12"..$ 130.00–165.00

Black

12"..$ 155.00–175.00

Caracul wig, **original outfit**

10"..$ 150.00–225.00

GILBERT TOYS

1909–1966, New Haven, Connecticut. company founded on the invention of the Erector Set, went on to make dolls based on popular television characters. Dolls listed are in very good condition with all original clothing and accessories, mint-in-box can bring double the value listed.

Honey West(**Anne Francis**), **1965, vinyl head and arms, hard plastic torso and legs, rooted blond hair, painted eyes, painted beauty spot near mouth, head marked "K73" with leopard**

11½" ....$ 125.00–150.00

Accessories **MOC**..............................$ 100.00–400.00

The Man From U.N.C.L.E. characters from TV show of the 1960s

Ilya Kuryakin (**David McCallum**)

12¼" ....$ 80.00–100.00

11.5" Honey West, Gilbert Toys, vinyl, MIB: $257. **Photo courtesy of Morphy Auctions.**

Napoleon Solo (**Robert Vaughn**)

12¼" .... $ 90.00–120.00

James Bond, **Secret Agent 007, character from James Bond movies**

12¼" .... $ 125.00–150.00

Odd Job $150.00–200.00

GIRL SCOUT DOLLS

1917 on, listed chronologically. Dolls made for the Girl Scouts of America, various manufacturers. Dolls listed are in good condition with original clothing, MIB can bring double the values listed.

1917, **all-composition doll, painted features, mohair wig**

6½" .... $ 225.00–250.00

1920s Girl Scout **doll in camp uniform, pictured in Girls Scout 1920 handbook, all-cloth, mask face, painted features, wigged, gray green uniform**

13" .... $ 600.00+

Grace Corry Rockwell, **Scout 1929, composition shoulder head, designed by Grace Cory, cloth body with crier, molded hair, painted features, original uniform, mark on shoulder plate: "by Grace Corry," body stamped "Madame Hendren Doll//Made in USA"**

13" .... $ 350.00–450.00

Averill Mfg. Co, **1936, all-cloth, printed and painted features**

16" .... $ 300.00–350.00

Georgene Novelties

1940–1946, **all-cloth, flat-faced painted features, yellow yarn curls, wears original silver green uniform with red triangle tie, hang tag reads: "Genuine Georgene Doll//A product of Georgene Novelties, Inc., NY//Made in U.S.A."**

15" .... $ 200.00–250.00

8" Girl Scout, Black
Fluffie, Effanbee,
vinyl: $100.
**Photo courtesy
of Memories
of Things Past
Antiques.**

1946–1955, **all-cloth, mask face, painted features and string hair**

13½" .... $ 125.00–175.00

1955–1957, **same as previous listing, but now has a stuffed vinyl head**

13" .... $ 150.00–200.00

Terri Lee, **1949–1958, hard plastic, felt hats, oilcloth saddle shoes**

16" .... $ 200.00–300.00

Tiny Terri Lee, **1955–1958, hard plastic, walker, sleep eyes, wig, plastic shoes**

10" .... $ 125.00–175.00

Walker, **hard plastic**

8" .... $ 60.00–90.00

Ginger, **1956–1958, made by Cosmopolitan for Terri Lee, hard plastic, straight-leg walker, synthetic wig**

7½"–8" .... $ 85.00–150.00

Effanbee Honey, **1949–1957, hard plastic, mohair wig**

14" .... $ 100.00–125.00

18" .... $ 200.00–250.00

Vogue, **Painted Lash Walker Ginny, 1954, hard plastic**

8" .... $ 250.00–275.00

Nancy Ann Storybook, **1957, Muffie, hard plastic**

8" .... $ 100.00–140.00

Effanbee, Patsy Ann, **1959 on, all-vinyl jointed body, saran hair, with sleep eyes, freckles on nose, Brownie or Girl Scout**

15" .... $ 75.00–125.00

Effanbee Suzette, **ca. 1960, jointed vinyl body, sleep eyes, saran hair, thin body, long legs**

15" .... $ 250.00–300.00

Uneeda, 1961–1963, Ginny look-alike, vinyl head, hard plastic body, straight-leg walker, Dynel wig, marked "U" on head

8"..$ 30.00–40.00

Effanbee Fluffy, 1964–1972, vinyl dolls, sleep eyes, curly rooted hair, Brownie had blond wig, Junior was brunette, box had clear acetate lid, printed with Girl Scout trademark, and catalog number

8"..$ 45.00–55.00

Related, Fluffy Camp Fire Girl

8"..$ 55.00–65.00

Effanbee Fluffy Cadette, 1965, vinyl, rooted hair, sleep eyes

11"..$ 150.00–200.00

Effanbee Pun'kin Jr., 1974–1979, all-vinyl, sleep eyes, long straight rooted hair Brownie and Junior uniforms

11½"..$ 30.00–40.00

Related, Fluffy Camp Fire Girl

11½"..$ 45.00–55.00

Hallmark, 1979, all-cloth, Juliette Low, from 1916 handbook, wearing printed 1923 uniform

6½"..$ 10.00–12.00

Jesco, 1985, Katie, all-vinyl, sleep eyes, long straight rooted hair, look-alike Girl Scout, dressed as Brownie and Junior

9"..$ 35.00–45.00

Dakin, Ginny, 1986–1995, all vinyl

8"..$ 50.00–70.00

Madame Alexander, 1992, vinyl, unofficial Girl Scout, sleep eyes

8"..$ 35.00–45.00

Avon, 1995, Tender Memories series, porcelain, carries box of cookies

14"..$ 30.00–45.00

GLADDIE

1928–1930 on. Trade name of doll designed by Helen Webster Jensen, made in Germany, body made by K&K, for Borgfeldt. Flange heads made of bisque or biscaloid (a ceramic imitation of bisque), with molded hair, glass or painted eyes, open-closed mouth with two upper teeth and laughing expression, composition arms, lower legs, cloth torso, some with crier and upper legs, mark "copyriht" (misspelled). Dolls listed are in good condition, appropriately dressed.

20" Gladdie,
biscaloid: $800.
**Photo courtesy
of McMasters
Harris Apple Tree
Doll Auctions.**

Biscaloid ceramic head

16"... $ 700.00–800.00

18"–20".. $ 800.00–1,100.00

23"–24".. $ 1,200.00–1,500.00

29"... $ 1,500.00–1,900.00

Bisque head

14"... $ 2,600.00–2,800.00

18"–20".. $ 3,800.00–4,800.00

WM. AND F. & W. GOEBEL

1867–1930 on, Oeslau, Thüringia. Made porcelain and glazed china dolls, as well as bathing dolls, Kewpie-types, and others. Earlier mark was triangle with half moon. Supplied heads to other doll makers including Max Handwerck. Dolls listed are in good condition appropriately dressed. Exceptional dolls may be more.

Child, 1895

Socket head, **open mouth, composition body, sleep or set eyes, no mold number or mold 120**

5"–10"... $ 120.00–225.00

12"–16".. $ 160.00–200.00

17"–23".. $ 250.00–350.00

25"–27".. $ 400.00–$ 450.00

Baby body

13"... $ 130.00–160.00

Shoulder head, **open mouth, kid or cloth body, glass eyes**

20"–24".. $ 1750.00–200.00

6.5" Goebel, bisque, character with molded cap: $400. **Photo courtesy of Sara Bernstein's Dolls.**

Character Child, after 1909

Molded hair, **may have flowers or ribbons, painted features, with five-piece papier-mâché body**

5½"–7".. $ 200.00–250.00

Molded on bonnet **or hat, closed mouth, five-piece papier-mâché body, painted features**

6"–9".. $ 400.00–500.00

Character Baby, **after 1909, open mouth, sleep eyes, five-piece bent-leg baby body**

11"–15".. $ 220.00–270.00

18"–21".. $ 325.00–375.00

Toddler body

11"–14".. $ 450.00–550.00

GOOGLY

Popular 1900–1925, various manufacturers. Doll with exaggerated side-glancing eyes. Round eyes were painted, glass, tin, or celluloid, when they move to side they are called flirty eyes. Most doll manufacturers of the period made dolls with googly eyes. With painted eyes, they could be painted looking to side or straight ahead; with inserted eyes, the same head can be found with and without flirty eyes. May have closed smiling mouth, composition or papier-mâché body, molded hair or wigged. Dolls listed are in good condition appropriately dressed. Exceptional dolls can be more.

All-Bisque, **jointed shoulders, hips, molded shoes, socks**

Painted intaglio eyes, **no maker's mark**

3".. $ 250.00–350.00

5"–6"... $ 400.00–500.00

Rigid neck, **glass eyes, no maker's mark**

3".. $ 325.00–375.00

4" googly, mold 217, all bisque: $625. **Photo courtesy of Alderfer Auction Company, Inc.**

8" googly, mold 608, Bähr & Proschild, bisque, glass eyes: $1,800. **Photo courtesy of McMasters Harris Apple Tree Doll Auctions.**

4"–5" .... $ 500.00–550.00

6"–7" .... $ 600.00–775.00

Swivel neck, **glass eyes, no maker's mark**

5" .... $ 525.00–600.00

7" .... $ 800.00–850.00

No mold number, **jointed knees**

7" .... $ 2,500.00–2,800.00

Marked by maker, **Molds 217, 218, 330, 501**

4"–5" .... $ 625.00–675.00

6"–7" .... $ 700.00–900.00

Hertwig, **molded clothing, wire jointed at shoulders and hips, painted eyes**

4"–7" .... $ 100.00–125.00

Hertel & Schwab, **Mold 189**

5"–6.5" .... $ 800.00–1,300.00

8" .... $ 1,500.00–$ 1,600.00

Molds 165

6"–10" .... $ 900.00–1,500.00

Kestner **Mold 111, jointed knees and elbows**

4½"–6" .... $ 1,700.00–2,300.00

Molds 192, 292, **Glass eyes, watermelon smile**

4"–5" .... $ 975.00–1,500.00

Mold 211, **with jointed elbows, knees, neck**

5" .... $ 2,800.00–3,000.00

Too few in database for reliable range.

7" .... $ 3,750.00–4,200.00

Too few in database for reliable range.

Our Fairy, **mold 222, ca. 1914, wigged, glass eyes**

4½"–5"...$ 800.00–1,000.00

6"–7"...$ 1,500.00–1,800.00

11"...$ 2,000.00–2,200.00

Painted eyes, **molded hair**

5"...$ 450.00–550.00

8"...$ 750.00–850.00

12"...$ 950.00–1,500.00

Limbach, **Mold 1920, molded cloche, painted eyes, jointed shoulders**

7½"...$ 450.00–500.00

Peek-a-boo kids, **designed by Chloe Preston, 1914 on, bisque immobile with painted features including wide lashes**

1 3/4"–2.5"...$ 35.00–50.00

4"–5"...$ 135.00–250.00

Bisque Head, **painted or glass eye, composition body**

Bähr & Pröschild, **marked "B.P.," mold 608, ca. 1914, glass eyes, wigged**

8"–9"...$ 1,800.00–2,000.00

Demacol, **made for Dennis Malley & Co., London, bisque socket head, glass eyes, closed watermelon mouth, mohair wig, five-piece composition toddler body**

8"–13"...$ 800.00–1,200.00

Goebel, **mold 208, 268, others**

Painted eyes

6"–7"...$ 600.00–650.00

9"–10"...$ 800.00–850.00

12"...$ 900.00–1000.00

Glass eyes

7"–8"...$ 900.00–1,200.00

10"–11"...$ 1,500.00–1,600.00

13"...$ 2,200.00–2,500.00

Round open/closed mouth, **molded painted hair, toddler body, resembles Recknagel mold 50**

Painted eyes

7"...$ 900.00–1,050.00

Glass eyes

9½"...$ 3,400.00–3,600.00

 6.5" googly, mold 208, Goebel, bisque, glass eyes, wigged: $625. **Photo courtesy of Morphy Auctions.**

 14" googly, mold 165, Hertel & Schwab, bisque: $ 4,000. **Photo courtesy of Ann Lloyd Antique Dolls.**

Handwerck, Max

Marked "Elite," **Molded Military helmet, bisque socket head, glass eyes, closed mouth**

 10"–14"..$1,800.00–2,500.00

Marked "Elite," **Bellhop style molded hat**

 11"–12"..$2,000.00–2200.00

Marked "Elite," **two faced**

 12"..$3,000.00–3,200.00

Hertel Schwab & Co., **1914 on**

Mold 163, **solid dome, glass eyes, molded hair, closed smiling mouth, toddler body**

 12"..$6,000.00–7,500.00

 16"–18"..$8,600.00–9,000.00

 21½"..$12,000.00

Jubilee, **Jubilee, socket head, glass eyes, closed smiling mouth**

Mold 165 Toddler

 10"–12"..$2,200.00–3,000.00

 15"–18"..$4,500.00–6,000.00

Mold 172 Baby, solid dome

 11"–12"..$4,000.00–4,500.00

 16"–18"..$5,500.00–6,000.00

Mold 173, **solid dome, glass eyes, closed smiling mouth**

Baby

 10"–11"..$2,500.00–2,800.00

 16"..$4,800.00–5,200.00

Toddler

 10"–12"..$3,000.00–3,5000.00

 16"..$6,000.00–6,400.00

7.5" googly, mold 9573, Gebruder Heubach, bisque: $850. **Photo courtesy of McMasters Harris Apple Tree Doll Auctions.**

10" googly, Hug Me Kiddie, composition: $850. **Photo courtesy of Morphy Auctions.**

Heubach, Ernst

Molds 262, 264, ca. 1914, "EH" painted eyes, closed mouth

6"–8"...$400.00–500.00

10"–12"...$600.00–800.00

Mold 276, **bug molde on nose, gooly crossed eyes**

7"...$2,500.00–3,000.00

Mold 318, **ca. 1920, "EH" character, closed mouth**

11"...$1,100.00–1,285.00

14"...$1,900.00–2,050.00

Mold 319, **ca. 1920, "EH" character, painted eyes, tearful features**

12"...$24,000.00 at auction

Mold 417, **character, small eye cuts, glass eyes, closed mouth with pursed lips, wigged**

11"...$750.00–900.00

Heubach, Gebruder

No mold number, **painted eyes**

6"–7"...$600.00–675.00

9"–11"...$900.00–1,100.00

13"...$1,500.00–1,700.00

Mold 8590, **painted eyes, molded touseled hair with pronounced curl on top**

15"–16"...$6,500.00–6,700.00

Mold 8676, **painted eyes**

9"...$800.00–850.00

11"...$950.00–1,050.00

Mold 8678, **glass eyes**

6"–7"...$900.00–1,000.00

9"–11"...$1,400.00–1,600.00

Mold 8723, 8995, **glass eyes**

   13"...$2,600.00–2,900.00

Mold 8764, **Einco, shoulder head, glass eyes, closed mouth, for Eisenmann & Co.**

   11"...$4,500.00–5,000.00

   18"–20".......................................$11,500.00–13,500.00

Mold 9058, **painted eyes, watermelon mouth, molded hair**

   7"–8"..$500.00–600.00

Mold 9141, **winker, one eye painted closed**

   7"–10"...$900.00–1,100.00

Mold 9573, **glass eyes**

   6"–8"..$800.00–900.00

   9"–11"...$1,000.00–1,200.00

Mold 10342, **glass eyes, wigged, rosebud mouth**

   8"..$1,300.00–1,600.00

Hitt, Oscar

Mold **1409 26 Virginia Short for Ginny 368379 copr. by Oscar Hitt Germany**
15", wigged, round glass eyes, pursed lips sold at auction for $27,120.00
Mold **1409/30 Virginia Short for Ginny 368379 copr. by Oscar Hitt Germany**
14", painted hair, round glass eyes, pursed lips sold at auction for $14,690.00

Kämmer & Reinhardt

Mold 131, **ca. 1914, "S&H//K*R," glass eyes, closed mouth**

   7"–8½"..$4,500.00–5,500.00

   11"–13".......................................$5,000.00–6,500.00

   15"–16".......................................$8,500.00–9,500.00

Kestner

Mold, 221, **ca. 1913, "JDK ges. gesch," character, glass eyes, smiling closed mouth**

   7"..$4,000.00–4,500.00

   11"–13".......................................$4,500.00–5,500.00

   14"–16".......................................$5,500.00–6,500.00

Kley & Hahn, **mold 180, ca. 1915, "K&H" by Hertel Schwab & Co. for Kley & Hahn, character, glass eyes, laughing open-closed mouth**

   14"–15".......................................$6,000.00–6,500.00

Lenci: See Lenci category.

Limbach, **marked with crown and cloverleaf, socket head, large round glass eyes, pug nose, closed smiling mouth**

   7"–8"..$1,400.00–1,600.00

Armand Marseille

Mold 200, **ca. 1911, glass eyes, closed mouth**

8"–9".. $800.00–900.00

11"–14".. $1,050.00–1,200.00

Mold 210, **ca. 1911, painted intaglio eyes, character, solid-dome head, painted eyes, closed mouth**

6"–8".. $400.00–500.00

11"–12".. $700.00–800.00

Mold 232, **ca. 1913, character, closed mouth**

7".. $900.00–1,000.00

10"–11".. $1,100.00–1,200.00

Mold 240, **molded hair with top knot & side curls, glass eyes**

10" sold for $2,260.00 at auction

Molds 241, **ca. 1914, wigged, glass eyes, closed mouth**

9"–10".. $2,900.00–3,100.00

Mold 253, **"AM Nobbikid Reg. U.S. Pat. 066 Germany," ca. 1925**

6"–7".. $700.00–800.00

9"–11".. $1,400.00–1,800.00

Mold 254, **ca. 1912, "AM" dome, painted eyes, closed mouth**

6".. $400.00–450.00

8"–9".. $500.00–550.00

Mold 320, **dome, painted eyes, watermelon smile**

6"–7".. $275.00–325.00

Mold 322, **"AM," ca. 1914, dome, painted eyes**

8"–9".. $600.00–650.00

11".. $800.00–850.00

Mold 323, **1914–1925, glass eyes, also composition**

7"–9".. $475.00–575.00

11"–12".. $750.00–800.00

Mold 325, **ca. 1915, character, closed mouth**

9".. $675.00–725.00

14".. $900.00–1,000.00

Nippon, **baby, painted eyes, five-piece body**

6½"–7½" $90.00–110.00

14" glass eyes with molded tuft of hair $735.00 at auction

10" googly, mold 323, Armand Marseille, bisque: $625. **Photo courtesy of Alderfer Auction Company, Inc.**

10" googly pair, mold 241, Armand Marseille, bisque: $6,200 pair. **Photo courtesy of Sweetbriar Auctions.**

Peek-a-boo kids, **designed by Chloe Preston, 1914 on, bisque flange neck head on cloth body**

4"–5" $275.00–350.00

P.M. Porzellanfabrik Mengersgereuth, **ca. 1926, "PM" character, closed mouth, previously thought to be made by Otto Reinecke, mold 950**

6½"–7" $1,100.00–1,300.00

10" $1,750.00–1,800.00

Recknagel,

Mold 32, **Moritz, intaglio eyes, hair tuft, watermelon smile**

6"–7" $700.00–800.00

Mold 45, 46, 49,54,55, **intaglio eyes, molded hair, closed mouth**

7"–9" $300.00–400.00

Mold 50, **round open/closed mouth, intaglio eyes, molded hair**

7"–8" $500.00–650.00

Simon Halbig

Mold 605, **socket head, sleep eyes**

8"–10" $1,900.00–2,100.00

S.F.B.J.

Mold 245, **glass eyes**

7"–8" $1,600.00–1,900.00

Fully jointed body

10"–14" $6,500.00–7,500.00

Steiner, Herm, **mold 133, ca. 1920, "HS," closed mouth, papier-mâché body**

7"–8" $1,000.00–1,100.00

Molded headwear, **hairbow, cap, etc., socket head, sleep eyes**

10"–12" $1,500.00–3,500.00

Walthur & Sohn, **mold 208, ca. 1920, "W&S" closed mouth, five-piece papier-mâché body, painted socks/shoes**

7"–9" $550.00–700.00

Composition Face, 1911–1914, all-composition head or composition mask face, cloth body, includes Hug Me Kids, Little Bright Eyes, and others.

9"–12" $850.00–950.00

12"–14" $1,300.00–1,600.00

LUDWIG GREINER

28" Greiner, papier-mâché, 1858 patent mark: $900. **Photo courtesy of Withington Auction Inc.**

1840–1874. Succeeded by sons, 1890–1900, Philadelphia, Pennsylvania. Papier-mâché shoulder head dolls, with molded hair, painted/glass eyes, usually made up to be large dolls. Dolls listed are in good condition appropriately dressed. Some wear is acceptable for these dolls but highly worn condition examples will bring half the value of good condition examples.

With "1858" label

12"–13" $800.00–900.00

15"–17" $700.00–800.00

20"–23" $800.00–1,000.00

28"–30" $1,100.00–1,300.00

Glass eyes

24"–26" $1,600.00–2,100.00

With "1872" label

15" $250.00–350.00

18"–24" $500.00–625.00

26"–30" $650.00–700.00

32"–33" $800.00–950.00

GUND

20" Nancy Lou, Gund, mask face, cloth, MIB: $200. **Photo courtesy of Alderfer Auction Company, Inc.**

1898 on, Connecticut and New York. Adolph Gund founded the company making stuffed toys.

Character

Cloth mask face, **painted features, cloth body**

    14"–16" $70.00–80.00

    19"- 24" $100.00–150.00

Little Lulu

    16" $40.00–50.00

Flat faced cloth

    6½" $25.00–30.00

Mary Poppins, **crepe fabric over wire armature**

    11"–13" $30.00–35.00

Plastic mask face, **1940s–1950s, cloth body, Perki and others**

    14"–16" $40.00–55.00

Vinyl mask face, **1950s–1960s, on plush body, included characters such as Popeye, Disney Pinocchio, Seven Dwarves, and others**

    9"–12" $35.00–40.00

Christopher Robin, **cloth body**

    18" $100.00–140.00

The Now Kids, **1970s, cloth dolls, yarn hair, hippies named Desmond and Rhoda**

    Pair $25.00–40.00

Harry Potter, Ron Weasley, Hermionie Granger, Hagrid (16"), **2001, felt heads, poseable cloth bodies**

    12" $25.00–30.00

HALF DOLLS

3.75"half doll, bisque, bald for wigging, both arms away, molded gloves: $450. **Photo courtesy of Gloria's Antique Dolls.**

6" half doll, one arm away and back, china, on original base with lower legs: $. **Photo courtesy of Alderfer Auction Company, Inc.**

1900–1930s, Germany, Japan. Half dolls can be made of bisque, china, composition, or papier-mâché, and were used not only for pincushions but on top of jewelry or cosmetic boxes, brushes, lamps, and numerous other items of decor. The hardest to find have arms molded away from the body as they were easier to break with the limbs in this position and thus fewer survived. Dolls listed are in good condition. Add more for extra attributes. Common examples or those of low quality bring half or less of the value of good-quality examples. Differences in quality can be seen in detail of molding and painting of the features. Rare examples will bring more.

Dolls listed are German except where otherwise noted.

Arms Away

Lady, **good quality, molded hair, marked by maker or mold number**

3"–4" $100.00–150.00

5"–6" $225.00–400.00

8" $375.00–500.00

12" $850.00–900.00

Bald head with wig

4"–6" $150.00–300.00

High quality, **makers such as Galluba & Hoffman, Aelteste Volkstedter Porzellanfabrick, Dressel Kister, others**

4"–5" $375.00–500.00

7½" $500.00–1,200.00

Child, **molded hair**

2½" $55.00–70.00

Elaborate Hat or special headwear, or applied decoration in hair, **high quality, makers such as Galluba & Hoffman, Aelteste Volkstedter Porzellanfabrick, Dressel Kister, others**

3½"–4½" $450.00–550.00

5"–6" $500.00–600.00

Holding items in hand, **such as letter, flower, book, etc.**

3½"–4" $300.00–400.00

4½"–5" $500.00–600.00

High quality, **makers such as Galluba & Hoffman, Aelteste Volkstedter Porzellanfabrick, Dressel Kister, others**

3½"–4" $400.00–700.00

4½"–5" $500.00–900.00

Flapper, **good quality**

3½"–4" $100.00–150.00

4½"–5" $200.00–300.00

High quality

3½"–4" $350.00–450.00

4½"–5" $500.00–600.00

Both arms away and back to body, **good quality**

2½"–3½" $30.00–40.00

5" $45.00–75.00

7" $60.00–130.00

High quality

4"–5" $500.00–800.00

One Arm Away and back to body, **common German type**

2"–3½" $40.00–80.00

4½"–6½" $60.00–120.00

Arms In, **close to figure**

3"–4" $40.00–100.00

5"–6" $75.00–125.00

Bald head, wigged

3"–4" $50.00–60.00

6" $80.00–100.00

Decorated bodice, **necklace, fancy hair or holding article**

3"–5" $200.00–400.00

Double faced

2½"–3½" $325.00–375.00

Man

.... $375.00–400.00

Papier-mâché or composition

2"–3½".. $20.00–30.00

5"–6"... $45.00–60.00

China lady, **marked Japan**

3".. $15.00–25.00

6".. $40.00–50.00

Occupied Japan

3".. $55.00–60.00

Jointed Shoulders

China or bisque, **high quality, molded hair**

3"–4½".. $50.00–80.00

5"–7"... $120.00–200.00

High quality

3"–4½".. $250.00–350.00

5"–7"... $350.00–500.00

HEINRICH HANDWERCK

1855–1932, Waltershausen, Thüringia, Germany. Made composition doll bodies, sent Handwerck molds to Simon & Halbigto make bisque heads. Trademarks included an eight-point star with French or German wording, a shield, and ìBÈbÈ Cosmopolite,î ìBÈbÈ de Reclame,î and ìBÈbÈ Superior.î Sold dolls through Gimbels, Macy's, Montgomery Wards, and others. Bodies marked "Handwerk" in red on lower back torso. Patented a straight wrist body. Dolls listed are in good condition appropriately dressed. Exceptional dolls may be more.

Socket Head Child, 1885 on. Open mouth, sleep or set eyes, ball-jointed body, bisque socket head, pierced ears, appropriate wig, nicely dressed

Molds 69, 79, 89, 99, 109, 119, or No Number

10"–12".. $ 375.00–425.00

14"–16".. $ 425.00–525.00

18"–24".. $ 450.00–550.00

26"–28".. $ 550.00–675.00

30"–35".. $ 800.00–900.00

28" mold 109, Heinrich Handwerck, bisque, dolly face: $500. **Photo courtesy of McMasters Harris Apple Tree Doll Auctions.**

Mold 79, 89 **closed mouth**

15".. $ 1,500.00–1,600.00

18"–20".. $ 2,000.00–2,100.00

24".. $ 2,500.00–2,700.00

Mold 189, **open mouth**

15".. $ 700.00–750.00

18"–22".. $ 850.00–1,000.00

Bébé Cosmopolite

19"–20".. $ 800.00–900.00

24"–28".. $ 1,000.00–1,200.00

Shoulder Head Child, 1885 on, open mouth, glass eyes, kid or cloth body

Molds 139 or no numbers

12".. $ 120.00–145.00

15"–16".. $ 150.00–185.00

18"–22".. $ 200.00–250.00

24"–25".. $ 275.00–300.00

MAX HANDWERCK

1899–1928, Waltershausen, Thüringia, Germany. Made dolls and doll bodies, registered trademark, "Bébé Elite."

Used heads made by Goebel.

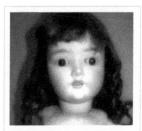

25" Max Handwerck, bisque, undressed: $325. **Photo courtesy of Gloria's Antique Dolls.**

Child

Bisque socket head, open mouth, sleep or set eyes, jointed composition body. Size numbers only or molds 283, 285, 286, 291, 297, 307, and others

> 16"–18" .... $ 300.00–325.00

> 22"–26" .... $ 375.00–475.00

> 28"–32" .... $ 600.00–675.00

Bébé Elite, **1900 on, bisque socket head, mohair wig, glass sleep eyes, mohair lashes, open mouth, pierced ears, jointed composition/wood body, marks: "Max Handwerck Bébé Elite 286 12 Germany" on back of head, 1/3 less if on baby body**

> 13"–15" .... $ 275.00–325.00

> 19"–21" .... $ 375.00–425.00

> 27"–29" .... $ 450.00–525.00

Googly: See Googly category.

HARD PLASTIC

Hard plastic was developed during WWII and became a staple of the doll industry after the war ended. Numerous companies made hard plastic dolls from 1948 through the 1950s; dolls have all hard plastic jointed bodies, sleep eyes, lashes, synthetic wig, open or closed mouths. Marks: none, letters, little known, or other unidentified companies.

Hard Plastic Child, **1950s, maker unknown, some marked U.S.A., some on "magic skin" lytex bodies, original clothing and wig**

> 14"–16" .... $ 100.00–150.00

> 18"–20" .... $ 175.00–225.00

Advance Doll & Toy Company, **1954 on. Made heavy walking hard plastic dolls, metal rollers on molded shoes, named Winnie and Wanda, later models had vinyl heads**

> 18"–24" .... $ 100.00–150.00

16" Sweet Dolly, unknown maker, hard plastic, mint condition: $200. **Photo courtesy of Alderfer Auction Company, Inc.**

27" Rita, Pan's Doll Co, hard plastic, mint condition: $300. **Photo courtesy of McMasters Harris Apple Tree Doll Auctions.**

Artisan Novelty Company, **1950s, hard plastic, wide crotch**

Raving Beauty

20"..$ 100.00–150.00

Black ....$ 225.00–275.00

Duchess Doll Corporation, **1948–1950s, made small hard plastic adult dolls, mohair wigs, painted or sleep eyes, jointed arms, stiff or jointed neck, molded and painted shoes, about 7"–7½" tall, costumes stapled onto body, elaborate costumes, exceptional dolls may be more**

7"..$ 8.00–10.00

Eugenia Doll Co., **1950s, New York City**

16"–20"...$ 70.00–120.00

Fortune Doll Company, **a subsidiary of the Beehler Arts Company**

Pam **(Ginny-type), hard plastic, sleep eyes, synthetic wig, closed mouth, strung or walker. Elaborate costumes bring higher end of range**

8"..$ 40.00–50.00

Black ....$ 60.00–75.00

Imperial Crown Toy Co. (Impco), **1950s, made hard plastic or vinyl dolls, rooted hair, synthetic wigs**

Hard Plastic Walker

14"..$ 35.00–50.00

20"..$ 40.00–60.00

Vinyl

16"..$ 65.00–75.00

Kendall Company

Miss Curity, **1953, hard plastic, jointed only at shoulders, blond wig, blue sleep eyes, molded-on shoes, painted stockings, uniform sheet vinyl, "Miss Curity" marked in blue on hat**

7½" ....$ 30.00–40.00

18" Wanda Walker, Advance Doll and Toy Company, hard-plastic, Mint with box: $175. **Photo courtesy of McMasters Harris Apple Tree Doll Auctions.**

Nun Doll, **all hard plastic, sleep eyes, unmarked**

7½" .... $ 18.00–25.00

12" .... $ 45.00–65.00

17" .... $ 100.00–125.00

Pedigree Dolls & Toys, **England, 1950s on, made hard plastic and vinyl dolls**

Posey Walker, **walker, sleep eyes, wig**

20"–22" .... $ 225.00–300.00

Black

16"–22" .... $ 150.00–250.00

Roberta Doll Co.

Walker

14" .... $ 40.00–50.00

Roddy of England, **1950–1960s, made by D.G. Todd & Co. Ltd., Southport, England, hard plastic walker, sleep or set eyes**

11"–12½" .... $ 40.00–50.00

22" .... $ 125.00–175.00

Rosebud of England, **1950s–1960s, started in Raunds, Northamptonshire, England, by T. Eric Smith shortly after WWII**

Miss Rosebud, **hard plastic, various shades of blue sleep eyes, glued-on mohair wig, jointed at the neck and hips, marked "Miss Rosebud" in script on her back and head and "MADE IN ENGLAND" on her upper back, more for rare examples or mint-in-box dolls**

7½" .... $ 85.00–120.00

Ross Products

Tina Cassini, **designed by Oleg Cassini, hard plastic, marked on back torso, "TINA CASSINI," clothes tagged "Made in British Crown Colony of Hong Kong"**

12" .... $ 100.00–120.00

Costume, **MIB** .... $ 100.00–125.00

Royal Doll Co.

Hard plastic girl, **1950s, similar to Sweet Sue by American Character**

Wearing formal

20"...$ 40.00–50.00

Virga, **a subsidiary of the Beehler Arts Company, marketed Ginny type dolls under various lines**

Playmates

8"...$ 50.00–65.00

Lolly Pop dolls, **hair colors such as pink, blue, bright yellow**

8"...$ 55.00–75.00

CARL HARTMANN

8.5" Globe baby, Carl Hartmann, bisque: $300. **Photo courtesy of McMasters Harris Apple Tree Doll Auctions.**

1889–1930s, Neustadt, Germany. Made and exported bisque and celluloid dolls, especially small dolls in regional costumes, called Globe Babies.

Child, **bisque socket head, open mouth, jointed composition and wood body**

22"–24" ....$ 350.00–425.00

Shoulder-head, **kid body**

22"–26" ....$ 100.00–150.00

Globe Baby, **bisque socket head, glass sleep eyes, open mouth, four teeth, mohair or human hair wig, five-piece papier-mâché or composition body with painted shoes and stockings**

8"–12" ....$ 300.00–400.00

KARL HARTMANN

24", Karl Hartmann, bisque: $475.
Photo courtesy of McMasters Harris Apple Tree Doll Auctions.

1911–1926, Stockheim, Germany. Doll factory, made and exported dolls. Advertised ball-jointed dolls, characters, and papier-mâché dolls. Marked "KH."

Child, **bisque socket head, open mouth, glass eyes, composition body**

No Mold Number

16"–18"	$ 200.00–250.00
22"–26"	$ 450.00–500.00
27"–32"	500.00–550.00

Mold 283, 285, 287, 305

22–24"	$ 300.00–350.00

HASBRO

1923, Pawtucket, Rhode Island. Founded by the Hassenfeld Brothers. Began making toys in 1943. One of their most popular toys was the G.I. Joe series which came out in 1964. Dolls listed are in good condition with original clothing and accessories, mint-in-package usually brings double the value listed. Dolls in played with condition bring one-third to one-half the value of complete examples.

Aimee, **1972, rooted hair, amber sleep eyes, jointed vinyl body, long dress, sandals, earrings**

18"	$ 35.00–45.00

Baby Alive, **1992, east, drinks, wets, vinyl**

14"	$ 30.00–35.00

4.5" Dolly Darling, Hasbro, vinyl, MIB: $90. **Photo courtesy Fourty Fifty Sixty.**

24" My Buddy (black) Hasbro, vinyl, MIB: $200. **Photo courtesy of Doll Hugs Shop.**

Bridal Sewing doll, **1950s, hard plastic doll, boxed with fabric and sewing supplies**

    1 doll set .... $ 40.00–45.00

    6 doll set .... $ 100.00–120.00

Charlie's Angels, **1977, vinyl, Jill, Sabrina, Kelly, Kris**

    8½" .... $ 20.00–25.00

Dolly Darling, **1965**

    4½" .... $ 35.00–45.00

    Hat Box Series, **molded hair** ....$ 40.00–50.00

Flying Nun

    4⅞" .... $ 35.00–40.00

    12" .... $ 75.00–100.00

Jem: See Jem section.

Leggie, **1972**

    10" .... $ 35.00–45.00

    Black .... $ 40.00–50.00

Little Miss No Name, **1965**

    15" .... $ 100.00–125.00

Maxie, **1987, and her friends Rob, Ashley, Kimberly and others, vinyl fashion doll**

    11½" .... $ 15.00–20.00

Moon Dreamers, **1986, vinyl**

    5½" .... $ 30.00–35.00

My Beautiful Doll, **1989, vinyl, painted eyes**

    17½" .... $ 35.00–45.00

My Buddy, **1985, vinyl and cloth boy**

    24" .... $ 75.00–95.00

12" GI Joe Action Soldier, Hasbro, vinyl, MIB: $250. **Photo courtesy of Morphy Auctions.**

12.5" Rock N'Curl Jem, Hasbro, vinyl, MIB: $125. **Photo courtesy of Charlotte's Web Vintage Dolls and Collectibles.**

My Buddy's Kid Sister

20"... $ 40.00–50.00

Peteena Poodle, **1966, vinyl fashion doll poodle**

9½" .... $ 175.00–225.00

Pippi Longstocking, **1973, vinyl**

12"... $ 20.00–30.00

Real Baby, **1984, designed by J. Turner**

18"... $ 45.00–60.00

Show Biz Babies, **1967, 4"**

Mama & Papas $150.00–175.00each

Peter Noone, Herman's Hermits $120.00–140.00

Monkees

Individual $75.00–80.00

Set of four..$325.00–350.00

Storykins, **1967, 3", includes Cinderella, Goldilocks, Prince Charming, Rumpelstiltskin, Sleeping Beauty**

.... $ 30.00–40.00 each

Sweet Cookie, **1972, vinyl, with cooking accessories**

18"... $ 75.00–95.00

World of Love Dolls, **1971**

Love, Peace, Flower

9"... $ 18.00–25.00

Music... $ 40.00–50.00

Soul (black) .... $ 45.00–55.00

Adam... $ 30.00–40.00

G.I. Joe Action Figures, 1964, hard plastic head with facial scar, painted hair, and no beard. Dolls listed are in good condition with original clothing and accessories. MIB can bring double the values listed.

G.I. Joe Action Soldier, **flocked hair, Army fatigues, brown jump boots, green plastic cap, training manual, metal dog tag, two sheets of stickers**

11½" .... $ 125.00–175.00

Painted hair $125.00–250.00

Black .... $ 300.00–350.00

Green Beret, **teal green fatigue jacket, four pockets, pants, Green Beret cap with red unit flashing, M-16 rifle, 45 automatic pistol with holster, tall brown boots, four grenades, camouflage scarf, and field communication set**

11" .... $ 125.00–175.00

G.I. Joe Action Marine, **camouflage shirt, pants, brown boots, green plastic cap, metal dog tag, insignia stickers, and training manual**

11" .... $ 125.00–175.00

G.I. Joe Action Sailor, **blue chambray work shirt, blue denim work pants, black boots, white plastic sailor cap, dog tag, rank insignia stickers**

11" .... $ 175.00–200.00

G.I. Joe Action Pilot, **orange flight suit, black boots, dog tag, stickers, blue cap, training manual**

11" .... $ 175.00–250.00

Dolls only, **nude** .... $ 55.00–75.00

G.I. Joe Action Soldier of the World, **1966, figures in this set may have any hair and eye color combination, no scar on face, hard plastic heads**

Australian Jungle Fighter

.... $ 395.00–450.00

British Commando, **boxed**

.... $ 525.00–600.00

French Resistance Fighter

.... $ 425.00–500.00

German Storm Trooper

.... $ 500.00–600.00

Japanese Imperial Soldier

.... $ 300.00–400.00

Russian Infantryman

.... $ 475.00–500.00 300

Talking G.I. Joe, 1967–1969, talking mechanism added, semi-hard vinyl head, marks: **"G.I. Joe®//Copyright 1964//By Hasbro®//Pat. No. 3,277,602//Made in U.S.A."**

Talking G.I. Joe Action Soldier, **green fatigues, dog tag, brown boots, insignia, stripes, green plastic fatigue cap, comic book, insert with examples of figure's speech**

....$ 200.00–250.00

Talking G.I. Joe Action Sailor, **denim pants, chambray sailor shirt, dog tag, black boots, white sailor cap, insignia stickers, Navy training manual, illustrated talking comic book, insert examples of figure's speech**

....$ 250.00–350.00

Talking G.I. Joe Action Marine, **camouflage fatigues, metal dog tag, Marine training manual, insignia sheets, brown boots, green plastic cap, comic, and insert**

....$ 175.00–225.00

Talking G.I. Joe Action Pilot, **blue flight suit, black boots, dog tag, Air Force insignia, blue cap, training manual, comic book, insert**

....$ 250.00–350.00

G.I. Joe Action Nurse, **1967, vinyl head, blond rooted hair, jointed hard plastic body, nurse's uniform, cap, Red Cross armband, white shoes, medical bag, stethoscope, plasma bottle, two crutches, bandages, splints, marks: "Patent Pending//©1967 Hasbro®//Made in Hong Kong"**

2,000.00–2,500.00

G.I. Joe, Man of Action, **1970–1975, flocked hair, scar on face, dressed in fatigues with Adventure Team emblem on shirt, plastic cap, marks: "G.I. Joe®//Copyright 1964//By Hasbro®//Pat. No. 3, 277, 602//Made in U.S. A."**

Kung Fu Grip ....$ 200.00–275.00

Talking ....$ 250.00–300.00

G.I. Joe, Adventure Team, **marks: "©1975 Hasbro ®//Pat. Pend. Pawt. R.I.," flocked hair and beard, six team members:**

Air Adventurer, **orange flight suit**

....$ 175.00–225.00

Astronaut, **talking, white flight suit, molded scar, dog tag pull string**

....$ 150.00–200.00

Land Adventurer, **black, tan fatigues, beard, flocked hair, scar**

....$ 275.00–300.00

Land Adventurer, **talking, camouflage fatigues**

....$ 200.00–225.00

Sea Adventurer, **light blue shirt, navy pants**

....$ 250.00–300.00

Talking Adventure Team Commander, **flocked hair, beard, green jacket, and pants**

....$ 400.00–450.00

G.I. Joe Land Adventurer, **flocked hair, beard, camouflage shirt, green pants**

....$ 100.00–150.00

G. I. Joe Negro Adventurer, **flocked hair**

.... $ 250.00–300.00

G. I. Joe, **"Mike Powers, Atomic Man"**

.... $ 65.00–95.00

G.I. Joe Eagle Eye Man of Action

.... $ 100.00–125.00

G.I. Joe Secret Agent, **unusual face, mustache**

.... $ 400.00–450.00

Sea Adventurer w/Kung Fu Grip

.... $ 125.00–145.00

Bulletman, **muscle body, silver arms, hands, helmet, red boots**

.... $ 225.00–275.00

Others

G.I. Joe Air Force Academy, Annapolis, or West Point Cadet

.... $ 300.00–350.00

G.I. Joe Secret Service Agent, **limited edition of 200**

.... $ 225.00–275.00

Jem, 1986–1987, **Jem dolls were patterned after characters in the animated Jem television series, ca. 1985–1988, and include a line of 27 dolls. All-vinyl fashion type with realistically proportioned body, jointed elbows, wrists, and knees, swivel waist, rooted hair, painted eyes, open or closed mouth, and hole in bottom of each foot. All boxes say "Jem" and "Truly Outrageous!" Most came with cassette tape of music from Jem cartoon, plastic doll stand, poster, and hair pick. All 12½" tall, except Starlight Girls, 11".**

Dolls listed are in excellent condition, wearing complete original outfit. MIB can bring double.

Jem and Rio

Jem/Jerrica **1ˢᵗ issue**

4000 .... $ 55.00–75.00

Jem/Jerrica, **star earrings**

.... $ 55.00–75.00

Glitter 'n Gold Jem

4001 .... $ 40.00–55.00

Rock 'n Curl Jem

4002 .... $ 45.00–55.00

Flash 'n Sizzle Jem

4003 .... $ 48.00–56.00

Rio, 1st issue

    4015 .... $ 35.00–45.00

Glitter 'n Gold Rio

    4016 .... $ 25.00–35.00

Glitter 'n Gold Rio, **pale vinyl**

    4016 .... $ 125.00–150.00

Holograms

Synergy

    4020 .... $ 40.00–50.00

Aja, 1st issue

    4201/4005 .... $ 50.00–600.00

Aja, 2nd issue

    4201/4005 .... $ 75.00–90.00

Kimber, 1st issue

    4202/4005 .... $ 40.00–50.00

Kimber, 2nd issue

    4202/4005 .... $ 70.00–80.00

Shana, 1st issue

    4203/4005 .... $ 45.00–55.00

Shana, 2nd issue

    4203/4005 .... $ 100.00–125.00

Danse

    4208 .... $ 35.00–40.00

Video

    4209 .... $ 25.00–30.00

Raya

    4210 .... $ 100.00–125.00

Starlight Girls, **11", no wrist or elbow joints**

Ashley**4211/4025**, Krissie **4212/4025**, Banee **4213/4025**

    .... $ 30.00–45.00

Misfits

Pizzazz, 1st issue

    4204/4010 .... $ 80.00–95.00

Pizzazz, 2nd issue

    4204/4010 .... $ 65.00–75.00

Stormer, 1st issue

4205/4010 .... $ 50.00–60.00

Stormer, **2nd issue**

4205/4010 .... $ 60.00–70.00

Roxy, **1st issue**

4206/4010 .... $ 65.00–70.00

Roxy, **2nd issue**

4206/4010 .... $ 50.00–60.00

Clash

4207/4010 .... $ 65.00–75.00

Jetta

4214 .... $ 40.00–45.00

Accessories

Concert Clash game, by Milton Bradley, 1986

.... $ 25.00

Glitter 'n Gold Roadster

.... $ 100.00–150.00

Rock 'n Roadster............................. $ 35.00–40.00

JEm Guitar....................................... $ 30.00–40.00

Backstager.. $ 30.00–35.00

Star Stage... $ 40.00–45.00

MTV jacket **(promo)** .... $ 100.00–125.00

Integrity Toys reissues, 2012

Hollywood Jem, sold for   **$ 633.00 online**

HERTEL SCHWAB & CO.

1910–1930s, Stutzhaus, Germany. Porcelain factory founded by August Hertel and Heinrich Schwab, both designed doll heads used by Borgfeldt, Kley and Hahn, Koenig & Wernicke, Louis Wolf, and others. Made china and bisque heads as well as all-porcelain, most with character faces. Molded hair or wig, painted blue or glass eyes (often blue-gray), open mouth with tongue or closed mouth, socket or shoulder heads. Usually marked with mold number and "Made in Germany" or mark of company that owned the mold.

Baby, **1910 on, bisque head, molded hair or wig, open or open-closed mouth, teeth, sleep or painted eyes, bent-leg baby composition body**

 23" mold 151, Hertel & Schwab, bisque: $400. **Photo courtesy of Alderfer Auction Company, Inc.**

 18" mold 140, Hertel & Schwab, bisque: $5,000. **Photo courtesy of Ann Lloyd Antique Dolls.**

Mold 130, 142, 150, 151, 152, 159

8"–12"...$ 200.00–300.00

15"–16"...$ 300.00–350.00

19"–20"...$ 300.00–400.00

22"–24"...$ 500.00–550.00

25"–27"...$ 550.00–650.00

Toddler body

14"...$ 400.00–450.00

20"...$ 400.00–500.00

Molds 125, 127 (**so-called Patsy Baby**)

9"–12"...$ 1,100.00–1,200.00

Molds 120, 126 (**so-called Skippy Baby**)

9"–12"...$ 825.00–900.00

Child

Mold 111, **character face, closed mouth, glass sleep eyes, wigged**
11" 7,200.00–7,400.00

17"–18"...$ 16,000.00–17,000.00

Mold 127, **ca. 1915, character face, solid dome with molded hair, sleep eyes, open mouth, Patsytype**

15"...$ 1,500.00–1,800.00

17"...$ 2,000.00–2,400.00

Mold 134, **ca. 1915, character face, sleep eyes, closed mouth**

15"–18"...$ 6,000.00–6,900.00

Mold 136, **ca. 1912, "Made in Germany," dolly face, open mouth**

7"–8"...$ 22500–275.00

18"–20"...$ 300.00–340.00

24"–25"...$ 350.00–400.00

Mold 140, **ca. 1912, character, glass eyes, open-closed laughing mouth**

    12"–18" .... **$ 3,400.00–5,000.00**

Mold 141, **ca. 1912, character, painted eyes, open-closed mouth**

    12"–14" .... **$ 2,500.00–2,900.00**

Mold 149, **ca. 1912, character, glass eyes, closed mouth, wigged**
18" sold for $5,280.00 at auction

Mold 178, **character, open/ closed mouth, wigged, ball-jointed body**

    6"–7" .... **$ 375.00–435.00**

Mold 182, **dolly face, open mouth, wigged, ball-jointed body**

    18"–23" .... **$ 450.00–575.00**

Googly: See Googly category.

HERTWIG & CO.

4" Hertwig Half-bisque: $125. **Photo courtesy of Private Collector.**

1864–1940s, Kutzhütte, Thüringia, Germany. Porcelain factory producing china and bisque dolls. Some distributed by Butler Brothers.

Half-Bisque Dolls, 1911 on, bisque head and torso, molded clothing, lower body cloth, lower arms and legs bisque

Child

    4½" **$125.00–150.00**

Adult

    6½" **$175.00–225.00**

All Bisque: including animals in crochet outfits, See All-Bisque section.

China Name Dolls: See China section.

Bisque Bonnet-Head: See Bonnet-Head section.

ERNST HEUBACH

15.5" mold 275, Ernst Heubach, bisque, shoulder head: $175.
Photo courtesy of Minton's Doll and Curiosity Shop.

1887–1930s, Köppelsdorf, Germany. In 1919, the son of Armand Marseille married the daughter of Ernst Heubach and merged the two factories. Mold numbers range from 250 to 452. They made porcelain heads for Dressel (Jutta), Revalo, and others. Dolls listed are in good condition, appropriately dressed.

Child, 1888 on

Mold 1900, 225, 275, or Horseshoe Mark, **shoulder head, open mouth, glass eyes, kid or cloth body**

  10"–12" $75.00–150.00

  18"–22" $175.00–200.00

  26"–28" $275.00–300.00

Molds 250, 251, 302, and others, **socket head, composition body, open mouth, glass eyes**

  8"–10" $150.00–200.00

  8"–9" on flapper body $250.00–300.00

  13"–15" $225.00–250.00

  16"–19" $225.00–275.00

  23"–25" $300.00–350.00

  27"–32" $400.00–450.00

  36" $500.00–575.00

Painted bisque

  8"–12" $80.00–90.00

  16" $100.00–125.00

Baby, 1910 on, open mouth, glass eyes, socket head, wig, five-piece bent-leg composition body, add more for toddler body, flirty eyes

Molds 267, 300, 320, 321, 342, and others

5"–6½"...................................$225.00–250.00

8"–11"...................................$125.00–175.00

14"–17"...................................$225.00–275.00

19"–21"...................................$325.00–375.00

25"–27"...................................$425.00–475.00

Painted bisque, **flirty eyes**

16"–24"...................................$300.00–425.00

Character Child, **1910 on, painted eyes**

Molds 261, 262, 271, and others, **bisque shoulder head, cloth body**

12"...................................$225.00–300.00

Mold 312 **(for Seyfarth & Reinhard)**

14"...................................$250.00–275.00

18"...................................$325.00–350.00

28"...................................$450.00–525.00

Mold 417 Elisabeth, **glass eyes, resembles Armand Marseille Just Me**

7"...................................$1,800.00–1,900.00

11"–12"...................................$1,700.00–1,800.00

Baby, Newborn, **1925 on solid dome, molded and painted hair, glass eyes, closed mouth, cloth body, composition or celluloid hands**

Molds 338, 339, 340, 348, 349

10"–12"...................................$150.00–225.00

14"–16"...................................$275.00–375.00

17"...................................$400.00–450.00

Black, **mold 399, 444**

9"–12"...................................$250.00–375.00

GEBRÜDER HEUBACH

1910–1938, Lichte, Thüringia, Germany. Porcelain factory founded in 1804 but did not make dolls until 1910. Made bisque heads and all-bisque dolls, characters, either socket or shoulder head, molded hair or wigs, sleeping or intaglio eyes, in heights from 4" to 26". Provided heads to other companies including Bauersachs, Cuno & Otto Dressel, Eisemann & Co., and Gebruder Ohlhaver. Mold numbers from 556 to 10633. Sunburst or square marks, more dolls with square marks. Dolls listed are in good condition, appropriately dressed.

16" mold 7407, Gebruder Heubach, bisque, closed mouth, socket head: $2,900. **Photo courtesy of Sweetbriar Auctions.**

12" mold 7622, Gebruder Heubach, bisque, socket head: $900. **Photo courtesy of Withington Auction Inc.**

Marked "Heubach," **no mold number**

Closed mouth, **intaglio eyes, wigged**

8"... $300.00–500.00

Closed mouth pouty, **intaglio eyes, painted hair**

6½"–8"... $250.00–375.00

10"–15"... $375.00–450.00

Smile, painted eyes

15"... $3,400.00–3,500.00

Lady doll, **open or closed mouth, glass eyes, mold 7625, 7635, 7925, 7926, others**

10"–11"... $2,000.00–2,400.00

14"–16"... $2,800.00–3,500.00

22"... $4,000.00–4,500.00

Animal head, **bears, cats, etc on five-piece composition child doll bodies**

6"–8"... $1,600.00–1,800.00

Too few in database for reliable range.

Marked Heubach Googly: See Googly category.

Character Child

Shoulder Head

Mold 5392, **Boy, molded hair, closed mouth, painted eyes**

17"–19"... $300.00–400.00

Mold 5777, **Dolly Dimple, shoulder head version**

17"–19"... $1,200.00–1,500.00

Mold 6688, 6692, **ca. 1912, shoulder head version, sunburst, intaglio eyes, closed mouth pouty**

14"–16"... $450.00–550.00

20"–23"... $600.00–700.00

14" mold 8221, Gebruder Heubach, bisque, shoulder head: $700. **Photo courtesy of Joyce Romer.**

Mold 6736, **ca. 1912, square mark, painted eyes, laughing mouth**

9"–13"...$250.00–350.00

16"..$700.00–750.00

Mold 7072, **ca. 1912, closed mouth, molded hair, painted eyes**

22"–..$750.00–850.00

Mold 7184, **ca. 1912, open-closed mouth, crying, intaglio eyes**

12"..$750.00–800.00

Mold 7644, **ca. 1910, "Our Pet," sunburst or square mark, painted eyes, open-closed laughing mouth**

9"–10"..$375.00–425.00

14"..$650.00–700.00

17"..$800.00–900.00

20"..$1,000.00–1,200.00

Mold 7802, **ca. 1912, closed mouth pouty, molded hair, intaglio eyes**

14"–16"...$150.00–200.00

Mold 7844, **ca. 1912, open/closed laughing mouth, molded hair, intaglio eyes**

14"–23"...$300.00–400.00

Mold 7850, **ca. 1912, "Coquette," open-closed mouth**

10"–12"...$650.00–750.00

15"..$825.00–875.00

Mold 7853, **ca. 1912, downcast eyes**

14"..$1,600.00–1,800.00

Mold 8221, **square mark, dome, intaglio eyes, open-closed mouth**

14"..$650.00–700.00

Mold 8714, **Whistler, intaglio eyes, hair molded**

14"..$650.00–700.00

Mold 9139,**open-closed mouth singing, intaglio eyes, hair molded**

19"...$2,600.00–2,800.00

Mold 9355, **ca. 1914, square mark, glass eyes, open mouth**

13"...$800.00–850.00

19"...$1,100.00–1,250.00

Socket-Head

Mold 5636, **ca. 1912, glass eyes, open-closed laughing mouth, teeth**

12"–13"...$950.00–1,000.00

15"–18"...$1,100.00–1,500.00

21"...$1,700.00–1,800.00

Mold 5689, **ca. 1912, sunburst mark, smiling open mouth**

14"...$1,100.00–1,200.00

17"...$1,400.00–1,600.00

20"–22"...$1,800.00–2,200.00

Mold 5730, **"Santa," ca. 1912, sunburst mark, made for Hamburger & Co.**

14"–16"...$650.00–700.00

19"–22"...$800.00–1,000.00

24"–26"...$1,200.00–1,500.00

Mold 5777, **"Dolly Dimple," ca. 1913, open mouth, for Hamburger & Co.**

12"–14"...$900.00–1,000.00

16"–19"...$1,000.00–1,400.00

22"–24"...$1,600.00–2,000.00

Mold 6894, **intaglio eyes, closed mouth**

9"–12"...$400.00–450.00

20"–22"...$800.00– $900.00

Mold 6969, **ca. 1912, socket head, square mark, glass eyes, closed mouth**

7"–9"...$1,050.00–1,200.00

12"–13"...$1,200.00–1,500.00

16"–18"...$2,200.00–2,800.00

24"–26"...$3,500.00–4,000.00

Mold 6970, **ca. 1912, sunburst, glass eyes, closed mouth**

7"–9"...$900.00–1,000.00

12"–13"...$1,400.00–1,600.00

16"–18"...$1,800.00–2,100.00

20"–24"...$2,500.00–3,000.00

Molds 7246, 7247, 7248, **ca. 1912, sunburst or square mark, closed mouth, glass eyes**

7"–10" $700.00–900.00

12"–13" $1,200.00–1,8000.00

16"–18" $2,200.00–2,500.00

20"–24" $2,900.00–3,400.00

26"–28" $3,300.00–3,500.00

Mold 7407, **character, glass eyes, open-closed mouth**

16" $2,800.00–3,000.00

Mold 7550, **character, glass eyes, open-closed mouth**

12" $1,200.00–1,500.00

Mold 7602, 7603, **ca. 1912, molded hair tufts, intaglio eyes**

10"–12" $500.00–600.00

15"–18" $700.00–800.00

Mold 7604, **ca. 1912, open-closed mouth, intaglio eyes**

12"–14" $650.00–700.00

20" $1,100.00–1,200.00

Mold 7608, **pouty**

9"–11" $300.00–400.00

Mold 7622, 7623, **ca. 1912, intaglio eyes, closed or open-closed mouth**

16"–18" $1,100.00–1,300.00

Mold 7644, **ca. 1912, open/closed laughing child, intaglio eyes, molded hair**

12"–13" $500.00–600.00

Mold 7711, **ca. 1912, glass eyes, open mouth, flapper body**

9"–10" $1,000.00–1,200.00

18" $6,000.00–7,000.00

Molds 7763, 7788, 7850 (**Coquette**), **ca. 1912, molded hair with bow**

9"–11" $650.00–850.00

14"–15" $1,100.00–1,300.00

18"–20" $1,600.00–1,800.00

Mold 7764, **ca. 1912, open-closed mouth singing, intaglio eyes, molded hair**

17" $3,500.00–3,700.00

Mold 7911, **ca. 1912, open-closed mouth with tongue, intaglio eyes, molded hair**

16" $1,200.00–1,300.00

Mold 8004, **ca. 1912, intaglio eyes, closed mouth, molded hair**

9"–11" $500.00–550.00

Mold 8178, **ca. 1912, open-closed mouth with teeth, intaglio eyes, wigged**

    15".. $1,000.00–1,200.00

Mold 8191, **"Crooked Smile," ca. 1912, square mark, intaglio eyes, laughing mouth**

    11"–12".. $800.00–1,000.00

    14"–16".. $1,200.00–1,500.00

Mold 8193, **dolly face, sleep eyes, open mouth**

    11"–13".. $750.00–800.00

Mold 8317, **wig, open-closed smiling mouth, eight teeth, glass eyes**

    16".. $3,200.00–3,400.00

    19".. $4,600.00–4,800.00

Mold 8381, **"Princess Juliana," molded hair, ribbon, painted eyes, closed mouth**

    14"–16".. $8,500.00–10,000.00

Mold 8413, **ca. 1914, wig, sleep eyes, open-closed mouth with teeth**

    16".. $2,800.00–3,437.00

Mold 8774, **"Whistling Jim," ca. 1914, smoker or whistler, square mark, flange neck, intaglio eyes, molded hair, cloth body, bellows**

    9".. $600.00–700.00

    13"–14".. $775.00–825.00

Mold 9390, **closed mouth, molded hair with bow one side, intaglio eyes,**

    9"–12".. $200.00–300.00

Mold 9457, **ca. 1914, square mark, dome, intaglio eyes, Princess Angeline, Native American woman, wrinkled face, downcast eyes, wigged, believed to be a portrait of the daughter of Chief Seattle**

    13"–15".. $2,000.00–2,700.00

    18".. $3,800.00–4,000.00

Mold 9590, **closed mouth, intaglio eyes, molded page boy hairstyle with molded bow**

    7"–10".. $550.00–700.00

Mold 10532, **ca. 1920, square mark, open mouth, five-piece toddler body**

    8½".. $800.00–900.00

    13½".. $1,000.00–1,100.00

    20"–22".. $1,400.00–1,600.00

    25".. $1,700.00–1,900.00

Mold 11173, **"Tiss Me," socket head, wig**

    8".. $2,000.00–2,500.00

Too few in database for reliable range.

Character Baby, **socket head, 1911 on, bisque head, bent-limb body**

Mold 6894, 6897, 7759, 7602, 7604, **all ca. 1912, sunburst or square mark, intaglio eyes, closed mouth, molded hair**

    6"–7".. $275.00–325.00

    9"–13"... $425.00–500.00

    15"... $600.00–700.00

    20"... $800.00–900.00

Toddler

    14".. $625.00–675.00

Mold 7620, **open-closed mouth with 2 teeth, molded hair, intaglio eyes**

    8"–12"... $175.00–300.00

Molds 7877, 7977, **"Baby Stuart," ca. 1912, socket head, molded bonnet, closed mouth, painted eyes**

    6"–9".. $650.00–800.00

    11"–13"... $1,300.00–1,600.00

    15"... $1,700.00–2,000.00

Mold 7975, **"Baby Stuart," ca. 1912, socket head, glass eyes, removable molded bisque bonnet**

    9"–13"... $2,200.00–2,400.00

Molds 8326, **"Baby Stuart," shoulder head, molded bonnet, closed mouth, painted eyes**

    11"–13"... $500.00–600.00

Mold 8420, **ca. 1914, square mark, glass eyes, closed mouth**

    10".. $650.00–750.00

    15"... $1,200.00–1,400.00

All Bisque: See All-Bisque section.

E. I. HORSMAN

1878–1980s, New York City. Founded by Edward Imeson Horsman as company importing, assembling, wholesaling, and distributing various dolls and doll lines. From 1909 to 1919 they distributed Aetna Doll & Toy company's dolls. In 1919 the two companies merged. Eventually Horsman made their own dolls as well as distributing other lines. They took out their first patent for a complete doll in 1909 for a Billiken doll. They made dolls of composition, rubber, hard plastic, and vinyl.

Early Composition on Cloth Body, **composition head, sometimes lower arms, cloth body. Dolls listed are in good condition with original clothing, add more for exceptional doll.**

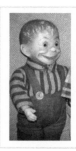

13" Mike, Gene Carr Kid, Horsman, composition: $300. **Photo courtesy of My Dear Dolly.**

20" Brite Star, Horsman, composition, Mint condition w/hang tag: $475. **Photo courtesy of Dollyology Vintage Dolls**

Baby Bumps, **1910–1917, composition head, cloth cork stuffed body, blue and white cloth label on romper, copy of K*R #100 Baby mold**

    11".. **$225.00–$250.00**

    Black **$250.00–300.00**

Baby Butterfly, **1914 on, composition head, hands, cloth body, painted hair and features**

    13".. **$250.00–300.00**

    15".. **$350.00–400.00**

Billiken, **1909, composition head, molded hair, slanted eyes, smiling closed mouth, on stuffed mohair or velvet body, cloth label on body, "Billiken" on right foot**

    12".. **$400.00–450.00**

Campbell Kids, **1910 on, designed by Helen Trowbridge, based on Grace Drayton's drawings, composition head, painted and molded hair, side-glancing painted eyes, closed smiling mouth, composition arms, cloth body and feet, mark: "EIH © 1910"; cloth label on sleeve, "The Campbell Kids// Trademark by //Joseph Campbell// Mfg. by E.I. Horsman Co."**

    12".. **$200.00–250.00**

Can't Break "Em Characters, **1911 on**

Child, **boy or girl**

    11"–13".. **$275.00–325.00**

Cotton Joe, **black**

    13".. **$300.00–375.00**

Little Mary Mix-up

    15".. **$325.00–350.00**

Master & Miss Sam, **in patriotic outfits**

    15".. **$350.00–375.00**

Polly Pru

    13".. **$325.00–350.00**

Fairy, **1911, composition head and hands, molded hair, painted side-glancing eyes, cloth body, designed by Helen**

20" Jackie, Horsman, vinyl: $100. **Photo courtesy of My Dear Dolly.**

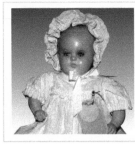

11" baby, Horsman, composition: $70. **Photo courtesy of Enchantments by Rhonda.**

Trowbridge, based on Little Fairy Soap advertising by N.K. Fairbanks Co., mark "EIH © 1911"

13" $325.00–400.00

Gene Carr Kids, **1915–1916, composition head, molded and painted hair, painted eyes, open/closed smiling mouth with teeth, big ears, cloth body, composition hands, original outfit, cloth tag reads: "MADE GENE CARR KIDS U.S.A.//FROM NEW YORK WORLD'S//LADY BOUNTIFUL COMIC SERIES//By E.I. HORSMAN CO. NY"**

Blink, Lizzie, Mike, Skinney

14" $250.00–300.00

Snowball, **black** $450.00–500.00

Gold Medal Baby, **1911 on, line of baby dolls with composition head and limbs, upper and lower teeth, included Baby Suck-a-Thumb, Baby Blossom, Baby Premier, and others**

10" $125.00–150.00

12" $150.00–175.00

19" $150.00–200.00

Early All-Composition Dolls

Peek-a-Boo, **1913, designed by Grace Drayton**

8" $150.00–175.00

Peterkin, **1914–1930**

11"–13" $175.00–200.00

Puppy & Pussy Pippin, **1911, designed by Grace Drayton, composition head, plush body**

.... $300.00–350.00

Composition Dolls on Cloth Body, **1920 on**

Brother & Sister, **1937, marked: "Brother//1937//Horsman//©"& "Sister//1937//Horsman//©"**

Brother 21" and Sister 23"

.... $175.00–225.00 each

Ella Cinders, 1928–1929, based on a cartoon character, composition head, black painted hair or wig, round painted eyes, freckles under eyes, open/closed mouth, also came as all-cloth, mark: "1925//MNS"

    14"...$300.00–450.00

    18"...$750.00–850.00

Jackie Coogan, "The Kid," 1921–1922, composition head, hands, molded hair, painted eyes, turtleneck sweater, long gray pants, checked cap, button reads: "HORSMAN DOLL// JACKIE// COOGAN// KID// PATENTED"

    13½" $450.00–500.00

    15½" $550.00–600.00

Jeanie Horsman, 1937, composition head and limbs, painted molded brown hair, sleep eyes, mark: "Jeanie© Horsman"

    14"...$225.00–275.00

All-Composition Dolls, 1930 on

Body Twist, 1930, with jointed waist

    11"...$275.00–425.00

Bright Star, 1937–1946,

    14"...$100.00–150.00

    20"...$200.00–250.00

Campbell Kids, 1930–1940s, all-composition

    13"...$200.00–250.00

Child, including Gold Medal child

    13"–14"..$50.00–75.00

    16"–18"..$125.00–150.00

    21"...$175.00–200.00

HEbee-SHEbees, 1925–1927, based on drawings by Charles Twelvetrees, painted features, molded undershirt and booties or various costumes

    10½" $140.00–175.00

All-bisque HEbee & SHEbee: See All-Bisque section.

JoJo, 1937, blue sleep eyes, wigged, over molded hair, toddler body, mark: "HORSMAN JO JO//©1937"

    13"...$100.00–150.00

Naughty Sue, 1937, jointed body

    16"...$650.00–700.00

Patsy-Type, names such as Sue, Babs, Joan were given to the various sizes

    12"...$100.00–125.00

    14"...$150.00–200.00

16" Naughty Sue, Horsman, composition: $675. **Photo courtesy of Sara Bernstein's Dolls.**

Roberta, **1937, all-composition**

16"..$325.00–375.00

Sweetheart, **1938, composition, hard rubber arms**

24"–28"..$300.00–350.00

Composition Baby, **1920s–1940s**

Buttercup, **1931, composition flange neck head, arms, legs, cloth body, closed mouth, sleep, marked**

12"–19"..$400.00–800.00

Dimples, **1927–1937 on, composition head, arms, cloth body, bent-leg body or bent-limb baby body, molded dimples, open mouth, sleep or painted eyes, marked "E.I. H."**

13"–14"..$125.00–175.00

16"–18"..$175.00–275.00

20"–22"..$250.00–350.00

Toddler

20"..$300.00–350.00

24"..$400.00–425.00

Tynie Baby, **ca. 1924–1929, bisque or composition head, sleep or painted eyes, cloth body, some all-bisque, marks: "©1924//E.I. HORSMAN//CO. INC." or "E.I.H. Co. 1924" on composition or "©1924 by//E I Horsman Co. Inc//Germany//37" incised on bisque head**

All-bisque, **with wardrobe, cradle**

9"..$2,500.00–3,000.00

Bisque, **closed mouth sleep eyes**

8"–10"..$90.00–150.00

12" –15"..$200.00–250.00

Composition, **heads and arms, cloth body**

14"...$100.00–125.00

18"...$150.00–175.00

21"...$175.00–200.00

Vinyl, **1950s, boxed**

15"...$40.00–50.00

1974 reissue, boxed

12"...$15.00–20.00

1991 reissue, boxed

12"...$10.00–15.00

Mama Dolls, 1920 on, **composition head, arms, and lower legs, cloth body with crier and stitched hip joints so lower legs will swing, painted or sleep eyes, mohair or molded hair, models including Peggy Ann, Rosebud, and others**

14"–15"...$100.00–125.00

19"–24"...$150.00–200.00

Hard Plastic and Vinyl, **dolls listed are in excellent condition with original clothing and tags, allow more for mint-in-box doll, add more for accessories or wardrobe**

Angelove, **1974, plastic/vinyl made for Hallmark**

12"...$12.00–15.00

Answer Doll, **1966, button in back moves head**

10"...$18.00–25.00

Baby Dimples, **1990, vinyl reissue**

19"–21"...$30.00–40.00

Baby First Tooth, **1966, vinyl head, limbs, cloth body, open/closed mouth with tongue and one tooth, molded tears on cheeks, rooted blond hair, painted blue eyes, mark: "©Horsman Dolls Inc. //10141"**

16"...$30.00–40.00

Baby Grow Up, **1966, vinyl, one body with interchangable child arms & legs, girl's head, baby arms & legs, and baby head**

16"...$15.00–20.00

Baby Sofskin, **1972 on, vinyl**

12"–15"...$20.00–25.00

Baby Tweaks, **1967, vinyl head, cloth body, inset eyes, rooted saran hair, mark: "54// HORSMAN DOLLS INC.//Copyright 1967/67191" on head**

20"...$50.00–60.00

Ballerina, **1957, vinyl, one-piece body and legs, jointed elbows**

18"...$60.00–75.00

Betty, **1951, all-vinyl, one-piece body and limbs**

14" $50.00–60.00

Vinyl head, **hard plastic body**

16" $20.00–25.00

Betty Ann, **vinyl head, hard plastic body**

19" $40.00–50.00

Betty Jane, **vinyl head, hard plastic body**

25" $65.00–75.00

Betty Jo, **vinyl head, hard plastic body**

16" $20.00–30.00

Bright Star, **ca. 1952 on, all hard plastic**

15" $55.00–65.00

1989, reissue, vinyl

17" $25.00–30.00

Bye-Lo Baby, **1972, reissue, molded vinyl head, limbs, cloth body, white nylon organdy bonnet dress, mark: "3 (in square)//HORSMAN DOLLS INC.//©1972"**

14" $30.00–40.00

1980–1990s

14" $15.00–20.00

Celeste, **portrait doll, in frame, eyes painted to side**

12" $25.00–30.00

Cinderella, **1965, vinyl head, hard plastic body, painted eyes to side**

11½" $30.00–40.00

Cindy, **1950s, all hard plastic child, "170"**

15" $75.00–100.00 100

17" $100.00–125.00

19" $150.00–175.00

Cindy Fashion-type doll, **vinyl head, soft vinyl stuffed high-heel body**

15" $60.00–80.00

18" $75.00–150.00

Solid Vinyl Body, **jointed at shoulders and hips, high-heel foot**

10½" $35.00–50.00

Cindy Kay, **1950s+, all-vinyl child with long legs**

15" $70.00–80.00

20" $110.00–125.00

27" $200.00–225.00

Crawling Baby, **1967, vinyl, rooted hair**

 14".. $20.00–25.00

Disney Exculsives, **1981, Cinderella, Snow White, Mary Poppins, Alice in Wonderland**

 8".. $20.00–35.00

Mouseketeer, 1971, **vinyl, boy or girl**

 8".. $18.00–25.00

Elizabeth Taylor, **1976, set came with extra outfits**

 11½"... $25.00–35.00

Floppy, **1958, vinyl head, foam body and legs**

 18".. $20.00–25.00

Flying Nun, **1965, TV character portrayed by Sally Field**

 12".. $85.00–115.00

Gold Medal Doll, **1953, vinyl head, soft vinyl foam stuffed body, molded hair**

 17"–26"...................................... $80.00–125.00

1954, **vinyl, boy**

 12".. $35.00–40.00

 15".. $65.00–75.00

Hansel & Gretel, **1963, vinyl head, hard plastic body, rooted synthetic hair, closed mouth, sleep eyes, marks: "MADE IN USA" on body, on tag, "HORSMAN, Michael Meyerberg, Inc.," "Reproduction of the famous Kinemins in Michael Myerberg's marvelous Technicolor production of Hansel and Gretel"**

 15".. $60.00–70.00 pair

HEbee-SHEbees, **1987, vinyl reissues**

 .... $15.00–25.00

Jackie, **1961, vinyl doll, rooted hair, blue sleep eyes, long lashes, closed mouth, high-heeled feet, small waist, nicely dressed, designed by Irene Szor who says this doll named Jackie was not meant to portray Jackie Kennedy, mark: "HORSMAN//19©61//BC"**

 18"–25"...................................... $80.00–100.00

Lil' David & Lil' Ruth, **1970s, all vinyl, anatomically correct babies**

 12".. $15.00–20.00

Tyine David & Tynie Ruthie

 6".. $15.00–20.00

Lullabye Baby, **1967–1968, vinyl bent-leg body, rooted hair, inset blue eyes, drink and wet feature, musical mechanism, Sears 1968 catalog, came on suedette pillow, in terry-cloth p.j.s, mark: "2580//B144 8 //HORSMAN DOLLS INC//19©67"**

 12".. $40.00–50.00

Mary Poppins, **1965, all in good condition with original clothing, mint-in-box can bring double the value listed**

12"..$30.00–40.00

16"..$60.00–70.00

26", 1966...$70.00–80.00

36"..$250.00–325.00

Mary Poppinss set with extra outfits, **1965**

12 ....$60.00–70.00

Mary Poppins with Michael and Jane, **1966**

12" and 8" $75.00–100.00

1970s version Mary Poppins

12"..$20.00–30.00

Patty Duke, **ca. 1965, vinyl, rooted hair, painted eyes**

12"..$80.00–$100.00

Peggy Pen Pal, **ca. 1970, vinyl, rooted hair, came with writing desk and pen**

18"..$30.00–40.00

Black..$40.00–50.00

Pipi Longstocking, **ca. 1972, vinyl, rooted hair, painted eyes**

11"..$35.00–50.00

Police Woman, **ca. 1976, vinyl, plastic fully articulated body, rooted hair**

9"..$20.00–30.00

Poor Pitiful Pearl, **1963, from cartoon by William Steig, marked on neck: "Horsman 1963"**

11"..$30.00–40.00

17"..$50.00–60.00

Ruthie, **1962**

15"..$25.00–35.00

19"..$45.00–50.00

Softee, **1959, vinyl baby**

15"..$20.00–25.00

Thirsty Walker, **1962**

26"..$25.00–30.00

Ventriloquist dolls, **1973 on, Tessi Talk, Willie Talk, Simon Sez**

16"..$40.00–50.00

MARY HOYER DOLL MFG. CO.

14" Mary Hoyer, hard plastic: $325. **Photo courtesy of Alderfer Auction Company, Inc.**

18" Gigi, Mary Hoyer, hard plastic: $. **Photo courtesy of Morphy Auctions.**

1937–1968, 1990–present, Reading, Pennsylvania. Designed by Bernard Lipfert, all-composition, later hard plastic, then vinyl, swivel neck, jointed body, mohair or human hair wig, sleep eyes, closed mouth, original clothes, or knitted from Mary Hoyer patterns, company reopened by Hoyer's granddaughter in 1990. Dolls listed are in good condition with appropriate clothing, dolls in hard to find outfits bring high end of range.

Composition, **less for painted eyes**

14"..$250.00–450.00

Hard Plastic, **circa 1946 on**

In knit outfit

14"...$250-00–400.00

In tagged Hoyer outfit

14"..$300.00–500.00

Boy in original wig

14"..$425.00–475.00

Modern, **values are for secondary market dolls, dolls are still available at retail**

14"...$125.00–200.00 MIB

Gigi, **circa 1950, with round Mary Hoyer mark found on 14" dolls, only 2,000 made by the Frisch Doll Company**

18"..$800.00–1,200.00

Vinyl, **circa 1957 on**

Vicky, **all-vinyl, high-heeled doll, body bends at waist, rooted saran hair, two larger sizes 12" and 14" were discontinued**

10½"..$90.00–100.00

Margie, **circa 1958, toddler, rooted hair, made by Unique Doll Co.**

10"...$80.00–100.00

Cathy, **circa 1961, infant, made by Unique Doll Co.**

10"...$20.00–25.00

Janie, **circa 1962, baby**

8"...$20.00–25.00

Becky, **circa 1967, girl**

14"...$75.00–100.00

ADOLPH HÜLSS

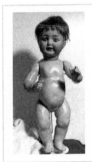

17" mold 156, Adolph Hülss, toddler body, bisque, no clothing: $325. **Photo courtesy of Minton's Doll and Curiosity Shop.**

1915–1930+, Waltershausen, Germany. Made dolls with bisque heads, jointed composition bodies. Trademark: "Nesthakchen," "h" in mold mark often resembles a "b." Heads made by Simon & Halbig.

Baby, bisque socket head, sleep eyes, open mouth, teeth, wig, bent-leg baby, composition body, add more for flirty eyes

Mold 156

9"...$250.00–300.00

14"–15"...$400.00–450.00

17"–19"...$600.00–650.00

23"...$750.00–800.00

Toddler

8"–10"...$500.00–600.00

16"–17"...$550.00–650.00

20"...$700.00–775.00

Painted bisque

22"...$150.00–175.00

Child, **bisque socket-head, wig, sleep eyes, open mouth, teeth, tongue, jointed composition body**

Mold 176

15"..$500.00–550.00

18"..$575.00–650.00

22"..$700.00–775.00

MAISON HURET

18" Huret, bisque, wood body, metal hands, glass eyes: $18,000. **Photo courtesy of McMasters Harris Apple Tree Doll Auctions.**

18" Huret, bisque, Prevost era: $7,500. **Photo courtesy of Morphy Auctions.**

1812–1930 on, France. May have pressed, molded bisque, or china heads, painted or glass eyes, closed mouths, bodies of cloth, composition, gutta-percha, kid, or wood, sometimes metal hands. Used fur or mohair for wigs, had fashion-type body with defined waist. Look for dolls with beautiful painting on eyes and face; painted eyes are more common than glass, but the beauty of the painted features and/or wooden bodies increases the price.

Poupée

Bisque shoulder head, **kid body with bisque lower arms, glass eyes**

15"..$13,000.00–14,000.00

17"–18"..$16,000.00–20,000.00

Round face, **painted blue eyes, kid or cloth body**

16"–18"..$14,000.00–16,000.00

Wood body

17"..$18,000.00–22,000.00

China shoulder head, **kid body, china lower arms**

17"..$12,000.00–17,000.00

Wood body

17"..$19,000.00–23,000.00

Gutta percha body

   17"...$15,000.00–20,000.00

Huret Bébé, **1878, bisque head, glass eyes, closed mouth**

Composition body

   13"...$7,000.00–11,000.00

   20"–..$19,000.00–21,000.00

Gutta percha body

   18"...$70,000.00–80,000.00

Wooden body

   18"...$25,000.00–34,000.00

Prevost Era Lady or Gentleman, **1914–1918, elongated face on composition body**

   17"–18"..$6,000.00–9,000.00

IDEAL NOVELTY AND TOY CO.

22" Princess Beatrix, Ideal, composition: $500. **Photo courtesy of Charlotte's Web Vintage Dolls and Collectibles.**

14" Flossie Flirt, Ideal, composition, MIB: $250. **Photo courtesy of Morphy Auctions.**

1906–1980s, Brooklyn, New York. Produced their own composition dolls in early years. Later made dolls of rubber, hard plastic, vinyl, and cloth. Up to 1950 dolls listed are in good condition with appropriate clothing. After 1950 dolls listed are in excellent condition with original clothing and tags for values listed.

Cloth

Dennis the Menace, **1976, all-cloth, printed doll, comic strip character by Hank Ketcham, blond hair, freckles, wearing overalls, striped shirt**

   7"..$10.00–15.00

   14"..$30.00–35.00

13.5" Baby Snooks (Fannie Brice), Ideal, composition: $200. **Photo courtesy of Alderfer Auction Company, Inc.**

21" Gulliver, Ideal, Deanna Durbin mold, composition: $1,400. **Photo courtesy of Gandtiques.**

Internationals, **1920s on, cloth mask faces, cloth bodies**

    13"... $65.00–90.00

Peanuts Gang, **1976–1978, all-cloth, stuffed printed dolls from Peanuts cartoon strip by Charles Schulz, Charlie Brown, Lucy, Linus, Peppermint Patty, and Snoopy**

    7"... $16.00–20.00

    14"... $22.00–28.00

Snow White and the Seven Dwarves, **1939 on, cloth mask face dolls, cloth body**

Snow White, **black mohair wig, dress with dwarves printed on skirt**

    16"... $250.00–300.00

Dwarves

    10"... $150.00–175.00 each

Strawman, **1939, all-cloth, scarecrow character played by Ray Bolger in Wizard of Oz movie, yarn hair, all original, wearing dark jacket and hat, tan pants, round paper hang tag**

    17"... $900.00–1,200.00

    21"... $1,400.00–1,500.00

Composition

Early Composition Character Children, **composition heads, lower arms and sometimes shoes on cloth body, excelsior stuffed**

Cracker Jack Boy, **1917, sailor suit, carries package of Cracker Jacks**

    14"... $300.00–325.00

Happy Hooligan, **1910**

    21"... $375.00–425.00

Liberty Boy, **1917, molded uniform**

    12"... $150.00–200.00

Naughty Marietta (**Coquette-type**), 1912

    14"... $250.00–300.00

Snookums, **1910, plush body**

14".................................... $500.00–600.00

Uneeda Kid, **1914–1919, original clothing including rain slicker and biscuit box**

15".................................... $350.00–425.00

Zu Zu**Kid, 1916–1917**

14".................................... $175.00–225.00

Child or Toddler, **1913 on, composition head, molded hair, or wigged, painted or sleep eyes, cloth or composition body, may have Ideal diamond mark or hang tag, original clothes**

13".................................... $155.00–225.00

15"–16".................................... $230.00–255.00

18".................................... $295.00–325.00

Baby Doll, **1913 on, composition head, molded hair or wigged, painted or sleep eyes, cloth or composition body, models such as Baby Mine, Our Pet, Prize baby, and others**

15"–18".................................... $250.00–400.00

Mama Doll, **1921 on, composition head and arms, molded hair or wigged, painted or sleep eyes, cloth body with crier and stitched swing leg, lower part composition**

16"–18".................................... $125.00–200.00

20"–24".................................... $225.00–325.00

Babies, **mid 1920s–1940s, composition head, arms and legs, cloth body**

Flossie Flirt, **1924–1931, composition head, limbs, cloth body, crier, tin flirty eyes, open mouth, upper teeth, original outfit, dress, bonnet, socks, and shoes, mark: "IDEAL" in diamond with "U.S. of A"**

14"–16".................................... $120.00–160.00

18"–20".................................... $140.00–180.00

20"–22".................................... $170.00–200.00

24"–28".................................... $200.00–400.00

Tickletoes, **1928–1939, composition head, rubber arms, legs, cloth body, squeaker in each leg, flirty sleep eyes, open mouth, two painted teeth, original organdy dress, bonnet, paper hang tag, marks: "IDEAL" in diamond with "U.S. of A." on head**

14".................................... $125.00–175.00

17".................................... $140.00–200.00

20".................................... $185.00–240.00

Snoozie, **1933 on, composition head, painted hair, hard rubber hands and feet, cloth body, open yawning mouth, molded tongue, sleep eyes, designed by Bernard Lipfert, marks: "©B. Lipfert//Made for Ideal Doll & Toy Corp. 1933" or "©by B. Lipfert" or "IDEAL SNOOZIE//B. LIPFERT" on head**

14"–16".................................... $120.00–225.00

18"–20".................................... $250.00–350.00

9" Jiminy Cricket, Ideal, composition and wood: $400. **Photo courtesy of Phillip Weiss Auctions.**

12" Captain Action, Ideal, vinyl, with box: $425. **Photo courtesy of Morphy Auctions.**

Princess Beatrix, **1938–1943, represents Princess Beatrix of the Netherlands, composition head, arms, legs, cloth body, flirty sleep eyes, fingers molded into fists, original organdy dress and bonnet**

> 14"...$300.00–350.00
>
> 16"–18"..$400.00–450.00
>
> 20"– 22" $500.00–600.00
>
> 26"..$550.00–650.00

Soozie Smiles, **1923, two-faced composition doll with smiling face, sleep or painted eyes, and crying face with tears, molded and painted hair, cloth body and legs, composition arms, original clothes, tag, also in gingham check romper**

> 15"–17"..$225.00–275.00

Composition Child, **1920s–1940s**

Buster Brown, **1929, composition head, hands, legs, cloth body, tin eyes, red outfit. mark: "IDEAL" (in a diamond)**

> 17"..$325.00–375.00

Charlie McCarthy, **1938–1939, hand puppet, composition head, felt hands, molded hat, molded features, wire monocle, cloth body, painted tuxedo, mark: "Edgar Bergen's//©CHARLIE MCCARTHY//MADE IN U.S.A."**

8" 150.00–200.00

Cinderella, **1938–1939, all-composition, brown, blond, or red human hair wig, flirty brown sleep eyes, open mouth, six teeth, same head mold as Ginger, Snow White, Mary Jane with dimple in chin, some wore formal evening gowns of organdy and taffeta, velvet cape, had rhinestone tiara, silver snap shoes, Sears catalog version has Celanese rayon gown, marks: none on head; "SHIRLEY TEMPLE//13" on body**

> 13"..$300.00–325.00
>
> 16"..$325.00–350.00
>
> 20"..$350.00–375.00
>
> 22"..$375.00–400.00
>
> 25"..$400.00–425.00
>
> 27"..$425.00–450.00

12" Tiny Pebbles & Bam Bam, Ideal, all vinyl, circa 1964-1966: $400. **Photo courtesy of Withington Auction Inc.**

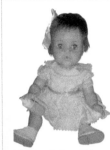

13.5" Betsy Wetsy, Ideal, vinyl: $80. **Photo courtesy of Charlotte's Web Vintage Dolls and Collectibles.**

Deanna Durbin, **1938–1941, all-composition, fully jointed, dark brown human hair wig, brown sleep eyes, open mouth, six teeth, felt tongue, original clothes, pin reads: "DEANNA DURBIN//A UNIVERSAL STAR," more for fancy outfits, marks: "DEANNA DURBIN//IDEAL DOLL" on head; "IDEAL DOLL//21" on body**

15"..$400.00–500.00 600

18"..$600.00–700.00 800

21"..$800.00–900.00

24"..$750.00–850.00

Flexy, **1938–1942, composition head, gauntlet hands, molded and painted hair, painted eyes, wooden torso and feet, flexible wire tubing for arms and legs, original clothes, paper tag, marks: "IDEAL DOLL//Made in U.S. A." or just "IDEAL DOLL" on head**

Black Flexy, **closed smiling mouth, tweed patched pants, felt suspenders**

13½" $275.00–300.00

Baby Snooks, **(Fannie Brice), open/closed mouth with teeth**

13½" 175.00–225.00

Clown Flexy, **looks like Mortimer Snerd, painted white as clown**

13½" $225.00–275.00

Mortimer Snerd, **Edgar Bergen's dummy, smiling closed mouth, showing two teeth**

13½" $200.00–250.00

Soldier, **closed smiling mouth, in khaki uniform**

13½" $175.00–225.00

Sunny Sam and Sunny Sue, **girl bobbed hair, pouty mouth, boy as smiling mouth**

13½" $175.00–200.00

Judy Garland

1939–1940, **as Dorothy from** *The Wizard of Oz,* **all-composition, jointed, wig with braids, brown sleep eyes, open mouth, six teeth, designed by Bernard Lipfert, blue or** red checked rayon jumper, white blouse, marks: "IDEAL" on head plus size number, and "USA" on body

13"... $500.00–600.00

15½"... $1,000.00–1,200.00

18"... $1,300.00–1,5 00.00

1940–1942, teen, all-composition, wig, sleep eyes, open mouth, four teeth, original long dress, hang tag reads: "Judy Garland// A Metro Goldwyn Mayer//Star//in//'Little Nellie//Kelly," original pin reads "JUDY GARLAND METRO GOLDWYN MAYER STAR," marks: "IN U.S.A." on head, "IDEAL DOLLS," a backwards "21" on body

15"... $600.00–700.00

21"... $900.00–1,000.00

Gulliver, **Deanna Durbin mold, from movie *Gulliver's Travels***

21"... $1,200.00–1,600.00

Lone Ranger (or Tonto), **composition head, cloth body, hat marked**

20"... $350.00–450.00

Seven Dwarfs, **1938 on, composition head and cloth body, head turns, removable clothes, each dwarf has name on cap, pick, and lantern**

12"... $125.00–175.00 each

Dopey, **1938, one of Seven Dwarfs, a ventriloquist doll, composition head and hands, cloth body, arms, and legs, hinged mouth with drawstring, molded tongue, painted eyes, large ears, long coat, cotton pants, felt shoes sewn to leg, felt cap with name, can stand alone, mark: "IDEAL DOLL" on neck**

20"... $350.00–400.00

Snow White, **1938 on, all-composition, jointed body, black mohair wig, flirty glass eyes, open mouth, four teeth, dimple in chin, used Shirley Temple body, red velvet bodice, rayon taffeta skirt pictures seven Dwarfs, velvet cape, some unmarked, marks: "Shirley Temple/18" or other size number on back**

11½"... $425.00–475.00

13"–14"... $400.00–450.00

19"–21"... $450.00–500.00

Snow White, **1938–1939, as above, but with molded and painted bow and black hair, painted side-glancing eyes, add 50 percent more for black version, mark: "IDEAL DOLL" on head**

14½"... $300.00–350.00

17½"–19½"................................... $450.00–550.00

Shirley Temple, **1934 on: See Shirley Temple section.**

Composition and Wood Dolls, **1940 on, segmented wooden body, strung with elastic**

Gabby, **from movie *Gulliver's Travels***

10½"... $525.00–600.00

24" Baby Crissy, Ideal, vinyl, MIB: $200. **Photo courtesy of Charlotte's Web Vintage Dolls and Collectibles.**

8.25" Mini Monster, Ideal, vinyl: $250. **Photo courtesy of Morphy Auctions.**

Jiminy Cricket

    8"–9" $375.00–425.00

Ferdinand the Bull

    9" $175.00–2050.00

King Little, **from movie** *Gulliver's Travels*

    13 .... $900.00–1,000.00

Pinocchio, **1939**

    8" $140.00–180.00

    11" $250.00–325.00

    17"– 20" $700.00–800.00

Superman, **1940s, painted features**

    13" $1,000.00–1,400.00

Magic Skin Dolls, 1940 on, latex body, stuffed, original clothing. These doll bodies are prone to disintegration.

Baby Coos, 1948–1953, also Brother and Sister Coos, designed by Bernard Lipfert, hard plastic head, jointed arms, sleep eyes, molded and painted hair, closed mouth, squeeze box voice, later on cloth and vinyl body, marks on head, "16 IDEAL DOLL// MADE IN U. S. A." or unmarked

    14" $100.00–150.00

    16"–18" $165.00–180.00 16 90

    20"–22" $175.00–200.00

    27"–30" $225.00–250.00

Bonnie Braids, **1951–1953, comic strip character, daughter of Dick Tracy and Tess Trueheart, vinyl head, jointed arms, one-piece body, open mouth, one tooth, painted yellow hair, two yellow saran pigtails, painted blue eyes, coos when squeezed, long white gown, bed jacket, toothbrush, Ipana toothpaste, mark: "©1951//Chi. Tribune// IDEAL DOLL//U.S.A." on neck**

 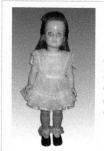

30" Miss Ideal, Ideal, vinyl: $225. **Doll from Private Collection.**

18" Pattite, Ideal, vinyl: $350. **Photo courtesy of MoMos Dolls and Vintage Goodies.**

Baby

11½" $90.00–110.00

14" $250.00–300.00

Toddler, **1953, vinyl head, jointed hard plastic body, open-closed mouth with two painted teeth, walker**

11½" $70.00–110.00

13½" $80.00–140.00

Magic Skin Baby, **1940, 1946–1949, hard plastic head, one-piece body and legs, jointed arms, sleep eyes, molded and painted hair, some with fancy layettes or trunks, latex usually darkened**

13"–14" $35.00–55.00

15"–16" $55.00–70.00

17"–18" $90.00–110.00

20"–22" $100.00–150.00

Joan Palooka, **1953, daughter of comic strip character, Joe Palooka, vinyl, head, "Magic Skin" body, jointed arms and legs, yellow molded hair, topknot of yellow saran, blue painted eyes, open/closed mouth, smells like baby powder, original pink dress with blue ribbons, came with Johnson's baby powder and soap, mark: "©1952//HAM FISHER//IDEAL DOLL" on head**

14"–18" $100.00–150.00

Snoozie, **1951, open/closed mouth, vinyl head**

11"–16" $95.00–110.00

20"–22" $125.00–175.00

Sparkle Plenty, **1947–1950, hard plastic head, "Magic Skin" body may be dark, yarn hair, character from Dick Tracy comics**

14" $175.00–225.00

Hard Plastic and Vinyl Dolls, **all in good condition with original clothing, mint-in-box can bring double the value listed**

Baby

    11"...$25.00–35.00

    14"...$40.00–55.00

    20"...$60.00–70.00

Child

    14"...$25.00–35.00

Andy Gibb, **1979**

7½" 18.00–25.00

April Shower, **1969, vinyl, battery operated, splashes hands, head turns**

    14"...$25.00–30.00

Baby Pebbles, **1963–1964, character from the Flintstone cartoons, Hanna Barbera Productions, vinyl head, arms, legs, soft body, side-glancing blue painted eyes, rooted hair with topknot and bone, leopard print nightie and trim on flannel blanket, also as an all-vinyl toddler, jointed body, outfit with leopard print**

    14"...$150.00–200.00

Tiny Pebbles, **1964–1966, hard vinyl body, came with plastic log cradle in 1965, prices reflect doll in original clothing, allow more for cradle**

    8"...$100.00–125.00

    12"...$190.00–210.00

    16"...$225.00–250.00

Bamm-Bamm, **1964, character from Flintstone cartoon, Hanna Barbera Productions, all-vinyl head, jointed body, rooted blond saran hair, painted blue side-glancing eyes, leopard skin suit, cap, club**

    12"...$180.00–200.00

    16"...$95.00–115.00

Batgirl and Super Girl, **1967–1968, all-vinyl, posable body, rooted hair, painted side-glancing eyes, dressed in costume**

    11½" ....$700.00–900.00 each

Belly Button Babies, **1971, Me So Glad, Me So Silly, Me So Happy, vinyl head, rooted hair, painted eyes, press button in belly to move arms, head, and bent legs, both boy and girl versions**

White

    9½"...$25.00–30.00

Black

    9½"...$35.00–40.00

Betsy McCall, **1952–1953: See Betsy McCall section.**

Betsy Wetsy, **1937–1938, 1954–1956, 1959–1962, 1982–1985, open mouth for bottle, drinks, wets, came with bottle, some in layettes, marks: "IDEAL" on head, "IDEAL" on body**

Hard rubber head, **soft rubber body, sleep or painted eyes**

11"...$95.00–125.00

13½" $150.00–175.00

15" 200.00–225.00

17"..$225.00–250.00

19"..$275.00–300.00

Hard plastic head, **vinyl body**

11½" $150.00–175.00

13½" $185.00–225.00

16"..$250.00–300.00

20"..$325.00–350.00

All-vinyl

8".. $60.00– $75.00

11½" $75.00–100.00

13½" $80.00–110.00

16"..$100.00–150.00

Reissue, **all vinyl, sleep eyes**

16" 25.00–30.00

Bizzie-Lizzie, **1971–1972, vinyl head, jointed body, rooted blond hair, sleep eyes, plugged into power pack, she irons, vacuums, uses feather duster, two D-cell batteries, doll without accessories will bring half of the value listed**

White

18"..$60.00–85.00

Black

18"..$75.00–90.00

Blessed Event, **crying baby, vinyl head, squinting eyes**

21"..$150.00–200.00

Butterick Sew Easy Designing Set, **1953, hard vinyl mannequin of adult woman, molded blond hair, came with Butterick patterns and sewing accessories**

14"..$125.00–150.00

Captain Action" Superhero, **1966–1968, represents a fictional character who changes disguises to become a new identity, vinyl articulated figure, dark hair and eyes. MIB brings double**

Captain Action

12"..$200.00–250.00

Batman disguise $200.00–250.00

Aquaman $200.00–275.00

22" Saucy Walker, Ideal, hard plastic: $200. **Photo courtesy of Morphy Auctions.**

16" Toni, Ideal, marked P91, hard plastic: $275. **Photo courtesy of Charlotte's Web Vintage Dolls and Collectibles.**

Capt. Flash Gordon...........................$75.00–100.00

Dr. Evil...$200.00–225.00

Phantom set....................................$85.00–100.00

Steve Canyon disguise $150.00–200.00

Superman set w/dog.........................$500.00–600.00

Lone Ranger outfit only....................$100.00–150.00

Spiderman ....$500.00–$600.00

Tonto outfit only..............................$125.00–175.00

Ultraman $450.00–550.00

Action Boy

9"...$250.00–300.00

Clarabell, 1954, clown from Howdy Doody TV show, mask face, cloth body, dressed in satin Clarabelle outfit with noise box and horn, later vinyl face

16"...$1750.00–200.00

20"...$200.00–225.00

Crissy® Family of Dolls, 1969–1974, 1982, vinyl grow-hair dolls, all in good condition with original clothing, mint-in-box can bring double the value listed

Baby Crissy, 1973–1976, all-vinyl, jointed body, legs and arms foam filled, rooted auburn grow hair, two painted teeth, brown sleep eyes, mark: "©1972//IDEAL TOY COPR.//2M 5511//B OR GHB-H-225" on back

White

24" 85.00–100.00

Black

24"...$150.00–200.00

Beautiful Crissy, 1969–1974, all-vinyl, dark brown eyes, long hair, turn knob in back to make hair grow, some with swivel waist (1971), pull string to turn head (1972), pull string to talk (1971), reissued ca. 1982–1983, first year hair grew to floor length

White

18"... $70.00–80.00

Black

17½" $100.00–200.00

1982 doll..$35.00–40.00

Brandi, Kerry, & Tressy, **Crissy's friends, Brandi, 1972–1973; Kerry, 1971; Tressy, 1970 (Sears Exclusive), vinyl head, painted eyes, rooted growing hair, swivel waist**

White

18"... $100.00–150.00

Black

18"... $1100.00–160.00

Cinnamon, **Velvet's Little Sister, 1972–1974, vinyl head, painted eyes, rooted auburn growing hair, orange polka dotted outfit, additional outfits sold separately, marks: "©1971//IDEAL TOY CORP.//G-H-12-H18//HONG KONG//IDEAL 1069-4 b" head; "©1972//IDEAL TOY CORP.//U.S. PAT-3-162-976//OTHER PAT. PEND.// HONG KONG" on back**

White

13½" $40.00–45.00

Black

13½" $90.00–150.00

Cricket, Mia, & Dina, **Cricket, 1971–1972 (Sears Exclusive); Dina, 1972–1973; Mia, 1971, vinyl, members of the Crissy' family, growing hair dolls, painted teeth, swivel waist**

15"... $65.00–75.00

Tara, **1976, all-vinyl black doll, long black rooted hair that "grows," sleep eyes, marked "©1975//IDEAL TOY CORP//H-250//HONG KONG" on head and "©1970// IDEAL TOY CORP//GH-15//M5169-01//MADE IN HONG KONG" on buttock**

15½" $150.00–200.00

Velvet, **1971–1973,** *Crissy's* **younger cousin, talker**

15"... $80.00–125.00

1974, **non-talker, other accessories,**

grow hair

White

15"... $65.00–75.00

Black

15"... $60.00–65.00

Daddy's Girl, 1961, vinyl head and arms, plastic body, swivel waist, jointed ankles, rooted saran hair, blue sleep eyes, closed smiling mouth, preteen girl, label on dress reads "Daddy's Girl," marks: "IDEAL TOY CORP.//g-42-1" on head, "IDEAL TOY CORP.//G-42" on body

38" $1,200.00–1,400.00

42" $1,500.00–1,700.00

Davy Crockett and his horse, 1955–1956, all-plastic, can be removed from horse, fur cap, buckskin clothes

4¾" $50.00–60.00

Diana Ross, 1969, from the Supremes (singing group), all-vinyl, rooted black bouffant hairdo, gold sheath, feathers, gold shoes, or chartreuse mini-dress, print scarf, and black shoes

17½" $250.00–300.00

Dorothy Hamill, 1978, Olympic skating star, vinyl head, plastic posable body, rooted short brown hair, comes on ice rink stand with skates; also extra outfits available

11½" $18.00–24.00

Evel Knievel, 1974–1977, all-plastic stunt figure in white suit, helmet, more with stunt cycle

7" $35.00–40.00

Flatsy, 1969, flat vinyl doll with wire armature, rooted hair

6" $20.00–50.00

Giggles, 1960, vinyl head, giggling doll, allow 1/3 for non-working good condition

18" $175.00–250.00

Harmony, 1972, vinyl, battery operated, makes music with guitar, allow 1/3 for non-working or doll only

21" $125.00–175.00

Harriet Hubbard Ayer, 1953, cosmetic doll, vinyl stuffed head, hard plastic (Toni) body, wigged or rooted hair, came with eight-piece H. H. Ayer cosmetic kit, beauty table and booklet, marks: "MK 16//IDEAL DOLL" on head "IDEAL DOLL//P-91" on body

14" $50.00–75.00

16" $80.00–100.00

19" $110.00–130.00

21" $120.00–150.00

Honeybunch, 1956–1957, soft vinyl head, vinyl body and limbs are stuffed with cotton, curlable hair

15"–23" $50.00–100.00

Honeymoon, –1965, comic strip character, daughter of Dick Tracy Jr., all vonyl, white yarn hair, clear plastic space helmut

16" $75.00–100.00

Hopalong Cassidy, 1949–1950, vinyl stuffed head, vinyl hands, molded and painted gray hair, painted blue eyes, one-piece body, dressed in black cowboy outfit, leatherette boots, guns, holster, black felt hat, marks: "Hopalong Cassidy" on buckle

    20".. $185.00–200.00

    24".. $200.00–225.00

Plastic, with horse, Topper

    4½" $45.00–60.00

Howdy Doody, 1950–1953, television personality, hard plastic head, red molded and painted hair, freckles, ventriloquist doll, mouth operated by pull string, cloth body and limbs, dressed in cowboy outfit, scarf reads "HOWDY DOODY," mark: "IDEAL" on head

    18".. $400.00–450.00

    20".. $450.00–500.00

    24".. $500.00–525.00

1954, with vinyl hands, wears boots, jeans

    20½".. $275.00–300.00

    25".. $325.00–375.00

Jet Set Dolls, 1967, vinyl head, posable body, rooted straight hair, mod fashions, earrings, strap shoes, Chelsea, Stephanie, and Petula

    24".. $45.00–55.00

Jody, An Old Fashioned Girl, 1975, vinyl, long rooted red hair

    9".. $20.00–25.00

Joey Stivic, Archie Bunker's grandson, 1976, vinyl, rooted hair

    14".. $45.00–60.00

Judy Splinters, 1949–1950, vinylite, TV character ventriloquist doll, open/closed mouth

    18".. $70.00–90.00

    22".. $125.00–150.00

    36".. $180.00–200.00

Baby

    15".. $175.00–200.00

Kissy, 1961–1964, vinyl head, rigid vinyl toddler body, rooted saran hair, sleep eyes, jointed wrists, press hands together and mouth puckers, makes kissing sound, original dress, panties, t-strap sandals, marks: "©IDEAL CORP.//K-21-L" on head "IDEAL TOY CORP.// K22//PAT. PEND." on body

White

    22½" $75.00–100.00

Black

    22½" $125.00–150.00

*Kissy Baby*Error! Bookmark not defined., **1963–1964, all-vinyl, bent legs**

22" $65.00–85.00

Tiny Kissy, **1963–1968, smaller toddler, red outfit, white pinafore with hearts, marks: "IDEAL CORP.//K-16-1" on head "IDEAL TOY CORP./K-16-2" on body**

White

16" $70.00–80.00

Black

16" $90.00–100.00

Lori Martin, **1961, character from *National Velvet* TV show, all-vinyl, swivel waist, jointed body, including ankles, blue sleep eyes, rooted dark hair, individual fingers, dressed shirt, jeans, black vinyl boots, felt hat, marks: "Metro Goldwyn Mayer Inc.//Mfg. by//IDEAL TOY CORP//38" on head, "©IDEAL TOY CORP.//38" on back**

30" $425.00–475.00

38" $475.00–525.00

Little Lost Baby, **1968, three faced doll**

22" $75.00–100.00

Mary Hartline, **1952, from TV personality on *Super Circus* show, hard plastic, fully jointed, blond nylon wig, blue sleep eyes, lashes, black eye shadow over and under eye, red, white, or green drum majorette costume and baton, red heart paper hang tag, with original box, marks: "P-91//IDEAL DOLL//MADE IN U.S.A." on head, "IDEAL DOLL//P-91 or IDEAL//16" on body**

7½" $30.00–45.00

16" $100.00–125.00

22½" $350.00–400.00

Mini Monsters, **1865, Wolfy, Vampy, Franky, others**

8 ¼" $200.00–250.00

Miss Clairol, Glamour Misty, **1965–1966, vinyl head and arms, rigid plastic legs, body, rooted platinum blond saran hair, side-glancing eyes, high-heeled feet, teen doll had cosmetics to change her hair, all original, marks: "©1965//IDEAL TOY CORP//W-12-3" on neck, "©1965 IDEAL" in oval on lower rear torso**

12" $45.00–55.00

Centered eyes

12" $85.00–95.00

Miss Curity, **1953, hard plastic, saran wig, sleep eyes, black eye shadow, nurse's outfit, navy cape, white cap, Bauer & Black first aid kit and book, curlers, uses Toni body, mark: "P-90 IDEAL DOLL, MADE IN U.S.A." on head**

14½" $100.00–150.00

Miss Ideal, 1961, all-vinyl, rooted nylon hair, jointed ankles, wrists, waist, arms, legs, closed smiling mouth, sleep eyes, original dress, with beauty kit and comb, marks: "©IDEAL TOY CORP.//SP-30-S" head, "©IDEAL TOY CORP.//G-30-S" back

    25"..$150.00–200.00

    30"..$200.00–250.00

Miss Revlon, 1956–1959, vinyl, hard plastic teenage body, jointed shoulders, waist, hips, and knees, high-heeled feet, rooted saran hair, sleep eyes, lashes, pierced ears, hang tag, original dress, some came with trunks, mark: "VT 20//IDEAL DOLL." Dolls listed are in good condition with original clothing, mint-in-box examples can bring double the values listed

    15"..$225.00–275.00

    18"..$200.00–275.00

    20"..$250.00–325.00

    23"..$225.00–350.00

    26", 1957 only.................................$300.00–350.00

Little Miss Revlon, 1958–1960, vinyl head and body, jointed head, arms, legs, swivel waist, high-heeled feet, rooted hair, sleep eyes, pierced ears with earrings, original clothes, with box, many extra boxed outfits available

    10½"..$100.00–150.00

Mitzi, 1961–1962, vinyl fashion doll similar to Mattel's Barbie®

    11.5"..$65.00–80.00

Plassie, 1942, hard plastic head, molded and painted hair, composition shoulder plate, composition limbs, stuffed pink oilcloth body, blue sleep eyes, original dress, bonnet, mark: "IDEAL DOLL//MADE IN USA//PAT.NO. 225 2077" on head

    16"..$160.00–180.00

    19"–22"...$150.00–175.00

    24"..$180.00–200.00

Play N Jane, 1971, hard vinyl, plays tic tak toe, horseshoes and basketball, allow half for non-working condition

    16"..$75.00–100.00

Play Pal family of Dolls, 1959–1962

Patti, all-vinyl, jointed wrists, sleep eyes, curly or straight saran hair, bangs, closed mouth, blue or red and white check dress with pinafore, three-year-old size, reissued in 1981 and 1982 from old molds, more for redheads, mark: "IDEAL TOY CORP.//G 35 OR B-19-1" on head

    35"..$400.00–700.00

Reissue Patti, **Ashton Drake**

    35"..$200.00–225.00

Bonnie Play Pal, **1959**, Patti's three-month-old sister, made only one year, rooted blond hair, blue sleep eyes, blue and white check outfit, white shoes and socks

    24"..$550.00–600.00

Johnny Play Pal, **1959, blue sleep eyes, molded hair, Patti's three-month-old brother**

24"... $500.00–550.00

Pattite, **1960, rooted saran hair, sleep eyes, red and white check dress, white pinafore with her name on it, looks like Patti Playpal**

18"... $300.00–400.00

Penny Play Pal, **1959, rooted blond or brown curly hair, blue sleep eyes, wears organdy dress, vinyl shoes, socks, Patti's two-year-old sister, made only one year, marks: "IDEAL DOLL//32-E-L" or "B-32-B PAT. PEND." on head, "IDEAL" on back**

32"... $300.00–450.00

Peter Play Pal, **1960–1961, gold sleep eyes, freckles, pug nose, rooted blond or brunette hair, original clothes, black plastic shoes, marks: "©IDEAL TOY CORP.// BE-35-38" on head, "©IDEAL TOY CORP.//W-38//PAT. PEND." on body**

38"... $500.00–600.00

Walker

38"... $850.00–875.00

Saucy Play Pal, **1960**

32"... $300.00–375.00

Suzy Play Pal, **1959, rooted curly short blond saran hair, blue sleep eyes, wears purple dotted dress, Patti's one-year-old sister**

28"... $400.00–450.00

Petite Princess Doll House Family of 4, **vinyl**

3"–5"... $50.00–75.00 set

Posie Walker, **1954–1956, vinyl head, hard plastic body**

17"... $75.00–100.00

23"... $100.00–150.00

25"... $175.00–225.00

Rub-A-Dub Dolly, **1974, allow more for doll with accessories such as tugboat shower**

15"–18"... $60.00–70.00

Samantha, **1965–1966, from TV show *Bewitched*, vinyl head, body, rooted saran hair, posable arms and legs, wearing red witch's costume, with broom, painted side-glancing eyes, other costume included negligee, mark: "IDEAL DOLL//M-12-E-2" on head**

12"... $200.00–250.00

Saucy Walker, **1951–1955, all hard plastic, walks, turns head from side to side, flirty blue eyes, crier, open/closed mouth, teeth, holes in body for crier, saran wig, plastic curlers, came as toddler, boy, and "Big Sister"**

14"... $150.00–175.00

16"... $150.00–200.00

22"... $170.00–220.00

293

Black

16"... $250.00–275.00

Big Sister, **1954**

25"... $425.00–475.00

Snoozie

1958–1965, **all-vinyl, rooted saran hair, blue sleep eyes, open/closed mouth, cry voice, knob makes doll wiggle, close eyes, crier, in flannel pajamas**

14"... $60.00–70.00

1964–1965, **vinyl head, arms, legs, soft body, rooted saran hair, sleep eyes, turn knob, she   squirms, opens and closes eyes, and cries**

20"... $150.00–200.00

Storybook dolls, **1985, all-vinyl, rooted hair**

8"... $10.00–15.00

Tabatha, **1966, baby from TV show** *Bewitched,* **vinyl head, body, rooted platinum hair, painted blue side-glancing eyes, closed mouth, came in pajamas, mark: "©1965//Screen Gems, Inc.//Ideal Toy Corp.//T.A. 18-6//H-25" on head**

14"... $260.00–300.00

Tammy Family Dolls, **dolls listed are in good condition wearing original clothing, mint-in-box examples can bring double the values listed.**

Tammy, **1962+, vinyl head, arms, plastic legs and torso, head joined at neck base, marks: "©IDEAL TOY CORP.//BS12" on head, "©IDEAL TOY CORP.//BS-12//1" on back, scarcer outfit brings higher end of range**

White

12"... $25.00–75.00

Black

12"... $55.00–90.00

Pos'n

12"... $20.00–50.00

Mom

12½".. $35.00–45.00

Dad

13"... $30.00–40.00

Dodi

9"... $65.00–75.00

Ted

12½".. $25.00–35.00

Patti, **1964 Montgomry Ward exclusive**

9"... $500.00–600.00

Pepper

   9".. $40.00–50.00

Pos'n Pepper

   9".. $30.00–40.00

Salty

   9".. $65.00–85.00

   Clothing (MIP)................................ $50.00–90.00

Tearie Dearie, **1964**

   9".. $45.00–55.00

Thumbelina

1961–1962, **vinyl head and limbs, soft cloth body, painted eyes, rooted saran hair, open/closed mouth, wind knob on back moves body, crier in 1962**

   16".. $130.00–165.00

   20".. $200.00–300.00

1982–1983, **all-vinyl one-piece body, rooted hair, non-moving, comes in quilted carrier, also black**

   7".. $30.00–40.00

1982, 1985, **reissue from 1960s mold, vinyl head, arms, legs, cloth body, painted eyes, crier, open mouth, molded or rooted hair, original with box**

   18".. $60.00–75.00

Thumbelina, Ltd. Production Collector's Doll, **1983–1985, porcelain, painted eyes, molded and painted hair, beige crocheted outfit with pillow booties, limited edition 1,000**

   18".. $65.00–75.00

Tiny Thumbelina, **1962–1968, vinyl head, limbs, cloth body, painted eyes, rooted saran hair, wind key in back makes body head move, original tagged clothes, marks: "IDEAL TOY CORP.//OTT 14" on head, "U.S. PAT. #3029552" on body**

   14".. $150.00–225.00

Newborn Thumbelina, **1968, vinyl head and arms, foam stuffed body, rooted hair, painted eyes, pull-string to squirm**

   9".. $150.00–200.00

Toddler Thumbelina, **1969–1971, vinyl head and arms, cloth body, rooted hair, painted eyes**

   9".. $80.00–100.00

Tiffany Taylor, **1974–1976, all-vinyl, rooted hair, top of head turns to change color, painted eyes, teenage body, high-heeled, extra outfits available**

   19".. $50.00–60.00

Black

19" 60.00–70.00

Tuesday Taylor, **1976–1977, vinyl, posable body, turn head to change color of hair, clothing tagged "IDEAL Tuesday Taylor"**

11½" $50.00–75.00

Tuesday Taylor's Boyfriend Eric, **1976, vinyl, posable body, turn head to change color of hair, clothing tagged "IDEAL Tuesday Taylor"**

12" $40.00–50.00

Tippy Tumbles, **1977**

17" $55.00–65.00

Toni, **1949, designed by Bernard Lipfert, all hard plastic, jointed body, DuPont nylon wig, usually blue eyes, rosy cheeks, closed mouth, came with Toni wave set and curlers in original dress, with hang tag, marks: "IDEAL DOLL//MADE IN U.S.A." on head, "IDEAL DOLL" and P-series number on body. MIB can bring double**

P-90

14" $200.00–300.00

P-91

16" $250.00–350.00

P-92

19" $300.00–400.00

P-93

21" $350.00–450.00

P-94.

22½" $500.00–650.00

Tubsy, **1967, with accessories**

18" $150.00–200.00

Whoopsie, **1978–1981, vinyl, reissued in 1981, marked: "22//©IDEAL TOY CORP// HONG KONG//1978//H298"**

13" $30.00–45.00

Wizard of Oz Series, **1984–1985, Tin Man, Lion, Scarecrow, Dorothy, and Toto, all-vinyl, six-piece posable bodies**

9" .... $15.00–20.00 each

JULLIEN

1827–1904, Paris, France. After 1904 became a part of S.F.B.J. Had a porcelain factory, won some awards, purchased bisque heads from Francois Gaultier. Dolls listed are in good condition, appropriately dressed.

15" bébé, Jullien, bisque, open mouth: $1,900. **Photo courtesy of Sweetbriar Auctions.**

Child, bisque socket head, wig, glass eyes, pierced ears, open mouth with teeth or closed mouth, on jointed composition body

Closed mouth

17"–19"	$3,600.00–4,100.00
24"–26"	$4,600.00–5,000.00

Open mouth

18"–20"	$2,300.00–2,500.00
23"–26"	$2,100.00–4,000.00
29"–30"	$2,400.00–2,600.00

JUMEAU

1842–1899, Paris and Montreuil-sous-Bois; in 1899 joined in S.F.B.J. which continued to make dolls marked Jumeau through 1958. Founder Pierre Francois Jumeau made fashion dolls with kid or wood bodies, head marked with size number, bodies stamped "JUMEAU//MEDAILLE D'OR//PARIS." Early Jumeau heads were pressed pre-1890. By 1878, son Emile Jumeau was head of the company and made Bébé Jumeau, marked on back of head, on chemise, band on arm of dress. Tête Jumeaux have poured heads. Bébé Protige and Bébé Jumeau registered trademarks in 1886, Bee mark in 1891, Bébé Marcheur in 1895, Bébé Francaise in 1896. Mold numbers of marked EJs and Têtes approximate the following heights: 1–10", 2–11", 3–12", 4–13", 5–14", 6–16", 7–17", 8–18", 9–20", 10–21", 11–24", 12–26", 13–30". Dolls listed are in good condition, nicely wigged, and with appropriate clothing. Exceptional dolls may be much more.

Poupée Jumeau (so-called French Fashion-type), 1860s on, marked with size number on swivel head, closed mouth, paperweight eyes, pierced ears, stamped kid body, add more for original clothes

Poupée Peau **(kid body)**

11"–13"	$2,500.00–3,500.00
15"–16"	$2,000.00–4,000.00

21" Portrait Poupée, Jumeau, bisque, wood body: $12,000. **Photo courtesy of McMasters Harris Apple Tree Doll Auctions.**

13" Portrait Jumeau, 1st series, bisque: $14,000. **Photo courtesy of Withington Auction Inc.**

17"–18"...$4,000.00–6,500.00

20"...$6,000.00–8,000.00

Poupée Bois (**wood body**), **bisque lower arms**

10"–11"..$7,000.00–8,000.00

14"–16"..$9,000.00–10,000.00

So-called Portrait face

17"–19"..$4,000.00–7,000.00

21"–23"..$5,000.00–8,000.00

Wood body

19"–21"......................................$10,000.00–12,000.00

Portrait Child Doll, **1877–1883, closed mouth, paperweight eyes, pierced ears, wigged (sometimes skin wig), straight wristed composition body with separate balls at joints, head marked with size number only.**

First Series, **almond eye**

12"–14½"

....$11,000.00–15,000.00

16"–18½"

....$15,000.00–20,000.00

19"–20".....................................$16,000.00–22,000.00

23"–25".....................................$25,000.00–28,000.00

25"..$24,000.00–30,000.00

Second Series

11"–12"..$5,500.00–7,000.00

13"–15"..$6,500.00–8,000.00

18"–20"...$7,500.00–9,000.00

22"..$9,000.00–11,000.00

25"..$12,000.00–15,000.00

22" E.J. Jumeau, bisque: $15,000. **Photo courtesy of McMasters Harris Apple Tree Doll Auctions.**

22" Triste (Long Face) Jumeau, bisque: $24,000. **Photo courtesy of Withington Auction Inc.**

Long Face Triste Bébé, 1879–1886, head marked with number only, pierced applied ears, closed mouth, paperweight eyes, straight wrists on Jumeau marked body

> 20"–23" $20,000.00–25,000.00
>
> 26"–27" $22,000.00–28,000.00
>
> 31"–33" $28,000.00–32,000.00

Premiere, 1880, unmarked bébé, allow more for exceptional couturier outfit

> 9"–12" $7,000.00–9,000.00
>
> 15"–16" $9,000.00–12,000.00
>
> 17"–19" $10,000.00–14,000.00

E.J. Bébé, 1881–1886, earliest "EJ" mark above with number over initials, pressed bisque socket head, wig, paperweight eyes, pierced ears, closed mouth, jointed body with straight wrists

> 12"–16" $10,000.00–11,000.00
>
> 17"–18" $10,000.00–14,000.00
>
> 19"–21" $12,000.00–15,000.00
>
> 23"–24" $16,000.00–20,000.00

EJ/A marked Bébé

> 25" $32,000.00–36,000.00

Mid "EJ," mark has size number centered between E and J (E 8 J), later with Déposé above

10"–14" 6,000.00–10,000.00

> 16"–20" $8,000.00–11,000.00
>
> 23"–26" $9,000.00–14,000.00

Déposé Jumeau, 1886–1889, poured bisque head marked, "Déposé Jumeau," and size number, pierced ears, closed mouth, paperweight eyes, composition and wood body with straight wrists marked "Medaille d'Or Paris"

> 10"–14" $6,500.00–8,000.00
>
> 16"–18" $7,000.00–9,000.00

24" Jumeau, bisque, closed-mouth tête, all original (hat added): $7,500. **Photo courtesy of Withington Auction Inc.**

20" mold 1907, Jumeau, bisque: $1,600. **Photo courtesy of McMasters Harris Apple Tree Doll Auctions.**

20"–23"..$8,000.00–11,000.00

25"–26"..$10,000.00–13,000.00

33"...$15,000.00–17,000.00

Tête Jumeau, **1885 on, poured bisque socket head, red stamp on head, stamp or sticker on body, wig, glass eyes, pierced ears, closed mouth, jointed composition body with straight wrists, may also be marked E.D. with size number when Douillet ran factory, uses tête face. The following sizes were used for Têtes: 0–9", 1–10", 2–11", 3–12", 4–13", 5–14½", 6–16", 7–17", 8–19", 10–21½", 11–24", 12–26", 13–29", 14–31", 15–33", 16–34"–35"**

Bébé **(Child), closed mouth**

9"–10"..$4,000.00–5,000.00

12"–13"..$4,000.00–5,000.00

16"–17"..$5,000.00–6,000.00

19"–22"..$5,500.00–7,000.00

24"–26"..$7,000.00–8,000.00

29"–31"..$7,500.00–9,000.00

Lady body

14"–16"..$4,000.00–5,000.00

18"–22"..$7,000.00–8,000.00

Open mouth, **child**

10"–12"..$2,000.00–2,500.00

17"–22"..$2,100.00–2,500.00

24"–25"..$3,000.00–4,000.00

27"–29"..$3,000.00–4,500.00

32"–35"..$4,000.00–5,000.00

10" Great Lady of
Fashion, Jumeau,
bisque: $450.
**Photo courtesy
of The Museum
Doll Shop.**

B. L. Bébé, **1892 on, marked "B. L." for the Louvre department store, socket head,
wig, pierced ears, paperweight eyes, closed mouth, jointed composition body**

13"–16" $4,500.00–5,500.00

18"–23" $6,500.00–7,000.00

Phonographe Jumeau, **1894–1899, bisque head, open mouth, phonograph in torso,
working condition**

24"–25" $6,000.00–8,000.00

R.R. Bébé, **1892 on, wig, pierced ears, paperweight eyes, closed mouth, jointed
composition body with straight wrists**

21"–23" $4,400.00–4,800.00

Open mouth

18"–26" $3,300.00–3,600.00

Child mold 1907, **1907 on, some with Tété Jumeau stamp, sleep or set eyes, open
mouth, jointed French body**

14"–16" $9 00.00–1,100.00 1000

19"–20" $1,300.00 1,800.00

23"–26" $1,900.00–2,200.00

29"–32" $2,200.00–2,800.00

35" $3,000.00–3,200.00

Character Child

Mold 203, 208, and other 200 series, **1882–1899, glass eyes**

20"–28" $70,000.00–100,000.00

24" mold 201 sold at auction for $285,000.00

Mold 217, **crier**

20" example sold at auction for $188,100.00

Too few in database for reliable range.

Mold 230 child, **1910 on, open mouth socket-head, glass eyes, wig, composition body**

12"–14" $650.00–700.00

20–23" $1,100.00–1,300.00

Two-Faced Jumeau, **crying and smiling**

18" .... $13,000.00–$16,000.00

Princess Elizabeth, made after Jumeau joined SFBJ and adopted Unis label, mark will be "71 Unis//France 149//306//Jumeau//1938//Paris," bisque socket head with high color, closed mouth, flirty eyes, jointed composition body

Mold 306

15" $1,600.00–1,900.00

18"–19" $2,200.00–2,600.00

32"–33" $5,000.00–6,000.00

Great Ladies of Fashion, Mold 221, 1940s–1950s, bisque head, five-piece composition body with hole in one foot for stand, elaborate costumes and wigs representing Queen Victoria, Marie Antoinette, etc.

10" $400.00–500.00

Accessories

Marked Jumeau shoes

5"–6" $300.00–400.00

7"–10" $600.00–700.00

KAMKINS

18" Kamkins, cloth: $2,000. **Photo courtesy of Withington Auction Inc.**

1919–1928, Philadelphia, Pennsylvania, and Atlantic City, New Jersey. Cloth doll made by Louise R. Kampes Studio. Clothes made by cottage industry workers at home. All-cloth, molded mask face, painted features, swivel head, jointed shoulders and hips, mohair wig. Dolls listed are in good, clean, unfaded condition, allow 50 percent less for soiled or faded examples.

18"–20" $2,000.00–3,000.00

KÄMMER & REINHARDT

30" Kämmer & Reinhardt, bisque: $1,000. **Photo courtesy of Oldeclectics**.

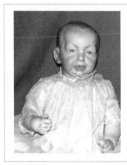

15" mold 100 baby, Kämmer & Reinhardt, bisque: $450. **Photo courtesy of The Museum Doll Shop.**

1885–1933, Waltershausen, Germany. Registered trademark K✡R, Majestic Doll, Mein Leibling, Die Kokette, Charakterpuppen (character dolls). Designed doll heads, most bisque were made by Simon & Halbig; in 1918, Schuetzmeister & Quendt also supplied heads; Rheinische Gummi und Celluloid Fabrik Co. made celluloid heads for Kämmer & Reinhardt. Kämmer & Reinhardt dolls were distributed by Bing, Borgfeldt, B. Illfelder, L. Rees & Co., Strobel & Wilken, and Louis Wolfe & Co. Also made heads of wood and composition, later cloth and rubber dolls. Mold numbers identify heads starting with (1) bisque socket heads, (2) shoulder heads, as well as socket heads of black or mulatto babies, (3) bisque socket heads or celluloid shoulder heads, (4) heads having eyelashes, (5) googlies, black heads, pincushion heads, (6) mulatto heads, (7) celluloid heads, bisque head walking dolls, (8) rubber heads, (9) composition heads, some rubber heads. Other letters refer to style or material of wig or clothing. All dolls listed are in good condition with appropriate clothing.

Child

Bisque Socket head child

Mold 192 **(possibly as early as 1892), jointed composition body, sleep eyes**

Closed mouth

6"–7"	$350.00–450.00
10"–11"	$600.00–800.00
16"–18"	$1,900.00–2,100.00
22"–24"	$2,400.00–2,600.00

Open mouth

7"–8"	$375.00–450.00
12"–14"	$450.00–550.00
16"–18"	$675.00–800.00
20"–22"	$900.00–1,100.00
26"–28"	$1,600.00–1,900.00

Child, Dolly Face, **1910 to 1930s, bisque head with open mouth, jointed composition body, sleep eyes**

No Mold Number or Molds 191, 401, 402, 403

On five-piece flapper style body

> 5"–6" $300.00–400.00

> 7"–8" $400.00–450.00

> 9"–11" $700.00–800.00

Jointed composition body

> 8"–10" $350.00–400.00

> 12"–14" $450.00–500.00

> 16"–18" $550.00–650.00

> 19"–21" $700.00–750.00

> 23"–26" $750.00–800.00

> 28"–30" $950.00–1,200.00

Child Shoulder Head Doll, **kid body**

> 14" $300.00–350.00

> 19"–22" $375.00–400.00

Character Dolls, **1909 on**

Mold 100, **Baby often referred to by collectors as "Kaiser Baby," solid dome head, intaglio eyes, open-closed mouth, composition bent-limb body. Allow more for toddler body.**

> 11"–12" $300.00–400.00

> 14"–15" $400.00–450.00

> 18"–20" $600.00–700.00

Mold 101, **Peter or Marie, painted eyes, closed mouth, jointed body**

> 7–8" $1,300.00–1,500.00

> 10"–12" $1,600.00–2,000.00

> 14"–15" $2,100.00–2,300.00

> 17"–18" $2,600.00–3,000.00

> 19"–20" $3,500.00–4,000.00

Glass eyes

> 12" $7,000.00–8,000.00

> 18"–20" $9,000.00–12,500.00

Mold 102, **Elsa or Walter, painted eyes, molded hair, closed mouth, very rare**

> 12" $19,000.00–22,000.00

> 22" $35,000.00–50,000.00

16" mold 116A baby, Kämmer & Reinhardt, bisque: $1,400. **Photo courtesy of Sweetbriar Auctions.**

18" mold 117, Kämmer & Reinhardt, bisque, flirty eyes: $4,500. **Photo courtesy of Sweetbriar Auctions.**

Mold 103, **painted eyes, closed mouth**

    19"–23" **$70,000.00–80,000.00**

Too few in database for reliable range.

Mold 104, **ca. 1909, painted eyes, laughing closed mouth, very rare**

    20" example sold at auction for   **$216,660.00**

Too few in database for reliable range.

Mold 105, **painted eyes, open-closed mouth, very rare**

    18" example sold at auction for   **$226,102.00**

Too few in database to give reliable range.

Too few in database for reliable range.

Mold 107, **Karl, painted intaglio eyes, closed mouth**

    21"–22" **$40,000.00–55,000.00**

Too few in database to give reliable range.

Mold 108,

    25" example sold at auction for   **$321,582.00**

Too few in database for reliable range.

Mold 109, **Elise, painted eyes, closed mouth**

    9"–10" **$6,000.00–8,000.00**

    12"–14" **$10,000.00–14,000.00**

    20"–24" **$16,000.00–19,000.00**

Mold 112, **painted open-closed mouth**

    9" **$5,000.00**

    13"–15" **$11,000.00–13,000.00**

    17"–18" **$14,000.00–16,000.00**

Glass eyes

    12"–16" **$14,000.00–18,000.00**

Too few in database for reliable range.

Mold 112X, **flocked hair**

    17"...$13,000.00–15,000.00

Mold 114, **Hans or Gretchen, painted eyes, closed mouth**

    8"–9"...$2,000.00–2,200.00

    12"–15"..$3,000.00–4,000.00

    18"–20"...$5,000.00–6,000.00

    23"–25"..$6,500.00–7,500.00

Glass eyes

    15"–20"..$7,000.00–9,000.00

Mold 115, **solid dome, painted hair, sleeping eyes, closed mouth, toddler**

    12"–15"..$3,000.00–4,000.00

Mold 115A, **sleep eyes, closed mouth, wig**

Baby, **bent-leg body**

    10"–12"..$900.00–1,400.00

    14"–16"..$1,600.00–2,000.00

    19"–22"..$2,500.00–3,000.00

Toddler, **composition, jointed body**

    15"–16"..$3,750.00–4,300.00

    18"–22"..$4,900.00–5,500.00

Mold 116, **dome head, sleep eyes, open-closed mouth**

    10"–13"..$1,500.00–1,800.00

Mold 116A, **sleep eyes, open-closed mouth or open mouth, wigged, bent-leg**

Baby

    10"–12"..$800.00–1,000.00

    15"–18"..$1,200.00–1,800.00

    21"–23"..$2,000.00–2,400.00

Toddler **body**

    15"–18"..$3,000.00–3,800.00

    21"–23"..$4,000.00–5,000.00

Mold 117, 117A Mein Liebling (My Darling), **glass eyes, closed mouth**

    8"–11"..$3,200.00–3,600.00

    14"–16"..$3,800.00–4,000.00

    18"–20"..4,500.00–5,000.00

21.5" mold 127, Kämmer & Reinhardt, child body, bisque: $1,200. **Photo courtesy of Morphy Auctions.**

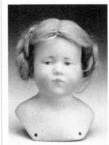

16" mold 201, Marie, Kämmer & Reinhardt, bisque, shoulderhead, no body: $1,000. **Photo courtesy of Morphy Auctions.**

22"–24" $5,500.00–6,000.00

28"–30" $7,000.00–8,000.00

Flapper body

8" $3,500.00

Too few in database for reliable range.

Mold 117N, Mein Neuer Liebling (My New Darling), **flirty eyes, open mouth**

14"–16" $1,500.00–1,900.00

20"–22" $2,200.00–2,600.00

28"–30" $3,000.00–3,400.00

Mold 117X, **socket head, sleep eyes, open mouth**

14"–16" $1,200.00–1,600.00

22"–24" $1,800.00–2,000.00

30"–32" $2,100.00–2,500.00

Molds 118, 118A, **sleep eyes, open mouth, baby body**

11" $1,100.00–1,200.00

15" $1,300.00–1,500.00

18" $1,900.00–2,200.00

Mold 119, **sleep eyes, open-closed mouth, marked "Baby," five-piece baby body**

24"–25" $16,000.00

Too few in database for reliable range.

Molds 121, 122, **sleep eyes, open mouth**

Baby

10"–11" $450.00–500.00

15"–16" $600.00–700.00

20"–26" $650.00–850.00

12" character, Kämmer & Reinhardt, cloth: $400. **Doll courtesy of Alfred Edward.**

Toddler body

10"...$500.00–600.00

13"–14"...$750.00–850.00

18"–20"...$900.00–1,000.00

Mold 123 Max and Mold 124 Moritz **flirty sleep eyes, laughing/closed mouth, special body with molded shoes**

16"...$40,000.00–50,000.00 pair

Mold 126 Mein Liebling Baby (My Darling Baby), **sleep or flirty eyes, bent-leg, values are for sleep eyes, allow more for flirty or naughty eyes, or wobble tongue.**

Baby

10"–12"...$300.00–350.00

14"–16"...$375.00–450.00

18"–20"...$400.00–500.00

22"–24"...$550.00–650.00

Toddler body

Five-piece body, **with "starfish" hands**

6"–8"...$400.00–500.00

9"–10"...$500.00–600.00

15"...$800.00–900.00

20"–25"...$900.00–1,100.00

Mold 127, 127N, **domed head-like mold 126, bent-leg body, add more for flirty eyes**

Baby

10"–11"...$750.00–800.00

14"–15"...$900.00–1,000.00

18"–22"...$1,100.00–1,200.00

Toddler body

    15"–16" $1,300.00–1,500.00

    20"–23" $1,700.00–2,000.00

    26" $1,900.00–2,000.00

Mold 128, **sleep eyes, open mouth, baby body**

    10" $450.00–500.00

    13"–15" $600.00–700.00

    20"–24" $800.00–1,000.00

Mold 131: See Googly category.

Mold 135, **sleep eyes, open mouth, baby body**

    13"–16" $950.00–1,100.00

Mold 201, **shoulder head, painted eyes, closed mouth, similar to mold 101, muslin body**

    16" $2,100.00–2,500.00

Too few in database for reliable range.

Mold 314, **socket head, composition body, painted eyes, flocked hair**

    14" $6,250.00

Puz, **composition head, cloth body**

    16"–17" $900.00–1,000.00

    23"–25" $1,100.00–1,300.00

Cloth Character Dolls, **1927, wire armature body, needle-sculpted stockinette heads, painted features, wooden feet, all in good clean, unfaded condition**

    12"–13" $300.00–450.00

Composition, **1930s on, sleep eyes, wigged**

Baby, Mold 926

    13" $275.00–350.00

Adult

Fat Character Man & Woman pair

    8" $600.00–800.00

Too few in database for reliable range.

Celluloid: See Celluloid section.

KENNER

11.5" Blythe, Kenner, vinyl: $1,500. **Photo courtesy of McMasters Harris Apple Tree Doll Auctions.**

12" Luke Skywalker, Kenner, vinyl, MIP: sold at auction $2,880.00. **Photo courtesy of Philip Weiss Auctions.**

1947 to 2000, Cincinnati, Ohio. Purchased by Tonka Toys in 1987 and then by Hasbro in 1991, run as a separate division by both. Dolls listed are in very good condition with all original clothing and accessories. **MIB can bring double.**

Baby Alive, **1990, vinyl head, eats and drinks**

    16"..$35.00–40.00

Baby Bundles

    16"..$50.00–60.00

Baby Yawnie, **1974, vinyl head, cloth body**

    15"..$12.00–18.00

Blythe, **1972, pull string to change color of eyes, "mod" clothes**

    11½" $1,500.00–2,000.00

Butch Cassidy or Sundance Kid

    4"..$30.00–40.00

    with horses $40.00–50.00

Cover Girls, **1978, posable elbows and knees, jointed hands**

Dana, **black**

    12½"..$70.00–80.00

Darci, **1979**

    12½"..$25.00–30.00

Erica, **redhead**

    12½"..$25.00–30.00

Crumpet, **1970, vinyl and plastic**

    18"..$50.00–60.00

Dusty, 1974, vinyl teenage doll

11"..$20.00–30.00

Skye, black, teenage friend of Dusty

11"..$20.00–30.00

Gabbigale, 1972

White

18"..$40.00–50.00

Black

18"..$45.00–55.00

Garden Gals, 1972, hand bent to hold watering can

6½"..$10.00–15.00

Glamour Gal, 1982, similar to Deluxe Reading's Dawn doll

6"..$10.00–14.00

Hardy Boys, 1978, Shaun Cassidy, Parker Stevenson

12"..$15.00–20.00

Hug A Bunch, 1985, plush doll, synthetic eyes

18"..$18.00–22.00

International Velvet, 1976, Tatum O'Neill

11½"..$15.00–20.00

Jenny Jones and baby, 1973, all-vinyl, Jenny, 9", Baby, 2½"

Set..$20.00–25.00

Nancy Nonsense, 1975, pull string taker

17"..$40.00–50.00

Rose Petal, 1984, scented, various flowers and colors

7"..$18.00–20.00

Sabrina the Teenage Witch, 1997, TV show starring Mellissa Joan Hart

11.5"..$10.00–15.00

Sea Wees, 1979–1984, mermaid dolls

7"..$18.00–25.00

Six Million Dollar Man Figures, 1975–1977, TV show starring Lee Majors, MIB can bring triple, or more on rare figures

Big Foot

13"..$75.00–85.00

Fembot

13"..$85.00–95.00

Jaime Sommers, Bionic Woman

13"...$40.00–50.00

Masketron Robot

13"...$100.00–125.00

Oscar Goldman, **1975–1977, with exploding briefcase**

13"...$40.00–50.00

Steve Austin, The Bionic Man

13"...$100.00–125.00

Steve Austin, Bionic Grip, **1977**

13"...$100.00–125.00

Transport and Repair playset

...$90.00–110.00

Star Wars Figures, 1974–1978, large size action figures. Dolls listed are complete dolls in excellent condition. Never-removed-from-box would bring triple the price or more.

Ben-Obi-Wan Kenobi

12"...$225.00–250.00

MIB example sold for $1,440.00 at auction

Boba Fett

13"...$155.00–175.00

C-3PO

12"...$65.00–75.00

Chewbacca

12"...$120.00–140.00

Darth Vader

12"...$180.00–200.00

MIB example sold for $2,100.00 at auction

Han Solo

12"...$600.00–700.00

IG-88

15"...$300.00–350.00

Jawa

8½"...$100.00–130.00

Leia Organa

11½"...$125.00–150.00

Luke Skywalker

12"...$200.00–225.00

R2-D2

7½" $90.00–100.00

Stormtrooper

12" $175.00–200.00

Steve Scout, **1974,**

9" $30.00–40.00

Bob Scout, **Steve's black friend**

9" $35.00–45.00

Strawberry Shortcake, **ca. 1980–1986, and friends**

5" $25.00–45.00

Baby Strawberry Shortcake, **blows kisses**

15" $35.00–45.00

Sweet Cookie, **1972**

18" $25.00–30.00

Terminator, **Arnold Schwarzenegger, 1991, talks**

13½" $20.00–25.00

Upsy Baby, **ca. 1985, battery operated, stands up from crawling position, rooted hair, paintd eyes**

14" $20.00–25.00

J.D. KESTNER

16" mold 169, Kestner, bisque, socket head, closed mouth: $2,500. **Photo courtesy of Sweetbriar Auctions.**

16" mold XI, Kestner, bisque: $4,300. **Photo courtesy of Sweetbriar Auctions.**

1805–1938, Waltershausen, Thüringia, Germany. Kestner was making dolls by the 1820s and was one of the first firms to make dressed dolls. Besides wooden dolls, papier-mâché, wax over composition, and Frozen Charlottes, Kestner made bisque dolls with leather or composition bodies, chinas, all-bisque dolls, and celluloid dolls. Supplied bisque heads to Catterfelder Puppenfabrik. Borgfeldt, Butler Bros., Century Doll Co., Horsman, R.H.

Macy, Sears, Siegel Cooper, F.A.O. Schwarz, and others were distributors for Kestner. Early bisque heads with closed mouths marked X or XI, turned shoulder head, and swivel heads on shoulder plates are thought to be Kestners. After 1892, dolls were marked "made in Germany" with mold numbers.

Bisque heads with early mold numbers are stamped "Excelsior DRP No. 70 685," heads of 100 number series are marked "dep." Some early characters are unmarked or only marked with the mold number. After "211" on, it is believed all dolls were marked "JDK" or "JDK, Jr." Registered the "Crown Doll" (Kronen Puppe) in 1915, used crown on label on bodies and dolls.

The Kestner Alphabet was registered in 1897 as a design patent. It is possible to identify the sizes of doll heads by this key. Letter and number always go together: B/6, C/7, D/8, E/9, F/10, G/11, H/12, H ¾ /12 ¾, J/13, J ¾ /13 ¾, K/14, K ½ /14 ½, L/15, L ½ /15 ½, M/16, N/17.

Dolls listed are in good condition with original clothes or appropriately dressed. Exceptional dolls may be more.

Early Socket-head Child, bisque socket head, 1880 on. Closed or open-closed mouth, plaster pate, may be marked with size numbers only, glass eyes, may sleep, composition ball-jointed body, sometimes with straight wrists, appropriate wig and dress, in good condition, more for original clothes.

Mold 128, 169, or no mold number, **closed mouth, round or long face styles**

10"–12"	$1,200.00–1,800.00
14"–16"	$2,000.00–2,500.00
19"–21"	$2,400.00–2,800.00
24"–25"	$2,400.00–3,600.00

Square face, **closed mouth, some with white space between lips, no mold number**

14"–16"	$2,300.00–2,700.00
19"–21"	$2,900.00–3,200.00
24"–25"	$3,300.00–3,400.00

A.T. look, **closed mouth, glass eyes, marked only with size number such as 15 for 24"**

12"–15"	$7,000.00–8,000.00
21"	$10,000.00–12,000.00
26"	$13,000.00–14,000.00

Bru **look, closed mouth with space between lips, glass eyes, resembles circle dot Bru**

14"–15"	$5,500.00–6,000.00
19"–22"	$6,000.00–6,500.00

Mold X

15"	$2,900.00–3,300.00

Mold XI

16"	$4,0000.00–4,600.00

13" Kestner, bisque, pouty, straight wrists: $1,800. **Photo courtesy of Sweetbriar Auctions.**

13" mold 129, Kestner, bisque, socket head: $900. **Photo courtesy of Withington Auction Inc.**

Mold XII

17".. $4,200.00–4,400.00

Mold 103, **pouty closed mouth**

28"– 30"...................................... $2,500.00–3,000.00

Pouty, **no mold mark, closed mouth**

10"–14"...................................... $1,600.00–2,000.00

18"–20"...................................... $2,500.00–3,000.00

22"–24"...................................... $3,500.00–4,000.00

Early Shoulder Head Child, 1880 on, bisque shoulder head, glass eyes, plaster pate, wig, kid body with bisque lower arms, marked with size numbers or letter only

Closed mouth

10"–12"...................................... $400.00–525.00

14"–16"...................................... $550.00–650.00

20"–22"...................................... $700.00–800.00

25"–26"...................................... $900.00–1,000.00

33"–36"...................................... $1,200.00–1,500.00

AT look, **closed mouth**

11"... $2,300.00–2,700.00

21"–25"...................................... $7,000.00–7,500.00

Open mouth

16"–18"...................................... $250.00–300.00

22"–24"...................................... $400.00–450.00

Turned shoulder head, **closed mouth**

16"–18"...................................... $550.00–650.00

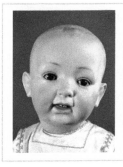

24" Kestner, baby, bisque, marked "JDK": $550. **Photo courtesy of Withington Auction Inc.**

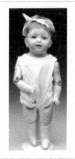

11" Kestner mold 238, shoulderhead baby, bisque: $750. **Photo courtesy of Morphy Auctions.**

22"–25"..$750.00–850.00

28"...$900.00–1,000.00

Shoulder Head Child, **1892 on, bisque shoulder head with sleep eyes, open mouth, plaster pate, wigged, kid body**

Molds 145, 147, 148, 154, 166, 195

10"–14"..$200.00–300.00

15"–18"..$300.00–350.00

20"–22"..$350.00–400.00

26"–32"..$500.00–900.00

Bisque Socket Head Child, **open mouth, glass eyes, Kestner ball-jointed body**

Mold 142, 144, 146, 164, 167, 171, 214

8"–12"..$550.00–600.00

14"–16"..$550.00–650.00

18"–22"..$700.00–750.00

24"–26"..$800.00–950.00

28"–32"..$1,000.00–1,100.00

Mold 171, **18" size only called "Daisy"**

18"...$2,000.00–2,500.00

Mold 129, 130, 149, 152, 160, 161, 168, 173, 174

10"–12"..$800.00–900.00

14"–16"..$900.00–1,000.00

18"–26"..$700.00–1,000.00

Mold 155, **open mouth, glass eyes, five-piece or fully jointed body**

8"–11"..$500.00–650.00

18" mold 245, Hilda, Kestner, bisque: $2,200. **Photo courtesy of Sweetbriar Auctions.**

15" mold 182, Kestner, bisque, painted eyes: $. **Photo courtesy of Sweetbriar Auctions.**

Molds 196, 215

18"–20"...$650.00–750.00

26"–28"...$800.00–850.00

32"...$900.00–950.00

Character Baby, **1910 on, socket head with wig or solid dome with painted hair, glass eyes, open mouth with bent-leg baby body, more for toddler body**

Marked "JDK," **solid dome bisque socket head, glass sleep eyes, molded and/or painted hair, composition bent-leg baby body, add more for body with crown label and/or original clothes**

12"–14"...$250.00–300.00

16"–18"...$400.00–475.00

21"–25"...$500.00–600.00

So-called Baby Jean, **solid dome, fat cheeks, marked JDK**

11"–13"...$600.00–700.00

15"–18"...$800.00–1,000.00

22"–24"...$1,100.00–1,200.00

Molds 211, 226, 236, 257, 260, **allow 25 percent more for toddler body or flocked hair**

8"–13"...$400.00–500.00

16"–18"...$600.00–650.00

20"–22"...$700.00–800.00

24"–26"...$900.00–1,000.00

Molds 210, 234, 235, 238, **shoulder head, solid dome, sleep eyes, open-closed mouth or open mouth**

12"–14"...$850.00–1,000.00

Mold 220, **sleep eyes, open-closed mouth**

18"...$5,500.00–6,000.00

18" Kestner, mold 183, bisque: $4,000. **Photo courtesy of Sweetbriar Auctions.**

16" mold 212 character, Kestner, bisque: $11,00. **Photo courtesy of Sweetbriar Auctions.**

Toddler

16"–20" $6,500.00–7,500.00

Hilda, molds 237, 245, 1070 **(bald solid dome), sleep eyes, open mouth**

11"–13" $2,200.00–2,500.00

16"–18" $2,000.00–2,200.00

20"–22" $2,100.00–2,800.00

25"–26" $2,500.00–3,000.00

Mold 243, **Asian baby, sleep eyes, open mouth**

13"–14" $1,600.00–2,200.00

16"–18" $3,000.00–3,500.00

Mold 247, **socket-head, open mouth, sleep eyes**

14"–18" $900.00–1,000.00

Toddler

16"–21" $1,200.00–1,600.00

Mold 255, **marked "O.I.C. made in Germany," solid dome flange neck, glass eyes, large open-closed screamer mouth, cloth body**

11"–13" $3,000.00–4,000.00

Character Child, **1910 on, socket head, wig, glass eyes, composition and wood jointed body**

Mold 143 **(1897 on, precursor to character dolls), open mouth, glass eyes, jointed body**

8"–10" $750.00–850.00

12"–14" $750.00–1,000.00

16"–20" $1,100.00–1,500.00

Mold 178, 179, 180, 181, 182, 184, 185, 186, 187, 189, 190, 191

Painted eyes

9"–12" $2,500.00–3,000.00

20" Kestner, Gibson
girl, bisque: $2,200.
**Photo courtesy
of Sweetbriar
Auctions.**

15" $3,750.00–4,000.00

18" $4,000.00–5,000.00

Glass eyes

12" $2,400.00–2,900.00

15" $3,500.00–3,800.00

18" $3,500.00–4,500.00

Mold 206, **fat cheeks, closed mouth, glass eyes child or toddler**

12"–15" $12,000.00–14,000.00

19" $24,000.00–26,000.00

Too few in database for reliable range.

Mold 208, **for all-bisque, see that category**

Painted eyes

12" $13,500.00–15,500.00

Glass eyes

16" $16,000.00–18,000.00

Too few in database for reliable range.

Mold 212, **fat cheeks, closed mouth, small eye cuts, glass eyes**

17" $11,000.00–12,000.00

Mold 239, **socket head, open mouth, sleep eyes**

Toddler, **also comes as baby**

15"–17" $2,500.00–3,000.00

Mold 241, **socket head, open mouth, sleep eyes**

17"–18" $3,500.00–4,000.00

21"–22" $4,200.00–4,400.00

24"–25" $4,6000.00–5,000.00

28"–30" $5,400.00–6,000.00

Other Character dolls

Mold 279 socket head with molde bob hairstyle, open mouth, glass eyes, on composition body

15"... $500.00–600.00

Max & Moritz socket head on composition body

13"... $6,700.00–7,200.00 each

Lady Doll, 1898 on, bisque socket head, open mouth, glass eyes, composition body, slender waist and molded breasts

Mold 162

16"–22".. $2,500.00–3,000.00

Mold 172 "Gibson Girl," shoulder head, closed mouth, glass eyes, kid body, bisque forearms

10"–13".. $80.00–1,000.00

15"–17".. $1,500.00–2,000.00

18"–21".. $2,000.00–2,500.00

Wunderkind, set includes doll body with four interchangeable heads, some with extra apparel

With heads 174, 178, 184, and 185

11"... $9,000.00–9,500.00

With heads, 171, 179, 182, and 183

14½"... $12,650.00

Too few in database for reliable range.

Celluloid shoulder head doll, sleep eyes, kid body, wigged

Molds 200, 201

16"–20".. $250.00–350.00

KEWPIE

1913 on, designed by Rose O'Neill. Manufactured by Borgfeldt, later Joseph Kallus, and then Jesco in 1984, and various companies with special license, as well as unlicensed companies. They were made of all–bisque, celluloid, cloth, composition, rubber, vinyl, zylonite, and other materials. Kewpie figurines (action Kewpies) have mold numbers 4843 through 4883. Kewpies were also marked with a round paper sticker on back, "KEWPIES DES. PAT. III, R. 1913; Germany; REG. US. PAT. OFF." On the front, was a heart-shaped sticker marked "KEWPIE//REG. US.// PAT. OFF." May also be incised on the soles of the feet, "O'Neill." Dolls listed are in good condition. Add more for label, accessories, original box, or exceptional doll.

 4.25" Kewpie, all bisque, jointed shoulders, special painted footwear with fancy bows: $400. **Photo courtesy of Withington Auction Inc.**

 2.75" Doodledog, all bisque: $1,000. **Photo courtesy of Withington Auction Inc.**

All-Bisque

Immobiles, **standing, legs together, immobile, no joints, blue wings, molded and painted hair, painted side-glancing eyes**

2"–3½ " $100.00–125.00

4"–5" $125.00–160.00

6" $200.00–225.00

Jointed shoulders

2"–2½" $75.00–95.00

3"–4" $110.00–120.00

5"–6" $130.00–220.00

7"–8" $230.00–260.00

10"–12" $500.00–700.00

Jointed hips and shoulders

4" $700.00–850.00

5"–6" $900.00–1,000.00

7"–8" $950.00–1,050.00

10" $1,150.00–1,250.00

12½" $1,300.00–1,350.000

Jointed shoulders with any article of molded clothing

2½"–4½" $400.00–700.00

5"–6" $800.00–900.00

8" $1,000.00–1,100.00

With Mary Jane shoes

4½" $375.00–400.00

6½" $425.00–500.00

4.75" Kewpie soldier, Saxony Infantry, all bisque: $1,200. **Photo courtesy of Withington Auction Inc.**

11" Kewpie socket head, bisque: $4,000. **Photo courtesy of Morphy Auctions.**

Bisque Action Figures

Arms folded

6"..$525.00–600.00

Aviator

8½"..$775.00–850.00

Back, **laying down, kicking one foot**

4"..$250.00–300.00

Basket and ladybug, **Kewpie seated**

4"..$1,400.00–1,700.00

"Blunderboo," **Kewpie falling down**

4½"..$400.00–425.00

Baby bottle **with Kewpie and Baby Kewpie**

3½"..$1,600.00–1,700.00

Bottle, **green beverage, Kewpie standing, kicking out**

2½"..$525.00–575.00

Bottle stopper

2"..$100.00–150.00

Box, **heart shaped, with Kewpie kicker atop**

4"..$650.00–750.00

Bride and Groom

3½"..$300.00–350.00

5" &400.00–450.00

Boutonnière

1½"..$85.00–110.00

2"..$120.00–135.00

Bunny **in lap of seated Kewpie**

2"..$425.00–475.00

Candy container

    4"...$400.00–500.00

Carpenter, **wearing tool apron**

    8½"...$975.00–1,100.00

Cat, **on lap of seated Kewpie**

    3"–3½"......................................$525.00–575.00

Chick **with seated Kewpie**

    2"...$525.00–575.00

Christmas Ornament, **molded bisque clip on back**

    2"...$500.00–550.00

Cowboy

    10"...$700.00–800.00

Dog, **with Red Cross Kewpie**

    4"...$250.00–300.00

Doodle Dog **alone**

    1½"..$700.00–800.00

    3"...$1,000.00–1,200.00

Doodle Dog **with Kewpie**

    2½"..$1,000.00–1,500.00

Drum **on brown stool, with Kewpie**

    3½"..$2,000.00–2,200.00

Farmer

    6½"..$800.00–900.00

Feeding baby, **larger Kewpie feeding smaller Kewpie with spoon**

    2½" **sold at auction for**...................$1,0,830.00

Fireman in helmut

4½" sold at auction for $3,078.00

Flowers, **Kewpiewith bouquet in right hand**

    5"...$825.00–925.00

Gardener

    4"...$300.00–350.00

Governor

    2½"..$325.00–375.00

    3¼"..$400.00–475.00

Guitar, **Standing Kewpie playing**

    3½"..$400.00–450.00

Hatbox (turquoise), held by seated Kewpie

  3".. $1,500.00–1,600.00

Hottentot, **black Kewpie**

  3½" $425.00–500.00

  5"... $625.00–675.00

  9".. $925.00–975.00

Huggers

  2½" $75.00–100.00

  3½" $100.00–175.00

  4½" $250.00–300.00

Inkwell, **with writer Kewpie**

  4½" $475.00–525.00

Jack-O-Lantern **between legs of Kewpie**

  2".. $450.00–500.00

Jester, **with white hat on head**

  4½" $500.00–575.00

Kneeling

  4".. $475.00–550.00

Lying on Back

  4"long.. $375.00–425.00

Lying on Tummy

  3¼"long $325.00–375.00

Mailing label in hand

  2¼" $550.00–650.00

Mandolin, **green basket and seated Kewpie**

  2".. $450.00–550.00

Mayor, **seated Kewpie in green wicker chair**

  4".. $375.00–425.00

Minister

  5"... $200.00–250.00

Policeman

  4½" $1,100.00

Reader Kewpie **seated with book**

  2"... $200.00–250.00

  3½" $250.00–300.00

  4"... $350.00–400.00

Reader Kewpie in green armchair, **seated with book**

    5½" $1,350.00

Rose in hand Kewpie **on place card holder**

    2" $60.00–75.00

Salt Shaker

    2" $150.00–175.00

Seated on bench, **feeeding bottle to doodledog**

    3½" long sold at auction for $4,845.00

Sitting on Elephants Lap

    3½" sold at auction for $14,820.00

Sailor

    5" $2,900.00

Soldier, **Confederate**

    4" $225.00–250.00

Soldier, **Confederate, lying on stomach aiming rifle**

    3" $450.00–500.00

Soldier **in Prussian helmet**

    5½" $900.00–1,100.00

Soldier **in Prussian helmet with rifle and saber**

    3¾" $950.00–1,200.00

Soldier **lying on stomach aiming rifle**

    3" $400.00–450.00

Soldier **vase, vase looks like tree**

    6½" $850.00–800.00

Soldier

    2¾" $450.00–500.00

    4½" $500.00–550.00

Stomach, **Kewpie laying flat, arms and legs out**

    4" $375.00–450.00

Sweeper **with dust bin by leg**

    3½"–4" $300.00–400.00

Teddy Bear **held in arm of Kewpie**

    3¾" $625.00–650.00

Teddy Bear **vase, teddy bear in arms of Kewpie**

    3¾" $500.00–550.00

Thinker

4"–6" $175.00–200.00

Traveler with dog and umbrella

3½" $1,200.00–1,300.00

Traveler with umbrella and bag

4" $350.00–400.00

5" $500.00–550.00

Vase kewpie Gardener standing to side of vase

6½" $900.00–1,000.00

Writer, seated Kewpiewith pen in hand

2" $325.00–375.00

4" $375.00–450.00

Writer, seated Kewpiewith pen in hand on bisque tray with note written on it

2.5 X 4.5 .... $175.00–225.00

Carnival chalk Kewpiewith jointed shoulders

13" $75.00–125.00

Bisque Socket Head, made by Kestner, glass eyes, composition body

12"–14" $4,000.00–5,000.00

Bisque Flange-neck Head, painted eyes, cloth body with bisque hands

11" $3,800.00–4,300.00

Bisque Shoulder Head, on cloth body

Painted eyes

7"–10" $525.00–800.00

Glass eyes

12" $2,500.00–2,800.00

Celluloid

Bride and Groom

4" $15.00–40.00

Jointed arms, heart label on chest

5" $80.00–100.00

8" $165.00–185.00

12" $275.00–325.00

China

Cigarette Lighter, Green Japserware with Kepie figures

4" sold at auction for $1,254.000

Perfume holder, **one-piece with opening at back of head**

    4½" $550.00–1,100.00

Salt Shaker

    1¼" $85.00–165.00

Dishes, **china by Royal Rudolstadt, Germany, early 20th century**

Individual pieces

    .... $25.00–100.00

    German jasperware creamer $70.00–80.00

    German jasperware hatpin holder, 4½"

    .... $275.00–300.00

Cloth

Richard Krueger "Kuddle Kewpie **silk screened face, stockinette or sateen body, tagged**

    8"–10" $200.00–300.00

    13"–14" $350.00–400.00

    18"–23" $575.00–650.00

R. John Wright, **1999 on, molded felt, jointed shoulders, values listed are for secondary market dolls, dolls also available at retail**

    6" $20.00–400.00

Composition, **made by Cameo Doll Co., Mutual Doll Co., and Rex Doll Co.**

Hottentot, **all-composition, heart decal to chest, jointed arms, red wings, ca. 1946**

    11"–13" $400.00–450.00 150

All-composition, **jointed body, blue wings**

    8" $125.00–150.00

    11"–13" $200.00–300.00

Composition head, **cloth body, flange neck, composition forearms, tagged floral dress**

    11" $250.00–300.00

Talcum container

One-piece composition talcum shaker with heart label on chest

    11" $200.00–225.00

Hard Plastic

Kewpie **1950s, Kewpie design**

    8½" $140.00–210.00

    12" $300.00–325.00

Sleep eyes, **five-piece body with starfish hands**

    14" $300.00–350.00

Metal

Figurine, **cast steel on square base, excellent condition**

    5½" $40.00–55.00

Sitting on a stamp box

    4" $300.00–400.00

Soap

Kewpie soap figure with cotton batting, **colored label with rhyme, marked "R.O. Wilson, 1917"**

    4" $90.00–110.00

Vinyl

Knickerbocker, **late 1950s on, vinyl mask face on plush body**

    8"–12" seated $75.00–90.00

Bunny Kuddles, **Kewpie mask faced bunny wearing vinyl hat**

    11" seated $50.00–60.00

Cameo Dolls, **1960s, in very good condition with original clothing**

    10"–12" $35.00–45.00

    14"–16" $60.00–70.00

    27" $100.00–125.00

Jesco Dolls, **1980s, mint, all-original condition**

    8" $20.00–35.00

    10"–12" $40.00–50.00

    15"–18" $65.00–75.00

    24"–27" $75.00–100.00

KLEY & HAHN

1902–1930s, Ohrdruf, Thüringia, Germany. Bisque heads, jointed composition or leather bodies, composition and celluloid head dolls. Was an assembler and exporter; bought heads from Bähr & Pröschild, Kestner (Walkure), Hertel Schwab & Co, and Rheinische Gummi. Dolls listed are in good condition, appropriately dressed.

Character Baby, **bisque socket head, bent limb composition body, molds such as 133, 135, 138, 158, 160, 161, 167, 176, 525, 571, 680, and others**

    9"–13" $400.00–475.00

    16"–18" $500.00–600.00

    20"–22" $700.00–775.00
    24"–28" 800.00–900.00

31" Walkure mold, Kley & Hahn, bisque: $650. **Photo courtesy of McMasters Harris Apple Tree Doll Auctions.**

21" mold 520, Kley & Hahn, character girl, bisque: $5,100. **Photo courtesy of Ann Lloyd Antique Dolls.**

Toddler body

14"–16" $800.00–900.00

18"–21" $1,000.00–1,200.00

26" $1,300.00–1,400.00

Mold 567 (made by Bähr & Pröschild) character multi-face, laughing face, glass eyes, open mouth; crying face, painted eyes, open-closed mouth

11" $1,000.00–1,400.00

15" $1,950.00–2,100.00

17" $2,200.00–2,400.00

19" $2,400.00–2,600.00

Child, 1920, dolly face, sleep eyes, open mouth, molds 250, 282, or Walkure

12"–13" $175.00–275.00

16"–18" $300.00–375.00

22"–24" $350.00–400.00

28"–30" $500.00–600.00

33"–36" $700.00–800.00

Mold 325, "Dollar Princess," open mouth

18"– 20" $325.00–375.00

23"–25" $375.00–425.00

Character Child, 1912, bisque socket head, jointed composition body

Mold numbers 154, 166, 169

Closed mouth

14"–16" $1,800.00–2,100.00

19"–20" $2,200.00–2,300.00

27" $2,500.00–2,600.00

Open mouth

    17"–20"... $1,000.00–1,200.00

Painted eye character, **molds 520, 526, 531**

    14"–16"... $3,600.00–3,800.00

    17"–19"... $3,900.00–4,100.00

    20"–23"... $5,000.00–6,000.00

Mold 525, **solid dome head, open/closed mouth, intaglio eyes**

    15"–20"... $450.00–500.00

Mold 536, **open/closed mouth, intaglio eyes**

    12"–15"... $3,000.00–3,200.00

Mold 546, 549, **ca. 1912, character face**

    12"–14"... $3,300.00–3,500.00

    15"–16"... $3,500.00–4,000.00

    18"–21"... $4,200.00–4,4,000.00

Mold 554, 568, **ca. 1912, character face**

    21"... $1,400.00

Mold 567, **2-faced character baby with protruding ears, smiling, scowling**

    13"–15""... $1,800.00–2,000.00

C.F. KLING & CO.

1834–1940s, Ohrdruf, Thüringia, Germany. Porcelain factory that began making doll heads in 1879, made china, bisque, and all-bisque dolls, and snow babies. Often mold number marks are followed by size number. Dolls listed are in good condition, appropriately dressed, more for exceptional doll with elaborate molded hair or bodice.

Bisque Shoulder Head, 1880 on

Painted eyes, **molded hair, cloth or kid body, molds such as 123, 124, 131, 167, 178, 182, 186, 189, and others**

    12"–14"... $350.00–450.00

    15"–16"... $525.00–625.00

    18"–20"... $675.00–775.00

    23"–25"... $800.00–900.00

Glass eyes, **molded hair, cloth or kid body, molds such as 128, 131, 190, 203, 204, 214, 217, 247, 254, and others**

    15"–16"... $550.00–650.00

    22"–23"... $800.00–900.00

14" mold 131-5, Kling, bisque, shoulder head: $500. **Photo courtesy of McMasters Harris Apple Tree Doll Auctions.**

Wigged, **straight or turned shoulderhead, closed mouth, cloth or kid body, molds such as 123, 166, 167, and others**

15"–18" $600.00–800.00

20"–28" $700.00–1,100.00

Tinted or Untinted Bisque Lady, **painted eyes or glass, molded bodices, fancy hair, molds such as 135,144, 170, and others**

15"–17" $1,000.00–1,200.00

19"–21" $1,400.00–2,000.00

China Shoulder Head, **1880 on, molded hair, painted eyes, closed mouth, molds such as 131, 188, 189, 202, 220, 285, and others**

11"–15" $150.00–250.00

18"–20" $300.00–400.00

24"–25" $500.00–600.00

Mold 188, glass eyes

18"–20" $450.00–500.00

Bisque socket head, **1900 on, open mouth, sleep eyes, jointed body, molds such as 182, 370, 372, 373, 377**

13"–15" $225.00–350.00

17"–22" $375.00–500.00

All-Bisque: See All-Bisque section.

KLUMPE

1952–1970s, Barcelona, Spain. Caricature figures made of felt over wire armature with painted mask faces. Figures represent professionals, hobbyists, Spanish dancers, historical characters, and contemporary males and females performing a wide variety of tasks. Of the two hundred or more different figures, the most common are Spanish dancers, bull fighters,

11" Klumpe, surgeon, cloth: $110. **Photo courtesy of Joan & Lynette Antique Dolls and Accessories.**

and doctors. Some Klumpes were imported by Effanbee in the early 1950s. Originally the figures had two sewn-on identifying cardboard tags. Dolls listed are in good condition.

Average figure

10½" $70.00–140.00

Elaborate figure, **with tags & accessories**

10½" $150.00–300.00

KNICKERBOCKER DOLL & TOY CO.

1927–1980s, New York, New York. Made dolls of cloth, composition, hard plastic, and vinyl.

Cloth

Clown

17"... $18.00–25.00

Disney characters

Donald Duck, **all-cloth**

10½"–12"...................................... $575.00–800.00

Little Lulu, **mask face**

18".. $100.00–150.00

Mickey Mouse, **ca. 1930s, oil-cloth eyes**

10"–12"... $900.00–2,000.00

16" example in excellent condition sold for $7,930.00 at auction

Cowboy Mickey

12"–17"... $1,500.00–2,000.00

Pinocchio, **cloth and plush**

13".. $200.00–250.00

12" Mickey Mouse, Knickerbocker, cloth: $800. **Photo courtesy of Morphy Auctions.**

10" Jiminy Cricket, Knickerbocker, composition: $450. **Photo courtesy of McMasters Harris Apple Tree Doll Auctions.**

Seven Dwarfs, **1939 on, mask face, mohair beard, up-turned toes**

14"... **$125.00–150.00 each**

Snow White, **all-cloth, mask face**

16"... **$250.00–300.00**

Flintstones

6½"... **$15.00–18.00**

Holly Hobbie, **1970s, cloth, later vinyl**

Cloth

7"–9"... **$12.00–16.00**

14"–16"... **$25.00–35.00**

26"–33"... **$40.00–55.00**

Vinyl

6"... **$10.00–16.00**

11"... **$25.00–35.00**

Baby Holly Hobbie, **vinyl and cloth**

15"... **$15.00–18.00**

Levi's Big E Jeans dolls, **1973**

10"–16"... **$35.00–40.00**

Little Orphan Annie, **1977**

16"... **$20.00–28.00**

Composition

"Blondie" **comic strip characters, composition, painted features, hair**

Alexander Bumstead, **molded hair**

9"... **$325.00–400.00**

Blondie Bumstead, **mohair wig**

11"... **$425.00–500.00**

Dagwood Bumstead, **molded hair**

    14"..$425.00–500.00

Child, **1938 on, mohair wig, sleep eyes**

    15"..$120.00–200.00

    18"..$225.00–300.00

Mickey Mouse, **1930s–1940s, composition, cloth body**

    18"..$900.00–1,100.00

18" Cowboy Mickey sold for $2,074.00 at auction

Jiminy Cricket, **all-composition**

    10"..$400.00–450.00

Pinocchio, **all-composition**

    10"–12"...$200.00–225.00

    14"–17"...$300.00–400.00

Seven Dwarfs, **1939+**

    9"..$ 130.00–150.00 each

Sleeping Beauty, **1939+, bent right arm**

    15"..$150.00–200.00

    18"..$300.00–350.00

Snow White, **1937+, all-composition, bent right arm, black wig**

    15"..$425.00–525.00

    20"..$475.00–550.00

Molded hair and ribbon, **mark: "WALT DISNEY//1937//KNICKERBOCKER"**

    13"..$325.00–400.00

    15"..$525.00–600.00

boxed set of 13" Snow White and 9" Dwarfs

    ....$1,800.00–2,000.00

Plastic and Vinyl Mask Face Dolls, **1950s–1960s**

Plush Body

Pinocchio

    13"..$40.00–60.00

Baby Santa Claus, **1955 on**

    7"seated...$30.00–35.00

Sleepy Head

    13"–23"...$30.00–35.00

Cloth Body

Knick the Clown

19"...$35.00–45.00

Lovely Lori

15"...$65.00–75.00

Vinyl head on cloth body

Soupy Sales

13"...$120.00–180.00

Quickdraw MacGraw

16½ " $80.00–100.00

Winnie Witch

13"...$85.00–100.00

Hard Plastic and Vinyl

Betsy Clark, **1974, all vinyl**

6"...$20.00–25.00

Vinyl head & Hands, **on cloth body**

15"...$25.00–50.00

Bozo Clown

14"...$18.00–25.00

17"–24"..$40.00–60.00

28"–30"..$60.00– 80.00

Cinderella, **two faces, one sad, one with tiara**

16"...$15.00–20.00

Flintstone characters

17"...$40.00–50.00

Kewpies: See Kewpiesection.

Little House on the Prairie, **1978**

12"...$25.00–30.00

Little Orphan Annie **comic strip characters, 1982**

Little Orphan Annie, **vinyl**

6"...$12.00–16.00

11"...$18.00–22.00

Daddy Warbucks

7"...$7.00–9.00

Punjab

7"...$9.00–12.00

Miss Hannigan

    7"...$5.00–10.00

Molly

    5½" $7.00–11.00

Rattle Dolls, **hard plastic, jointed shoulders, painted side-glancing eyes**

    6"...$15.00–20.00

Snoopy or Belle, **Charles Schultz character, 1965**

    8"...$16.00–19.00

    Outfits **MOC**..................................$12.00–20.00

Two-faced dolls, **1960s, vinyl face masks, one crying, one smiling**

    12"..$22.00–28.00

Dolly Pops, **1979 on, molded vinyl with synthetic hair, molded changeable vinyl clothing**

    2½" $11.00–18.00

Dolly Pops Poptown playset

    1982 ....$30.00–45.00

GEBRUDER KNOCH

20" mold 216, Gebruder Knoch, bisque, open/closed mouth, intaglio eyes: $350. **Photo courtesy of Sweetbriar Auctions.**

1887–1919, Neustadt, Thüringia, Germany. Porcelain factory that made bisque doll heads with cloth or kid body.

Shoulder Head

Dolly face

    9"–15"...$75.00–90.00

    20"–22"...$200.00–300.00

Mold 203, 205, **ca. 1910**

Mold 203, **character face, painted eyes, closed mouth, stuffed cloth body**

Mold 205, **"GKN" character face, intaglio eyes, open-closed mouth, molded tongue**

12"–13"...$450.00–550.00

14"–15"...$625.00–700.00

Mold 216, **ca. 1912, "GKN" solid dome, intaglio eyes, laughing, open-closed mouth**

16"–18"...$250.00–325.00

Socket Head

Mold 179, 181, 190, 192, 193, 201, **ca. 1900, mold 201 also came as black, dolly face, glass eyes, open mouth, ball jointed composition body**

7"–8" on five-piece body

....$70.00–80.00

10"–13"...$150.00–200.00

18"–25"...$300.00–450.00

Mold 204, 205, **ca. 1910, character face**

15"...$800.00–900.00

Mold 229: See All-Bisque category.

Mold 230, **ca. 1912, molded bonnet, character shoulder head, painted eyes, open-closed mouth laughing, mold 232, ca. 1912, molded bonnet, character shoulder head, laughing**

13"...$675.00–900.00

15"...$1,200.00–1,600.00

KÖNIG & WERNICKE GMBH

1912–1930s, Waltershausen, Germany. Had doll factory, made bisque or celluloid dolls with composition bodies, later dolls with hard rubber heads. Bought bisque heads from Bähr & Pröschild, Hertel & Schwab and Armand Marseille. Made "My Playmate" for Borgfeldt. Dolls listed are in good condition, appropriately dressed.

Bisque Baby

Mold 98, 99, **ca. 1910,** *Mold 1070,* **ca. 1915 "made in Germany" (made by Hertel Schwab & Co.), character, socket head, sleep eyes, open mouth, teeth, tremble tongue, wigged, composition bent-leg baby body**

9"–12"...$200.00–250.00

15"–16"...$275.00–450.00

18"–22"...$350.00–500.00

24"–27"...$550.00–650.0

14" mold 1070, toddler, König & Wernicke, bisque: $500. **Photo courtesy of Alderfer Auction Company, Inc.**

Toddler

    11"–13" **$550.00–600.00**

    15"–17" **$600.00–800.00**

    19"–20" **$700.00–1,000.00**

Child, **socket head, composition body**

Dolly face

    15" **$375.00–425.00**

    26"–29" **$700.00–800.00**

    36" **$800.00–900.00**

Mold 1070, **character child, sleep eyes**

    15" **$600.00–700.00**

    18"–20" **$800.00–1,100.00**

    30" **$1,800.00–2,000.00**

Painted bisque child, **regional dress**

    18" **$125.00–175.00**

Low Fire Bisque Child, **resembles composition, on five-piece or fully jointed body, open mouth, sleep eyes, add more for flirty eyes**

    14" **$225.00–300.00**

    16" **$350.00–450.00**

Celluloid Child, **mold 777, celluloid socket head, glass eyes, wigged**

    13"–15" **$125.00–150.00**

    17"–21" **$175.00–200.00**

RICHARD KRUEGER

20" Krueger, cloth mask face, cloth body, all original: $120. **Doll from Private Collection.**

1907–1950s, New York City. Made cloth mask faced dolls.

Child, **1930 on**

Cloth body

10"	**$55.00–65.00**
12"	**$45.00–75.00**
16"	**$75.00–100.00**
20"	**$100.00–120.00**

Oilcloth body

10"	**$45.00–60.00**
14"–18"	**$55.00–100.00**

Walt Disney and other characters

Dwarf, **plush beard**

12½"	**$125.00–175.00**

Snow White

18"	**$250.00–300.00**

Three Little Pigs

7"	**$100.00–150.00 each**

Pinocchio

16"	**$400.00–500.00**

Kuddle Kewpie: See Kewpie section.

Scootles, **1935, designed by Rose O'Neill, yarn hair**

10"...$750.00–800.00

18"...$825.00–875.00

18" in excellent conditon sold at auction for $7,080.00

KÄTHE KRUSE

1910 to present, Prussia, after WWII, Bavaria. Made cloth dolls with molded stockinette heads and waterproof muslin bodies, heads, hair, and hands oil painted. Early dolls are stuffed with deer hair. Early thumbs are part of the hand; after 1914 they are attached separately, later they're again part of the hand. Marked on the bottom of the left foot with number and name "Käthe Kruse," in black, red, or purple ink. After 1929, dolls had wigs, but some still had painted hair. Later dolls have plastic and vinyl heads. Original doll modeled after bust sculpture "Fiamingo" by Francois Duquesnois. Dolls listed are in good condition, appropriately dressed. Allow significantly less for dirty or faded examples.

Cloth

Doll I Series, **1910–1929, all-cloth, jointed shoulders, wide hips, painted eyes and hair, three vertical seams in back of head, marked on left foot**

16"...$5,000.00–6,500.00

Ball-jointed knees, **1911 variant produced by Kämmer & Reinhardt**

17"...$11,000.00–13,000.00

Later model, **1929+, now with slim hips**

17"...$2,500.00–4,000.00

Doll IH Series, **wigged version, 1930+**

17"...$1,500.00–2,000.00

Bambino, **a doll for a doll, circa 1915–1925**

8"...$500.00

Too few in database for reliable range.

Doll II Series, **"Schlenkerchen," ca. 1922–1936, smiling baby, open-closed mouth, stockinette covered body and limbs, one seam head**

13"...$12,000.00–13,000.00

Doll V, VI, **Sandbabies Series, 1920s+, "Traumerchen" (closed eyes) and "Du Mein" (open eyes) were cloth dolls with painted hair, weighted with sand or unweighted, with or without belly buttons, in 19⅝" and 23⅝" sizes, one- or three-seam heads or cloth over cardboard, later heads were made in the 1930s from a heavy composition called magnesit**

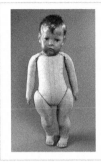

16" Doll I, Käthe Kruse, cloth, wide hips: $2,500. **Photo courtesy of McMasters Harris Apple Tree Doll Auctions.**

20" Käthe Kruse, model VIII: $2,400. **Photo courtesy of Morphy Auctions.**

19⅝"–23½"

.... $6,000.00–7,500.00

Magnesit head, **circa 1930s+**

20".. $2,000.00–3,000.00

Doll VII Series, **circa 1927–1952, two versions were offered**

Smaller 14" Du Mein open eye baby, **painted hair or wigged, three-seam head, wide hips, sewn on thumbs, 1927–1930**

14".. $3,500.00–4,000.00

Doll I version, **with wide hips, separately sewn on thumbs, painted hair or wigged, after 1930–1950s slimmer hips and with thumbs formed with hand**

14".. $3,500.00–4,000.00

Doll VIII Series

Deutsche Kind, the "German child," 1929 on, **modeled after Kruse's son, Friedebald, hollow head, swivels, one vertical seam in back of head, wigged, disk-jointed legs, later made in plastic during the 1950s**

20".. $1,800.00–2,400.00

Doll IX Series

"The Little German Child," 1929 on, **wigged, one seam head, a smaller version of Doll VIII**

14".. $2,000.00–2,600.00

Doll X Series, **1935 on, smaller Doll I with one-seam head that turns**

14".. $2,500.00–2,800.00

Doll XII Series, **1930s, Hampelchen with loose legs, three vertical seams on back of head, painted hair, button and band on back to make legs stand. The 14" variation has head of Doll I; the 16" variation also has the head of Doll I, and is known after 1940s as Hempelschatz, Doll XIIB**

14".. $1,600.00–2,000.00

18".. $2,000.00–3,000.00

341

Hard Plastic, **1948–1975, celluloid and other synthetics**

US Zone mark

    14"–19"..$900.00–1,400.00

Turtle Mark Dolls, **1955–1961, synthetic bodies**

    14"...$125.00–175.00

    16"...$200.00–250.00

    18"...$300.00–350.00

1975 to date, **marked with size number in centimeters, B for baby, H for hair, and G for painted hair**

    10"...$100.00–125.00

    13"–15"...$125.00–225.00

    17"–19"...$200.00–250.00

GEBRUDER KUHNLENZ

9" Gebruder Kuhnlenz, mold 44.18: $225. **Photo courtesy of McMasters Harris Apple Tree Doll Auctions.**

1884–1935, Kronach, Bavaria, Germany. Porcelain factory made dolls, doll heads, movable children, and swimmers. Butler Bros. and Marshall Field distributed their dolls.

Closed Mouth Child

Mold 22 **bisque solid dome socket head, closed mouth, glass eyes, pierced ears, wig, wood and composition jointed body**

    10"–12"...$525.00–575.00

Mold 28, 31, 32, 39, **ca. 1890, bisque socket head, closed mouth, glass eyes, pierced ears, wig, wood and composition jointed body**

    8"–10"...$900.00–1,400.00

    15"–16"...$1,500.00–1,800.00

    21"–23"...$2,200.00–2,500.00

Mold 34, **Bru type, paperweight eyes, closed mouth, pierced ears, composition jointed body**

12½"–15"..$2,900.00–4,000.00

18"–20"..$4,500.00–6,300.00

Mold 38, **solid dome turned shoulder head, closed mouth, pierced ears, kid body**

12"–15"..$550.00–625.00

17"–20"..$800.00–1,000.00

Open Mouth Child

Mold 41, 44, **socket head, glass eyes, open mouth, composition body**

6"–8"..$200.00–250.00

9"–10"..$375.00–425.00

15"–19"..$500.00–600.00

24"–26"..$700.00–800.00

30"–31"..$900.00–1,000.00

Mold 165, 185, **ca. 1900, socket head, sleep eyes, open mouth, teeth**

16"–18"..$200.00–275.00

22"–24"..$400.00–500.00

28"–30"..$550.00–650.00

Mold 47, 61, 170 **shoulder head**

14"–16"..$100.00–150.00

18"–20"..$175.00–200.00

Character dolls

Mold 205, **shoulder head, open/closed mouth, intaglio eyes, molded painted hair**

20"..$500.00–550.00

No mold #, **open/closed laughing mouth, glass eyes**

15"..$1,000.00–1,200.00

Small Dolls, **44 marked "Gbr. K" in sunburst, socket head, glass eyes, open mouth, five-piece body composition body**

7"–8"..$175.00–225.00

All-Bisque, **swivel neck, molds 31, 41, 44, 56, others, glass eyes, more elaborate footwear, original costumes and larger sizes bring high end of range**

4"–7"..$350.00–1,000.00

A. LANTERNIER
& CIE.

16" Toto, Lanternier, bisque: $500. **Photo courtesy of Withington Auction Inc.**

1915–1924, Limoges, France. Porcelain factory, made dolls and heads. Lady dolls were dressed in French provincial costumes, bodies by Ortyz; dolls were produced for Association to Aid War Widows.

Adult, ca. 1915

Marked "Masson," "Lorraine," "Favorite," bisque socket head, open-closed mouth with teeth, composition adult body

12"– 13"	$700.00–900.00
16"–18"	$1,000.00–1,100.00
19"–22"	$1,100.00–1,400.00

Painted eyes

18"	$1,100.00–1,200.00

Child, dolly face **no mold name or "Cherie," "Favorite," "La Georgienne," bisque socket head, open mouth with teeth, wig, composition jointed body**

12"–14"	$500.00–600.00
16"–20"	$625.00–700.00
22"–24"	$550.00–600.00
25"–26"	$700.00–800.00

Character Child, marked "Toto"

"Caprice," **open/closed mouth with teeth, glass eyes, wigged**

19"	$600.00

"Toto," **marked on head, chubby cheeks**

15"–18"	$450.00–650.00

LEATHER

Leather was an available resource for Native Americans to use for making doll heads, bodies, or entire dolls. It was also used by American doll makers such as Darrow and by French and Moroccan doll makers, as well as others. Some examples of Gussie Decker's dolls were advertised as "impossible for child to hurt itself" and leather was fine for teething babies.

Darrow, American, molded rawhide. These dolls are almost always found with very little original paint remaining. Value listed reflects this condition

   12"... $200.00–250.00

   18"–22" $300.00–400.00

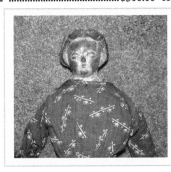

16" Darrow, leather: $275. **Photo courtesy of The Museum Doll Shop.**

French all-leather baby, molded head, jointed body, painted eyes

   4"–4½"... $2,800.00–3,500.00

French budoir-type doll, 1960s, appliqued mouth, fur eye lashes

   23".. $75.00–85.00

Moroccan leather dolls, 1900–1940s, souvenir type dolls depicting regional characters

   9"–11" $25.00–45.00

Native American Dolls

Plains tribes, various, **1900 on**

   5"–8"... $130.00–225.00

   13"–15" $400.00–650.00

   23".. $700.00–850.00

Eskimo, **ca. 1940**

   10"–12" $100.00–125.00

Todhunter, M. 1926 on, England, leather over molded clay face, wire armature body wrapped with suede

   10"–12" $100.00–125.00

LENCI

16" Lenci, 400 series, felt: $2,600. **Photo courtesy of Sara Bernstein's Dolls.**

17.5" Lenci, 1500 series girl, felt: $2,100. **Photo courtesy of Alderfer Auction Company, Inc.**

1919 to 2003, Turino, Italy. Lenci was the trademark and name of firm started by Enrico and Elena di Scavini that made felt dolls with pressed faces, also made composition head dolls, wooden dolls, and porcelain figurines and dolls. Early Lenci dolls have tiny metal button, hang tags with "Lenci//Torino//Made in Italy." Ribbon strips marked "Lenci//Made in Italy" were found in the clothes ca. 1925–1950. Some, not all, dolls have Lenci marked in purple or black ink on the sole of the foot. Some with original paper tags may be marked with a model number in pencil. Dolls have felt swivel heads, oil-painted features, often side-glancing eyes, jointed shoulders and hips, third and fourth fingers are often sewn together, sewn-on double felt ears, often dressed in felt and organdy original clothes, excellent condition. May have scalloped socks.

The most sought after are the well-constructed early dolls from the 1920s and 1930s, when Madame Lenci had control of the design and they were more elaborate with fanciful, well-made accessories. They carried animals of wood or felt, baskets, felt vegetables, purses, or bouquets of felt flowers. This era of dolls had eye shadow, dots in corner of eye, two-tone lips, with lower lip highlighted and, depending on condition, will command higher prices.

After WWII the company was purchased by the Garella Brothers. The later dolls of the 1940s and 1950s have hard cardboard-like felt faces, with less intricate details, like less elaborate appliqués, fewer accessories, and other types of fabrics such as taffeta, cotton, and rayon, all showing a decline in quality and should not be priced as earlier dolls. The later dolls may have fabric covered cardboard torsos. Model numbers changed over the years, so what was a certain model number early, later became another letter or number.

Lenci characteristics include double-layer ears, scalloped cotton socks. Early dolls may have rooted mohair wig. 1930s dolls may have "frizzed" played-with wigs. Later dolls are less elaborate with hard cardboard-type felt faces. Dolls listed are in clean condition and wearing original clothing. Soiled, faded examples will bring significantly less. Add more for tags, boxes, or accessories. Exceptional dolls and rare examples may go much higher.

Baby

13"–15"..$1,700.00–1,900.00

18"–22"..$2,700.00–3,000.00

16" model 164 sold at auction for $5,985.00

346

15" Lenci Boudoir doll, felt, ca. 1933: $1,900. **Photo courtesy of Sweetbriar Auctions.**

1930s, Bambino, **felt over metal baby**

　　16"... $5,000.00–6,500.00

Too few in database for a reliable range.

Child

1920s–1930s, **softer face, more elaborate costume, face model numbers 300, 109, 149, 159, 110, 111**

　　12"–14".. $1,000.00–1,200.00

　　16"–22".. $1,500.00–4,000.00

Model 1500, **scowling face**

　　17"–19".. $2,000.00–3,000.00

Model 400

　　14"–16".. $2,200.00–2,600.00

Model 500

　　21"... $2,000.00–2,200.00

1940s–1950s+, **hard face, less intricate costume**

　　13"... $300.00–400.00

　　15"... $400.00–500.00

　　17"... $500.00–600.00

Small Dolls

Mascottes and Miniatures, **9"**

　　Regional costume $300.00–400.00

　　Child.. $300.00–500.00

More Eleborate Character

　　... $500.00–700.00

Long Limbed Lady Dolls, **with adult face, flapper or boudoir body with long slim limbs**

    17"–20"..$2,200.00–3,000.00

    24"–28"..$3,000.00–4,000.00

    32"..$5,000.00–5,600.00

Rarities

Celebrities

Jackie Coogan

    21"..$3,500.00–3,600.00

Dorothy Gish (long limbed lady)

    31" **sold for**....................................$4,250.00 at auction

Mozart

    11"..$1,400.00–1,800.00

    14"..$2,000.00–2,200.00

Pastorelle

    14"..$2,900.00–3,100.00

Shirley Temple (series 950)

    28"–32"..$3,200.00–3,500.00

Characters

Aladdin

    14"..$7,000.00–7,750.00

Aviator, **girl with felt helmet**

    18"..$2,900.00–3,200.00

Becassine

    11"..$925.00–975.00

20" glass eyes

    ....$2,900.00–3,100.00

Benedetta

    19"..$2,000.00–2,400.00

Black Clown

    13"..$2,500.00–3,000.00

Cowboy

    14"–18"..$1,000.00–2,000.00

Cupid

    17"..$4,900.00–5,200.00

Elf, **ca. 1926, black**

7"...$3,000.00 at auction

Fascist Boy, **rare**

14"...$3,500.00–4,000.00

Flower Girl, **ca. 1930**

20"...$1,200.00–1,400.00

Henriette

26"...$2,200.00–2,800.00

Indian

17"...$3,200.00–3,600.00

Laura

16"...$950.00–1,100.00

Pierrot

17"–21"...$2,300.00–2,700.00

Pinocchio

11"...$1,100.00

Rajah, **seated on cushion**

12"...$2,100.00–2,400.00

Smoker

Painted eyes

28"...$2,500.00–3,000.00

Glass eyes

24"...$4,000.00–4,200.00

Snake Charmer, **seated, light brown felt**

17"...$8,000.00–8,500.00

Sport Series

16"–18"...$3,000.00–6,000.00

Polo player

16"–17"...$9,000.00–12,000.00

Val Gardena

19"...$800.00–900.00

Winking Boy

11"...$950.00–1,100.00

Ethnic or Regional Costume

Asian, boy with lantern

25"...$4,500.00–5,000.00

Black Girl

    18"... $2,50.00–3,000.00

Italian girl

    18"... $1,000.00–1,200.00

Madame Butterfly, **ca. 1926**

    17"... $3,000.00–3,200.00

    25"... $4,300.00–4,800.00

Marenka, **Russian girl, ca. 1930**

    19"... $3,000.00–3,200.00

Sarda, Italian girl, **ca. 1930**

    19"... $800.00–900.00

Scotish boy

    18"... $1,700.00–1,900.00

Spanish girl, **ca. 1930**

    14"... $1,200.00–1,400.00

    19"... $2,500.00–3,000.00

Tyrol boy or girl, **ca. 1935**

    18"... $2,000.00–2,500.00

Eye Variations

Glass eyes

    16"... $1,400.00–1,600.00

    22"... $2,800.00–3,000.00

Flirty glass eyes

    15"–20"... $1,000.00–1,800.00

Surprise eye, **widow, "O" shaped eyes and mouth**

    19"–20"... $1,800.00–2,200.00

Modern, **1979 on**

    12"–14"... $90.00–120.00

    21"–26"... $100.00–300.00

Pinocchio, **1981**

    18"... $100.00–120.00

Accessories

    Lenci Dog... $100.00–150.00

    Purse... $175.00–225.00

    9½" jester purse sold at auction for $570.00

LENCI-TYPE

1920–1950. These were made by many English, French, or Italian firms like Anili, Gre-Poir, or Nicette from felt with painted features, mohair wig, original clothes. These must be in very good condition, tagged or unmarked. Usually Lenci-types have single felt ears or no ears. Elaborate costume or those that closley resemble lenci bring higher end of range.

17" Gre Poir, cloth face: $400. **Photo courtesy of Morphy Auctions.**

Child

Low quality

    10"–17"..$120.00–165.00

High quality

    11"–15"..$300.00–500.00

    17"–20"..$400.00–600.00

Regional costume, **makers such as Alma, Vecchiotti, and others,**

    8"–9"...$65.00–250.00

    11"–15"..$175.00–300.00

Smoker

    16"...$160.00–300.00

Alma, **dolls have elastic strung heads**

Child

    11"..$200.00–275.00

    15"–17"..$400.00–650.00

    21"..$775.00–875.00

Anili, **founded by the daughter of Elena Di Scavini (Lenci), molded felt dolls**

Child

    15"–21"..$70.00–175.00

Gre Poir, **France, New York City, 1927–1930s, Eugenie Poir made felt or cloth mask face dolls, unmarked on body, no ears, white socks with three stripes, hang tag 16"–18"**

       Cloth face $325.00–400.00

       Felt face $800.00–900.00

Messina-Vat, **1923 on, Turin, Italy**

       20" $400.00–450.00

LIBERTY OF LONDON

11" Henry the Eight, Liberty of London, cloth: $190. **Photo courtesy of The Museum Doll Shop.**

1906 to 1950s, London, England. Liberty of London was founded in 1873. In 1920 they registered the name "Liberty" for their line of needle-sculpted cloth art dolls.

British Characters and Historical Figures, such as Shakespeare, John Bull, Queen Victoria, and others

       9"–10" $100.00–300.00

       Beefeater $90.00–130.00

Coronation dolls

       9"–10" $150.00–225.00

Princess Elizabeth or Margaret

       7" $200.00–275.00

A.G. LIMBACH

5.5" all bisque baby, Limbach, bisque: $150. **Photo courtesy of Alderfer Auction Company, Inc.**

1772–1927 on, Limbach, Thüringia, Germany. This porcelain factory made bisque head dolls, china dolls, bathing dolls, and all-bisque dolls beginning in 1872. Usually marked with three leaf clover. Beware of all bisque fakes with unusual or character head which are currently flooding the market.

All-Bisque

Child, **small doll, molded hair or wigged, painted eyes, molded and painted shoes and socks, may have mark "8661," and cloverleaf, more for exceptional dolls**

  3½" $35.00–50.00

  4"–7" $50.00–150.00

  11"–12" $275.00–325.00

Paper sticker marked "Our Mary," **all-bisque, glass sleep eyes, wigged**

  6"–8" $175.00–225.00

Baby, **mold 8682, character face, bisque socket head, glass eyes, clover mark, bent-leg baby body, wig, open-closed mouth**

  8½"–11" $275.00–350.00

Child

Bisque Socket Head, **dolly face may have name above mold mark, such as Norma, Rita, Wally, glass eyes, clover mark, wig, open mouth**

  18"–20" $600.00–700.00

  22"–24" .... $700.00–8`00.00

Character Head, **child or baby**

  8"–12" $800.00–2,000.00

Bisque Shoulder Head, **open mouth, glass eyes, kid body**

  10"–15" $80.00–100.00

Lady "The Irish Queen": See Parian-type, Untinted Bisque.

MAROTTES

12" Marotte,
German, bisque:
$700. **Photo
courtesy of
The Museum
Doll Shop.**

1860 on and earlier. Doll's head on wooden or ivory stick, sometimes with whistle, when twirled some play music. Bisque head on stick made by various French and German companies.

Bisque

German head, **open mouth dolly face mold, various German makers such as Armand Marseille, Gebruder Heubach, etc.**

> 9"–14" $425.00–750.00
>
> 16"–18" $775.00–900.00

Character mold

> 9"–14" $900.00–1,500.00

French head

> 10"–12" $700.00–1,000.00
>
> 14"–16" $1,000.00–1,400.00

Celluloid

> 11"–15" $200.00–350.00

ARMAND MARSEILLE

1884–1950s, Sonneberg, Köppelsdorf, Thüringia, Germany. One of the largest suppliers of bisque doll heads, ca. 1900–1930, to such companies as Amberg, Arranbee, Bergmann, Borgfeldt, Butler Bros., Dressel, Montgomery Ward, Sears, Steiner, Wiegand, Louis Wolfe, and others. Made some doll heads with no mold numbers, but names, such as Alma, Baby Betty, Baby Gloria, Baby Florence, Baby Phyllis, Beauty, Columbia, Duchess, Ellar, Florodora, Jubilee, Mabel, Majestic, Melitta, My Playmate, Nobbi Kid, Our Pet, Princess,

23" mold 1894, Armand Marseille, bisque, socket head, no clothes or wig: $250. **Photo courtesy of Joan & Lynette Antique Dolls and Accessories.**

20" mold 390, Armand Marseille, bisque: $300. **Photo courtesy of Morphy Auctions.**

Queen Louise, Rosebud, Superb, Sunshine, and Tiny Tot. Some Indian dolls had no mold numbers. Often used Superb kid bodies, with bisque hands. After WWII and into the 1950s the East German government continued to produce dolls marked AM. Dolls listed are in good condition, appropriately dressed.

Child Doll, 1890 on, bisque socket head, open mouth, glass eyes, wig, composition fully jointed body. Dolls listed are in good condition, appropriately dressed. Allow more for flirty eyes.

Socket head, composition body, **no mold number, or just marked "A.M.," and molds 390, Floradora, 1894**

9"–10"	$100.00–125.00
12"–14"	$150.00–200.00
16"–18"	$250.00–300.00
20"–24"	$300.00–350.00
28"–30"	$350.00–400.00
32"–36"	$500.00–650.00
40"–42"	$700.00–800.00

Five-piece flapper body, **high quality**

6"–7"	$150.00–200.00
10"–13"	$250.00–300.00

Five-piece body, **low quality**

10"–12"	$130.00–145.00
14"–16"	$160.00–185.00

Molds Queen Louise, Rosebud

12"–13"	$200.00–225.00
15"–17"	$225.00–275.00
22"–24"	$300.00–325.00
26"–28"	$350.00–400.00
31"–34"	$500.00–650.00

17" mold 230 "Fany", Armand Marseille, bisque: $5,000. **Photo courtesy of Joan & Lynette Antique Dolls and Accessories.**

7.5" mold 310 Just Me, Armand Marseille, painted bisque: $525. **Photo courtesy of McMasters Harris Apple Tree Doll Auctions.**

Mold Baby Betty

14"–16" $300.00–350.00

18"–20" $350.00–400.00

Shoulder head, kid body

Shoulder heads mold 370, 1894, 3200, **Alma, Beauty, Floradora, Lily, Mabel, My Playmate, Princess, Rosebud**

10"–12" $85.00–100.00

14"–16" $100.00–150.00

18"–20" $200.00–250.00

22"–26" $220.00–280.00

Molds 1890, 1892, 1895, 1897, 1899, 1901, 1902, 1903, 1909

10"–12" $125.00–175.00

14"–16" $225.00–275.00

18"–20" $275.00–350.00

22"–24" $375.00–400.00

Character Baby

Molds Kiddiejoy, 256, 259, 326, 327, 328, 329, 360a, 750, 790, 900, 927, 970, 971, 975, 990, 991, 992 Our Pet, 995, 996, 1330, **bisque solid-dome or wigged socket head, open mouth, glass eyes, composition bent-leg baby body, add more for toddler body or flirty eyes or exceptional doll**

8"–10" $225.00–250.00

12"–15" $225.00–250.00

17"–21" $250.00–300.00

24"–26" $350.00–400.00

Mold 233

8" $300.00–375.00

12"–13" $400.00–450.00

15" $500.00–550.00

Mold 250, **open/closed mouth with two lower teeth, molded hair, intaglio eyes**

8"–9" $350.00–400.00

Mold 251/248

Open/closed mouth

10"–12" $500.00–600.00

Closed mouth

12" $325.00–350.00

Mold 410, **two rows of retractable teeth**

12" $900.00–1,100.00

Mold 500, **intaglio eye, bent-limb composition body**

13"–15" $475.00–600.00

Mold 518

16"–18" $400.00–600.00

Mold 560A

8"–9" $150.00–225.00

12"–16" $400.00–500.00

Mold 580, 590

11"–13" $475.00–525.00

15"–16" $750.00–950.00

Mold 920

21" $650.00

Too few in database for reliable range.

Melitta, **toddler**

16" $800.00–900.00

Character Child

No mold #, **marked A (size #) M, bisque socket head, intaglio eyes, closed mouth, wigged, composition jointed body**

20"–25" $20,000.00–30,000.00

34" sold for .... $40,000.00 at auction

Too few in database for reliable range.

Mold 225, **ca. 1920, bisque socket head, glass eyes, open mouth, two rows of teeth, composition jointed body**

14" $3,000.00–3,600.00

19" $4,000.00–4,650.00

13" mold 550, Armand Marseille, bisque, character socket head: $1,600. **Photo courtesy** *of* **Ann Lloyd Antique Dolls.**

8.5" mold 560a, Armand Marseille, bisque, character socket head: $650. **Photo courtesy of Joan & Lynette Antique Dolls and Accessories.**

Fany, **ca. 1912, can be child, toddler, or baby**

230, **molded hair**

13"–16" $4,000.00–5,000.00

17"–18" $5,000.00–6,000.00

231 **(wigged)**

13"–15" $5,000.00–5,500.00

Mold 250, **ca. 1912, domed**

9"–13" $575.00–600.00

15" $600.00–650.00

18" $750.00–875.00

Mold 251, **ca. 1912, socket head, open-closed mouth**

10"–13" $650.00–750.00

17"–18" $1,000.00–1,200.00

Mold 253: See Googly section.

Mold 310, **Just Me, ca. 1929, bisque socket head, wig, flirty eyes, closed mouth, composition body**

7½"–8" $750.00–800.00

9"–10" $850.00–900.00

11" $1,200.00–1,500.00

13" $1,700.00–2,000.00

Painted bisque, **with Vogue labeled outfits**

7"–8" $500.00–700.00

10" $1,000.00–1,100.00

Mold 340, **pouty**

Painted intaglio eyes

10"–12" $1,400.00–1,600.00

22" mold 351, Armand Marseille, bisque, bent limb composition body: $350. **Photo courtesy of Morphy Auctions.**

Mold 350, **ca. 1926, glass eyes, closed mouth**

    16"..$1,950.00–2,250.00

    20"..$2,500.00–2,850.00

Mold 360a, **ca. 1913, open mouth**

    12"..$350.00–400.00

Mold 400, 401, **ca. 1926, glass eyes, closed mouth**

    13"–15"...$1,600.00–1,800.00

    20"–24"...$1,900.00– $2,100.00

Mold 449, **ca. 1930, painted eyes, closed mouth**

    13"..$575.00–625.00

    18"..$700.00–800.00

Painted bisque

    11"..$200.00–250.00

    15"..$375.00–450.00

Mold 450, **glass eyes, closed mouth**

    14"..$575.00–700.00

Mold 500, 600, **ca. 1910, domed shoulder head, molded/painted hair, painted intaglio eyes, closed mouth**

    10"–12"...$900.00–1,000.00

    13"–16"...$1,300.00–1,750.00

Mold 520, **ca. 1910, domed head, glass eyes, open mouth**

Composition body

    12"..$675.00–750.00

    19"..$1,800.00–2,000.00

Kid body

    16"..$800.00–900.00

    20"..$1,200.00–1,400.00

Mold 550, **ca. 1926, domed, glass eyes, closed mouth**

    13"–15"..$1,600.00–1,900.00

Mold 560, 560a, **ca. 1910, character, domed, painted eyes, open-closed mouth or 560A, ca. 1926, wigged, glass eyes, open mouth**

    9"–14"...$600.00–900.00

    17"–22"..$900.00–1,200.00

Mold 570, **ca. 1910, domed, closed mouth**

    12"...$1,600.00–1,750.00

Mold 590, **ca. 1926, sleep eyes, open-closed mouth**

    16"...$900.00–1,000.00

    18"–20"..$1,100.00–1,200.00

Mold 600, **shoulder head, solid dome with molded hair, closed mouth, intaglio eyes**

    12"–15"..$650.00–750.00

Mold 640, **shoulder head, closed mouth, ontaglio eyes, wig**

    12"...$575.00–675.00

Mold 700, **ca. 1920, closed mouth**

Painted eyes

    12½"..$1,800.00–2,000.00

Glass eyes

    10"–14"..$1,200.00–1,500.00

Mold 800, **ca. 1910, socket head, 840 shoulder head**

    18"...$2,000.00–2,200.00

Lady, 1910 on, bisque head, wigged, sleep eyes, open or closed mouth, composition lady body

Molds 400, 401,

9"–14"

    Open mouth.....................................$900.00–1,300.00

    Closed mouth $1,000.00–1,500.00

    Painted Bisque $800.00–900.00

Newborn Baby, 1924 on, newborn, bisque solid-dome socket head or flange neck, may have wig, glass eyes, closed mouth, cloth body with celluloid or composition hands

Mold 341, My Dream Baby, 351, 345, 352, Rock-A-Bye Baby, **marked "AM."**

    8"...$75.00–100.00

    10"–12"..$125.00–150.00

    14"–16"..$175.00–225.00

    22"–24"..$275.00–400.00

On bent-limb composition body

11"–12".. $200.00–250.00

16"... $275.00–300.00

With toddler body

28".. $600.00–700.00

Pillow puppet

10"... $195.00–210.00

Baby Gloria, **solid dome, open mouth, painted hair**

12"... $350.00–400.00

15"... $450.00–500.00

Baby Phyllis, **head circumference:**

9"–10"... $200.00–225.00

13"–15".. $250.00–275.00

Composition Child, **1940s–1950s, mold 2966 and others. sleep eyes, synthetic wig, five-piece composition body (very thin cardboard-like composition)**

22"–28".. $145.00–160.00

MARX TOY CORP.

18" Miss Seventeen, Marx, hard plastic, MIB: $150. **Photo courtesy of Alderfer Auction Company, Inc.**

1919 to present, Sebring, Ohio. Founded in 1919 as Louis Marx & Co. in New York City. Dolls listed are in perfect condition with original clothing.

Archie and Friends, **characters from comics, vinyl, molded hair or wigged, painted eyes, in package**

Archie, Betty, Jughead, Veronica

8½"... $9.00–16.00

Freddy Krueger, 1989, vinyl, pull string talker horror movie *Nightmare on Elm Street* character played by Robert England

10"..$10.00–15.00

Johnny West Family of Action Figures, 1965–1976, adventure or Best of the West Series, rigid vinyl, articulated figures, molded clothes, came in box with vinyl accessories and extra clothes, had horses, dogs, and other accessories available, dolls listed are complete with box and all accessories, allow more if never removed from box or special sets, half as much if without box

Bill Buck, brown molded-on clothing, 13 pieces, coonskin cap

11½"..$300.00–370.00

Captain Tom Maddox, blue molded-on clothing, brown hair, 23 pieces

11½"..$50.00–65.00

Chief Cherokee, tan or light color molded-on clothing, 37 pieces

11½"..$50.00–65.00

Daniel Boone, tan molded-on clothing, coonskin cap

11½"..125.00–150.00

Dangerous Dan, blue figure, flocked hair and beard

11½"..200.00–225.00

Fighting Eagle, tan molded-on clothes, with Mohawk hair, 37 pieces

11½"..$70.00–90.00

General Custer, dark blue molded-on clothing, yellow hair, 23 pieces

11½"..$55.00–75.00

Geronimo, light color molded-on clothing

11½"..$55.00–75.00

Jamie West, dark hair, molded-on tan clothing, 13 accessories

9"..$70.00–85.00

Jane West, blond hair, turquoise molded-on clothing, 37 pieces

11½"..$40.00–50.00

Janice West, dark hair, turquoise molded-on clothing, 14 pieces

9"..$35.00–45.00

Jay West, blond hair, tan molded-on clothing, 13 accessories, later brighter body colors
9" 55.00–75.00

Jed Gibson, c. 1973, black figure, molded-on green clothing

12"..$200.00–250.00

Johnny West, brown hair, molded-on brown clothing, 25 pieces

12"..$60.00–75.00

Johnny West, **with quick draw arm, blue clothing**

    12".. $90.00–115.00

Josie West, **blond, turquoise molded-on clothing, later with bright green body**

    9".. $30.00–40.00

Princess Wildflower, **off-white molded-on clothing, with papoose in vinyl cradle, 22 pieces of accessories**

    11½" $55.00–75.00

Sam Cobra, **outlaw, with 26 accessories**

    11½" $130.00–150.00

Sheriff Pat Garrett **(Sheriff Goode in Canada), molded-on blue clothing, 25 pieces of accessories**

    11½" $130.00–150.00

Zeb Zachary, **dark hair, blue molded-on clothing, 23 pieces**

    11½" $170.00–200.00

Mike Hazard Double Agent, **1967, vinyl, trench coat, acessories, and box**

    12".. $140.00–150.00

Knight and Viking Series, **ca. 1960s, action figures with accessories, values for doll with box and accessories**

Gordon, the Gold Knight, **molded-on gold clothing, brown hair, beard, mustache**

    11½" $50.00–75.00

Sir Stuart, Silver Knight, **molded-on silver clothing, black hair, mustache, goatee**

    11½" $50.00–65.00

Brave Erik, Viking **with horse, ca. 1967, molded-on green clothing, blond hair, blue eyes**

    11½" $100.00–150.00

Odin, the Viking, **ca. 1967, brown molded-on clothing, brown eyes, brown hair, beard**

    11½" $60.00–75.00

Miss Seventeen, **1961, hard plastic, high heeled, fashion-type doll, modeled like the German Bild Lilli (Barbie doll's predecessor), came in black swimsuit, black box, fashion brochure pictures 12 costumes, she was advertised as "A Beauty Queen"**

    18".. $120.00–150.00

Miss Marlene, **hard plastic, high heeled, Barbie-type, ca. 1960s, blond rooted wig**

    11".. $100.00–125.00

Miss Toddler, **also know as Miss Marx, vinyl, molded hair, ribbons, battery operated walker, molded clothing**

    18".. $45.00–55.00

PeeWee Herman, 1987 TV character, vinyl and cloth, ventriloquist doll in gray suit, red bow tie

    25"..$40.00–50.00

    Pull string talker, **18"** $20.00–30.00

Sindy, ca. 1963+, in England by Pedigree, a fashion-type doll, rooted hair, painted eyes, wires in limbs allow her to pose, distributed in U.S. by Marx c. 1978–1982

    11"..$30.00–40.00

Pedigree **50.00–65.00**

Gayle, **Sindy's friend, black vinyl**

    11"..$80.00–95.00

    Outfits $75.00–95.00

Soldiers, ca. 1960s, articulated action figures with accessories

Buddy Charlie, **Montgomery Wards, exclusive, a buddy for G.I. Joe, molded-on military uniform, brown hair**

    11½" $80.00–100.00

Stony "Stonewall" Smith, **molded-on Army fatigues, blond hair, 36-piece accessories**

    11½" $80.00–100.00

Twinkie, doll with vinyl clothing and wigs

    4½" $40.00–60.00

MATTEL

1959 to present, founded by Ruth and Elliot Handler. Many dolls of the 1960s and 1970s designed by Martha Armstrong Hand. Dolls listed are in excellent condition with all original clothing and accessories. Allow double for mint-in-box examples.

Baby Beans, 1971–1975, vinyl head, bean bag dolls, terry cloth or tricot bodies filled with plastic and foam

    12"..$25.00–35.00

Talking

    12"..$55.00–75.00

Baby Come Back, 1976, battery-operated walker, rooted hair,

    16"..$25.00–30.00

Baby First Step, 1965–1967, battery-operated walker, rooted hair, sleep eyes, pink dress

    18"..$35.00–45.00

10" Talking Buffy, Mattel, vinyl: $45. **Photo courtesy of Memories of Things Past.**

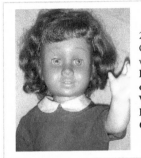

20" Chatty Cathy, Mattel, vinyl: $165. **Photo courtesy of Charlotte's Web Vintage Dolls and Collectibles.**

Talking

    18"...$50.00–60.00

Longer hair, **pink outfit**

    18"...$50.00–60.00

Baby Go Bye-Bye and Her Bumpety Buggy, **1970, doll sits in car, battery operated, 12 maneuvers**

    11"...$90.00–110.00

Baby Pattaburp, **1964–1966, vinyl, drinks milk, burps when patted, pink jacket, lace trim**

    16"...$60.00–70.00

Baby Play-A-Lot, **1972–1973, posable arms, fingers can hold things, comes with 20 toys, moves arm to brush teeth, moves head, no batteries, has pull string and switch**

    16"...$50.00–60.00

Baby That-A-Way **1974, crawls**

    15"...$45.00–55.00

1984 model, **curly hair**

    15"...$35.00–45.00

Baby Say 'N See, **1967–1968, eyes and lips move while talking, white dress, pink yoke**

    17"...$55.00–65.00

Baby Skates, **1982, vinyl face and hands, rooted blonde hair, battery-operated roller skating doll**

    15"...$30.00–40.00

Baby Secret, **1966–1967, vinyl face and hands, stuffed body, limbs, red hair, blue eyes, whispers 11 phrases, moves lips**

    18"...$75.00–90.00

Baby Small Talk, **1968–1969, says eight phrases, infant voice, additional outfits available**

    10¾" $20.00–30.00

13" My Child, Mattel, cloth: $150. **Photo courtesy of Charlotte's Web Vintage Dolls and Collectibles.**

3" Bunson Bernie, Mattel, vinyl: $75. **Doll from private collection.**

Black

    10¾" $55.00–65.00

In Nursery Rhyme outfit

    10¾" $25.00–35.00

Baby Tender Love, 1970–1973, baby doll, realistic skin, wets, can be bathed

Newborn

    13" $35.00–45.00

Living

    19" $40.00–50.00

Talking

    16" $40.00–50.00

Bless You, **1974, sneezes**

    14" $30.00–40.00

Baby Magic, **1978**

    14" $25.00–35.00

Tiny Baby Tender Love, **molded vinyl hair, 972**

    11½" $35.00–45.00

Brother, **sexed**

    11½" $35.00–45.00

Baby Walk 'n Play, 1968

    11" $10.00–15.00

Baby Walk 'n See

    18" $20.00–25.00

Barbie: See that section.

Big Jim Series, vinyl action figures, many boxed accessory sets available

Big Jim, **black hair, muscular torso**

    9½" $20.00–30.00

Big Jim with Talking Field Radio

9½" $30.00–35.00

Big Jack, **African American**

9½" $55.00–65.00

Big Josh, **dark hair, beard**

9½" $40.00–50.00

Dr. Steele, **bald head, silver tips on right hand**

9½" $60.00–75.00

Sports Camper set

.... $60.00–75.00

Beanie, **From Beanie & Cecile TV show, 1962, vinyl head, hands, feet, cloth body, pull string talker**

18" $75.00–100.00

Bozo, **1964**

18" $50.00–60.00

Buffy and Mrs. Beasley, 1967–1974, characters from TV sitcom *Family Affair*

Buffy, **vinyl, rooted hair, painted features, holds small Mrs. Beasley, vinyl head, on cloth body**

6½" $55.00–65.00

Talking Buffy, **vinyl, 1969–1971, holds tiny 6" rag Mrs. Beasley**

10¾" $50.00–60.00

Mrs. Beasley

1965, **vinyl head, cloth body**

16" $150.00–175.00

1973, **non-talker**

15½" $65.00–80.00

Captain Kangaroo, **1967, cloth, Sears only, talking character, host for TV kids program**

19" $60.00–75.00

Captain Laser, **1967, vinyl, painted features, blue uniform, silver accessories, batteries operate laser gun, light-up eyes**

12" $100.00–125.00

Casper, the Friendly Ghost

1964

16" $125.00–150.00

1971

5" $25.00–35.00

10" Jimmy Osmond, Mattel, vinyl, MIB: $40. **Photo courtesy of Phillip Weiss Auctions.**

16" Sister Belle, Mattel, vinyl: $55. **Photo courtesy Fourty Fifty Sixty.**

Chatty Cathy Series

Chatty Cathy, **1960–1963, vinyl head, hard plastic body, pull string activates voice, dressed in pink and white checked or blue party dresses, 1963–1965, says 18 new phrases, red velvet and white lace dress, extra outfits available**

20"..$150.00–225.00

Black

20"..$500.00–550.00

Canadian version.............................$450.00–550.00

1995 Reissue doll $60.00–75.00

Charmin' Chatty, **1963–1964, talking doll, soft vinyl head, closed smiling mouth, hard vinyl body, long rooted hair, long legs, five records placed in left side slot, one-piece navy skirt, white middy blouse, with red sailor collar, red socks and saddle shoes, glasses, five disks; extra outfits and 14 more disks available**

24"..$125.00–175.00

Chatty Baby, **1962–1964, red pinafore over rompers**

18"..$65.00–95.00

Brown haired, brown eyed, MIB sold at online auction for $719.00

Tiny Chatty Baby, **1963–1964, smaller version of Chatty Baby, blue rompers, blue, white striped panties, bib with name, talks, other outfits available**

15½" $100.00–125.00

Black

15½" $150.00–175.00

Tiny Chatty Brother, **1963–1964, boy version of Tiny Chatty Baby, blue and white suit and cap, hair parted on side**

15½" $100.00–125.00

Cheerful Tearful, **1966–1967, vinyl, blond hair, face changes from smile to pout as arm is lowered, feed her bottle, wets and cries real tears**

13"..$45.00–55.00

Tiny Cheerful Tearful

    7".. $45.00–55.00

Dancerella, **1978 battery operated**

    19".. $55.00–65.00

Dancerina, **1969–1971, battery operated, posable arms, legs, turns, dances with control knob on head, pink ballet outfit**

    24".. $75.00–100.00

Baby Dancerina, **1970, smaller version, no batteries, turn-knob on head, white ballet outfit**

    16".. $50.00–65.00

Black

    16".. $125.00–150.00

Teeny Dancerina

    12".. $25.00–35.00

Debbie Boone, **1978**

    11½".. $20.00–25.00

Dick Van Dyke, **1969, as Mr. Potts in movie, Chitty Chitty Bang Bang, all-cloth, flat features, talks in actor's voice, mark: "© Mattel 1969" on cloth tag**

    24".. $60.00–75.00

Drowsy, **1965–1974, vinyl head, stuffed body, sleepers, pull-string talker**

    15½".. $60.00–75.00

Reissue, 2001

    15".. $40.00–45.00

Dr. Dolittle, **1968, character patterned after Rex Harrison in movie version, talker, vinyl with cloth body**

    24".. $40.00–50.00

All vinyl

    6".. $20.00–30.00

Gramma Doll, **1970–1973, Sears only, cloth, painted face, gray yarn hair, says ten phrases, talker, foam-filled cotton**

    11".. $12.00–16.00

Grizzly Adams, **1971**

    10".. $30.00–40.00

Guardian Goddesses, **1979**

    11½".. $30.00–40.00

Herman Munster, **1965, cloth doll, talking TV character, The Munsters**

    21".. $275.00–375.00

Liddle Kiddles, 1966 on, small dolls of vinyl over wire frame, posable, painted features, rooted hair and came with bright costumes and accessories, packaged on 8½" x 9½" cards, mark: "1965//Mattel Inc.//Japan" on back, dolls listed are in excellent condition with all accessories, add double for mint in package (or card) and never removed from package, less for worn dolls with missing accessories

1966, First Series

3501 Bunson Bernie

    3"...$70.00–80.00

3502 Howard "Biff" Boodle

    3½"..$55.00–75.00

3503 Liddle Diddle

    2¾"...$80.00–100.00

3504 Lola Liddle

    3½"..$75.00–100.00

3505 Babe Biddle

    3½"..$45.00–60.00

3506 Calamity Jiddle

    3"...$80.00–90.00

3507 Florence Niddle

    2¾"...$85.00–95.00

3508 Greta Griddle

    3"...$65.00–85.00

3509 Millie Middle

    2¾"...$100.00–120.00

3510 Beat A Diddle

    3½"..$85.00–95.00

1967, Second Series

3513 Sizzly Friddle

    3"...$70.00–90.00

3514 Windy Fiddle

    2½"..$60.00–90.00

3515 Trikey Triddle

    2¾"...$90.00–100.00

3516 Freezy Sliddle

    3½"..$70.00–90.00

3517 Surfy Skiddle

    3"...$70.00–80.00

3518 Soapy Siddle

    3½" **$75.00–90.00**

3519 Rolly Twiddle

    3½" **$90.00–100.00**

3548 Beddy Bye Biddle (with robe)

    .... **$70.00–90.00**

3549 Pretty Priddle

    3½" **$75.00–100.00**

1968, Third Series

3587 Baby Liddle

    2¾" **$50.00–70.00**

3551 Telly Viddle

    3½" **$80.00–110.00**

3552 Lemon Stiddle

    3½" **$60.00–75.00**

3553 Kampy Kiddle

    3½" **$80.00–100.00**

3554 Slipsy Sliddle

    3½" **$75.00–100.00**

Storybook Kiddles, **1967–1968**

    .... **$75.00–150.00**

Skediddle Kiddles, **1968–1970**

    4" **$25.00–40.00**

Kiddles 'N Kars, **1969–1970**

    2¾" **$50.00–70.00**

Tea Party Kiddles, **1970–1971**

    3½" **$50.00–80.00**

Lucky Locket Kiddles, **1967–1970**

    2" **$25.00–40.00**

Kiddle Kolognes, **1968–1970**

    2" **$60.00–75.00**

Kiddle Kones, **1968–1969**

    2" **$60.00–75.00**

Kola Kiddles, **1968–1969**

    2" **$40.00–50.00**

Kosmic Kiddle, **1968–1969**

    2½" $140.00–160.00

Sweet Treat Kiddles, **1969–1970**

    2" $65.00–80.00

Liddle Kiddle Playhouses, **1966–1968**

    .... $55.00–65.00

Matty Mattel

    16" $65.00–75.00

Mork & Mindy, **1979**

    9" .... $25.00–35.00 each

My Child, **1986, cloth over vinyl head, cloth body, synthetic wig**

    13" $95.00–150.00

Myrtle, **1968, talking puppet, from television show** *My Three Sons,* **vinyl head**

    14" $100.00–125.00

Osmond Family

Donny or Marie Osmond, **1978**

    12" $15.00–20.00

Jimmy Osmond, **1979**

    10" $15.00–20.00

Rainbow Brite, **1983 vinyl head, cloth body, orange yarn hair**

    18½" $65.00–75.00

Rock Flowers, **1970, vinyl mod dolls**

    6" $15.00–25.00

Saucy, **1972, vinyl, makes funny faces when arms is rotated**

    15" $55.00–65.00

Scooba Doo, **1964, vinyl head, rooted hair, cloth body, talks in Beatnik phrases, blond or black hair, striped dress**

    23" $95.00–110.00

Shogun Warrior, **all plastic, battery operated, robot**

    23½" $250.00–300.00

Shrinkin' Violette, **1964–1965, cloth, yarn hair, pull-string talker, eyes close, mouth moves**

    16" $100.00–150.00

Sister Belle, **1961–1963, vinyl, pull string talker, cloth body**

    16" $50.00–60.00

Sister Small Talk, 1967, talkers, painted eyes

10" 45.00–55.00

Space 1999, 1972, characters from television show of same name, articulated vinyl

   10"...$40.00–60.00

Star Spangled dolls, uses Sunshine Family adults, marked "1973"

Pioneer Daughter, Native American, Revolutionary, Southern, etc.

   9"...$20.00–30.00

Sunshine Family, vinyl, posable, come with Idea Book, Father, Mother, Baby

   Family of 3 ....$45.00–55.00

Steve

   9"...$10.00–15.00

Stephie

   7½" $12.00–18.00

Swingy, 1968, mechanical dancing doll

   18"..$40.00–50.00

Tatters, 1965–1967, talking cloth doll, wears rag clothes

   19"..$75.00–125.00

Teachy Keen, 1966–1970, Sears only, vinyl head, cloth body, ponytail, talker, tells child to use accessories included, buttons, zippers, comb

   16"..$70.00–90.00

Timey Tell 1969, talking,

   17"..$50.00–70.00

Tippee Toes, 1968–1970, battery operated, legs move, rides accessory horse, tricycle, knit sweater, pants

   17"..$70.00–80.00

Truly Scrumptious, character from movie Chitty Chitty Bang Bang

   11½" $175.00–225.00

   Talking...$150.00–200.00

Welcome Back Kotter, 1973, characters from TV sitcom

Freddie "Boom Boom" Washington, Arnold Horshack

   9"...$35.00–45.00

Vinnie Barbarino (John Travolta)

   9"...$30.00–35.00

Gabe Kotter

   9"...$15.00–20.00

MAWAPHIL

15.5"
Mawaphil,
cloth mask
face: $100.
**Doll courtesy
of private
collection.**

1920–1942, Atlanta, Georgia. Dolls designed by Mary Waterman Philips, manufactured by the Rushton Co. Stockinette crib dolls and cloth mask face dolls.

Crib doll, **all cloth, stockinette or velveteen**

　　8"–12" $45.00–60.00

Cloth mask face doll, **cloth body, appropriately dressed**

　　12"–15" $85.00–125.00

MEGO CORPORATION

11.5" Lenny &
Squiggy from
Laverne and
Shirley, Mego,
vinyl, circa
1977, MOC:
$120. **Photo
courtesy of
Phillip Weiss
Auctions.**

1954 to 1982. Made many vinyl "action figure" dolls during the 1970s. Prices shown are for excellent condition dolls with all appropriate clothes and accessories. Allow double values listed for mint in box examples.

12.5", Kiss, Mego, vinyl, MIB set: $1,100. **Photo courtesy of Morphy Auctions.**

Action Jackson, 1971–1972, vinyl head, plastic body, molded hair, painted black eyes, action figure, many accessory outfits, mark: "©Mego Corp//Reg. U.S. Pat. Off.//Pat. Pend.//Hong Kong//MCMLXXI"

8"...$20.00–30.00

Black

8"...$50.00–60.00

Dinah-mite, **Black**.............................$30.00–35.00

Jungle House Playset **MIB at online auction for $199.00**

Baby Sez So, 1976

16"...$25.00–30.00

Bubble Yum Baby, 1978, blows up "gum"

14"...$20.00–25.00

Black $30.00–35.00

Candi, 1979, fashion doll

11½" $10.00–12.00

18"...$22.00–28.00

Captain and Tennille, Daryl Dragon and Toni Tennille, 1977, recording and TV personalities, Toni Tennille doll has no molded ears

12½" ....$18.00–28.00 each

Charlie's Angels, 1977, **TV** show dolls based on characters played by Farrah Fawcett, Jaclyn Smith, Kate Jackson, and Cheryl Ladd, vinyl dolls, rooted hair

9"...$10.00–15.00

12½" $35.00–65.00

Cher, 1976, TV and recording personality, husband Sonny Bono, all-vinyl, fully jointed, rooted long black hair, also as grow-hair doll

Cher

12"...$25.00–35.00

Growing Hair Cher, **1976**

12"...$50.00–65.00

Sonny Bono

12"...$25.00–35.00

CHiPs, **1977, California Highway Patrol TV show, Jon Baker (Larry Wilcox), Frank "Ponch" Poncherello (Erik Estrada)**

8"...$18.00–25.00

Conan the Barbarian, **1978, film character, all-vinyl, fully jointed**

8"...$85.00–100.00

Diana Ross, **1977, recording and movie personality, all-vinyl, fully jointed, rooted black hair, long lashes**

12½" $55.00–75.00

Dukes of Hazzard, **1982, from TV show, Bo, Luke, Boss Hogg, Cletus, Rosco**

8"–9"..$20.00–25.00

Flash Gordon Series, **ca. 1976, vinyl head, hard plastic articulated body**

Dale Arden

9"...$60.00–70.00

Dr. Zarkov

9½" $40.00–50.00

Flash Gordon

9½" $90.00–125.00

Ming, the Merciless

9½" $60.00–70.00

Happy Days Series, **1976, characters from** *Happy Days* **TV sitcom, Henry Winkler starred as Fonzie, Ronnie Howard as Richie, Anson Williams as Potsie, and Donny Most as Ralph Malph**

Fonzie

8" 35.00–45.00

Richie, Potsie, Ralph, **each**

8"...$25.00–35.00

James Bond Moonraker, **1979, film character played by Roger Moore**

12"...$35.00–45.00

Joe Namath, **1970, football player, actor, soft vinyl head, rigid vinyl body, painted hair and features**

12"...$60.00–75.00

KISS, 1978, rock group, with Gene Simmons, Ace Frehley, Peter Cris, and Paul Stanley, all-vinyl, fully jointed, rooted hair, painted features and makeup

12½" .... $75.00–125.00 each

Kristy McNichol, 1978, actress, starred in TV show, *Family,* all-vinyl, rooted brown hair, painted eyes, marked on head: "©MEGO CORP.//MADE IN HONG KONG," marked on back: "©1977 MEGO CORP.//MADE IN HONG KONG"

9" $25.00–35.00

Laverne and Shirley, 1977, TV sitcom; Penny Marshall played Laverne, Cindy Williams played Shirley, also, from the same show, David Lander as Squiggy, and Michael McKean as Lenny, all-vinyl, rooted hair, painted eyes

11½" .... $20.00–30.00 each

Marvel Super Heros, 1974 on, vinyl head, rooted black hair, painted eyes, plastic body, MIB will bring much more, *NOT TO BE CONFUSED with the recent reissues. 8"

Aquaman	$90.00–120.00
Batgirl	$75.00–95.00
Batman	$125.00–160.00
Catwoman	$65.00–80.00
Falcon	$40.00–45.00
Flash	$50.00–75.00
Green Goblin	$75.00–85.00
Ironman	$85.00–100.00
Joker	$55.00–75.00
Mr. Fantastic	$75.00–95.00
Mr. Mxyzptlk	$60.00–80.00
Riddler	$125.00–150.00
Robin	$60.00–80.00
Spiderman	$60.00–80.00
Superman	$60.00–80.00
Supergirl	$100.00–125.00

MOC at online auction $1,011.00

Tarzan	$45.00–55.00
Wonderwoman	$90.00–100.00

Our Gang, 1975, from *Our Gang* movie shorts, that replayed on TV, included characters Alfalpha, Buckwheat, Darla, Mickey, Porky, and Spanky

6" $10.00–15.00

Planet of the Apes

Planet of the Apes Movie Series, **ca. 1970s**

Astronaut

    8"..**$40.00–45.00**

Cornelius

    8"..**$30.00–40.00**

Dr. Zaius

    8"..**$30.00–40.00**

Zira

    8"..**$45.00–55.00**

Planet of the Apes TV Series, **ca. 1974**

Alan Verdon

    8"..**$55.00–65.00**

Galen

    8", Palitoy....................................**$35.00–45.00**

General Urko

    8"..**$60.00–70.00**

General Ursus

    8"..**$80.00–100.00**

Peter Burke

    8"..**$55.00–65.00**

    Forbidden Zone Palyset..................**$150.00–200.00**

Star Trek

Star TV Series, **ca. 1973–1975**

Captain Kirk

    8"..**$35.00–40.00**

Dr. McCoy

    8"..**$30.00–35.00**

Klingon

    8"..**$35.00–45.00**

Lt. Uhura

    8"..**$25.00–30.00**

Mr. Scott

    8"..**$60.00–70.00**

Mr. Spock

    8"..**$25.00–35.00**

Star Trek Aliens, **ca. 1975–1976**

Andorian

    8"..\$110.00–130.00

Cheron

    8"..\$45.00–55.00

Neptunian

    8"..\$65.00–75.00

Mugato

    8"..\$140.00–160.00

Talos

    8"..\$120.00–150.00

The Gorn

    8"..\$40.00–55.00

The Romulan

    8"..\$100.00–125.00

Star Trek Movie Series, **ca. 1979, 12½" dolls**

    Acturian \$80.00–100.00

    Captain Kirk....................................\$45.00–55.00

    Commander Decker..........................\$30.00–50.00

    Ilia..\$30.00–40.00

    Klingon \$65.00–75.00

    Mr. Spock.......................................\$40.00–50.00

Starsky and Hutch, 1976, police TV series, Paul Michael Glaser as Starsky, David Soul as Hutch, Bernie Hamilton as Captain Dobey, Antonio Fargas as Huggy Bear, also included a villain, Chopper, all-vinyl, jointed waists

    7½" \$20.00–30.00

Suzanne Somers, 1978, actress, TV personality, starred as Chrissy in *Three's Company,* all-vinyl, fully jointed, rooted blond hair, painted blue eyes, long lashes

    12½" \$25.00–35.00

Waltons, The, 1975, from TV drama series, set of two 8" dolls per package, all-vinyl

    John Boy and Mary Ellen set................\$15.00–20.00

    Mom and Pop set...............................\$15.00–20.00

    Grandma and Grandpa set......................\$20.00–25.00

Wizard of Oz, 1974, Dorothy, Glinda, Cowardly Lion, Scarecrow, Tin Man, Wizard, **Wicked Witch**

    8"..\$20.00–30.00

Munchkins $50.00–60.00

14" **Dorothy, Cowardly Lion, Scarecrow, Tin Man**

.... $125.00–150.00

Wonder Woman Series, ca. 1976–1977, vinyl head, rooted black hair, painted eyes, plastic body

Lt. Diana Prince

12½" $55.00–65.00

Nubia

12½" $80.00–90.00

Nurse

12½" $30.00–40.00

Queen Hippolyte

12½" $55.00–65.00

Steve Trevor

12½" $50.00–6000

Wonder Woman

12½" $85.00–115.00

METAL HEADS

12" metal shoulderhead, Minerva, sleep eyes: $125. **Photo courtesy of Joan & Lynette Antique Dolls and Accessories.**

1850–1930 on. Made in Germany, Britain and America, by various manufactures, including Buschow & Beck (Minerva), Alfred Heller (Diana), Karl Standfuss (Juno), and Art Metal Works. Various metals used were aluminum, brass, and others, and they might be marked with just a size and country of origin or unmarked. Dolls listed are in good condition with original or appropriate dolls. Dolls with chipped paint will bring significantly less.

Metal shoulder head, cloth or kid body, molded and painted hair, glass eyes, more for wigged

12"–14" $125.00–150.00

16"–18" $150.00–200.00

20"–22" $225.00–250.00

Painted eyes

12"–14" $75.00–100.00

20"–22" $125.00–150.00

All metal or with composition body, **metal limbs**

Baby

11"–15" $80.00–100.00

16"–20" $120.00–150.00

Child

15" $300.00–350.00

20"–22" $450.00–500.00

Mama doll, **metal shoulder head, cloth body**

18" $200.00–250.00

Swiss: See Bucherer section.

MISSIONARY RAG BABY (BEECHER BABY)

21" Missionary Rag Baby, Beecher, cloth: $5,500. **Photo courtesy of McMasters Harris Apple Tree Doll Auctions.**

1893–1910, Elmira, New York. Julia Jones Beecher, wife of Congregational Church pastor Thomas K. Beecher, sister-in-law of Harriet Beecher Stowe. Made Missionary Ragbabies with the help of the sewing circle of her church. The dolls were made from old silk or cotton jersey underwear, with hand-painted and needle-sculpted features. All proceeds used for missionary work. Sizes 16" to 23" and larger. Dolls listed are in good condition, appropriately dressed. Exceptional examples will bring more.

16"..$3,500.00–4,000.00

21–23"...$4,500.00–5,5000.00

Black Beecher, **same construction and appearance as the white babies but from brown fabric with black yarn hair. Please note, this is not the black stockinette doll often erroneously referred to as "a black Beecher," which is quite different in construction from a true Black Beecher.**

21"–23"...$6,000.00–6,500.00

MOLLY-'ES

11" Maronska, International Series, Molly'es, cloth: $65. **Photo courtesy of Alderfer Auction Company, Inc.**

1920 to 1970s, Philadelphia, Pennsylvania. International Doll Co. was founded by Mollye Goldman. Molly-'es made cloth mask faced dolls, doll clothing, briefly Raggedy Ann, as well as composition and vinyl dolls. Her mask faced dolls had yarn or mohair hair, painted features, sewn joints at the shoulders and hips.

Cloth, fine line painted lashes, pouty mouth

Child

12" baby $50.00– $75.00

15"..$75.00–90.00

18"..$90.00–110.00

24"..$125.00–150.00

29"..$200.00–225.00

Internationals

11"..$45.00–65.00

15"..$70.00–90.00

27"..$120.00–135.00

Lady

    16"...$125.00–150.00

    21"...$175.00–225.00

Princess, Thief of Baghdad

Prince, cloth

    23"...$500.00–600.00

Princess

Composition

    18"...$700.00–825.00

Cloth

    18"...$500.00–550.00

Sabu, **composition**

    15"...$350.00–450.00

Sultan, **cloth**

    19"...$600.00–650.00

Composition

Baby

    15"...$120.00–140.00

    21"...$175.00–200.00

Cloth body

    18"...$80.00–100.00

Toddler

    15"...$150.00–250.00

    21"...$200.00–250.00

Child

    15"...$125.00–150.00

    19"...$175.00–200.00

Lady, **add more for ball gown**

    16"...$225.00–275.00

    21"...$325.00–400.00

Hard Plastic

Baby

    14"...$65.00–85.00

    20"...$100.00–135.00

Cloth body

    17"...$55.00–75.00

    25"...$100.00–125.00

Child

    14"...$130.00–150.00

    18"...$275.00–325.00

    25"...$375.00–400.00

Lady

    17"...$250.00–300.00

    20"...$325.00–375.00

    25"...$375.00–425.00

Vinyl

Baby

    8½"...$12.00–20.00

    12"...$18.00–25.00

    15"...$28.00–40.00

Child

    8"...$12.00–20.00

    10"...$18.00–25.00

    15"...$28.00–40.00

Little Women

    9"...$45.00–55.00

MONICA DOLLS

1941–1951. Monica Dolls from Hollywood, designed by Mrs. Hansi Share, made composition and later hard plastic with long face and painted or sleep eyes, eye shadow, unique feature is very durable rooted human hair, did not have high-heeled feet and unmarked, but wore paper wrist tag reading "Monica Doll, Hollywood," composition dolls had pronounced widow's peak in center of forehead.

Composition, 1941–1949, painted eyes, Veronica, Jean, and Rosalind were names of 17" dolls produced in 1942

    15"...$325.00–375.00

    17"...$350.00–500.00

    20"...$450.00–650.00

21" Monica, rooted hair, composition: $ask 500. **Photo courtesy of Minton's Doll and Curiosity Shop.**

Hard plastic, **1949–1951, sleep eyes, Elizabeth, Marion, or Linda**

14"–18".. $300.00–450.00

MORAVIAN

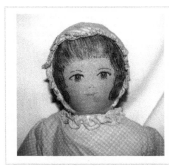

18" Moravian, cloth, early 20th century: $2,000. **Photo courtesy of Joan & Lynette Antique Dolls and Accessories.**

1872–present, Bethelhem, Pennsylvania. Cloth dolls made by the Ladies Sewing Society of the Moravian Church Guild. Fund raiser to support church work. Flat-faced rag doll with sewn joints at shoulders, elbows, hips, and knees, hand-painted faces, dressed in pink or blue gingham with apron and double bonnet.

Polly Heckewelder

19th–early 20th century doll

18"... $4,000.00–5,000.00

1920s–1950s doll

18"... $1,800.00–2,200.00

1960s to present

18"... $150.00–250.00

Benigna, **Miniature girls & Ladies**

5"- 6".. $200.00–400.00

MULTI-FACE, MULTI-HEAD DOLLS

11" Topsy Turvy doll, bisque, Simon Halbig mold 698 & so-called Belton head: $3,000. **Photo courtesy of Alderfer Auction Company, Inc.**

1866–1930 on. Various firms made dolls with two or more faces, or more than one head.

Bisque

French

Bru, **Surprise poupée, awake/asleep faces**

    12".. $12,000.00–14,000.00

Jumeau, **crying, laughing faces, cap hides knob**

    18".. $15,500.00–16,500.00

German

Bartenstein, **bisque socket head, papier-mâché hood and molded blouse shoulder plate, cloth over carton body with composition limbs, awake face with open mouth and glass eyes, crying face with open-closed mouth and glass eyes**

    20".. $1,400.00–1,500.00

Bergner, Carl, **bisque socket head, two or three faces, sleeping, laughing, crying, molded tears, glass eyes, on composition jointed body may have molded bonnet or hood, marked "C.B." or "Designed by Carl Bergner"**

    12"–15".. $1,500.00–1,700.00

Black face/white face doll

    13".. $2,800.00–3,000.00

Kestner, J. D., **ca. 1900+, Wunderkind, bisque doll with set of several different mold number heads that could be attached to body, set of one doll and body with additional three heads and wardrobe**

With heads 174, 178, 184 & 185

    11".. $4,000.00–6,000.00

With heads, 171, 179, 182 & 183

    14½" $6,000.00–8,000.00

Kley & Hahn, **solid-dome bisque socket head, painted hair, smiling baby and frowning baby, closed mouth, tongue, glass eyes, baby body**

13".. $1,500.00–1,700.00

Simon & Halbig, **smiling, sleeping, crying, turn ring at top of head to change faces, glass/painted eyes, closed mouth**

14½".. $3,000.00–3,200.00

Hermann Steiner **topsy turvy baby**

8"... $400.00–500.00

Cloth

Topsy-Turvy: **one black, one white head**

Painted face

13".. $750.00–850.00

Lithographed face

13".. $450.00–600.00

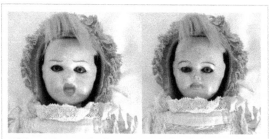

13" Bartenstein, two faced, composition or heavy paper mâche: $700. **Photo courtesy of Joan & Lynette Antique Dolls and Accessories.**

Bruckner

13".. $350.00–450.00

China

Youth & Age of Woman, **German, 19th century**

13".. $1,400.00–1,500.00

Topsy Turvy, **white head and black head, mid-19th century**

12".. $1,200.00–1,600.00

Composition

Berwick Doll Co., **Famlee Dolls, 1926 on, composition head and limbs, cloth body with crier, neck with screw joint, allowing different heads to be screwed into the body, painted features, mohair wigs and/or molded and painted hair, came in sets of two to 12 heads, with different costumes for each head**

Six-head set

16".. $400.00–700.00

Twelve-head set

16"..$1,200.00–1,400.00

Effanbee, **Johnny Tu Face**

16"..$275.00–325.00

Ideal, **1923, Soozie Smiles, composition, sleep or painted eyes on happy face, two faces, smiling, crying, cloth body, composition hands, cloth legs, original romper and hat**

15½"..$225.00–275.00

Three-in-One Doll Corp., **1946 on, Trudy, composition head with turning knob on top, cloth body and limbs, three faces, "Sleepy, Weepy, Smiley," dressed in felt or fleece snowsuit, or sheer dresses, more for exceptional doll**

15½"..$90.00–115.00

Papier-mâché

Smiling/crying faces, **glass eyes, cloth body, composition lower limbs**

19"..$650.00–700.00

Wax

Bartenstein, **glass eyes, carton body, crier**

Black face, white face

12"..$1,200.00–1,300.00

Smiling/crying faces

15"..$1,00.00–1,100.00

MUNICH ART DOLLS

12.5" Munich Art Doll, composition: $5,000. **Photo courtesy of Morphy Auctions.**

1908–1920s. Marion Kaulitz hand-painted heads designed by Marc-Schnur, Vogelsanger, and Wackerle, dressed in German or French regional costumes. Usually composition heads and bodies distributed by Cuno & Otto Dressell and Arnoldt Doll Co.

Composition, **painted features, wig, composition body, unmarked**

12"–14" $6,000.00–10,000.00

17"–18" $11,000.00–16,000.00

NANCY ANN STORYBOOK

5.25" Nancy Ann Storybook, Goldylocks, bisque: $350. **Photo courtesy of The Museum Doll Shop.**

1 8" Nancy Ann Style Show, Nancy Ann Storybook, hard plastic, circa 1954: $600. **Photo courtesy of McMasters Harris Apple Tree Doll Auctions.**

1936 on, San Francisco, California. Started by Nancy Ann Abbott. Made small painted bisque and hard plastic dolls with elaborate costumes. Also made an 8" toddler doll to compete with Vogue's Ginny, 10" fashion dolls and larger size "style show" dolls. Painted bisque, mohair wig, painted eyes, head molded to torso, jointed limbs, either sticker on outfit or hang tag, in box, later made in hard plastic.

Dolls listed are in good condition with original clothing and wrist tags. Allow more for mint-in-box, add 30 percent or more for black dolls. Prices ranges indicate more common examples to more rare costumes.

Painted Bisque

1936–1937, **pink/blue mottled or sunburst box with gold label, gold foil sticker on clothes "Nancy Ann Dressed Dolls," marked "87," "88," or "93," "Made in Japan," no brochure**

Baby

3½"–4½" $500.00–600.00

Child

5" $1,500.00–2,600.00

1938, early, **marked "America" (baby marked "87," "88," or "93" "Made in Japan"), colored box, sunburst pattern with gold label, gold foil sticker on clothes: "Judy Ann," no brochure**

Baby

3½"–4½" $475.00–525.00

Child

5" $800.00–1,000.00

1938, late, marked "Judy Ann USA" and "Story Book USA" (baby marked "Made in USA" and "88, 89, and 93 Made in Japan"), colored box, sunburst pattern with gold or silver label, gold foil sticker on clothes: "Storybook Dolls," no brochure

Judy Ann mold $350.00–500.00

Storybook mold $250.00–350.00

1939, child, Story Book Doll USA, molded socks and molded bangs (baby has star-shaped hands), colored box with small silver dots, silver label, gold foil sticker on clothes, "Storybook Dolls," no brochure

Baby

3½"–4½" $200.00–225.00

Child

5"... $375.00–450.00

1940, child has molded socks only (baby has star-shaped bisque hands), colored box with white polka dots, silver label, gold foil sticker on clothes, "Storybook Dolls," has brochure

Baby

3½"–4½" $90.00–115.00

Child

5"... $150.00–200.00

1941–1942, child has pudgy tummy or slim tummy, baby has star-shaped hands or fist, white box with colored polka dots, with silver label, gold foil bracelet with name of doll and brochure

Baby

3½"–4½" $100.00–160.00

Child

5"... $75.00–300.00

1943–1947, child has one-piece head, body, and legs ("stiff" legs), baby has fist hands, white box with colored polka dots, silver label, ribbon tie or pin fastener, gold foil bracelet with name of doll and brochure

Baby

3½"–4½" $40.00–55.00

Child

5"... $35.00–75.00

Hard Plastic

1947–1949, child has hard plastic body, painted eyes, baby has bisque body, plastic arms and legs, white box with colored polka dots with "Nancy Ann StorybookDollsî between dots, silver label, brass snap, gold foil bracelet with name of doll and brochure, more for special outfit

Baby

3½"–4½" $45.00–60.00

Child

5½" $40.00–70.00

1949 on, **hard plastic, both have black sleep eyes, white box with colored polka dots and "Nancy Ann Storybook Dolls" between dots, silver label, brass or painted snaps, gold foil bracelet with name of doll and brochure**

Baby

3½"–4½" $40.00–55.00

Child

5" $40.00–50.00

Special Dolls

Mammy and Baby, **marked "Japan 1146" or America mold**

5" $1,000.00–1,200.00

Storybook USA

5" $400.00–500.00

Topsy, **bisque black doll, jointed leg**

All-bisque $450.00–500.00

Plastic arms $150.00–200.00

All-plastic, **painted or sleep eye**

.... $125.00–150.00

White boots, **bisque jointed leg dolls**

5" **Add** $50.00

Series Dolls, **depending on mold mark**

All-Bisque

American Girl Series

Jointed legs $150.00–200.00

Stiff legs $35.00–50.00

Around the World Series

.... $600.00–1,000.00

Masquerade Series

Ballet Dancer, Cowboy, Pirate

.... $450.00–900.00

Clown sold at online auction for $1,808.00

Sports Series

.... $1,000.00–1,300.00

Margie Ann Series

Margie Ann $120.00–200.00

Powder & Crinoline Series

.... $75.00–100.00

Bisque or Plastic

Operetta or Hit Parade Series

.... $70.00–125.00

Hard Plastic

Big and Little Sister Series, or Commencement Series (**except baby**)

.... $75.00–100.00

Bridal, Dolls of the Day, Dolls of the Month, Fairytale, Mother Goose, Nursery Rhyme, Religious, and Seasons Series, **painted or sleep eye**

.... $60.00–75.00

Other Dolls

Audrey Ann, **toddler, marked "Nancy Ann Storybook12î**

6"... $900.00–975.00

Nancy Ann Style Show, **ca. 1954**

Hard plastic, **sleep eyes, long dress, unmarked**

18".. $400.00–900.00

Vinyl head, **plastic body, all original, complete**

18".. $300.00–600.00

Muffie

1953, **hard plastic, wig, sleep eyes, strung straight leg, non-walker, painted lashes**

8".. $175.00–250.00

1954, **hard plastic walker, molded eyelashes, brows**

8".. $150.00–200.00

1955–1956, **vinyl head, molded or painted upper lashes, rooted saran wig, walker or bent-knee walker**

8".. $60.00–80.00

1968+, **reissued, hard plastic**

8".. $40.00–50.00

Lori Ann

Vinyl

7½" $75.00–100.00

Tagged Lori Ann outfit

.... $50.00–70.00

Debbie

Hard plastic **in school dress, name on wrist tag/box**

10".. $175.00–200.00

Vinyl head, **hard plastic body**

    10".. $75.00–100.00

Hard plastic walker

    10½" $125.00–150.00

Vinyl head, **hard plastic walker**

    10½" $75.00–100.00

Little Miss Nancy Ann, **1959, high-heel fashion doll**

    8½" $75.00–150.00

Miss Nancy Ann, **1959, marked "Nancy Ann," vinyl head, rooted hair, rigid vinyl body, high-heeled feetIn undergarments or in day dress**

    10½" $120.00–150.00

Baby Sue Sue, **1960s, vinyl**

    10".. $60.00–100.00

NESBIT

7" - 8" House of Nesbit dolls, plastic, MIB: $50 each.
Photo courtesy of Phillip Weiss Auctions

House of Nesbit, 1956 on, England. Historical costume and character dolls designed by Peggy Nesbit. Hard plastic heads on vinyl bodies.

7"–10"

    Simple costumes $25.00–30.00

    Elaborate costumes......................... $50.00–70.00

GEBRUDER OHLHAVER

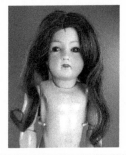

19" Gebruder Ohlhaver, bisque, marked Revalo: $300. **Photo courtesy of McMasters Harris Apple Tree Doll Auctions.**

13" Gebruder Ohlhaver, bisque, molded hair: $725. **Photo courtesy of Sweetbriar Auctions.**

1913–1930, Sonneberg, Germany. Had Revalo (Ohlhaver spelled backwards omitting the two *H*s) line; made bisque socket and shoulder head and composition dolls. Bought heads from Ernst Heubach, Gebrüder Heubach, and others. Dolls listed are in good condition with original or appropriate clothing.

Baby or Toddler, character face, bisque socket head, glass eyes, open mouth, teeth, wig, composition and wood ball-jointed body (bent-leg for baby)

Baby

10"	$90.00–110.00
15"–17"	$250.00–325.00
19"–21"	$425.00–500.00

Toddler

14"	$350.00–450.00
22"	$550.00–650.00

Child, Mold 150, or no mold number, bisque socket head, open mouth, sleep eyes, composition body

14"–16"	$400.00–500.00
18"–20"	$350.00–400.00
24"–28"	$500.00–600.00

Shoulder-head, **kid body**

18"–20"	$300.00–350.00

Character, bisque solid dome with molded and painted hair, intaglio eyes, composition body

Molded bob, **o/cl mouth, intaglio eyes, on five-piece body**

12"	$675.00–800.00

Coquette-type, **molded hair ribbon with bows**

High quality bisque

    12"–13"...**$800.00–900.00**

Low quality bisque

    11"–12"...**$475.00–550.00**

OLD COTTAGE DOLLS

10.5" Pearly King, Old Cottage, hard rubber: $60.00. **Photo courtesy of Morphy Auctions.**

Late 1948 on, England. Dolls were designed by Greta and Susi Fleischmann. Made with hard rubber or plastic heads, felt body, some with wire armature, oval hang tag has trademark "Old Cottage Dolls," special characters may be more

    8"–9"..**$50.00–80.00**

    11"–12"...**$60.00–100.00**

PAPIER-MÂCHÉ

Pre-1600 on. Papier-mâché is an elastic substance made of paper pulp and a variety of additives. Dolls of papier-mâché were being made in France as early as the sixteenth century. In Germany and France papier-mâché dolls were being mass produced in molds for heads after 1810. It reached heights of popularity by mid-1850s and was also used for bodies. Papier-mâché shoulder head, glass or painted eyes, molded and painted hair, sometimes in fancy hairdos. Usually no marks. Dolls listed are in good condition, nicely dressed. More for exceptional examples, considerably less for dolls that have been repainted.

Molded Hair Papier-mâché, so-called Milliner's Models, German, 1820–1860s, molded hair, a shapely waist, kid body, and wooden limbs, unusual variations or all original costume bring higher end of range

11" milliner's model (so called), German, papier-mâché, Apollo's Knot hairstyle: $1,800. **Photo courtesy of Alderfer Auction Company, Inc.**

23" papier-mâché, painted eyes: $1,700. **Photo courtesy of Withington Auction Inc.**

Apollo top knot, **side curls**

8"–10"	$1,400.00–1,700.00
12"–14"	$1,200.00–2,600.00
16"–18"	$3,000.00–4,000.00
20"–23"	$5,000.00–6,500.00

Applied hair, **some applied human hair included in the hairstyle**

16"–18"	$3,000.00–3,500.00

Braided bun, **side curls or long puffy side curls with simple bun**

7"–11"	$800.00–1,400.00
13"–15"	$1,600.00–2,200.00
19"	$2,900.00–3,100.00

Braided Coronet, **1840s style**

10"–12"	$1,800.00–2,500.00
18"	$2,200.00–2,800.00

Center part, molded bun

5"–10"	$800.00–1,000.00
13"–15"	$1,000.00–1,200.00
18"–24"	$1,400.00–1,800.00

Center part, sausage curls

11"–14"	$800.00–1,000.00

Coiled braids over ears, **braided bun**

9"–11"	$1,000.00–1,100.00
20"–21"	$2,100.00–2,300.00

Covered Wagon or Flat Top **hair style**

6"–10"	$500.00–800.00
14"–16"	$800.00–900.00

29" papier-mâché, Lerch & Co., American, painted eyes: $2,000. **Photo courtesy of Withington Auction Inc.**

28", papier-mâché, Pre-Greiner type: $2,000. **Photo courtesy of Morphy Auctions.**

Empire style short curls

8" $750.00–850.00

14"–20" $1,200.00–1,700.00

Long curls on shoulders

7"–14" $1,200.00–2,000.00

22" $3,000.00

Man, **molded hat, moustache, beard or other feature**

6"–10" $1,200.00–1,500.00

14"–18" $3,000.00–5,000.00

Molded comb, **side curls, braided coronet**

20"–25" $3,200.00–3,800.00

Early Type Shoulder Head, German, 1840s–1860s, cloth body; wooden limbs, with topknots, buns, puff curls, or braids, dressed in original clothing or excellent copy, may have some wear; more for painted pate, elaborate hairstyle or exceptional quality

Painted eyes

9"–14" $600.00–800.00

16"–18" $1,000.00–1,400.00

21"–24" $1,200.00–1,700.00

26"–30" $1,200.00–1,900.00

Glass eyes

10" 400.00–500.00

16"–18" $1,800.00–2,000.00

20"–24" $2,000.00–2,500.00

27"–30" .... $4,000.00 –4,500.00

Long curls

14" $1,100.00–1,500.00

21.5" papier-mâché, French type, glass eyes: $2,200.
Photo courtesy of Morphy Auctions.

12" papier-mâché, poupard (swaddling baby), French: $350.
Photo courtesy of Joan & Lynette Antique Dolls and Accessories.

16" $2,000.00–2,200.00

24" $3,200.00–3,500.00

Pre-Greiner Type, **1850s, German or American made shoulder head, molded painted black hair, black glass eyes, cloth body**

16"–18" $1,200.00–2,100.00

20"–25" $1,600.00–2,200.00

29"–31" $2,000.00–2,500.00

French Type, **1835–1850, made by German companies for the French trade, painted black hair, brush marks, solid-dome, shoulder head, some have nailed on wigs, open mouth, bamboo teeth, kid or leather body, appropriately dressed**

Glass eyes

11"–14" $1,200.00–1,600.00

18"–20" $1,800.00–2,100.00

22"–24" $2,200.00–2,500.00

28"–34" $3,400.00–3,800.00

Painted eyes

8"–12" $500.00–800.00

14"–16" $1,100.00–1,500.00

17"–20" $1,500.00–2,500.00

Papier-mâché, American, Greiner 1858–1883: See Greiner section.

Poupard, **French and German, all papier-mâché to represent a swaddled baby**

12" $225.00–350.00

Sonneberg Taufling (so-called Motschmann): See Sonneberg Taufling section.

Patent Washable, **1879–1910s, shoulder head with mohair wig, open or closed mouth, glass eyes, cloth body, composition limbs, made by companies such as F. M. Schilling and others**

30" Sonneberg-type papier-mâché, : $775. **Photo courtesy of Alderfer Auction Company, Inc.**

Better quality

12"–15" $275.00–375.00

18" $425.00–500.00

22"–24" $625.00–700.00

Lesser quality

10"–12" $100.00–125.00

14"–16" $175.00–200.00

23"–25" $250.00–300.00

Sonneberg-Type, 1880–1910, "M & S Superior," Muller & Strasburger, Cunno & Otto Dressel, and others shoulder head, with blond molded hair, painted blue or brown eyes, cloth body, with kid or leather arms and boots

11"–15" $200.00–250.00

18"–20" $325.00–400.00

24"–29" $400.00–500.00

Glass eyes

12"–16" $300.00–350.00

18"–21" $350.00–400.00

Wigged

18"–25" $375.00–500.00

Papier-mâché Child, 1920 on, head has brighter coloring, wigged, child often in ethnic costume, stuffed cloth body and limbs, or papier-mâché arms

French

9"–13" $80.00–100.00

13"–15" $175.00–225.00

German

10" $70.00–80.00

15" $95.00–115.00

Unknown maker

    8"..$50.00–60.00

    12"..$80.00–95.00

    16"..$110.00–135.00

Clowns, papier-mâché head, with painted clown features, open or closed mouth, molded hair or wigged, cloth body, composition or papier-mâché arms, or five-piece jointed body

High quality child body

    16"..$1,200.00–1,500.00

    20"..$1,500.00–1,800.00

Lower quality crude body type

    8"..$100.00–175.00

    14"..$250.00–325.00

PARIAN-TYPE,
SEE UNTINTED BISQUE

RONNAUG PETTERSSEN

12" Ronnaug Petterssen, Nisse, cloth: $300. **Photo courtesy of Morphy Auctions.**

1901–1980, Norway. Made cloth dolls, pressed felt head, usually painted side-glancing eyes, cloth bodies, intricate costumes, paper tags

Regional costumes

Early round faces

    7"–8" $200.00–250.00

Later faces

    7"–8" $100.00–150.00

Child, glass eyes, wigged

    17" $1,600.00–2,000.00

Nissa, gnome

    12–14" $200.00–400.00

DORA PETZOLD

Germany, 1919–1930+. Made and dressed dolls, molded composition head, painted features, wig, stockinette body, sawdust filled, short torso, free-formed thumbs, stitched fingers, shaped legs

    16"–18" $1,500.00–2,200.00

    20"–22" $2,400.00–3,000.00

18" Dora Petzold, composition: $1,200. **Photo courtesy of Oldeclectics**.

PHILADELPHIA BABY (SHEPPARD BABY)

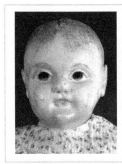

21" Philadelphia Baby, cloth: $4,000. **Photo courtesy of Withington Auction Inc.**

1900, Philadelphia, Pennsylvania. Rag baby sold by the J.B. Sheppard & Co. store. Molded stockinette, painted features, sewn joints at shoulders, hips, and knees. Dolls listed are in good condition, appropriately dressed. Allow more for exceptional condition.

18"–22".. **$5,000.00–6,000.00**

Doll in somewhat worn condition

18"–22".. **$1,400.00–2,000.00**

PLEASANT COMPANY

1985–present. Middleton, Wisconsin, founded by Pleasant T. Rowland. In 1998 the company was purchased by Mattel, Inc. Values listed are for excellent condition secondary market dolls in appropriate clothing. Many dolls are still available at retail as well.

18" Josefina, American Girl, Pleasant Company, vinyl: $175. **Photo courtesy of Alderfer Auction Company, Inc.**

American Girl®, **vinyl doll with wig**

18".. $100.00–150.00

Retired dolls $125.00–175.00

POLISH RELIEF DOLLS

11" Polish Relief, France, cloth: $900. **Photo courtesy of Sara Bernstein's Dolls.**

1914 on, Paris, France. Polish Relief dolls were created in the workshop of Madame Lazarski during and shortly after WWI. This project provided work for war refugees, and the money raised from the sale of the dolls aided Polish widows and orphans. Cloth dolls with embroidered features and floss hair.

Adult

19".. $900.00–1,500.00

Child

11"–17" $550.00–700.00

PRESBYTERIAN RAG DOLL

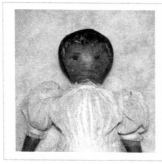

17" Presbyterian rag, cloth: $1,800. **Photo courtesy of The Museum Doll Shop.**

1885 on, Bucyrus, Ohio. The First Presbyterian Church made cloth dolls as a fund raiser, cloth doll with "pie-shaped gusseted" piece across top of head, flat face, painted hair and features, mitten hands, 17".

    1880s–1930s.................................. $3,500.00–4,000.00

    1950s–1980s.................................. 00.00–350.00

RABERY & DELPHIEU

15" Rabery et Delphieu, bébé, bisque: $3,800. **Photo courtesy of Morphy Auctions.**

1856–1930 and later, Paris. Became part of S.F.B.J. in 1899. Some heads pressed (pre-1890) and some poured, purchased some heads from Francois Gaultier. Dolls listed are in good condition, appropriately dressed. Exceptional dolls may be more.

Child

Closed mouth, **bisque socket head, paperweight eyes, pierced ears, mohair wig, cork pate, French composition and wood jointed body**

9"–10" $2,400.00–2,600.00

13"–16" $3,500.00–4,000.00

20"–24" $5,000.00–6,000.00

28" $6,500.00–7,500.00

Open mouth, **row of upper teeth**

18"–21" $1,600.00–1,900.00

24"–26" $2,000.00–2,500.00

RAGGEDY ANN & ANDY

15" Raggedy Ann, Volland, printed features, cloth: $1,200. **Photo courtesy of Morphy Auctions.**

14" Baby Ann, Mollye's, cloth: $. **Photo courtesy of Sara Bernstein's Dolls.**

1915 to present. Rag doll designed by Johnny Gruelle in 1915, made by various companies. Ann wears dress with apron, Andy, shirt and pants with matching hat.

P.J. Volland, 1918–1934, early dolls marked "Patented Sept. 7, 1915," all-cloth, tin or wooden button eyes, painted features, some have sewn knee or arm joints, sparse brown or auburn yarn hair, oversize hands, feet turned outward. Dolls listed are in clean unfaded condition, appropriately dressed.

Raggedy Ann and Andy, **15"–18"**

Painted face $1,600.00–1,800.00

Printed face $1,200.00–1,600.00

Beloved Belindy, **1926–1930 painted face, 1931–1934 print face**

15" $1,600.00–2,500.00

Pirate Chieftain **and other characters**

18" $3,000.00–4,000.00

Exposition, **1935**

Raggedy Ann, **no eyelashes, no eyebrows, outline nose, no heart, satin label on hem of dress**

18"..$5,500.00–7,000.00

Mollye Goldman, **1935–1937, marked on chest "Raggedy Ann and Andy Dolls Manufactured by Molly'es Doll Outfitters," nose outlined in black, red heart on chest, reddish-orange hair, multicolored legs, blue feet, some have oilcloth faces**

15"..$650.00–750.00

17"–21"...$700.00–900.00

Baby Ann

14"..$850.00–950.00

Georgene Novelties, **1938–1962, Ann has orange hair and a top knot, six different mouth styles, early ones had tin eyes, later ones had plastic, six different noses, seams in middle of legs and arms to represent knees and elbows, feet turn forward, red and white striped legs, all have hearts that say "I love you" printed on chest, tag sewn to left side seam, several variations, all say "Georgene Novelties, Inc."**

Raggedy Ann or Andy, **1930s–1960s**

Nose outlined with black, **1938–1944**

15"–17"...$350.00–450.00

19"–21"...$450.00–550.00

Awake/Asleep, **1940s**

Nose outlined black,

14"..$400.00–500.00

18" Beloved Belindy, Georgene Novelties, cloth: $800. **Photo courtesy of Morphy Auctions.**

24" Raggedy Ann & Raggedy Andy, Knickerbocker, cloth: $120 pair. **Photo courtesy of Morphy Auctions.**

Long nose face, **1944–1946**

19"..$1,200.00–1,450.00

Curved nose edges, **1946 on**

15"–19"...$100.00–150.00

20"–23"...$150.00–200.00

32"..$225.00–$250.00

Beloved Belindy, **1940–1944**

> 14"–18" $900.00–1,200.00

Knickerbocker, 1962–1982, printed features, hair color change from orange to red, there were five mouth and five eyelash variations, tags were located on clothing back or pants seam

Raggedy Ann or Andy

1964, cloud box

> 15" $200.00–275.00

Later examples

> 6" $12.00–15.00

> 15" $35.00–50.00

> 19" $45.00–55.00

> 30"–36" $100.00–125.00

Musical Ann

> 15" $55.00–65.00

Raggedy Ann Talking, **1972**

> 19" $75.00–100.00

Beloved Belindy, **ca. 1965**

> 15" $600.00–800.00

Camel with Wrinkled Knees

> 15" $150.00–175.00

Nasco/Bobbs-Merrill, 1972, vinyl head, hard plastic doll body, printed features, apron marked "Raggedy Ann"

> 24" $90.00–120.00

All hard vinyl, 1975, printed features, articulated body

> 9" $75.00–90.00

Bobbs-Merrill Co., 1974, ventriloquist dummy, hard plastic head, hands, foam body, printed face

> 30" $125.00–175.00

Applause Toy Company, 1981–present, owned by Hasbro which also markets Raggedy Ann through its Playskool line

> 8" $10.00–15.00

> 17" $30.00–35.00

> 48" $100.00–125.00

Limited Editions, **Applause marketed as part of their Dakin line, listings are for MIB**

75th anniversary Ann or Andy, **1992**

> 19" $45.00–65.00

8.5" Raggedy Ann & Raggedy Andy, R John Wright, cloth: $400 pair. **Photo courtesy of Alderfer Auction Company, Inc.**

Molly-E Raggedy Ann, **1993**

    18".. $40.00–50.00

Georgene reissues, **1996**

    15".. $30.00–40.00

Ann or Andy, **1994**

    13".. $70.00–80.00

US Patent Ann, **1995**

    17".. $65.00–85.00

Stamp Ann, **1997**

    17".. $35.00–45.00

Exposition Ann or Andy, **1998**

    17".. $35.00–45.00

R. John Wright, **present, molded felt doll, secondary market values, dolls still available retail**

Ann or Andy

    17".. $500.00–$600.00

Brass Key Productions, **1993 on, porcelain**

    7"–15" $8.00–15.00

JESSIE MCCUTCHEON RALEIGH

1916–1920, Chicago, Illinois. McCutcheon was a businesswoman who developed a line of dolls. These were distributed by Butler Brothers and perhaps others. She produced dolls of cloth and composition.

Shoebutton Sue, **flat face, painted spit curls, mitten hands, sewn on red shoes, shown in 1921 Sears catalog**

    15".. $300.00–500.00

18" child, Jessie McCutcheon Raleigh, composition body, composition: $1,100. **Photo courtesy of Morphy Auctions.**

Too few in database for reliable range.

Baby, **composition head on composition body**

    10"–12" $350.00–475.00

    18" $525.00–650.00

Child

Composition head on composition body, **wigged**

    11" $350.00–450.00

    13" $450.00–500.00

    18" $650.00–725.00

Molded hair

    11"–13" $600.00–800.00

    18"–22" $1,100.00–1,800.00

Composition head on cloth body **with composition lower arms and legs**

    22"–24" $325.00–400.00

RAYNAL

1922–1930 on, Paris. Edouard Raynal made dolls of felt, cloth, or with celluloid heads with widely spaced eyebrows. Dressed, some resemble Lenci, except fingers were together or their hands were of celluloid, marked "Raynal" on soles of shoes and/or pendant

Cloth, **1922, molded head, cloth body, sometimes celluloid hands**

    14"–16" $500.00–700.00

    17"–22" $1,000.00– 1,500.00

Baby Shirley type

    18"–22" $2,000.00–2,500.00

17" Raynal, cloth, France: $1,100. **Photo courtesy of Joan & Lynette Antique Dolls and Accessories.**

Pressed felt child, **cloth body**

14"–19".. $1,000.00–1,900.00

Felt body

14"–19".. $1,500.00–2,200.00

Celluloid, 1936, then Rhodoid

Baby

16"–24".. $400.00–475.00

Child, flirty eyes

18"–24".. $400.00–500.00

Vinyl, 1960s–1970s

Margareth

14"... $50.00–60.00

THEODOR RECKNAGEL

1886–1930, Alexandrienthal, Coburg, Germany. Made bisque and composition doll heads of varying quality, incised or raised mark, wigged or molded hair, glass or painted eyes, open or closed mouth, flange neck or socket head. Dolls listed are in good condition, appropriately dressed.

Baby

Solid dome infant, **1924, solid dome flange neck head, cloth body, glass eyes**

8"–9"... $125.00–150.00

Solid dome character baby, **1924, bent-limb baby body, painted or glass eyes**

6"–8"... $75.00–100.00

9"–12".. $125.00–150.00

8" Recknagel, open/closed mouth, bisque: $500. **Photo courtesy of Sweetbriar Auctions.**

Bonnet head baby, Mold 22, 23, 28, 44: **See bonnet head section.**

Child

Dolly face, **1890s–1914**

Mold 1907, 1909, 1914, others, **open mouth, glass eyes**

    7"–9"..$70.00–120.00

    10"–12"..$140.00–180.00

    15"–18"..$225.00–275.00

    22"–24"..$275.00–300.00

Character face, **ca. 1910+, may have crossed hammer mark**

    6"–7"...$350.00–400.00

    9"–12"..$450.00–500.00

Mold 57, **open/closed mouth with teeth, molded hair**

    9"–10"..$875.00–975.00

Mold 58, **open/closed mouth with teeth, molded hair with molded ribbon and three flowers**

    7"...$300.00–325.00

Mold 31, 32, **Max and Moritz**

    8"...$900.00–1,200.00 each

    12"...$1,300.00–1,500.00 each

Googly molds 43, 45, 46, 50, no mold number: See googly section.

REGIONAL DRESS DOLLS

14" German, bisque, mid quality: $250. **Photo courtesy of Alderfer Auction Company, Inc.**

12.5" Crow pair, by artist Rhonda Holy Bear, ca. 1970s, leather: sold at auction $2750. **Photo courtesy of Morphy Auctions.**

This category describes dolls costumed in regional dress to show different nationalities, facial characteristics, or cultural background. Examples are dolls in regional costumes that are commonly sold as souvenirs to tourists. These dolls became popular about 1875 and continue to be made today. A well-made beautiful doll with accessories or wardrobe may be more.

Bisque, German, **high quality brings high end of range**

High quality

6"–9" $250.00–350.00

10"–13" $375.00–425.00

Lower quality

6"–9" $70.00–125.00

10"–13" $150.00–200.00

French Fisherfolk, **bisque heads**

8"–12" $300.00–600.00

Painted bisque

4" $45.00–65.00

10" $95.00–130.00

Celluloid

8" $50.00–70.00

15" $90.00–115.00

Cloth

8" $100.00–155.00

13" $125.00–175.00

9" Skookums, Mary Frances Woods, crepe paper: each $350. **Photo courtesy of The Museum Doll Shop.**

Russian, **1920 on, all-cloth, molded and painted stockinette head, hands, in regional costumes**

7"... $65.00–80.00

15"... $225.00–350.00

18"... $350.00– 380.00

Composition

Child

8"... $100.00–125.00

13"–16"... $150.00–180.00

Walker in Dutch costume, **post-WWII era**

22".. $100.00–125.00

Jay Dolls, **Dublin, Ireland, molded heads, cloth wrapped bodies**

5"... $25.00–40.00

7½" $30.00–45.00

11"... $70.00–90.00

Native American Indian, **cloth, leather, natural fibers, etc, 19th and early 20th centuries**

5"–8"... $130.00–225.00

13"–15"... $400.00–650.00

23".. $700.00–850.00

Seminole, **woven Palmetto fiber**

4½"–6"... $30.00–45.00

Skookum, **1913 on, designed by Mary McAboy, painted features, with side-glancing eyes, mohair wigs, cloth figure wrapped in Indian blanket, with folds representing arms, wooden feet, later plastic, label on bottom of foot, box marked "Skookum Bully Good"**

4½" **papoose on mailer card** $35.00–45.00

6"–9"... $85.00–100.00

10–12"..$100.00–150.00

14"–16"..$200.00–300.00

18"–20"..$450.00–700.00

27"–33"..$900.00–1,100.00

Mary Frances Woods, **crepe paper faces**

10"–12"..$350.00–500.00

Hard Plastic, **regional dress, unmarked or unknown maker**

7"..$8.00–15.00

12"..$20.00–30.00

Baitz, Austria, **1970s, painted hard plastic, painted side-glancing eyes, open "o" mouth, excellent quality, tagged and dressed in regional dress**

8½"–9½" $60.00–75.00

Vinyl

6"..$20.00–25.00

12"..$40.00–45.00

Wood

Polish, **painted features, 1930s on**

7"..$600–11.00

RELIABLE TOY CO.

15" Barbara Ann Scott, Reliable Toy Co., composition: $250. **Photo courtesy of Morphy Auctions.**

1920 on, Toronto, Canada. Made composition, hard plastic and vinyl dolls.

Composition, **all-composition or composition shoulder head and arms on cloth body, some with composition legs. Dolls listed are in good condition, appropriately dressed.**

Baby, **1930s**

14"..$100.00–125.00

20"..$225.00–275.00

Baby Precious, **1947, Mama-style doll, sleep eyes, mohair wig**

    20".. $150.00–200.00

Barbara Scott Ice Skating Doll

    15".. $225.00–275.00

Her Highness

    15".. $200.00–225.00

Hiawatha or Indian child

    10½".. $45.00–55.00

    13".. $70.00–90.00

    16".. $110.00–125.00

Military Man

    14".. $175.00–225.00

Mountie

    17".. $100.00–125.00

Nurse, **painted eyes, mohair wig**

    18".. $100.00–120.00

Scottish child

    14".. $75.00–100.00

    17".. $100.00–130.00

Shirley Temple

    18"–22"... $400.00–800.00

Toddler

    13".. $125.00–175.00

Hard Plastic

Baby, **1958, sleep eyes, open mouth**

    8".. $30.00–40.00

Indian child, **all hard plastic**

    8".. $20.00–30.00

Toni, **P-90**

    14".. $275.00–325.00

Vinyl

Cindy Lou, **1961, vinyl head, rooted ponytail, sleep eyes**

    14".. $20.00–30.00

Eaton Baeuties, **1965, all vinyl, rooted hair, sleep eyes**

    14".. $45.00–65.00

Majorette, **1960s, vinyl head, rooted hair, sleep eyes**

    16".. $60.00–75.00

Mitzi, **1961-1962, vinyl head, rooted hair, Barbie-type**

    11½" $100.00–125.00

Patti Sue, **walker, 1960, Canadian version of Ideal's Patti Playpal**

    36".. $120.00–140.00

Suzy Steps, **walker, 1950, Canadian version of Ideal's Saucy Walker**

    13"–17" $75.00–100.00

Suzy Walker, **walker, 1950, Ginny-type**

    9".. $175.00–225.00

Tammy, **Canadian version of IdealTammy**

    12".. $75.00–100.00

REMCO INDUSTRIES

4.5" Beatles, Remco, vinyl, MIB: $300. **Photo courtesy of Morphy Auctions.**

1959–1974, Harrison, New Jersey. One of the first companies to market with television ads. Dolls listed are in good condition with original clothing and accessories. **Allow more for MIB.**

Addams Family, **1964**

Lurch

    5½" $70.00–120.00

Morticia

    4¾" $150.00–180.00

10.5" Libby Littlechap, Remco, vinyl: $25. **Photo courtesy of The Museum Doll Shop.**

Uncle Fester

    4½" $60.00–75.00

Baby Crawl-Along, **1967**

    20" $15.00–20.00

Baby Grow a Tooth, **1968, vinyl and hard plastic, rooted hair, blue sleep eyes, open/ closed mouth, one tooth, grows her own tooth, battery operated**

    15" $50.00–60.00

    Black $60.00–70.00

Baby Know It All, **1969**

    17" $40.00–50.00

Baby Laugh A Lot, **1970, rooted long hair, painted eyes, open/closed mouth, teeth, vinyl head, hands, plush body, push button, she laughs, battery operated**

    16" $300.00–350.00

Baby Look N'Love, **1978, vinyl, painted eyes, rooted hair, nods and turns head when squeezed.**

    14" $30.00–40.00

Beatles, **1964, vinyl and plastic, Paul McCartney, Ringo Starr, George Harrison, and John Lennon, Paul 4⅞", all others 4½" with guitars bearing their names, allow more for MIB**

    Set of 4 .... $500.00–600.00

    Individual Beatles **$100.00–150.00**

Daniel Boone, **1964, Fess Parker from TV show**

    4½" $80.00–100.00

Dave Clark Five, **1964, set of five musical group, vinyl heads, rigid plastic bodies**

    Set $160.00–180.00

Dave Clark

    5" $25.00–35.00

Other band members **have name attached to leg**

 3"...$15.00–20.00

Finger Dings, 1969 on, finger puppets, vinyl head

 6"...$35.00–45.00

The Monkees, **musical group**

30.00–40.00 each

Growing Sally, 1968, doll "grows" ¾", has extra clothes and additional wig

 6"...$20.00–30.00

 Black $30.00–40.00

Heidi and friends, 1967, in plastic case, rooted hair, painted side-glancing eyes, open/closed mouth, all-vinyl, press button and dolls wave

Heidi

 5½"..$25.00–30.00

Jan, **Asian**

 5½"..$25.00–30.00

Pip

 5½"..$30.00–40.00

Spunky

 4½"..$35.00–45.00

Winking Heidi, **1968**

 5½"..$15.00–20.00

Hildy

 4½"..$35.00–45.00

 Herby..$35.00–45.00

 TV Jones, dog.....................................$75.00–95.00

Hello Dolly, 1978, doll talks on phone

 13"..$25.00–35.00

Hug A Bug, 1971 butterfly

 4"..$90.00–125.00

Jeannie, I Dream of

 6"..$40.00–50.00

Plastic Bottle Playset, **6", Jeannie doll and all accessories**

 ....$400.00–450.00

Jumpsy, 1970, vinyl and hard plastic, jumps rope, rooted blond hair, painted blue eyes, closed mouth, molded-on shoes and socks

 14"..$50.00–60.00

Black

14"... $60.00–70.00

Kitty Karry All, 1969, featured on the TV show the Brady Bunch

20"... $150.00–200.00

Laurie Partridge, 1973

19"... $125.00–150.00

Littlechap Family, 1963+, vinyl head, arms, jointed hips, shoulders, neck, black molded and painted hair, black eyes, box, allow more for MIB.

Dr. John Littlechap

14½" $35.00–45.00

Judy Littlechap

12"... $35.00–35.00

Libby Littlechap

10½" $20.00–35.00

Lisa Littlechap

13½" $30.00–40.00

Littlechap Accessories

Dr. John's Office............................... $275.00–325.00

Master Bedroom $200.00–250.00

Family room $95.00–115.00

Dr. John Littlechap's outfits

Golf outfit..................................... $35.00 MIP

Medical .... $70.00 MIP

Suit .... $50.00 MIP

Tuxedo .... $70.00 MIP

Libby's outfits

Lingerie .... $50.00 MIP

Lisa's outfits

Black dress...................................... $40.00 MIP

Coat, **fur trim**................................. $50.00 MIP

Judy's outfits

Lingerie .... $50.00 MIP

Pajamas... $30.00 MIP

Dance dress...................................... $55.00 MIP

Mimi, 1973, vinyl and hard plastic, battery-operated singer, rooted long blond hair, painted blue eyes, open/closed mouth, record player in body, sings "I'd Like to Teach the World to Sing," song used for Coca-Cola' commercial, sings in different languages

19"...\$60.00–70.00

Black

19"...\$75.00–85.00

Monsters, 1976, Dracula, Frankenstein, others, jointed hard vinyl

9"...\$45.00–70.00

Munsters

Herman, pull string talker

20"...\$200.00–275.00

Lily #1822, 1964, vinyl, one-piece body, played by Yvonne DeCarl

4¾"...125.00–140.00

Grandpa, #1821, 1964, vinyl head, one-piece plastic body

4¾"...\$100.00–120.00

Herman, 1964, vinyl, one-piece body, played by Fred Gwynne

6¾"...\$155.00–175.00

Orphan Annie, 1967

15"...\$40.00–50.00

Polly Puff, 1970, vinyl, came with inflatable furniture

12"...\$30.00–35.00

Ronald MacDonald, 1976, vinyl

8"...\$20.00–25.00

Snuggle Bun, 1969, vinyl, push button makes headturn while doll crys

16"...\$40.00–50.00

Sweet April, 1971, vinyl

5½"...\$35.00–40.00

Black

5½"...\$45.00–50.00

Tippy Tumbles, 1968, vinyl, rooted red hair, stationary blue eyes, does somersaults, batteries in pocketbook

16"...\$40.00–50.00

Tumbling Tomboy, 1969, rooted blond braids, closed smiling mouth, vinyl and hard plastic, battery operated

17"...\$35.00–45.00

RICHWOOD TOYS INC.

8" Sandra Sue, Majorette, Richwood Toys, hard plastic, high heel feet: $135. **Photo courtesy Fourty Fifty Sixty.**

1950s–1960s, Annapolis, Maryland. Produced hard plastic dolls.

Sandra Sue, 8", 1940s, 1950s, hard plastic, walker, head does not turn, slim body, saran wigs, sleep eyes, some with high-heeled feet, only marks are number under arm or leg, all prices reflect outfits with original socks, shoes, panties, and accessories. Dolls listed are in good condition with appropriate clothing and tags, naked, played with dolls will bring one-fourth to one-third the value listed.

Flat feet

In camisole, slip, panties, shoes, and socks

.... $75.00–100.00

In school dress................................... $100.00–125.00

In party/Sunday dress

.... $125.00–175.00

Special coat, hat, and dress, **limited editions, Brides, Heidi, Little Women, Majorette**

.... $120.00–200.00

Sport or play clothes.......................... $100.00–125.00

High-heeled feet

Camisole, slip, panties, shoes, socks

.... $70.00–95.00

In school dress................................... $85.00–145.00

In party/Sunday dress $125.00–150.00

Special coat, hat and dress, **limited editions, Brides, Heidi, Little Women, Majorette**

.... $120.00–165.00

Sport or play clothes.......................... $95.00–125.00

Sandra Sue Outfits, **mint, including all accessories**

School dress $50.00–75.00

Party dress... $60.00–85.00

Specials... $75.00–100.00

Sport sets $75.00–85.00

Cindy Lou, 14", hard plastic, jointed dolls were purchased in bulk from New York distributor, fitted with double-stitched wigs by Richwood

In camisole, slip, panties, shoes, and socks

.... $125.00–175.00

In school dress...................................... $175.00–200.00

In party dress.. $200.00–225.00

In special outfits $200.00–250.00

In sports outfits.................................... $200.00–250.00

Cindy Lou Outfits, **mint, including all accessories**

School dress $75.00–100.00

Party dress... $95.00–125.00

Special outfit... $1,250.00–200.00

Sports clothes.. $100.00–150.00

GRACE CORRY ROCKWELL

14" Little Sister, Grace Corry Rockwell, composition: $350. **Photo courtesy of Dollyology Vintage Dolls.**

1926–1928, USA. Artist who designed dolls. Her bisque doll heads were made in Germany and were distributed by Borgfeldt. Her composition headed dolls were made by Averill.

Pretty Peggy, **bisque socket head, open mouth**

    12"–14" $4,000.00–4,800.00

    16"–19" $4,500.00–5,500.00

Little Sister & Brother, **composition, smiling mouth, molded hair**

    14" $300.00–350.00

ROHMER

15.5" Rohmer, poupée peau, bisque, glass eyes: $7,000. **Photo courtesy of McMasters Harris Apple Tree Doll Auctions.**

1857–1880, Paris, France. Mme. Rohmer held patents for doll bodies, made dolls of various materials. Dolls listed are in good condition, appropriately dressed, may be much more for exceptional dolls.

Poupée (so-called Fashion-type), bisque or china glazed shoulder or swivel head on shoulder plate, closed mouth, kid body with green oval stamp, bisque or wood lower arms

Glass eyes

    13"–16" $5,000.00–8,000.00

    17"–19" $9,000.00–12,000.00

    24" $16,000.00–17,000.00

Painted eyes

    13"–18" $5,000.00–7,5 00.00

14" with Provenance and trousseau sold for $25,800.00 at auction

ROLDAN

9.5" Guitar Player, Roldan, cloth: $175. **Photo courtesy of Morphy Auctions.**

1960s–1970s, Barcelona. Spain. Roldan characters are similar to Klumpe figures in many respects. They are made of felt over a wire armature with painted mask faces. Like Klumpe, Roldan figures represent professionals, hobbyists, dancers, historical characters, and contemporary males and females performing a wide variety of tasks. Some, but not all Roldans, were imported by Rosenfeld Imports and Leora Dolores of Hollywood. Figures originally came with two sewn-on identifying cardboard tags. Roldan characters most commonly found are doctors, Spanish dancers, and bull fighters. Roldan characters tend to have somewhat smaller heads, longer necks, and more defined facial features than Klumpe. Dolls listed are all in good, clean, unfaded condition, allow more for elaborate figure with many accessories.

9"–11"...$100.00–300.00

GERTRUDE F. ROLLINSON

27" Rollinson, cloth, "composition look", wigged: $3,000. **Photo courtesy of Sweetbriar Auctions.**

1916–1929, Holyoke, Massachusetts. Designed and made cloth dolls with molded faces, painted over the cloth on head and limbs, treated to be washable. Painted hair or wigged, some closed mouth, others had open/closed mouths with painted teeth. Some dolls closely resemble the dolls of the Chase Company while others are heavily sanded between coats of paint giving them a look of composition. Rollinson had her dolls made by the Utley Co. (later called New England Doll Company), and distributed by G. Borgfeldt, L. Wolfe, and Strobel & Wilken.

Chase-look doll **with painted hair or wig**

    13"–17" $1,400.00–1,800.00

    22"–26" $2,000.00–2,200.00

Composition look doll **with painted hair or wig**

    14"–16" $1,400.00–2,200.00

    22"–24" $1,600.00–2,500.00

RUBBER

15" Goodyear rubber doll, mid- 1800s: $450. **Photo courtesy of Joan & Lynette Antique Dolls and Accessories.**

1860s on, various European and American makers produced rubber dolls.

Goodyear Doll, **molded shoulder head doll in the style of the china and papier-mâché dolls of the era.**

    10"–18" $800.00–1,000.00

    20"–28" $1,000.00–1,700.00

American rubber doll, **1920s on**

Baby

    12"–15" $55.00–65.00

SANTONS

10" pair Santons, earthenware, MIB: $150.
Photo courtesy of Alderfer Auction Company, Inc.

Santons (little Saints) France, 1930 on. Character figures depicting elderly peasants. Earthenware heads, hand, and legs on wire armature bodies. Dressed in regional or occupational costume.

7"–8" **$35.00–55.00**

10"–12" **$65.00–90.00**

SASHA

16" Sasha, Frido/ Trendon, vinyl: $400.
Photo courtesy of Alderfer Auction Company, Inc.

1945–2001. Sasha dolls were created by Swiss artist Sasha Morgenthaler, who handcrafted 20" children and 13" babies in Zurich, Switzerland, from the 1940s until her death in 1975. Her handmade studio dolls had cloth or molded bodies, five different head molds, and were hand painted by Sasha Morgenthaler. To make her dolls affordable as children's playthings, she licensed Götz Puppenfabric (1964–1970 and 1995–2001) in Germany and

Frido Trendon Ltd. (1965–1986) in England to manufacture 16" Sasha dolls in series. The manufactured dolls were made of rigid vinyl with painted features.

Price range reflects rarity, condition, and completeness of doll, outfit, and packaging, and varies with geographic location. Dolls listed are in good condition, with original clothing. Allow more for mint-in-box.

Original Studio Sasha Doll, ca. 1940s–1974, made by Sasha Morgenthaler in Switzerland, some are signed on soles of feet, have wrist tags, or wear labeled clothing

20"...$10,000.00–14,000.00

Götz Sasha Doll, 1964–1970, Germany, girls or boys, two face molds, marked "Sasha Series" in circle on neck and in three-circle logo on back, three different boxes were used, identified by wrist tag and/or booklet

16"...$800.00–1,100.00

Frido-Trendon Ltd., 1965–1986, England, unmarked on body, wore wrist tags and current catalogs were packed with doll

Child

1965–1968, **packaged in wide box**

16"...$300.00–500.00

1969–1972, **packaged in crayon tubes**

16"...$400.00–550.00

Sexed Baby, **1970–1978, cradle, styrofoam cradles package or straw box and box, white or black**

....$120.00–140.00

Unsexed Baby, **1978–1986, packaged in styrofoam wide or narrow cradles or straw basket and box**

....$110.00–130.00

Child, **16"**

1973–1975, packaged in shoe box style box

1975–1980, white, shoe box style box

1980–1986, white, packaged in photo box with flaps

Sasha, 101, 103, sailing

....$150.00–175.00

Gingham 107

....$150.00–200.00

Marina

....$100.00–150.00

Caleb

....$130.00–180.00

Cora

.... $150.00–200.00

Gregor

.... $150.00–180.00

#1 Sasha Anniversary doll

16"... $100.00–120.00

1986, Sasha "Sari" 117S, black hair, estimated only 400 produced before English factory closed January 1986

16"... $400.00–700.00

130E Sasha "Wintersport," 1986, blond hair

16"... $250.00–300.00

Limited Editions

Made by Trendon Sasha Ltd. in England, packaged in box with outer sleeve picturing individual doll, limited edition Sasha dolls marked on neck with date and number, number on certificate matches number on doll's neck

1981 "Velvet," girl, light brown wig, 5,000 production planned

.... $250.00–300.00

1982 "Pintucks" girl, blond wig, 6,000 production planned

.... $175.00–225.00

1983 "Kiltie" girl, red wig, 4,000 production planned

.... $275.00–325.00

1984 "Harlequin" girl, rooted blond hair, 4,000 production planned

.... $200.00–250.00

1985 "Prince Gregor" boy, light brown wig, 4,000 production planned

.... $175.00–225.00

1986 "Princess Sasha" girl, blond wig, 3,500 production planned, but only 350 were made

.... $1,100.00–1,400.00

Götz Dolls Inc., 1995+, Germany, they received the license in September 1994; dolls introduced in 1995

Child, 1995–1996, marked "Götz Sasha" on neck and "Sasha Series" in three circle logo on back, about 1,500 of the dolls produced in 1995 did not have mold mark on back, earliest dolls packaged in generic Götz box, currently in tube, wear wrist tag, Götz tag, and have mini-catalog.

16½" $275.00–325.00

Baby, 1996, unmarked on neck, marked "Sasha Series" in three circle logo on back, first babies were packaged in generic Götz box or large tube, currently packaged in small "Baby" tube, wears Sasha wrist tag, Götz booklet and current catalog.

12"... $125.00–150.00

BRUNO SCHMIDT

18" marked BSW, Bruno Schmidt, bisque: $450. **Photo courtesy of Withington Auction Inc.**

1898–1930, Waltershausen, Germany. Made bisque, composition, and wooden head dolls, after 1913 also celluloid. Acquired Bähr & Pröschild in 1918. Often used a heart-shaped tag. Dolls listed are in good condition, appropriately dressed.

Character Baby, **bisque socket head, glass eyes, composition bent leg body**

Mold 2092, 2094, 2095, 2097 ca. 1920, Mold 2097, ca. 1911

> 13"–15"..$225.00–275.00
>
> 18"–20"..$325.00–400.00
>
> 33"..$550.00–650.00

Mold 2097, **toddler**

> 15"..$350.00–450.00
>
> 21"..$550.00–650.00
>
> 34"..$800.00–1,000.00

Child, **BSW, no mold numbers, bisque socket head, jointed body, sleep eyes, open mouth, add $50.00 more for flirty eyes**

> 14"..$325.00–425.00
>
> 18"–20"..$475.00–550.00
>
> 22"–24"..$550.00–600.00

Character

Asian, mold 500, **ca. 1905, yellow tint bisque socket head, glass eyes, open mouth, teeth, pierced ears, wig, yellow tint composition jointed body**

> 11"–14"..$900.00–1,200.00
>
> 18"..$1,500.00–1,900.00

Mold 529, **"2052," ca. 1912, painted eyes, closed mouth**

20"...$2,800.00–4,000.00

Mold 539, **"2023," ca. 1912, solid dome or with wig, painted eyes, closed mouth**

24"...$3,000.00–3,200.00

Mold 537, **"2033" (Wendy), ca. 1912, sleep eyes, closed mouth**

11"–13"...$8,000.00–10,000.00

15"–17"...$15,000.00–19,000.00

20"..22,000.00–22,000.00

Mold 2048, **ca. 1912, Tommy Tucker, 2094, 2096, ca. 1920, solid dome, molded and painted hair or wig, sleep eyes, open or closed mouth, composition jointed body**

Open mouth

12"–14"...$700.00–800.00

18"–20"...$800.00–1,000.00

26"–28"...$1,300.00–1,600.00

Mold 2072, **ca. 1920, sleep eyes, closed mouth**

16"..$2,200.00–2,450.00

19"..$2,500.00–2,900.00

Celluloid

Shoulder head doll, **kid body**

21"–23"...$90.00–110.00

FRANZ SCHMIDT

11" character baby, Franz Schmidt, bisque, wobbly tongue: $200. **Photo courtesy of Oldeclectics.**

1890–1937, Georgenthal, Thüringia, Germany. Made, produced, and exported dolls with bisque, composition, wood, and celluloid heads. Used bisque heads made by Simon & Halbig. Heads marked "S & C," mold 269, 293, 927, 1180, 1310. Heads marked "F.S. & C," mold 1250, 1253, 1259, 1262, 1263, 1266, 1267, 1270, 1271, 1272, 1274, 1293, 1295,

1296, 1297, 1298, 1310. Walkers: mold 1071, 1310. Dolls listed are in good condition, appropriately dressed.

Baby, bisque head, solid dome or cut out for wig, bent-leg body, sleep or set eyes, open mouth, some pierced nostrils, add more for flirty eyes

Mold 1271, 1272, 1295, 1296, 1297, 1310

10"–12"	$175.00–225.00
13"–14"	$250.00–400.00
18"–20"	$500.00–600.00
22"–24"	$650.00–750.00
27"	$900.00–1,100.00

Toddler

10"–12"	$300.00–400.00
16"–20"	$550.00–700.00
22"–24"	$750.00–850.00

Character Face

Mold 1237, **baby, open mouth, molded hair, breather, glass eyes**

13"	$1,200.00–1,300.00

Mold 1257, **baby, open mouth with wobble tongue, molded hair, breather, glass eyes**

13" Toddler	$900.00–1,000.00

Mold 1266, 1267, **ca. 1912, marked "F.S. & Co.," solid dome, painted eyes, closed mouth**

14"	$2,750.00–2,850.00
19"–23"	$3,400.00–3,800.00

Mold 1272, **ca. 1910, solid dome, sleep eyes, open mouth**

16"	$400.00–500.00

Child

Dolly face, **five-piece body, Mold 269, ca. 1890s, Mold 293, ca. 1900, marked "S & C," open mouth, glass eyes**

5"–7"	$275.00–350.00
10"–12"	$425.00–500.00
19"–23"	$500.00–575.00
27"–29"	$800.00–900.00

Character

Mold 1259, **ca. 1912, marked "F.S. & Co." character, sleep eyes, pierced nostrils, open mouth**

15"	$400.00–500.00

Mold 1262, 1263, **ca. 1910, marked "F.S. & Co.," painted eyes, closed mouth**

13"...$11,000.00–12,000.00

17"–24"..$20,000.00–24,000.00

Mold 1272, **ca. 1910, marked "F.S. & Co.," solid dome or wig, sleep eyes, pierced nostrils, open mouth**

9½"..$850.00–950.00

Mold 1286, **ca. 1915, marked "F.S. & Co. 1286/40 Germany," molded hair side-glancing glass eyes**

14"–16"..$8,000.00–12,000.00

SCHMITT & FILS

14" Schmitt & Fils, bisque, closed-mouth bébé: $18,000. **Photo courtesy of Sweetbriar Auctions.**

1854–1891, Noget-sur-Marne & Paris, France. Made bisque and wax-over-bisque or wax-over-composition dolls. Heads were pressed. Used neck socket like on later composition Patsydolls. Dolls listed are in good condition, appropriately dressed; more for exceptional doll with wardrobe or other attributes.

Child, **pressed bisque head, closed mouth, glass eyes, pierced ears, mohair or human hair wig, French composition and wood eight ball-jointed body with straight wrists**

Early round face

12"–14"..$15,000.00–18,000.00

15"–16"..$19,000.00–21,000.00

18"–24"..$23,000.00–28,000.00

Pear shaped face

14"–16"..$12,000.00–15,000.00

Long face modeling

16"–18"..$19,000.00–23,000.00

24"–26"..$26,000.00–32,000.00

Wax over papier-mâché, **swivel head, cup and saucer type neck, glass eyes, closed mouth, eight ball-jointed body**

   16"–17" $5,000.00–6,000.00

SCHOENAU & HOFFMEISTER

17" Hanna, toddler, Schoenau & Hoffmeister, bisque: $450. **Photo courtesy of Joan & Lynette Antique Dolls and Accessories.**

20" Princess Elizabeth, Schoenau & Hoffmeister, bisque: $2,800. **Photo courtesy of Sweetbriar Auctions.**

1901–1939, Burggrub, Bavaria. Had a porcelain factory, produced bisque heads for dolls, also supplied other manufacturers, including Bruckner, Dressel, Eckhardt, E. Knoch, and others. Dolls listed are in good condition, appropriately dressed. More for exceptional dolls.

Baby, bisque solid-dome or wigged socket head, sleep eyes, teeth, composition bent-leg body, closed mouth, newborn, solid dome, painted hair, cloth body, may have celluloid hands, add more for original outfit. Allow more for toddler body.

Solid dome infant

   10"–12" $300.00–400.00

   13"–15" $450.00–500.00

Mold 169, 170, 585 **(Porzellanfabrik Burggrub), bent-limb body**

   13"–15" $225.00–275.00

   18"–20" $375.00–425.00

   23"–25" $450.00–475.00

Hanna, **sleep eyes, open-closed mouth, bent-leg baby body, $100.00 more for toddler**

   13"–15" $300.00–350.00

   18"–20" $400.00–500.00

   22"–24" $550.00–650.00

Princess Elizabeth, **1929, socket head, sleep eyes, smiling open mouth, chubby leg toddler body**

   16"–17" $2,200.00–2,500.00

20"–22"...$2,800.00–3,200.00

25"..$3,500.00–4,000.00

Child, dolly face, bisque socket head, open mouth with teeth, sleep eyes, composition ball-jointed body

Mold 1906, 1909, 2500, 4000, 4600, 4700, 5000, 5500, 5700, 5800

10"–12"...$150.00–200.00

14"–16"...$225.00–300.00

18"–24"...$400.00–500.00

26"–28"...$600.00–750.00

32"–39"...$800.00–1,200.00

Mold 914, **ca. 1925, character**

24"–25"...$400.00–500.00

27"–28"...$550.00–600.00

31"..$600.00–700.00

Mold 4900, **ca. 1905, Asian, dolly-face**

8"–10"...$600.00–750.00

18"...$950.00–1,000.00

Shoulder head dolly, **open mouth with teeth, sleep eyes, kid body**

Mold 1800

14"–22"...$125.00–200.00

A. SCHOENHUT & CO.

15" Schoenhut Schnickel Fritz, wood, carved hair, repainted: $2,500. **Photo courtesy of Alderfer Auction Company, Inc.**

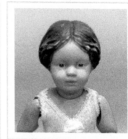

16" Schoenhut transitional period model 102, wood: $4,500. **Photo courtesy of Alderfer Auction Company, Inc.**

1872–1930 on, Philadelphia, Pennsylvania. Made all-wood dolls, using spring joints, had holes in bottoms of feet to fit into stands. Later made elastic strung with cloth bodies. Carved or molded and painted hair or wigged, intaglio or sleep eyes, open or closed mouth.

Later made composition dolls. Dolls listed are in good condition, appropriately dressed; more for exceptional doll.

Babies

Graziano Infants, **circa May 1911–1912**

Schnickel-Fritz, **carved hair, open-closed grinning mouth, four teeth, large ears, toddler**

15".. $3,600.00–4,000.00

Tootsie Wootsie, **carved hair, open-closed mouth, two upper teeth, large ears on child body**

15".. $4,600.00–5,000.00

Too few in database for reliable range.

Model 107, 107W (walker), **108, 108W (walker),** 1913–1926, 109W, 110W, 1921–1923

Baby, **nature (bent) limb**

13"–15"... $300.00–450.00

Toddler

11"–14"... $350.00–450.00

17".. $500.00–600.00

Elastic strung, **1924–1926**

14".. $675.00–750.00

Cloth body with crier

14".. $450.00–525.00

Bye-Lo Baby, **"Grace S. Putnam" stamp, cloth body, closed mouth, sleep eyes**

13".. $2,400.00–3,200.00

Child

Graziano Period, **1911–1912, dolls may have heavily carved hair or wigs, painted intaglio eyes, outlined iris, all with wooden spring-jointed bodies and are 16" tall, designated with 16 before the model number, like "16/100"**

Model 100, **girl, carved hair, solemn face**

Model 101, **girl, carved hair, grinning, squinting eyes**

Model 102, **girl, carved hair, bun on top**

Model 103, **girl, carved hair, loose ringlets**

Model 200, **boy, carved hair, short curls**

Model 201, **boy, carved hair, based on K*R 114**

Model 202, **boy, carved hair, forelock**

Model 203, **boy, carved hair, grinning, some with comb marks**

Model 300, **girl, long curl wig, face of 102**

Model 301, **girl, bobbed wig with bangs, face of 300**

Model 302, **girl, wig, based on K*R 101**

17" Miss Dolly, Schoenhut, wood, sleep eyes: $600. **Photo courtesy of McMasters Harris Apple Tree Doll Auctions.**

8.75" & 7" Maggie and Jiggs, Schoenhut, wood: $550. **Photo courtesy of Ladenburger Spielzeugauktion.**

Model 303, **girl, short bob, no bangs, grinning, squinting eyes**

Model 304, **girl, wig in braids, ears stick out**

Model 305, **girl, snail braids, grinning, face of 303**

Model 306, **girl, wig, long curls, face of 304**

Model 307, **girl, short bob, no bangs, "dolly-type" smooth eye**

Model 400, **boy, short bob, K*R 101 face**

Model 401, **boy, side part bob, face of 300/301**

Model 402, **boy, side part bob, grin of 303**

Model 403, **boy, dimple in chin**

Carved hair, **allow more for earlier examples and those in all original condition**

> 14"–16"..$3,500.00–4,500.00
>
> 19"–21"..$4,500.00–5,000.00

Wigged, **allow more for earlier examples and those in all original condition**

> 14"...$1,800.00–1,900.00
>
> 16"...$2,000.00–2,500.00
>
> 19"–21"..$3,000.00–4,000.00

Transition Period, **1911–1912, designs by Graziano and Leslie, dolls may no longer have outlined iris, some models have changed, dolls measure 16"–17", now have a groove above knee for stockings**

Model 100, **girl, same, no iris outline**

Model 101, **girl, short carved hair, bob/bow, round eyes/smile**

Model 102, **girl, braids carved around head, bow in back**

Model 103, **girl, heavy carved hair in front/fine braids in back**

Model 104, **girl, fine carved hair in front/fine braids in back**

Model 200, **boy, carved hair, same, no iris outline**

Model 201, **boy, carved hair, same, iris outline, stocking groove**

Model 202, **boy, carved hair, same, smoother**

Model 203, **boy, smiling boy, round eyes, no iris outline**

Model 204, **boy, carved hair brushed forward, serious face**

11.5" Hattie & Ty Pinn, Schoenhut, wooden, MIB: $275. **Photo courtesy of Alderfer Auction Company, Inc.**

Model 300, **girl, long curl wig, dimple in chin**

Model 301, **girl, bob wig, face of 102**

Model 302, **girl, wig, same like K*R 101**

Model 303, **girl, wig, similar to 303G, smiling, short bob, no bangs**

Model 304, **girl, wig, braids, based on K*R**

Model 305, **girl, wig, braids, face of 303**

Model 306, **girl, long curl wig, same face as 304**

Model 307, **girl, smooth eyeball**

Model 400, **boy, same (like K*R 101)**

Model 401, **boy, like K*R 114 (304)**

Model 402, **boy, smiling, round eyes**

Model 403, **boy, same as 300 with side part bob**

Model 404, **boy, same as 301, side part bob**

Carved hair, **allow more for earlier examples and those in all original condition**

    14"–16"...$3,500.00–5,000.00

    19"–21"...$4,000.00–5,500.00

Wigged, **allow more for earlier examples and those in all original condition**

    14"..$1,800.00–2,000.00

    16"..$2,400.00–2,800.00

    19"–21"...$2,900.00–3,500.00

Classic Period, **1912–1923, some models discontinued, some sizes added, those marked with * were reissued in 1930**

Model 101, **girl, short carved hair bob, no iris outline**

1912–1923, **14"**

1911–1916, **16"**

Model 102, **girl, heavy carved hair in front, fine braids in back with bow**

1912–1923, **14"**

1911–1923, **16"**

1912–1916, **19"–21"**

Model 105, **girl, short carved hair bob, carved ribbon around head**

1912–1923, **14"–16"**

1912–1916, **19"–21"**

Model 106, **girl, carved molded bonnet on short hair,**

1912–1916, **14", 16", 19"**

Model 203, **16" boy, same as transition**

Model 204, **16" boy, same as transition***

Model 205, **carved hair boy, covered ears**

1912–1923, **14"–16"**

1912–1916, **19"–21"**

Model 206, **19" carved hair boy, covered ears**

1912–1916

Model 207, **14" carved short curly hair boy**

1912–1916

Model 300, **16" wigged girl, same as transition period**

1911–1923

Model 301, **16" wigged girl, same as transition**

1911–1924

Model 303, **16" wigged girl, same as transition 305**

1911–1916

Model 307, **16" long curl wigged girl, smooth eye**

1911–1916

Model 308, **14" girl, braided wig**

1912–1916

1912–1924

19", bobbed hair

1917–1924

19"–21", bob or curls

Model 309, **16", 19"–21" wigged girl, two teeth, long curls, bobbed hair, 1912–1913**

19"–21"

Model 310, **14"–16", 19"–21" wigged girl, same as 105 face, long curls, 1912–1916**

Model 311, **14"–16" wigged girl, heart shape 106 face, bobbed wig, no bangs, 1912–1916**

1912–1913, **19"**

Model 312, **14", wigged girl, bobbed, 1912–1924, bobbed wig or curls, 1917–1924**

Model 313, wigged girl, long curls, smooth eyeball, receding chin, 1912–1916
14"–16"
19"–21"

Model 314, **19", wigged girl, long curls, wide face, smooth eyeball, 1912–1916**
19"

Model 315, **21", wigged girl, long curls, four teeth, triangular mouth, 1912–1916**

Model 403, **16", wigged boy, same as transition, bobbed hair, bangs, 1911–1924**

Model 404, **16", wigged boy, same as transition, 1911–1916**

Model 405, **14", 19" boy, face of 308, bobbed wig, 1912–1924**

Model 407, **19"–21", wigged boy, face of 310 girl, 1912–1916**

Carved hair, **allow more for earlier examples and those in all original condition**

    14"–16" $1,500.00–2,800.00

    19"–21" $2,000.00–3,800.00

Wigged, **allow more for earlier examples and those in all original condition**

    14" $900.00–1,500.00

    16" $1,500.00–2,000.00

    19"–21" $2,500.00–3,000.00

Miss Dolly

Model 316, **open mouth, teeth, wigged girl, curls or bobbed wig, painted or decal eyes, all four sizes, circa 1915–1925**

    15"–21" $350.00–500.00

Model 317, **sleep eyes, open mouth, teeth, wigged girl, long curls or bob, sleep eyes, four sizes, 1921–1928**

    15"–21" $450.00–800.00

Composition doll, **1924, molded curly hair, painted eyes, closed moth**

    13" $900.00–1,000.00

Manikin

Model 175, **man with slim body, ball-jointed waist, circa 1914–1918**

    19" $2,800.00–3,300.00

Small dolls, **such as circus figures, storybook and comic characters**

Circus performers, **rare figures may be much higher**

Bisque head

Bareback Lady Rider or Ringmaster, **all original**

    9" $275.00–325.00

Wood heads

Clowns

    8" $250.00–300.00

Ringmaster, Acrobat Gent, Lady
Bareback Rider, Lion Tamer

8"..$300.00–325.00

Animals, ***some rare animals may be**
much higher

Donkey, painted eyes

7"..$350.00

Kangaroo, glass eyes

11½" sold for $1,200.00 at online auction

Ostrich, painted eyes

9"..$250.00

Polar Bear, painted eyes

8"..$425.00

Barney Google & Sparkplug, **comic strip characters created by Billy De Beck Otto**
Messmer

7½" & 8" ....$400.00–600.00 pair

Felix the Cat, **comic strip characters created by Otto Messmer**

8"..$700.00–$800.00

Maggie and Jiggs **from cartoon strip "Bringing up Father"**

7"–9"..$450.00–550.00 pair

Max and Moritz **carved figures, painted hair, carved shoes**

8"..$500.00–550.00 each

Mary and her lamb $550.00–600.00

Teddy Roosevelt

8"..$1,600.00–2,000.00

Pinn Family, **all wood, egg-shaped head, original costumes, names such as Bobby**
Pinn, Hattie Pinn, Ty Pinn, etc.

5"–9"..$95.00–125.00

Black pinn dolls

9"..$250.00–300.00

Rolly-Dolly figures

9"–12"..$800.00–1,200.00

Schoenhut doll shoes

to fit 15"–20" $175.00–200.00

SCHUETZMEISTER
& QUENDT

20" Schuetzmeister & Quendt mold 101, bisque: $250. **Photo courtesy of Joan & Lynette Antique Dolls and Accessories.**

1889–1930 on, Boilstadt, Gotha, Thüringia. A porcelain factory that made and exported bisque doll heads, all-bisque dolls, and Nankeen dolls. Used initials "S & Q," mold 301 was sometimes incised "Jeannette." Dolls listed are in good condition, appropriately dressed.

Baby, **character face, bisque socket head, sleep eyes, open mouth, bent-leg body, allow more for toddler body**

Mold 201, 204, 300, 301, **ca. 1920**

10"–12"	$200.00–250.00
14"–17"	$300.00–350.00
19"–25"	$350.00–425.00

Mold 252, **ca. 1920, character face, black baby**

15"	$550.00–600.00

Child

Mold 101, 102, **ca. 1900, dolly face**

16"–17"	$300.00–350.00
19"–22"	$300.00–400.00

Mold 1376, **ca. 1900, character face**

19"	$475.00–550.00

S.F.B.J.

16" mold 301, S.F.B.J., bisque: $1,700. **Photo courtesy of Alderfer Auction Company, Inc.**

15" mold 227 boy, 14" mold 229, S.F.B.J., bisque: $1,600 each. **Photo courtesy of Sweetbriar Auctions.**

Société Francaise de Fabrication de Bébés & Jouets, 1899–1930+, Paris and Montreuil-sous-Bois. 1922–1930 on. Mark used by S.F.B.J. (Société Francaise de Fabrication de Bébés & Jouets) after 1922 is Union Nationale Inter-Syndicale. Competition with German manufacturers forced many French companies to join together including Bouchet, Fleischmann & Bloedel, Gaultier, Rabery & Delphieu, Bru, Jumeau, Pintel & Godchaux, Remignard and Wertheimer, and others. This alliance lasted until the 1950s. Fleischman owned controlling interest. 1922–1930 on. Mark used by S.F.B.J. (Société Francaise de Fabrication de Bébés & Jouets) after 1922 is Union Nationale Inter-Syndicale, UNIS FRANCE. Dolls listed are in good condition, appropriately dressed; more for exceptional dolls.

Child, bisque head, glass eyes, open mouth, pierced ears, wig, composition jointed French body

Jumeau type, **no mold number, open mouth**

13"–15"	$1,50.00–1,800.00
18"–22"	$1,100.00–1,300.00
24"–26"	$1,500.00–1,700.00
28"–33"	$2,000.00–2,900.00

Mold 301

6"–8" on five-piece body

	$300.00–350.00
8"–10"	$450.00–525.00
12"–14"	$600.00–750.00
16"–20"	$900.00–1,100.00
22"–24"	$900.00–1,200.00
26"–28"	$900.00–1,300.00

Bleuette: See Bleuette section.

13" Poulbot, mold 239, S.F.B.J., bisque: $1,600. **Photo courtesy of Morphy Auctions.**

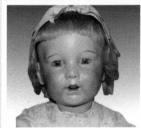

27" mold 251, S.F.B.J., bisque: $1,400. **Photo courtesy of Joan & Lynette Antique Dolls and Accessories.**

Kiss Thrower

15"–24"... $650.00–1,250.00

Mold 60

6"–8"... $250.00–300.00

12"–14"... $400.00–500.00

18"–21"... $700.00–800.00

25"–28"... $800.00–900.00

Mold 301 or 60, **papier-mâché head**

8"–10"... $125.00–150.00

13"–16"... $175.00–200.00

18"–22"... $250.00–300.00

Character Faces, bisque socket head, wigged or molded hair, set or sleep eyes, composition body, some with bent baby limb, toddler or child body, mold number 227, 235, and 236 may have flocked hair, add $100.00 for toddler body

Mold 226, **glass eyes, closed mouth**

14"–16"... $1,300.00–1,500.00

Mold 227, **open mouth, teeth, glass eyes**

14"... $1,500.00–1,600.00

17"... $1,600.00–1,800.00

19"–21"... $2,000.00–2,500.00

Mold 230, **glass eyes, open mouth, teeth**

12"–14"... $750.00–850.00

20"–23"... $1,200.00–1,500.00

Mold 233, **ca. 1912, crying mouth, glass eyes**

14"–16"... $3,600.00–4,000.00

Mold 234

18"... $2,800.00–3,050.00

Mold 235, **glass eyes, open-closed mouth**

    14"–15"...$900.00–1,250.00

    18"..$1,300.00–1,700.00

Mold 236, **glass eyes, laughing open/closed mouth**

Baby

    12"–13"...$550.00–650.00

    15"–17"...$700.00–800.00

    20"–22"...$1,000.00–1,200.00

Toddler

    13"..$1,000.00–1,200.00

    15"–18"...$1,300.00–1,400.00

    24"–26"...$1,200.00–1,400.00

Mold 237, **glass eyes, open-closed mouth**

    13"–14"...$1,000.00–1,200.00

    16"–17"...$1,300.00–1,500.00

Mold 238, **small open mouth**

    14"..$1,000.00–1,200.00

    18"..$1,800.00–2,000.00

Mold 239, **ca. 1913, designed by Poulbot**

    13"..$13,000.00–18,000.00

Mold 242, **ca. 1910, nursing baby**

    13"–15"...$2,500.00–2,800.00

Mold 247, **glass eyes, open-closed mouth**

Baby body

    6½" $550.00–650.00

Child or toddler

    13"–16"...$2,000.00–2,500.00

    20"..$2,000.00–2,300.00

    27"..$2,000.00–2,400.00

Mold 248, **ca. 1912, glass eyes, lowered eyebrows, very pouty closed mouth**

    10"–12"...$7,500.00–8,000.00

Mold 250, **open mouth with teeth**

    12"..$3,300.00 trousseau box

    18"–20"...$3,250.00–3,400.00

Mold 251, **open-closed mouth, teeth, tongue**

10"–12" $900.00–1,000.00

15"–18" $1,200.00–1,400.00

20"–24" $900.00–1,100.00

27" $1,300.00–1,500.00

Mold 252, **closed pouty mouth, glass eyes**

Baby

6"–8" $2,000.00–2,200.00

10" $2,600.00–3,000.00

Toddler

13"–15" $5,000.00–6,000.00

18"–20" $6,500.00–7,500.00

Unis France, **marked dolls, 1922–1930 on.**

Mold 60, 301, **bisque head, fully jointed composition/wood body, wig, sleep eyes, open mouth**

5"–6" $75.00–100.00

8"–10" $225.00–300.00

13"–15" $350.00– 400.00

21"–23" $500.00–600.00

5-piece composition body, **glass eyes**

5"–8" $175.00–200.00

10"–14" $250.00–300.00

Mold 247, 251, **toddler body**

15" .... $700.00–$950.00

7" .... $1,000.00–$1,200.00

SHIRLEY TEMPLE

1934 on, Ideal Novelty Toy Corp., New York. Designed by Bernard Lipfert. Dolls listed are in very good condition, all original. Add more for exceptional dolls or special outfits like Ranger or Wee Willie Winkie.

Composition, **1934–1940s, composition head and jointed body, dimples in cheeks, green sleep eyes, open mouth, teeth, mohair wig, tagged original dress, center-snap shoes, prototype dolls may have paper sticker inside head and bias trimmed wig. Rare costumes bring higher end of range or more.**

18" Baby Shirley Temple, Ideal, composition: $700. **Photo courtesy of Sweetbriar Auctions.**

19" Shirley, Ideal, vinyl: $225. **Photo courtesy of Alderfer Auction Company, Inc.**

Shirley Temple

11"..$450.00–700.00

13"..$400.00–550.00

16"..$450.00–800.00

16" in Heidi costume sold at online auction for

....$2,255.00

17"..$450.00–800.00

18"..$550.00–800.00

20"..$750.00–950.00

22"..$900.00–1,000.00

25"..$1,100.00–1,200.00

27"..$1,100.00–1,200.00

Baby Shirley

15"..$800.00–1,200.00

18"..$800.00–1,200.00

21"..$800.00–1,200.00

Hawaiian, "Marama," **Ideal used the composition Shirley Temple mold for this doll representing a character from the movie Hurricane, black yarn hair, wears grass skirt, Hawaiian costume**

13"..$450.00–500.00

18"..$850.00–900.00

Accessories:

Button, **three types**...........................$125.00

Buggy, **wicker or wood**....................$400.00–475.00

Dress, **tagged**...................................$125.00–575.00

Trunk..$175.00–225.00

Reliable Shirley Temple **composition, made in Canada**

18"–22"..$400.00–800.00

Japanese, unlicensed Shirley dolls

All-bisque

6"...$195.00–225.00

Celluloid

5"...$100.00–125.00

8"...$100.00–125.00

Composition **heavily molded brown curls, painted eyes, open-closed mouth with teeth, body stamped "Japan"**

7½"..$175.00–200.00

Celluloid

Dutch Shirley Temple **ca. 1937+, all-celluloid, open crown, metal pate, sleep eyes, dimples in cheeks, marked: "Shirley Temple" on head, may have additional marks, dressed in Dutch costume**

13"–15".......................................$475.00–550.00

Cloth

Wacker Manufacturing Co. **Chicago, painted features, side-glancing, molded face, mohair wig**

17"...$300.00–400.00

Vinyl, **dolls listed are in excellent condition, original clothes, accessories; the newer the doll, the more perfect it must be to command higher prices. Mib can bring double.**

1957, **all-vinyl, sleep eyes, synthetic rooted wig, open-closed mouth, teeth, came in two-piece slip and undies, tagged Shirley Temple, came with gold plastic script pin reading "Shirley Temple," marked on back of head: "ST//12"**

12"...$150.00–200.00

1958–1961, **marked on back of head: "S.T.//15," "S.T.//17," or "S.T.//19," some had flirty ("Twinkle") eyes; add more for flirty eyes or 1961 Cinderella, Bo Peep, Heidi, and Red Riding Hood**

15"..$130.00–200.00

17"..$150.00–225.00

19"..$200.00–250.00

1960, **jointed wrists, marked "ST–35–38–2"**

35"–36".......................................$800.00–1,100.00

1972, **Montgomery Wards reissue, plain box**

17"..$100.00–120.00

1973, **red dot "Stand Up and Cheer" outfit**

16"..$35.00–45.00

SIMON & HALBIG

20" mold 949 Simon & Halbig, bisque, socket head, open mouth: $1,700. **Photo courtesy of Sweetbriar Auctions.**

16" mold 1079, Simon & Halbig, bisque, socket head, open mouth: $600. **Photo courtesy of Alderfer Auction Company, Inc.**

1869–1930 on, Hildburghausen and Grafenhain, Germany. Porcelain factory, made heads for Jumeau (200 series), bathing dolls (300 series), porcelain figures (400 series), perhaps doll house or small dolls (500–600 series), bisque head dolls (700 series), bathing and small dolls (800 series), more bisque head dolls (900–1000 series). The earliest models of a series had the last digit of their model number ending with an 8, socket heads ended with 9, shoulder heads ended with 0, and models using a shoulder plate for swivel heads ended in 1.

Dolls listed are in good condition, appropriately dressed. All original or exceptional dolls may be more.

Molded hair lady, **1850s–60s, molded hair, painted or glass eyes**

10"–18".. $1,700.00–$2,400.00

Shoulder Head child, **1870s, molded hair, painted or glass eyes, closed mouth, cloth body with bisque lower arms, appropriately dressed, marked "S&H," no mold number**

10".. $800.00–1,000.00

13"–15".. $900.00–1,100.00

17" mold 153, Simon & Halbig, bisque, character, : $11,500. **Photo courtesy of Joan & Lynette Antique Dolls and Accessories.**

27" mold 1249, Simon & Halbig, bisque: $1,000. **Photo courtesy of McMasters Harris Apple Tree Doll Auctions.**

17"–19" $1,100.00–1,400.00

21"–23" $1,800.00–2,100.00

Swivel neck

9"–12" $2,000.00–2,800.00

Poupée (fashion-type doll), **1870s, bisque socket head with bisque shoulder plate on kid or twill over wood body, closed mouth, glass eyes, wigged**

Kid body

10" $1,800.00–2,000.00

15"–18" $2,400.00–2,600.00

Twill covered wood body

10"–11" $6,000.00–9,000.00

15"–16" $11,000.00–14,000.00

Closed-mouth Child, **1879, socket head, most on composition and wood body, glass eyes, wigged, pierced ears, appropriately dressed**

No mold #

16"–19" $4,000.00–6,000.00

Mold 719

16" $4,600.00–4,800.00

18"–22" $5,000.00–5,500.00

Edison phonograph mechanism in torso

23" $3,500.00–4,500.00

Mold 739

15"–20" $1,500.00–2,300.00

Mold 749

8"–9" $1,400.00–1,500.00

22" $3,000.00–4,000.00

19" mold 1299, Simon & Halbig, bisque, character: $900. **Photo courtesy of Gandtiques.**

Mold 905, 908

11"...$1,600.00–1,800.00

15"–17"...$2,100.00–3,300.00

Mold 919

15"...$5,300.00–7,200.00

19"...$6,000.00–8,150.00

Mold 929

14"–15"...$2,8.00–2,900.00

23"...$3,000.00–3,400.00

Mold 939

14"–16"...$1,700.00–1,900.00

18"–20"...$2,000.00–2,200.00

26"–27"...$2,700.00–2,800.00

Mold 949

10"–12"...$1,100.00–1,300.00

14"–16"...$1,400.00–1,700.00

18"–21"...$1,600.00–2,000.00

26"–31"...$3,500.00–4,000.00

Mold 720, 740, 940, 950, **dome shoulder head, kid body**

8"–10"...$350.00–450.00

14"–18"...$700.00–900.00

20"–22"...$1,200.00–1,600.00

All-bisque child: See All-Bisque, German section.

Open-mouth child, **1889–1930s, socket head on composition body (sometimes French), wigged, glass eyes may be stationary or sleep, appropriately dressed**

13.5" mold 1428 character, "Freddie," Simon & Halbig, bisque, glass eyes: $1,400. **Photo courtesy of Gloria's Antique Dolls.**

26" mold 1159, Simon & Halbig, bisque, lady body: $2,200. **Photo courtesy of Sweetbriar Auctions.**

Mold 530, 540, 550, 570, Baby Blanche

    17"–22"" **$450.00–600.00**

Mold 719, 739, 749, 759, 769, 939, 979

    5½"–6½" **$350.00–450.00**

    9"–13" **$1,000.00–1,200.00**

    15"–17" **$1,500.00–1,700.00**

    20"–22" **$1,900.00–2,100.00**

    26"–30" **$2,300.00–2,400.00**

Mold 905, 908

    12" **$1,800.00–2,000.00**

    18" **$1,90.00–2,200.00**

    22" **$1,425.00–2,600.00**

Mold 929, 949

    15"–17" **$900.00–1,100.00**

    22"–24" **$2,000.00–2,500.00**

    29"–32" **$2,100.00–2,600.00**

Mold 1009

    15"–16" **$700.00–750.00**

    19"–24" **$700.00–900.00**

    26"–28" **$1,600.00–1,800.00**

Mold 1029

    16"–18" **$475.00–575.00**

    24"–25" **$700.00–800.00**

    28" **$825.00–900.00**

Mold 1039, 1049, 1059, 1069, 1078, 1079

Flapper body

    8"–10"... **$250.00–400.00**

Child body

    10"–13"... **$775.00–900.00**

    16"–18"... **$600.00–700.00**

    21"–25"... **$600.00–700.00**

    27"–28"... **$800.00–1,000.00**

    30"–33"... **$700.00–900.00**

    36"... **$900.00–1,000.00**

Mold 1109

    13"... **$750.00–800.00**

    18"... **$1,000.00–1,000.00**

Mold 1248, 1249, Santa

    6"... **$550.00–650.00**

    10"–13"... **$750.00–850.00**

    15"–24"... **$900.00–1,000.00**

    26"–28"... **$1,100.00–1,300.00**

    35"– 38"... **$1,800.00–2,000.00**

Open-mouth shoulder head child, **1889–1930s, kid body**

Mold 1009, 1039

    12"–13"... **$250.00–300.00**

    19"... **$350.00–400.00**

    23"... **$400.00–450.00**

Mold 1010, 1040, 1070, 1080

    18"... **$450.00–500.00**

    23"–25"... **$750.00–850.00**

    28"–30"... **$950.00–1,050.00**

Mold 1250, 1260

    16"... **$400.00–450.00**

    18"–19"... **$500.00–600.00**

    23"–26"... **$650.00–750.00**

Character Face, **1909 on, bisque socket head, composition body, wig or molded hair, glass or painted eyes, open or closed mouth, appropriately dressed**

Mold 120, **similar to Kämmer & Reinhardt Mein Leibling mold**

    18"–22"... **$2,500.00–3,000.00**

Mold 150, **ca. 1912, intaglio eyes, closed mouth**

  21" sold at auction for...................$24,000.00

Too few in database for reliable range.

Mold 151, **ca. 1912, painted eyes, closed laughing mouth**

  15"–18"...$3,000.00–6,000.00

Mold 152, **lady, intaglio eyes**

  24" sold at auction for...................$36,480.00

Mold 153, **ca. 1912, molded hair, painted eyes, closed mouth**

  16–17"...$10,000.00–11,000.00

Too few in database for reliable range.

Mold 164, **sleep eyes, open mouth, wigged**

  23"..$5,000.00–6,000.00

Too few in database for reliable range.

Mold 600, **ca. 1912, sleep eyes, open mouth**

  16"–17"...$500.00–600.00

Mold 611, **solid dome**

  16"..$4,000.00–5,000.00

Mold 729, **ca. 1888, laughing face, glass eyes, open-closed mouth**

  16"..$1,900.00–2,550.00

Mold 769, **open mouth, paperweight eyes**

  17"..$2,500.00–3,000.00

Too few in database for reliable range.

Mold 969, **ca. 1887, open smiling mouth**

  17"–19"..$4,500.00–7,600.00

Too few in database for reliable range.

Mold 1019, **ca. 1890, laughing, open mouth**

  14"..$4,275.00–5,700.00

Too few in database for reliable range.

Mold 1269, 1279, **sleep eyes, open mouth**

  14"..$900.00–950.00

  16"–20"...$900.00–1,200.00

  22"–25"...$1,700.00–2,500.00

  33"..$3,800.00–4,000.00

Mold 1299, **ca. 1912, marked "S&H"**

  13"–19"..$750.00–900.00

Mold 1304, **clown**

    12"–13" $2,000.00–3,000.00

Mold 1448, **ca. 1914, bisque socket head, sleep eyes, closed mouth, pierced ears, composition/wood ball-jointed body**

    16"–18" $15,000.00–16,000.00

Too few in database for reliable range.

Little Women **(so-called), mold 1160 shoulder head lady, ca. 1909, fancy hairdo wig, closed mouth, glass eyes, cloth body with bisque lower limbs, appropriately dressed**

    5"–7" $150.00–200.00

    10"–12" $250.00–400.00

    13"–15" $500.00–600.00

Baby, character face, 1910 on, molded hair or wig, painted or glass eyes, open or closed mouth, bent-leg baby body, appropriately dressed, add more for flirty eyes or toddler body

Mold 1294, **ca. 1912, glass eyes, open mouth**

    16" $550.00–750.00

    19" $800.00–1,100.00

Mold 1294, **clockwork mechanism moves eyes**

    26"–31" $1,800.00–2,600.00

Mold 1428, **ca. 1914, glass eyes, open-closed mouth**

    13"–16" $1,200.00–1,400.00

Toddler

    12" $2,000.00–2,100.00

    16" $2,100.00–2,300.00

Mold 1488, **ca. 1920, glass eyes, open-closed or open mouth**

    12"–15" $3,000.00–3,500.00

    19"–20" $4,000.00–4,500.00

Mold 1489, **"Baby Erika," ca. 1925, glass eyes, open mouth, tongue**

    14"–16" $4,500.00–5,000.00

Mold 1498, **ca. 1920, solid dome, painted or sleep eyes, open-closed mouth**

    14" $3,200.00–3,500.00

Too few in database for reliable range.

Lady doll, 1910 on, bisque socket head, composition lady body, sleep eyes, wigged, appropriately dressed

Mold 1079, **open mouth, glass eyes**

    24" $1,500.00–2,000.00

Mold 1159, ca.1894, glass eyes, open mouth, Gibson Girl

Flapper body

    12"–15"..$1,200.00–2,000.00

Lady body

    18"–20"..$1,200.00–1,600.00

    22"–24"..$1,800.00–2,100.00

    28"..$2,300.00–2,600.00

Jumeaulady body

    20"–25"..$2,400.00–3,000.00

Mold 1303, ca. 1902, lady face, glass eyes, closed mouth

    14"..$5,815.00

Mold 1305, ca. 1902, old woman, glass eyes, open-closed laughing mouth

    23"..$18,000.00–20,000.00

Too few in database for reliable range.

Mold 1308, ca. 1902, old man, molded mustache/dirty face, may be solid dome

    18"..$4,200.00–5,600.00

Too few in database for reliable range.

Mold 1329, Asian

    14"–15"..$1,800.00–2,000.00

Too few in database for reliable range.

Mold 1468, 1469, ca. 1920, flapper, glass eyes, closed mouth

    14"–15"..$2,8,000.00–3,500.00

SNOW BABIES

1901–1930 on. All-bisque dolls covered with ground porcelain slip to resemble snow, made by Bähr & Pröschild, Hertwig, C.F. Kling, Kley & Hahn, and others, Germany. Mostly unjointed, some jointed at shoulders and hips. The Eskimos named Peary's daughter Marie, born in 1893, Snow Baby, and her mother published a book in which she called her daughter Snow Baby and showed a picture of a little girl in white snowsuit. These little figures have painted features, various poses.

Figure listed are in good condition. Allow more for exceptional figures.

New Snow Babies are being made today. Department 56 makes a line of larger-scale figures (see below), and reproductions of earlier Snow Babies are being produced in Germany and by individual artisans.

2.5" Snow Baby Polar Bear, bisque: $80. **Photo courtesy of Hatton's Gallery of Dolls.**

Single Snow Baby, **standing, sitting, or kneeling**

1½"–2½" $60.00–100.00

3"–4" 120.00–150.00

Snow Baby child with wire jointed limbs

3½"–5" $125.00–220.00

Action Babies

Baby with umbrella

2¾" $65.00–110.00

Cook & Peary with a Globe between them

5½" w X 3½ h" $300.00–350.00

Child on skis

4½" $300.00–325.00

Dog sled, 2 dogs & one baby

.... $100.00–125.00

Playing tennis

1½" $80.00–100.00

Polar Bear

1½" $75.00–85.00

Pushing a carriage with two babies in it

2½" $200.00–225.00

Riding on an airplane

.... $240.00–270.00

Riding on bear

.... $175.00–200.00

Riding on sled

2" $35.00–45.00

3"–4" $150.00–200.00

Riding on reindeer

    2½" $290.00–315.00

Santa on igloo with baby inside

    3½" $110.00–140.00

Santa riding camel, elephant or polar bear

    2½" $330.00–375.00

Skiing Down a hill, 2 babies

    2½" $200.00–250.00

Throwing Snowballs

    2½" $125.00–175.00

Two Snow Babies, **molded together**

    1½" $90.00–115.00

    3" $155.00–175.00

Three Snow Babies, **molded together**

    3" $250.00–300.00

Three on sled

    2½" $200.00–250.00

Snow Baby doll, **jointed hips, shoulders**

    3½"–5" $125.00–220.00

Snow Baby shoulder-head doll, ca. 1910, German, cloth body

    8"–10" $550.00–550.00

New Snow Babies, **today's commercial reproductions are by Dept. 56 and are larger, and the coloring is more like cream. Dept. 56 Snow Babies and their Village Collections are collectible on the secondary market. As with all newer collectibles, items must be mint to command higher prices. Values listed are for secondary market pieces. Many are still available at retail.**

Various ornaments and standing figures

    3"–5" $18.00–25.00

Characters from animated films and books such as Madeline, Eloise, Frosty, and Disney

    .... $35.00–65.00

SONNEBERG TAUFLING

1851–1900 on, Sonneberg, Germany. Various companies made an infant doll with special separated body with bellows and voice mechanism. Motchmann is erroneously credited with the body style, but he did patent the voice mechanism. Some bodies stamped

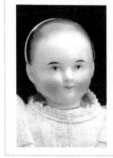

11" Sonneberg Taufling, china with "Alice": hairstyle: $5,500. **Photo courtesy of Morphy Auctions.**

"Motchmann" refer to the voice mechanism. The Sonneberg Taufling was made with head, shoulder plate, pelvis, lower arms, and lower legs of papier-mâché/composition, wax over papier-mâché, china, and bisque. Body parts put together with twill cloth in what are called "floating" joints. These dolls have glass eyes, closed mouth or open mouth, painted hair, or wigged. Dolls listed are in good condition.

Bisque: See also Jules Steiner

7"–12"...$3,500.00–5,500.00

14"–19"...$6,500.00–7,500.00

China

6"–7"...$3,200.00–4,500.00

10"–12"..$4,500.00–7,000.00

14"–16"..$5,000.00–8,000.00

Papier-mâché/composition or wax over papier-mâché. **Allow more for exceptional, early examples.**

8"–12"...$300.00–400.00

13"–15"..$550.00–1,000.00

18"–20"..$1,100.00–1,300.00

22"–24"..$1,000.00–1,600.00

Wood

Bébé tout en Bois, **carved wooden socket head, closed mouth, painted hair, glass eyes, twill and wood torso, nude**

9"–13"..$375.00–450.00

MARGARETE STEIFF

13" Steiff center seam pair of children, felt: each $5,000 pair. **Photo courtesy of Morphy Auctions.**

8" Young Hero Michel, Steiff, character boy, felt: $1,800. **Photo courtesy of McMasters Harris Apple Tree Doll Auctions.**

1877 to present, Giengen, Wurtemburg, Germany. Known today for their plush stuffed animals, Steiff made clothes for children, dolls with mask faces in 1889, clown dolls by 1898. Most Steiff dolls of felt, velvet, or plush have seam down the center of the face, but not all. Registered trademark button in ear in 1905. Button type eyes, painted features, sewn-on ears, big feet/shoes enable them to stand alone, all in excellent condition.

Values given are for dolls in good condition, for soiled, ragged, or worn dolls, use 35 percent of this price.

Adults

14½"–18"...$2,000.00–2,800.00

Characters, **center seam face, military men in uniform and conductors, firemen, English bobby, bellhop, etc.**

10½"–15"...$2,900.00–4,000.00

18"–22"..$5,000.00–10,000.00

Children

Center seam face

12"–14"..$2,000.00–3,000.00

16"–18"..$2,200.00–3,000.00

Molded felt face

12"–13"..$800.00–1,000.00

Made in U.S. Zone Germany, **1947–1953, glass eyes**

12"...$800.00–900.00

Rubber head doll, **cloth body**

12"–13"..$225.00–250.00

Vinyl characters, **wire armature in body**

Micki, Mecki, **hedgehogs, dressed**

7""...$35.00–45.00

Limited Edition Reissue Dolls, **1986–1987, felt, characters such as Tennis lady, Gentleman in morning coat, Peasant lady, Peasant Jorg**

MIB...$80.00–100.00

HERMANN STEINER

7" Hermann Steiner, Dolly face, bisque: $130. **Photo courtesy of McMasters Harris Apple Tree Doll Auctions.**

1909–1930 on, near Coburg, Germany. Porcelain and doll factory. First made plush animals, then made bisque, composition, and celluloid head dolls. Patented the Steinereye with moving pupils.

Baby

Mold 240, **circa 1925, newborn, solid dome, closed mouth, sleep eyes**

6"–8½"...$95.00–115.00

12"–16"...$175.00–225.00

Molds 245, 246, **circa 1926, character, solid dome, glass eyes, open-closed mouth, laughing baby, teeth, cloth or composition body**

13" -15"...$475.00–600.00

Mold 401, **shoulder head, solid dome, painted eyes, open-closed mouth, teeth, molded tongue**

15"..$350.00–475.00

Topsy Turvy baby doll

8"..$500.00–600.00

Child

Dolly face, **no mold number, open mouth, glass eyes, jointed composition body**

6"–10"...$125.00–175.00

6" on flapper body........................... $150.00–200.00

12"–16"... $150.00–200.00

18"–20"... $250.00–350.00

Shoulder Head child, **no mold number, open mouth, glass eyes, kid body**

18".. $100.00–120.00

Living Steiner **doll, character with molded hair and Steiner patented eye**

9"–10"... $500.00–650.00

Mold 128, **character bisque socket head, sleep eyes, open mouth, teeth, wig, composition/wood jointed body**

8"–9"... $250.00–300.00

14"... $400.00–500.00

JULES STEINER

18" Gigoteur, Steiner, bisque, all original: $3,300. **Photo courtesy of Gloria's Antique Dolls.**

24" Steiner, bisque, Fr A mark: $6,400. **Photo courtesy of McMasters Harris Apple Tree Doll Auctions.**

1855–1891 on, Paris. Made dolls with pressed heads, wigs, glass eyes, pierced ears on jointed composition bodies. Advertised talking, mechanical jointed dolls and bébés. Some sleep eyes were operated by a wire behind the ear, marked "J. Steiner May also carry the Bourgoin mark.

Dolls listed are in good condition, appropriately dressed. Add more for original clothes, rare mold numbers.

Baby with Taufling (Motchmann type) body, **solid dome bisque shoulder head, hips, lower arms and legs, with twill body in-between, closed mouth, glass eyes, wig**

12"–14"... 7,000.00–9,000.00

20"–22"... $10,000.00–12,500.00

Gigoteur, **crying, kicking child, key-wound mechanism, solid dome head, glass eyes, open mouth, two rows tiny teeth, pierced ears, mohair wig, papier-mâché torso**

Earlier, **paler doll head**

    17"–20" $3,000.00–4,000.00

Later, **more highly colored head**

    17"–20" $1,300.00–2,000.00

Round face Bébé, 1870s, early unmarked, pale pressed bisque socket head, rounded face, pierced ears, bulgy paperweight eyes, open mouth, two rows teeth, pierced ears, wig, composition/wood jointed body

    15"–18" $7,500.00–8,000.00

Closed mouth, **round face, dimples in chin**

    16"–18" .... $7,000.00–$10,000.00

Bébé with Series marks, 1880 on, bourgoin red ink, Caduceus stamp on body, pressed bisque socket head, cardboard pate, wig, pierced ears, closed mouth, glass paperweight eyes, French composition/papier-mâché (purple) body with straight wrists or bisque hands, Series C and A more common, marked with series mark: Sie and letter and number, rare Series B, E, F, and G models may be valued much higher

Series A or C

    8"–10" $4,5000.00–6,000.00

    14"–16" $5,500.00–7,000.00

    21"–23" $11,000.00–12,000.00

    27"–28" $11,000.00–12,000.00

    38" $18,000.00–21,000.00

Series E

    12"–15" .... $15,000 00–$20,000.00

Series F

10.5" 24,000.00–26,000.00

Series G

    16" $16,000.00–18,000.00

Bébé with Figure marks, 1887 on, bisque socket head, pierced ears, closed mouth, glass eyes, wig, composition/wood jointed French body, may use body marked "Le Parisien" or "Le Petit Parisien," head marked "Fire" and letter and number, and "J. Steiner figure marks included A, B, C, D, and E, A and C are the most often found

Closed mouth

A or C

    8"–10" $3,000.00–4,000.00

    12"–16" $3,500.00–4,500.00

    18"–24" $5,000.00–6,500.00

    28"–29" $8,000.00–9,000.00

Open mouth

Figure A

18"–23" $4,000.00–5,500.00

Figure B

19"–25" $6,000.00–7,500.00

38"–39" $10,000.00–11,000.00

Figure E

24"–26" $29,000.00–31,000.00

Phénix Baby, 1899 on, registered by Jules Mettais, successor of Jules Nicholas Steinerbisque socket head, closed mouth, composition body

17"–22" $3,500.00–4,000.00

SUN RUBBER

8" Squeeze dolls, Sun Rubber: $30 each. **Photo courtesy of Phillip Weiss Auctions**

1919–1950s, Barberton, Ohio. Made rubber and later vinyl dolls. Dolls listed are in excellent condition. Allow less for faded, cracked dolls or missing paint. MIB can bring double.

Psyllium, 1937, molded painted hard rubber, moving head, blue pants, white suspenders, black shoes and hat

10" $12.00–18.00

One-piece Squeeze dolls, 1940s, designed by Ruth E. Newton, molded clothes, squeaker, names such as Bonnie Bear, Happy Kappy, Rompy, and others

8" $30.00–35.00

So-Wee, 1941, molded hair, painted or sleep eyes

10"–12" $20.00–30.00

Black.. $40.00–50.00

Sunbabe, 1950, drink and wet baby, painted eyes, molded hair

    8"–13".. $30.00–35.00

    Black.. $35.00–45.00

BettyBows, 1953, molded hair with loop for ribbon, drink and wet baby, jointed body

    11".. $65.00–95.00

Constance Bannister Baby, 1954, molded hair, drink and wet, sleep eyes

    18".. $65.00–100.00

Tod L Dee, 1950s, all vinyl soft stuffed one-piece body, molded underclothes and shoes, molded painted hair, sleep eyes, open mouth, there is also a Tod L Tee & Tod L Tim

    10".. $20.00–30.00

Peter Pan, 1950s, all vinyl soft stuffed one-piece body, molded outfit, molded painted hair, sleep eyes

    10".. $20.00–25.00

Amosandra: See Black Dolls.

Gerber Baby: See Advertising Dolls.

SWAINE & CO.

11" Swaine & Co, bisque, glass eyes, marked "DIP": $775. **Photo courtesy of McMasters Harris Apple Tree Doll Auctions.**

1910–1927, Huttensteinach, Thüringia, Germany. Made porcelain doll heads. Marked "S & Co.," with green stamp. May also be incised "DIP" or "Lori."

Baby

Baby Lori, **marked "Lori," solid dome, open-closed mouth molded hair, sleep eyes**

    16"–18"... $1,400.00–1,600.00

    21"–23"... $1,900.00–2,100.00

Mold 232, **Lori variation, open mouth**

    12"–14"...$800.00–1,000.00

    20"–23"...$1,400.00–1,600.00

DI, **solid dome, intaglio eyes, closed mouth**

    10"–13"...$400.00–600.00

    17"...$900.00–1,000.00

DV, **solid dome, sleep eyes, closed mouth**

    13"...$775.00–825.00

    15"...$900.00–1,000.00

FP, S&C, **socket head, sleep eyes, closed mouth**

    8"–11"..$950.00–1,100.00

Child

BP, **socket head, open-closed smiling mouth, teeth, painted eyes**

    14½–17" $7,000.00–8,000.00

DIP, S&C, **socket head, sleep eyes, closed mouth**

    8"–10"..$600.00–700.00

    12"–14"...$850.00–950.00

Toddler body

    8"...$1,000.00–1,300.00

    13"–14"...$1,100.00–1,400.00

TERRI LEE

1946–1962, Lincoln, Nebraska, and Apple Valley, California. Company was founded by Violet Lee Gradwohl. The company went out of business in 1962. In 1997, Fritz Duda, Violet's nephew, was instrumental in founding Terri Lee Associates, which is making Terri Lee dolls now. First, dolls composition, then hard plastic and vinyl, the modern dolls are now being produced of a newer type of hard plastic. Closed pouty mouth, hand-painted features, wigged, jointed body. Values listed are for dolls in good condition and wearing original clothing. Allow significantly less for undressed, played-with dolls. Dolls in mint condition, with fancy costume, or additional wardrobe will bring more.

Terri Lee, **1946–1947**

    16"...$550.00–700.00

Painted hard plastic, **1947–1949, marked Pat. Pending**

    16"...$400.00–700.00

16" Bonnie Lou, hard plastic: $800. **Photo courtesy of Alderfer Auction Company, Inc.**

10" Tiny Terri Lee & Jerri Lee, hard plastic: $175 each. **Photo courtesy of McMasters Harris Apple Tree Doll Auctions.**

Flesh colored hard plastic, **1949–1952, marked Pat. Pending**

16"... $300.00–500.00

Vinyl, **less if sticky, 1950–1951**

16"... $200.00–300.00

Hard plastic, **1952–1962, marked Terri Lee**

16"... $175.00–400.00

Talking, **1960–1962**

16"... $250.00–300.00

Hard plastic, **1997–2005, values listed are secondary market values, dolls are available at retail as well**

16"... $20.00–40.00

Benji, painted plastic, brown, 1946–1962, black lamb's wool wig

16"... $900.00–1,100.00

Connie Lynn, 1955, hard plastic, sleep eyes, fur wig, bent-limb baby body

19"... $300.00–400.00

Gene Autry, 1949–1950, painted plastic

16"... $1,600.00–1,800.00

Jerri Lee, hard plastic, caracul wig

16"... $150.00–300.00

Linda Lee, 1950–1951, vinyl

12"... $60.00–75.00

1952–1958, **vinyl baby**

10"... $80.00–110.00

Mary Jane, Terri Lee look-alike, hard plastic walker

16"... $140.00–160.00

Patty Jo, black 1947–1949

    16"..$700.00–1,000.00

Bonnie Lou, black

    16"..$600.00–900.00

Tiny Terri Lee, 1955–1958

    10"..$150.00–200.00

Accessories

Terri Lee Outfits:

    Girl Scout/Brownie uniform....**$50.00**

    School dress **$40.00–100.00**

    Sunglasses **$35.00–45.00**

    Tiny Terri Lee dresses **$20.00–50.00**

A. THUILLIER

20" A Thullier, open mouth with teeth, bisque: $6,800. **Photo courtesy of Sweetbriar Auctions.**

1875–1893, Paris. Made bisque head dolls with composition, kid, or wooden bodies. Some of the heads were reported made by Francoise Gaultier. Bisque socket head or swivel on shoulder plate, glass eyes, pierced ears, cork pate, wig, nicely dressed, in good condition. Dolls listed are in good condition, appropriately dressed. Exceptionally beautiful dolls may run more.

Early Child, closed mouth with slightly parted lips

    11"–14"...$45,000.00–60,000.00

    18"–22"...$65,000.00–75,000.00

Later Child, 1890 Verdier and Gutmacher took over the firm, open mouth with molded teeth

    15"–29"...$6,500.00–7,000.00

ROBERT TONNER

16" Tyler Wentworth "Angelina," Tonner Doll Company, vinyl, MIB: $140. **Photo courtesy of McMasters Harris Apple Tree Doll Auctions.**

1991 to present, Hurley, New York. Robert Tonner is a fashion designer and sculptor who has created numerous dolls in porcelain and vinyl. Tonner Company also owns Effanbee Dolls.

Values listed are for secondary market dolls complete and in good condition. **Allow more for MIB**. Some of these dolls are still available retail as well.

American Models, 1993 on, vinyl, basic dolls at low end of value, dolls in elaborate costume at high end of value

    16"...$75.00–100.00

    19"...$65.00–120.00

    22"...$80.00–300.00

Ann Estelle, 1999, a Mary Engelbreit character, hard plastic, blond wig, glasses, basic dolls at low end of value, dolls in elaborate costume at high end of value

    10"...$55.00–80.00

    Sophie, **10"** $55.00–130.00

Ann Estelle, **8" version on Tiny Betsy body**

    ....$45.00–55.00

Betsy McCall, see Betsy McCall section.

Brenda Starr see Effanbee section.

Kripplebush Kids, 1997, hard plastic, Marni, Eliza, Hannah

    8"..$22.00–28.00

Kitty Collier, 2000

    18"...$45.00–55.00

Tiny Kitty Collier, vinyl, basic dolls at low end of value, dolls in elaborate costume at high end of value

    10"...$40.00–60.00

Tyler Wentworth, **1999, fashion-type, long, straight, brunette, blond, or red hair, allow more for special costumes**

    16"... $70.00–80.00

Twightlight Series

Various characters, **prices reflect complete doll on secondary market, no box**

    17.5"... $65.00–75.00

TROLLS

Trolls portray supernatural beings from Scandinavian folklore. They have been manufactured by various companies including Helena and Martii Kuuslkoski who made Fauni Trolls, ca. 1952+ (sawdust filled cloth dolls); Thomas Dam, 1960+; and Scandia House, later Norfin'; UneedaDoll and Toy Wishniks'; Russ Berrie; Ace Novelty; Treasure Trolls; Applause Toys; Magical Trolls; and many other companies who made lesser quality vinyl look-alikes, mostly unmarked, to take advantage of the fad. Most are all-vinyl or vinyl with stuffed cloth bodies.

Troll Figures

1960s, **by Thomas Dam**

    2½" $55.00–75.00

    5"... $60.00–75.00

    7"... $50.00–90.00

    Bank, 8" $25.00–30.00

    10"... $35.00–45.00

    12"... $40.00–85.00

    15"... $75.00–95.00

1977

    3"... $12.00–18.00

    9"... $30.00–40.00

    12"... $35.00–45.00

    Thumb sucker, 18" $85.00–110.00

Wishnik trolls, **by Uneeda**

    3"... $12.00–18.00

    7"... $25.00–35.00

1990s re-release

    6"... $10.00–15.00

Troll Animals, **Thomas Dam, 1964**

Cow

   6"...$75.00–125.00

Elephant

   2½" sold for ....$360.00 at online auction

Giraffe

   12"..$75.00–85.00

Monkey

   7½" ....sold for $295.00 at online auction

UNEEDA

14", Patsy-type, Uneeda, composition: $80. **Photo courtesy of Alderfer Auction Company, Inc.**

16" Magic Meg, Uneeda, grow hair doll, vinyl, MIB: $110. **Photo courtesy of The Museum Doll Shop.**

1917 on, New York City. Made composition head dolls, including Mama dolls and made the transition to plastics and vinyl.

Composition

Lucky Lindy, **1927, composition head and lower arms, cloth body, marked Uneeda, cardboard tag, oilcloth aviator suit**

   17"..$200.00–225.00

Rita Hayworth, as "Carmen," **1939, from The Loves of Carmen movie, all-composition, red mohair wig, unmarked, cardboard tag**

   14"..$300.00–400.00

Baby doll, **1930s, composition head, arms and legs on a cloth body**

   21"..$80.00– $100.00

Molded hair Girl (Patsy-type) **1930s, composition**

   14"..$70.00– $80.00

Hard Plastic and Vinyl

Baby Dollikins, **1960, vinyl head, hard plastic jointed body with jointed elbows, wrists, and knees, drink and wet**

    21"...$250.00–300.00

Baby Trix, **1965**

    19"...$18.00–25.00

Bareskin Baby, **1968**

    12½" $20.00–30.00

Blabby, **1962+**

    17"...$35.00–50.00

Chubby, **1976, vinyl, rooted hair, sleep eyes**

    18"...$15.00– 25.00

Debteen, **1967, all vinyl, rooted hair, side glancing staionary eyes**

    19"...$35.00–40.00

Dollikin, **1957 on, multi-joints, marked "Uneedacostumes or outstanding condition will bring more**

    19"...$150.00–220.00

Dolly Walker, **1967**

    36"...$100.00–150.00

Fairy Princess, **1961**

    32"...$90.00–110.00

Freckles, **1960, vinyl head, rigid plastic body, marked "22" on head**

    32"...$125.00–150.00

Granny & Me, **1978**

    11½" & 5½" ....$28.00–32.00 set

Jennifer, **1973, rooted side-parted hair, painted features, teen body, mod clothing**

    18"...$55.00–60.00

Little Sophisticates, **1967, large mod style head, closed eyes, painted smile, rooted hair**

    8½"...$50.00–65.00

Magic Meg, **w/Hair That Grows, vinyl and plastic, rooted hair, sleep eyes**

    16"...$50.00–60.00

Miss Dollikin, **also called Action Girl, 1957 on, fashion doll**

    11½" $32.00–42.00

Otis, **1973,ventriloquist doll, vinyl head, hands, rooted hair, cotton stuffed cloth body**

    30"...$95.00–120.00

Pee Wees, **1965 on, rooted hair, painted eyes**

3½"..$12.00– $20.00

Petal People, **1968, vinyl, rooted hair, came seated inside a vinyl flower in a pot (measured 12.5")**

2½" $20.00–30.00

1983 version, no flower pot

2½" $20.00–30.00

Pir-thilla, **1958, blows up balloons, vinyl, rooted hair, sleep eyes**

12½" $30.00–40.00

Plumpees, **1967, all vinyl with fat tummy, painted eyes**

8"...$9.00–12.00

Priscilla, **1960s**

12½" $15.00–18.00

Purty, **1973, when you press her tummy, she changes her facial expression**

11"..$20.00– $25.00

Pollyanna, **1960, for Disney**

11"..$30.00–40.00

17"..$50.00–70.00

31"..$100.00–150.00

Saranade, **1962, vinyl head, hard plastic body, rooted blond hair, blue sleep eyes, red and white dress, speaker in tummy, phonograph and records came with doll, used battery**

21"..$75.00–100.00

Suzette **(Carol Brent)**

12"..$50.00–60.00

*Thum-things***, 1973, vinyl, 3 faces**

4"..$15.00–20.00

Tiny Teen, **1957–1959, vinyl head, rooted hair, pierced ears, six-piece hard plastic body, high-heeled feet to compete with Little Miss Revlon, wrist tag**

10½" $35.00–45.00

Bob

11"..$25.00–30.00

Tinyteens, **1968 on, vinyl doll, rooted hair, posable body, rooted lashes, 12 dolls in series**

5"..$25.00–40.00

Wendy, **1960s Barbie®-type, rooted hair, painted eyes**

11½" ....$40.00–$55.00

UNTINTED BISQUE
(SO-CALLED PARIAN-TYPE)

16" untinted bisque (so-called parian), Alice style, painted eyes: $1,000. **Photo courtesy of Joan & Lynette Antique Dolls and Accessories.**

1850–1900 on, Germany. The term "parian" as used in doll collecting refers to dolls of untinted bisque. In other words, the doll's skin tone is white rather than tinted. These dolls were at the height of their popularity from 1860 through the 1870s. They are often found with molded blond hair, some with fancy hair arrangements and ornaments or bonnets, can have glass or painted eyes, pierced ears, may have molded jewelry or clothing, occasionally solid dome with wig, cloth body, nicely dressed in good condition. Dolls listed are in good condition, appropriately dressed. Exceptional examples may be much higher.

16" untinted bisque (so-called parian), Dolly Madison style, glass eyes, swivel neck: $900. **Photo courtesy of Oldeclectics.**

Lady

Common hair style

Painted eyes

Undecorated, **simple molded hair**

8"–12"	$150.00–300.00
14"–16"	$350.00–450.00
18"–25"	$500.00–600.00

Molded bodice, **fancy trim**

    8"..$200.00–275.00

    17"–23"..$550.00–800.00

Wigged, **bald head with period wig**

    10"–12"......................................$1,200.00–1,400.00

Glass eyes

    10"..$700.00–800.00

    12"–14"......................................$1,100.00–1,400.00

    16"–18"......................................$1,500.00–1,800.00

Fancy hair style, **with molded combs, ribbons, flowers, bands, or snoods, cloth body, untinted bisque limbs, more for very elaborate hairstyle**

Painted eyes, pierced ears

    7"–10"...$850.00–1,500.00

    14"–16"......................................$1,100.00–1,800.00

    18"–22"......................................$1,400.00–1,900.00

    24"–30"......................................$1,800.00–2,000.00

Decorated shoulder plate

Simple bodice or tie

    8½"..$275.00–300.00

    13"–15"......................................$450.00–600.00

    20"–23"......................................$650.00–750.00

More elaborate bodice and hair

    12"–16"......................................$1,700.00–2,100.00

    17"–21"......................................$2,500.00–3,000.00

Glass eyes, pierced ears

    12"–15"......................................$1,400.00–2,000.00

    18"–20"......................................$1,900.00–2,600.00

Swivel neck

    14"–15"......................................$2,100.00–2,400.00

Named Hairstyles, **painted eyes unless otherwise noted, names applied by modern collectors to describe style**

Alice in Wonderland, **molded head band or comb**

    14"–16"......................................$825.00–1,000.00

    19"–21"......................................$1,100.00–1,200.00

Countess Dagmar, **no mark, head band, cluster curls on forehead**

12" -15"... $750.00–900.00

18"–21"... $1,400.00–1,600.00

Currier & Ives

7"... $1,500.00–2,000.00

Dolly Madison

18"–22"... $750.00–1,200.00

Empress Eugenie, **headpiece snood**

12"–15"... $1,500.00–1,700.00

25"... $1,200.00–1,500.00

Irish Queen, **Limbach, clover mark, #8552**

14"–19"... $500.00–600.00

Molded hat, See bonnet head section.

Necklace, jewels, or standing ruffles

17"–20"... $1,800.00–2.800.00

Princess Augusta Victoria, **molded shoulder plate with cross necklace, glass eyes**

13"–15"... $900.00–1,000.00

22"... $1,000.00– $1,200.00

Men or Boys, center or side-part hair style, cloth body, decorated shirt and tie

Painted eyes

13"... $700.00–800.00

16"–17"... $900.00–1,100.00

Glass eyes

16"... $2,400.00–2,825.00

VINYL

1950s on. By the mid-1950s, vinyl (polyvinylchloride) was being used for dolls. Material that was soft to the touch and processing that allowed hair to be rooted were positive attractions. Vinyl became a desirable material, and the market was soon deluged with dolls manufactured from this product. Many dolls of this period are of little known manufacturers, unmarked, or marked only with a number. With little history behind them, these dolls need to be mint-in-box and complete to warrant top prices. With special accessories or wardrobe values may be more.

33" Charlie McCarthy, Juro Novelty Co., vinyl, all original: $110. **Photo courtesy of Phillip Weiss Auctions**

20" I Dream of Jeanie, Libby, vinyl: $200. **Photo courtesy of Morphy Auctions.**

Unknown Maker

Baby, **vinyl head, painted or sleep eyes, molded hair or wig, bent legs, cloth or vinyl body**

12".. $8.00–10.00

16".. $10.00–12.00

20".. $16.00–20.00

Child, **vinyl head, jointed body, painted or sleep eyes, molded hair or wig, straight legs**

14".. $10.00–14.00

22".. $18.00–25.00

Adult, **vinyl head, painted or sleep eyes, jointed body, molded hair or wig, smaller waist with male or female modeling for torso**

8".. $20.00–25.00

18".. $55.00–75.00

Known Maker

Baby Barry

Alfred E. Newman

20".. $450.00–500.00

Captain Kangaroo

16".. $100.00–130.00

19"–24".. $175.00–210.00

Christopher Robin

18".. $100.00–135.00

Daisy Mae

14".. $125.00–175.00

Emmett Kelly **(Willie the Clown)**

15".. $50.00–65.00

21".. $150.00–175.00

12" Mod Joy, Royal Doll Co., vinyl: $70. **Photo courtesy of Doll Hugs Shop.**

Li'l Abner

14"..$45.00–60.00

21"..$150.00–200.00

Mammy Yokum, **1957**

Molded hair

14"..$50.00–65.00

21"..50.00–75.00

Yarn hair

14"..$125.00–150.00

21"..$200.00–250.00

Nose lights up

23"..$275.00–325.00

Pappy Yokum, **1957**

14"..$30.00–45.00

21"..50.00–75.00

Nose lights up

23"..$275.00–325.00

Belle Doll & Toy Co, **Brooklyn, New York, 1950s**

Ballerina or Miss Revlon type

18"..$20.00–40.00

Little Miss Margie, **1955–1957. Little Miss Revlon type.**

10½" $30.00– $40.00

Dee & Cee, **Canada**

Calypso Bill & Jill, **1961, black, vinyl, marked "DEE CEE"**

16"..$35.00–50.00 each

Sweet Sue Teen Aged Doll, **Cissy17" $40.00–60.00**

Willy, **vinyl toddler, molded hair, sleep eyes**

    16".. $35.00–45.00

Flagg and Co., **Brookline, Massachusetts. 1947 on produced vinyl dolls with wire armatures.**

    8".. $10.00– $25.00

Furga, **Italy**

Alta Moda Series, **1965 on, Simonna, Sylvie, Sussannah, vinyl doll, rooted hair, inset langeld eye-lashes**

    17".. $250.00–350.00

Simonna outfit, **MIB**

    1967 .... $250.00–300.00

Lewis Galoob Toys, Inc., **San Francisco, CA, 1968, 1998 aquired by Hasbro**

Punky Brewster, **1984 based on television show character, painted eyes, rooted hair, vinyl head and hands on cloth body**

    18".. $40.00–50.00

Glad Toy/BrookGlad

Poor Pitiful Pearl, **1955, vinyl, some with stuffed one-piece vinyl bodies, others jointed**

    13".. $65.00–75.00

    17".. $75.00–125.00

Juro Novelty Co

Dick Clark, **1958, vinyl head, hands, feet, cloth body**

    26".. $125.00–175.00

Charlie McCarthy, **1977 Ventriloquist dummy**

    30"–35"... $85.00–150.00

Libby

I Dream of Jeannie, **1966**

    20".. $200.00–300.00

Lilli clones, **Hong Kong, various companies including Dura-Fam Ltd., Chang-Pi Su Co., and others. Dolls resemble Bild Lilli, marked Hong Kong**

    7".. $150.00–200.00

    11".. $70.00–150.00

Miss Curity, **sleep eyes, rooted hair**

    20".. $35.00–45.00

Playmates, **1985 on, made animated talking dolls using a tape player in torso powered by batteries, extra costumes, tapes, and accessories available, more for black versions. Double values for Mint-in-Box.**

Amazing Amy, **1998, vinyl, cloth body, interactive**

    20".. $55.00–75.00

Cricket, **1986+ on**

    25".. $50.00–70.00

Corky, **1987 on**

    25".. $50.00–70.00

Jill, **1987, hard plastic, jointed body**

    33".. $125.00–200.00

Harvey Rosenberg Inc., **1977, vinyl, came in box that looks like a closet**

Gay Bob

    13".. $50.00–70.00

Royal Doll Co.

Lonely Lisa, **1964, vinyl head, arms and legs, cloth body, doll with large sad eyes, designed by Keane**

    20".. $135.00–160.00

1965

    11½" $70.00–80.00

Mod Joy, **1965, vinyl, painted eyes, rooted hair**

    12".. $65.00–75.00

Sayco, **1907–1950s, New York City, first made composition dolls, then hard plastic and vinyl dolls**

Miss America Pageant, **1950s**

    11"–14".. $30.00–95.00

    20".. $125.00–175.00

Pouty girl, **soft vinyl head, rooted hair, sleep eyes, soft stuffed vinyl body**

    22".. $30.00–35.00

Walker, **costumed as a bride**

    28".. $55.00–65.00

Shindana, **1968–1983, Operation Bootstrap, Los Angeles, ethnic features**

    12"–15".. $35.00–45.00

Talking Tamu, **black, ethnic features**

    16".. $140.00–160.00

Susie Sad Eyes, **maker unknown, vinyl doll, made in Hong Kong, large painted "sad eyes," mod clothing**

    8".. $45.00–$55.00

Tomy

Kimberly, **1981–1985, closed mouth, more for black**

    17".. $50.00–60.00

Getting Fancy Kimberly, **1984, open mouth with teeth**

17"..$25.00–40.00

Tristar

Poor Pitiful Pearl, **circa 1955+, vinyl jointed doll came with extra party dress**

11"..$50.00–65.00

Unique

Ellie Mae Clampett, **1964**

11½" $25.00–35.00

Worlds of Wonder, **circa 1985–1987+, Fremont, California, made talking dolls and Teddy Ruxpin powered by batteries, had extra accessories, voice cards**

Pamela, The Living Doll, **1986+**

21"..$65.00–80.00

Julie, **1987 on**

24"..$75.00–100.00

Extra costume $20.00–30.00

Teddy Ruxpin, **1985+, animated talking bear**

20"..$95.00–120.00

VOGUE DOLL CO.

8" Toddles pair, Vogue, composition: $800. **Photo courtesy of Sweetbriar Auctions.**

8" strung Ginny, #74 Talon zipper series, Vogue, hard plastic: $475. **Photo courtesy of McMasters Harris Apple Tree Doll Auctions.**

1930s on, Medford, MA. Jennie Graves started the company and dressed "Just Me" and Arranbee dolls in the early years, before Bernard Lipfert designed Ginny. After several changes of ownership, Vogue dolls was purchased in 1995 by Linda and Jim Smith.

Composition dolls

Dora Lee, **sleep eyes, closed mouth**

11"..$250.00–375.00

8" bent knee walker Ginny, Vogue, hard plastic, MIB: $250. **Photo courtesy of McMasters Harris Apple Tree Doll Auctions.**

8" Ginny, Crib Crowd, Vogue, hard plastic: $1,200. **Photo courtesy of McMasters Harris Apple Tree Doll Auctions.**

Jennie, 1940s, sleep eyes, open mouth, mohair wig, five-piece composition body

13"...$325.00–375.00

19"...$375.00–425.00

Cynthia, 1940s, sleep eyes, open mouth, mohair wig, five-piece composition body

13"...$300.00–350.00

W.A.A.C. doll in Women's Army Auxiliary Corps uniform

13"...$500.00–600.00

Ginny Family

Toddles, composition, 1937–1948, name stamped in ink on bottom of shoe, some early dolls which have been identified as "Toodles" (spelled with two *o*'s) are blank dolls from various companies used by Vogue, painted eyes, mohair wig, jointed body, some had gold foil labels reading "Vogue." Dolls listed are in good condition with original clothes, more for fancy outfits such as Red Riding Hood or Cowboy/Cowgirl or with accessories

7½"–8"...$250.00–500.00

Painted Eye Ginny, 1948–1949, hard plastic, strung joints, marked "Vogueon head, ìVogue Dollî on body, painted eyes, molded hair with mohair wig, clothing tagged ìVogue Dollsî or ìVogue Dolls, Inc. Medford Mass.,î inkspot tag on white with blue letters, allow double or more for mint examples or rare outfits

8"...$150.00–300.00

Crib Crowd, 1950, baby with curved legs, sleep eyes, poodle cut (caracul) wig

8"...$1,000.00–1,200.00

Fluffy Bunny sold at auction for $2,242.00

Strung Ginny 1950–1953, hard plastic, sleep eyes, strung joints, marked "Vogue" on head, "Vogue Doll" on body, painted eyes, molded hair with mohair wig, clothing tagged "Vogue Dolls" or "Vogue Dolls, Inc. Medford Mass.," inkspot tag on white with blue letters

8"...$200.00–500.00

16" Brickette,
Vogue, vinyl, 1980,
MIB: $50 each.
**Photo courtesy of
Alderfer Auction
Company, Inc.**

Painted Lash Walker Ginny 1954, **sleep eyes, strung, dynel wigs, new mark on back torso: "GINNY//VOGUE DOLLS//INC.//PAT PEND.//MADE IN U.S.A."**

8"... $250.00–400.00

Black Ginny **1953–1954**

8"... $500.00–600.00

Molded Lash Walker Ginny **1955–1957, hard plastic, seven-piece body, sleep eyes, Dynel or saran wigs, marked: "VOGUE" on head, "GINNY//VOGUE DOLLS//INC.//PAT. NO. 2687594//MADE IN U.S.A." on back of torso**

8"... $150.00–300.00

Bent-knee Molded Lash Walker Ginny, **1957–1962, hard plastic, jointed knees, sleep eyes, dynel or saran wigs, marked "VOGUE" on head, "GINNY//VOGUE DOLLS//INC.// PAT.NO.2687594//MADE IN U.S.A."**

8"... $100.00–175.00

Ginny **1960, unmarked, big walker carried 8" doll dressed just like her**

36"... $350.00

Too few in database for reliable range.

Vinyl Walker Ginny **1963–1965, soft vinyl head, hard plastic walker body, sleep eyes, molded lashes, rooted hair, marked: "GINNY," on head, "GINNY//VOGUE DOLLS, Inc.//PAT. NO.2687594//MADE IN U.S.A." on back**

8"... $50.00–80.00

Ginny, 1965–1972, **all-vinyl, straight legs, non-walker, rooted hair, sleep eyes, molded lashes, marked "Ginny" on head, "Ginny//VOGUE DOLLS, INC." on back**

8"... $30.00–45.00

Ginny, 1972–1977, **all-vinyl, non-walker, sleep eyes, molded lashes, rooted hair, some with painted lashes, marked "GINNY" on head, "VOGUE DOLLS©1972//MADE IN HONG KONG//3" on back, made in Hong Kong by Tonka**

8"... $20.00–30.00

Ginny **1977–1979, "Ginny From Far-Away Lands," made in Hong Kong by Lesney, all-vinyl, sleep eyes, jointed, non-walker, rooted hair, chubby body, same** as Tonka doll overall, marked "GINNY" on head, "VOGUE DOLLS 1972// MADE IN HONG KONG//3", painted eyes, 1980–1981, marked "VOGUE DOLLS//©GINNYTIM//1977" on head, "VOGUE DOLLS©1977//MADE IN HONG KONG" on back

8"..$20.00–40.00

*Sasson Ginny*1981–*1982,* made in Hong Kong by Lesney, all-vinyl, fully jointed, bendable knees, rooted Dynel hair, sleep eyes in 1981, painted eyes in 1982, slimmer body, marked "GINNY" on head, "1978 VOGUE DOLLS INC//MOONACHIE N.J.// MADE IN HONG KONG" on back

8"..$18.00–25.00

*Ginny*1984–*1986,* made by Meritus' in Hong Kong, vinyl, resembling Vogue's 1963–1971 Ginny, marked "GINNY®" on head, "VOGUE DOLLS//(a star logo)//M.I.I. 1984//Hong Kong" on back, porcelain marked: "GW//SCD//5184" on head, "GINNNY//®VOGUE DOLLS//INC//(a star logo) MII 1984//MADE IN TAIWAN"

8"..$25.00–35.00

*Ginny*1986–*1995,* vinyl, by Dakin, soft vinyl, marked "VOGUE®DOLLS//©1984 R. DAKIN INC.//MADE IN CHINA" on back; hard vinyl, marked "VOGUE//®// DOLLS//©1986 R. DAKIN and Co.//MADE IN CHINA"

8"..$25.00–35.00

*Ginny*Baby, *1959–1982,* vinyl, jointed, sleep eyes, rooted or molded hair, a drink and wet doll, some marked "GINNY BABY//VOGUE DOLLS INC."

12"..$20.00–30.00

15"..$25.00–35.00

18"..$30.00–40.00

*Ginny*outfits

Talon Zipper outfit **MIB** $250.00

Vinyl shoes **MIB** $30.00

Ginnette

1955–1969, 1985–1986, vinyl, jointed, open mouth, 1955–1956 had painted eyes, 1956–1969 had sleep eyes, marked "VOGUE DOLLS INC"

8"..$100.00–150.00

1962–1963, rooted hair Ginnette

8"..$75.00–100.00

Jan, 1958–1960, 1963–1964, Jill's friend, vinyl head, six-piece rigid vinyl body, straight leg, swivel waist, rooted hair, marked "VOGUE," called Loveable Jan in 1963 and Sweetheart Jan in 1964

10½" $75.00–130.00

Jeff, 1958–1960, vinyl head, five-piece rigid vinyl body, molded and painted hair, marked "VOGUE DOLLS"

11"..$65.00–80.00

Jill, 1957–1960, 1962–1963, 1965, seven-piece hard plastic teenage body, bent-knee walker, high-heeled doll, big sister to Ginny(made in vinyl in 1965), extra wardrobe, marked ìJILL//VOGUE DOLLS//MADEI NU.S.A.//©1957î

10½"

Wearing leotard .... $85.00–$110.00

Wearing a street dress...................... $110.00–$200.00

Wearing a formal .... $175.00–$300.00

Jimmy, 1958, Ginnybaby brother, all-vinyl, open mouth, painted eye Ginnette, marked ìVOGUE DOLLS/INC.î

8"... $65.00–100.00

Little Miss Ginny 1965–1971, all-vinyl, promoted as a pre-teen, one-piece hard plastic body and legs, soft vinyl head and arms, sleep eyes, head marked "VOGUE DOLL//19©67" or "©VOGUE DOLL//1968" and back, "VOGUE DOLL"

12"... $25.00–30.00

Miss Ginny 1962–1964, soft vinyl head could be tilted, jointed vinyl arms, two-piece hard plastic body, swivel waist, flat feet; 1965–1980, vinyl head and arms, one-piece plastic body

15"–16"... $35.00–45.00

Hard Plastic and Vinyl

Baby Dear, 1959–1964, 18" vinyl baby designed by EloiseWilkin, vinyl limbs, cloth body, rooted topknot or rooted hair, white tag on body ìVogue Dolls, Inc.î; left leg stamped ì1960/E.Wilkins,î 12" size made in 1961

12"... $120.00–180.00

18"... $200.00–250.00

Baby Dear One, 1962, a one-year-old toddler version of Baby Dear, sleep eyes, two teeth, marked "C//1961//E.Wilkin//VogueDolls//Inc.î on neck, tag on body, mark on right leg

25"... $80.00–125.00

Baby Dear Musical, 1962–1963, 12" metal, 18" wooden shaft winds, plays tune, doll wiggles

12"... $170.00–200.00

18"... $200.00–250.00

Baby Too Dear, 1963–1965, two-year-old toddler version of Baby Dear, all-vinyl, open mouth, two teeth

17"... $150.00–200.00

23"... $250.00–300.00

Brikette, 1959–1961, 1979–1980, swivel waist joint, green flirty eyes in 22" size only, freckles, rooted straight orange hair, paper hang tag reads "I'm//Brikette//the//red headed//imp," marked on head "VOGUE INC.//19©60"

22"... $140.00–160.00

1960, **sleep eyes only, platinum, brunette, or orange hair**

    16"...$95.00–130.00

1980, **no swivel waist, curly pink, red, purple, or blond hair; allow double for MIB**

    16"...$25.00–30.00

Li'l Imp, **1959–1960,** Brikette's little sister, vinyl head, bent knee walker, green sleep eyes, orange hair, freckles, marked "R and B//44" on head and "R and B Doll Co." on back

    10½"...$85.00–120.00

Wee Imp, **1960,** hard plastic body, orange saran wig, green eyes, freckles, marked "GINNY//VOGUE DOLS//INC.//PAT.No. 2687594//MADE IN U.S.A."

    8"..$185.00–235.00

Littlest Angel, **1961–1963; 1967–1980**

1961–1963, **also called Saucy Littlest Angel, vinyl head, hard plastic bent knee walker, sleep eyes, same doll as Arranbee Littlest Angel, rooted hair, marked "R & B"**

    10½"...$90.00–110.00

1967–1980, **all-vinyl, jointed limbs, rooted red, blond, or brunette hair, looks older**

    11"...$40.00–50.00

    14"...$65.00–80.00

Love Me Linda (Pretty as a Picture), **1965,** vinyl, large painted eyes, rooted long straight hair, came with portrait, advertised as "Pretty as a Picture" in Sears and Montgomery Ward catalogs, marked "VOGUE DOLLS/©1965"

    15"...$75.00–95.00

Welcome Home Baby, **1978–1980,** newborn, designed by EloiseWilkin, vinyl head and arms, painted eyes, molded hair, cloth body, crier, marked ìLesneyî

    18"...$40.00–60.00

Welcome Home Baby Turns Two, **1980, toddler, designed by EloiseWilkin, vinyl head, arms, and legs, cloth body, sleep eyes, rooted hair, marked ì42260 Lesney Prod. Corp.//1979//Vogue Doll"**

    22"...$75.00–90.00

IZANNAH WALKER

1840s–1888, Central Falls, Rhode Island. Made cloth stockinette dolls, with pressed mask face, oil-painted features, applied ears, brush-stroked or corkscrew curls, stitched hands and feet, some with painted boots. All in good condition with appropriate clothing.

Very good condition

    17"–19"..$30,000.00–45,000.00

18" Izannah Walker, cloth: $16,000. **Photo courtesy of Morphy Auctions.**

Fair condition

17"–19"...$15,000.00–19,000.00

WAX

23" wax, slit head, English: $900. **Photo courtesy of Joan & Lynette Antique Dolls and Accessories.**

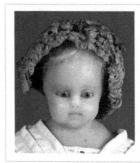

14" poured wax baby: $1,000. **Photo courtesy of Withington Auction Inc.**

1850–1930. Made by English, German, French, and other firms, reaching heights of popularity ca. 1875. Seldom marked, wax dolls were poured, some reinforced with plaster, and less expensive, but more durable with wax over papier-mâché or composition. English makers included Montanari, Pierotti, and Peck. German makers included Heinrich Stier.

Dolls listed are in good condition with original clothes, or appropriately dressed. More for exceptional dolls; much less for dolls in poor condition.

Slit-head wax, **English, 1830–1860s, wax over composition shoulder head, hair inserted into slit on center top of head, glass eyes may use wire closure**

11"–14"...$525.00–650.00

16"–19"...$700.00–900.00

23"–25"...$1,000.00–1,300.00

Poured Wax, **1850s–1900s**

Baby, **shoulder head, painted features, glass eyes, English Montanari type, closed mouth, cloth body, wig, or hair inserted into wax**

10"–13"..$800.00–1,200.00

18"–25"..$1,200.00–2,000.00

Child, **shoulder head, inserted hair, glass eyes, wax limbs, cloth body**

13"–15"..$700.00–1,000.00

18"–22"..$1,200.00–1,800.00

25"–27"..$2,500.00–3,500.00

Adult

Lady, **elaborate costume brings high end of price range**

11"–15"..$1,800.00–3,000.00

23"–27"..$2,000.00–4,000.00

Wax over Composition or Reinforced, **1860s–1890s**

Child

ca. 1860–1890, **early poured wax shoulder head, reinforced with plaster, inserted hair, glass eyes, cloth body**

10"–12"..$600.00–700.00

14"–16"..$700.00–800.00

20"–22"..$900.00–1,000.00

25"–29"..$1,100.00–1,300.00

25", **socket-head, glass eyes**

16"–18"..$1,500.00–1,800.00

Later wax over composition shoulder head, **open or closed mouth, glass eyes, wig, cloth body**

10"–12"..$250.00–300.00

15"–17"..$350.00–400.00

21"–23"..$525.00–675.00

Molded hair, **wax over composition, shoulder head, glass eyes, cloth body, wooden limbs, molded shoes**

13"–15"..$200.00–500.00

19"–23"..$500.00–700.00

Alice in Wonderland style, **with molded headband**

16"..$600.00–650.00

16" wax over composition: $800. **Photo courtesy of Withington Auction Inc.**

Lady

Wigged

12"–15" $300.00–600.00

22"–25" $400.00–700.00

Molded hair **and gloves**

15"–22" $1,000.00–3,000.00

Bonnethead: See Bonnet Head section.

Wax crèche figure, **1880–1910, poured wax Christ Child, inset hair, glass eyes**

6" $100.00–125.00

13"–23" $350.00–500.00

Wax fashion doll, **1910–1920, wax head, wire armature body, by makers such as LaFitte et Desirat and others, usually on wooden base**

11"–14" $500.00–600.00

NORAH WELLINGS

1926 to 1960, Wellington, Shropshire, England. The Victoria Toy Works was founded by Norah Wellings and her brother Leonard. Norah had previously worked as chief designer for Chad Valley. They made cloth dolls with molded heads and bodies of velvet, velveteen, plush, and felt, specializing in sailor souvenir dolls for steamship lines. The line included children, adults, blacks, ethnic, and fantasy dolls.

Baby, molded face, oil-painted features, some papier-mâché covered by stockinette, stitched hip and shoulder joints

10" $275.00–375.00

15" $425.00–600.00

22" $775.00–900.00

15" Norah Wellings, cloth: each $400. **Photo courtesy of Alderfer Auction Company, Inc.**

Child

Painted eyes

12"–14"	$200.00–350.00
16"–18"	$400.00–550.00
22"–23"	$600.00–750.00
26"–28"	$800.00–950.00
33" boy sold at auction for	**$2,124.00**

Glass eye

15"–18"	$800.00–1,100.00
22"–26"	$1,300.00–2,000.00

Characters in uniform, **regional dress, Pixie People, floppy limbed, painted eyes, Mounties, Sailors, Policemen, Scots, others**

8"–10"	$75.00–125.00
13"–14"	$135.00–175.00

Black or Asian

8"–13"	$125.00–175.00
16"–18"	$160.00–240.00

Black Islander, **glass eyes**

13"–14"	$140.00–220.00
16"	$250.00–300.00
28"	$400.00–450.00

Jolly Toddlers

11"	$120.00–180.00

WOODEN

17" wooden, English: sold at auction for $43,360. **Photo courtesy of Morphy Auctions.**

11" tuck comb wooden (so called): $1,200. **Photo courtesy of Morphy Auctions.**

Wooden dolls have been made from the earliest recorded times. During the 1600s and 1700s they became the luxury play dolls of the era. They were made commercially in England, Germany, Switzerland, Russia, United States, and other countries. By the late 1700s and early 1800s inexpensive German wooden dolls were the affordable doll of the masses and were exported worldwide.

English

William & Mary Period, **1690s–1700, carved wooden head, tiny multi-stroke eyebrow and eyelashes, colored cheeks, human hair or flax wig, wooden body, fork-like carved wooden hands, jointed wooden legs, cloth upper arms, medium to fair condition**

15"–22".. $40,000.00–56,000.00

Queen Anne Period, **early 1700s, dotted eyebrows, eyelashes, painted or glass eyes, no pupils, carved oval-shaped head, flat wooden back and hips, nicely dressed, good condition**

14"–18".. $25,000.00–55,000.00

Georgian Period, **1750s–1800, round wooden head, gesso coated, inset glass eyes, dotted eyelashes and eyebrows, human hair or flax wig, jointed wooden body, pointed torso, medium to fair condition**

13"–16".. $8,000.00–12,000.00

18"–25".. $8,000.00–10,000.00

1800–1840, **gesso-coated wooden head, painted eyes, human hair or flax wig, original clothing comes down below wooden legs**

10"–15".. $4,500.00–6,000.00

18"–22".. $4,000.00–5,000.00

Continental European, 18th century, early 19th century, very fine details

5"–6".. $5,000.00–6,000.00

20" Bébé
Tout en Bois,
wooden,
all original,
German: $600.
**Photo courtesy
of Withington
Auction Inc.**

14" wooden,
Swiss: $450.
**Photo courtesy
of Alderfer
Auction
Company**

12"–14"...$6,000.00–9,000.00

25"–32"...$14,000.00–20,000.00

German

1810–1850s, **delicately carved painted hair style, spit curls, some with hair decorations such as "tuck comb," all wooden head and body, pegged or ball-jointed limbs, allow more for exceptional original costume, wooden earrings, sideburn man, etc.**

4½"–9"...$750.00–1,200.00

12"–15"...$1,200.00–1,500.00

17"–18"...$3,500.00–4,000.00

21"...$6,000.00–6,500.00

1850s–1900

All wood with painted plain hair style, **may have spit curls**

1"...$100.00–125.00

4"–5"...$450.00–550.00

6"–8"...$600.00–800.00

14"–17"...$950.00–1,500.00

23"...$2,000.00–2,700.00

Wooden shoulder head, **fancy carved hair style, wood limbs, cloth body**

12"...$800.00–900.00

23"...$1,700.00–2,000.00

Bohemian, **with red painted torso**

8"–10"...$375.00–500.00

14"–16"...$650.00–800.00

1900 on, **turned wooden head, carved nose, painted hair, lower legs with black shoes, peg jointed**

8"–11"...$40.00– $90.00

15" Joel Ellis, Co-operative Manufacturing, Springfield, Vermont, wood: $900. **Photo courtesy of Alderfer Auction Company, Inc.**

5" Peggity, Tynietoy, wood: $900. **Photo courtesy of McMasters Harris Apple Tree Doll Auctions.**

Bébé Tout en Bois, **1900–1914, all-wooden doll made by German firms such as Rudolf Schneider, Schilling, and others, made for the French trade, child or baby, fully jointed body, glass eyes or painted, open mouth. Glass eyes bring higher end of price range.**

9"–13" $375.00–450.00

15"–18" $450.00–525.00

21"–23" $500.00–700.00

Kokeshi, 1900 on, Japan, traditional simple turned wooden dolls made for native and foreign tourist trade, values can be higher for unusual design or known artists.

1850s–1900

7"–14" $900.00–1,000.00

1900–1930

7"–9" $200.00–400.00

1950 to present

7"–9" $35.00–90.00

Matryoskia, Russian Nesting Dolls, 1900, set of wooden canisters that separate in the middle, brightly painted with a glossy finish to represent adults, children, storybook or fairytale characters, and animals. These come in sets usually of five or more related characters, the larger doll opening to reveal a smaller doll nesting inside, and so on, values can be much higher for unusual design, large sets, or known artists.

Set pre 1930s

4" $70.00–100.00

7" $115.00–150.00

9" $175.00–230.00

Set new

5" $12.00–120.00

7" $18.00–150.00

Political set: **Russian, American**

5" $20.00–35.00

7" $50.00–60.00

Swiss, **1900 on, carved wooden dolls with dowel jointed bodies, joined at elbow, hips, knees, examples with elaborate hair bring higher end of values**

> 8"–12".. $300.00–400.00

> 16"–18".. $500.00–700.00

Springfield, VT Woodens

Cooperative Manufacturing Co., 1873–1874, Joel Ellis manufactured wooden dolls with pressed heads and mortise and double tennon joints, with metal hands and feet painted black or blue, painted black molded hair sometimes blond, similar type wooden dolls were made by Jointed Doll Co. under patents by Martin, Sanders, Johnson, Mason & Taylor, a variety of head and jointing styles were used on these dolls.

Ellis, Joel (**Cooperative Manufacturing Co.**)

> 12"... $800.00–900.00

> 15"... $1,000.00–1,200.00

Jointed Doll Co.

> 11½"... $500.00–800.00

Tynietoy, **1917 on, Providence, Rhode Island, sold peg wooden type dolls called Peggity dolls.**

> 5".. $700.00–900.00

Ramp Walker dolls, **early to mid-20th century, such as Wilson Walkies, wooden body characters that walk down an incline**

> 4½" $35.00–50.00

> **Santa, Easter Bunny**........................ $80.00–120.00

Scarey Ann, 1928, push lever raises hair

> $200.00–250.00

Krahmer Dolls, **1947 on, Germany, wooden heads, cloth bodies**

1947–1960s

> 10"–13"... $250.00–$350.00

1970–80s

> 10"–13"... $100.00–$150.00

Schoenhut: See that section

WPA, VARIOUS PROJECTS

1935–1943, Works Progress Administration project to provide work for artisans and home workers. Other states also ran doll making projects under the WPA.

13" Alabama
WPA doll,
cloth: $300.
**Photo courtesy
of Morphy
Auctions.**

Milwaukee, WI project

Molded stockinette doll, **cloth body, cotton yarn hair, painted features, tab hinged joint
and hips**

22".. $800.00–1,200.00

Black $2,700.00–3,000.00

Flat face cloth doll, **embroidered features, cotton yarn hair**

11".. $400.00–425.00

14".. $450.00–500.00

19".. $700.00–800.00

Alabama project, **cloth, painted features, yarn hair**

13".. $300.00–400.00

Papier-mâché doll, **various prohects, dressed in regional or historic costume, often as
matched pair on one stand**

12"–16" .... $500.00–600.00 pair

BIBLIOGRAPHY

Johana Gast Anderton. *20ᵗʰ Century Dolls*. Des Moines: Wallace Homestead Book Co., 1971.

———. *More 20ᵗʰ Century Dolls, Vol. I & II*. Des Moines: Wallace Homestead Book Co., 1974.

———. *The Collector's Encyclopedia of Cloth Dolls*. Lombard: Wallace Homestead Book Co., 1984.

Genevieve Angione and Judith Whorton. *All Dolls Are Collectible*. New York: Crown Publishers, Inc, 1977.

Helen Bullard. *Crafts and Craftsmen of the Tennessee Mountains*. Falls Church: The Summit Press Ltd., 1976.

———. *The American Doll Artist*. Boston: the Charles T. Branford Co., 1965.

———. *The American Doll Artist*. Kansas City: Athens Publishing Co., 1975.

Jurgen and Marianne Cieslik. *German Doll Encyclopedia*. Cumberland: Hobby House Press, 1985.

Dorothy S., Elizabeth A., Evelyn J. Coleman. *The Collector's Encyclopedia of Dolls Vol. I & II*. New York: Crown Publishers, Inc., 1968 & 1986.

———. *The Collector's Book of Dolls' Clothes*. New York: Crown Publishers, Inc., 1975.

Suzanne**Error! Bookmark not defined.** DeMillar & Dennis Brevik. *Arranbee Dolls*. Paducah: Collector Books, 2004.

Linda Edward. *Cloth Dolls From Ancient to Modern*. Atglen: Schiffer Publishing, 1997.

Clara Hallard Fawcett. *Dolls A Guide for Collectors*. New York: H I Lindquist Publications, 1947.

———. *Dolls A New Guide for Collectors*. Boston: Charles T Branford Co., 1964.

Jan Foulke. *The Blue Book of Dolls and Values Vol. 2 through 14*. Cumberland: Hobby House Press, 1976, 1978, 1980, 1982, 1984, 1986, 1987, 1989, 1991, 1993, 1995, 1997, 1999.

Christiane Grafnitz. *German Paper-Mache Dolls 1760–1860*. Germany: Verlag Puppen & Spielzeug 1994.

Judith Izen. *American Character Dolls*. Paducah: Collector Books, 2004.

———. *Collector's Guide to Ideal Dolls*. Paducah: Collector Books, 2005.

Judith Izen & Carol Stover. *Collector's Encyclopedia of Vogue Dolls*. Paducah: Collector Books, 2005.

Flora Gill Jacobs. *Dolls' Houses in America*. New York: Charles Scribner's Sons, 1974.

———. *A History of Dolls' Houses*. New York: Charles Scribner's Sons, 1953.

Don Jensen. *Collector's Guide to Horsman Dolls*. Paducah: Collector Books, 2002.

Janet Pagter Johl. *The Fascinating Story of Dolls*. Watkins Glen, reissued Century House, 1970.

———. *More About Dolls*. New York: H. L. Lundquist Publications, 1946.

———. *Still More About Dolls*. New York: H. L. Lundquist Publications, 1950.

———. *Your Dolls and Mine*. New York: H. L. Lundquist Publications, 1952.

Polly Judd. *Cloth Dolls*. Cumberland: Hobby House Press, 1990.

Pam & Polly Judd. *Americas, Australia & Pacific Islands Costumed Dolls*. Grantsville: Hobby House Press, 1997.

Constance Eileen King. *The Collector's History of Dolls*. New York: Bonanza Books, 1981.

Wendy Lavitt. *American Folk Dolls*. New York: Alfred A. Knopf, Inc., 1982.

Doris Anderson Lechler. *Bleuette her Gautier-Languereau Ads and Catalogues of Fashion 1905–1960*. Self published.

———. *Bleuette — Her Faces, Fashions and Family.* Self published.

Sybill McFadden. *Fawn Zeller's Porcelain Dollmaking Techniques*. Cumberland: Hobby House Press, 1984.

Dorothy McGonagle. *A Celebration of American Dolls*. Grantsville: Hobby House Press, 1997.

Madeline Osborne Merrill. *The Art of Dolls*. Cumberland: Hobby House Press, 1985.

Madeline O. Merrill and Nellie O. Perkins. *Handbook of Collectible Dolls Vol. I.,* 1969.

Ursula Mertz. *Collector's Encyclopedia of Composition Dolls*. Paducah: Collector Books, 1999.

———. *Collector's Encyclopedia of Composition Dolls Vol. II*. Paducah: Collector Books, 2004.

Winifred Mills & Louise Dunn. *The Story of Old Dolls and How to Make New Ones*. New York: Doubleday, Doran & Co., Inc., 1940.

Estelle Patino. *American Rag Dolls*. Paducah: Collector Books, 1988.

Elaine Pardee & Jackie Robertson. *Encyclopedia of Bisque Nancy Ann Storybook Dolls*. Paducah: Collector Books, 2003.

Julie Pelletier Robertson. *Celluloid Dolls, Toys & Playthings*. Paducah: Collector Books, 2006.

Albert Christian Revi. *Spinning Wheel's Complete Book of Dolls*. New York: Galahad Books, 1975.

Lydia Richter. *Treasury of German Dolls*. Tucson: HP Books, 1984.

———. *The Beloved Kathe Kruse Dolls*. Cumberland: Hobby House Press, 1983.

Nancy Schiffer. *Indian Dolls*. Atglen: Schiffer Publishing Ltd., 1997.

Esther Singleton. *Dolls*. New York: Payson & Clark Ltd., 1927.

Eleanor St. George. *The Dolls of Yesterday*. New York and London: Charles Scribner's Sons, 1948.

———. *Dolls of Three Centuries*. New York and London: Charles Scribner's Sons, 1951.

Patricia Smith. *Antique Collector's Dolls Vol. 2*. Paducah: Collector Books, 1976.

Lewis Sorensen. *Lewis Sorensen's Doll Scrapbook*. Alhambra: Thor Publications, 1976.

Sydney Ann Sutton. *Scouting Dolls Through the Years*. Paducah: Collector Books, 2003.

Florence Theiriault. *Catalog Reprint Series*. Annapolis: Gold Horse Publishing, 1998.

Gillian Trotter. *Norah Wellings Cloth Dolls and Soft Toys*. Grantsville: Hobby House Press, 2003.

Joan Van Patton & Linda Lau. *Nippon Dolls & Playthings*. Paducah, Collector Books, 2001.

Blair Whitton. *Bliss Toys and Dollhouses*. New York: Dover Publications.

COLLECTOR RESOURCES

Antique Doll Dealers

Ann Lloyd Antique Dolls
5632 S. Deer Run Rd.
Doylestown, PA 18902
215-794-8164
Website: www.rubylane.com/shops/anntiquedolls

American Beauty Dolls
Nancy Stronczek
26 Bouker Street
Greenfield, Mass. 01301
413-774-3260
E-mail: njs@crocker.com
Website: www.rubylane.com/shops/americanbeautydolls

Aunt Mary's Antique Dolls
PO Box 198
Hawleyville, Ct 06440
203-426-9557
E-mail: mfurse@earthlink.net
Website: www.rubylane.com/shops/auntmarysantiquedolls

Charlotte's Web Vintage Dolls and Collectibles
Charlotte Adams-Scott
Bardstown, KY 40004
Tel: (502) 489-4581
Website: http://www.rubylane.com/shop/
charlottewebcollectible

Connectibles
Maida Webster
47 Buttery Road
New Canaan, Ct. 06840
203-253-1162
Websites: www.connectibles.net
www.buyconnectibles.com

Cybermogul Dolls
Marie Witherill
Statesville, NC 28677
E-mail: cybermogul@roadrunner.com
Website: www.rubylane.com/shops/cybermogul

Decades of Dolls
Rae-Ellen Koenig
848 Dunkels Church Rd
Kutztown, PA 19530-8821
Tel: (610) 894-9882
Website: http://www.rubylane.com/ni/shop/decadesofdolls

Dolls of the Golden Age
Website: http://www.rubylane.com/shop/dollsofthegoldenage

Doll Hugs Shop
Tammy Loranger
Website: http://www.rubylane.com/ni/shop/dollhugsshop
Dolls and Lace
PO Box 743
Lehi, Utah 84043 USA
E-mail: dollsandlace@hotmail.com
Website: www.dollsandlace.com

Dollyology Vintage Dolls
Kate Eaton
15516 Sunken Bridge Rd.
Grass Valley, CA 95949
Website: www.rubylane.com/shops/dollyologyvintagedolls
E-mail:dollyology@gmail.com

Emmie's Antique Doll Castle
Robbin Wilson
400 W. 32nd Court
Sand Springs, OK 74063
918-241-0269
Website: www.rubylane.com/shops/emmiesgirl

Enchantments by Rhonda
Rhonda Waters
3521 Nottingham Drive
Ponca City, OK 74604
580-765-0052
Website: /www.rubylane.com/shop/enchantments

Fourty Fifty Sixty
Ben Cassara/Joe Bucchi
Rutherford NJ 07070
Website: www.fourtyfiftysixty.com
Website: www.rubylane.com/shops/fourtyfiftysixty

Gandtiques
Gary Passamonte /Domenic Vecchioli
E-mail: gpassamonte@icloud.com
Website: www..rubylane.com/shop/gandtiques

Glenda Antique Dolls & Collectables
Gray's Antique Market, 1–7 Davies Mews, London W1K 5AB
Telephone 020 8367 2441 Mobile telephone 07970 722750
E-mail: glenda@glenda-antiquedolls.co.uk
Website: www.glenda-antiquedolls.co.uk

Gloria's Antique Dolls
Gloria & Mike Duddlesten
Website: www.rubylane.com/shop/dollstx
E-mail:dollstx@windstream.net

Hatton's Gallery of Dolls
Website: www.hattonsgallery.com
E-mail: info@hattonsgallery.com

Lynette Gross,
Joan & Lynette Antique Dolls and Accessories
13710 Smokey Ridge Trace
Carmel, IN 46033
Website: www.rubylane.com/shops/joan-lynetteantiquedolls

Joy's Antique Dolls
JoyFrizzell
PO Box 30
Westcliffe, CO 81252-0030
719-783-4500
Website: www.joysantiquedolls.com

Linda Kellermann 11013 Treyburn Drive Glen Allen, VA
23059 E-mail: lindas-antiques@erols.com
Doris Lechler
949 E. Cooke Rd.
Columbus, Ohio 43224
614-261-6659
E-mail: dorislechler@aol.com

Memories of Things Past
Elizabeth Schmahl
Website: www.rubylane.com/shops/memoriesofthingspastantiques

Minton's Doll and Curiosity Shop
Sherry Minton
4035 N. Orange Blossom Trail
Orlando, FL 32804
Tel: (407) 293-3164
Website: http://www.rubylane.com/shop/mintonsdollandcuriosityshop

Museum Doll Shop
104 Van Zandt Ave.
Newport, RI 02840
401-847-6866
Website: www.dollmuseum.com

Joy Macielle
Website: qualityvintagedollpatterns.com
E-mail: joy@qualityvintagedollpatterns.com

My Dear Dolly
PO Box 303
Sparta, NJ 07871
E-mail: mydeardollypat@yahoo.com
Website: mydeardolly.com

My Dolly Dearest
PO Box 909
8 S Village Circle
Adamstown, PA 19501
717-484-1137
E-mail: sidneyjeffrey@mydollydearest.com

N.A.D.D.A.
National Antique Doll Dealers Association
Website: www.nadda.org

Oldeclectics
Carla Thompson
Website: www.rubylane.com

Sara Bernstein's Dolls
Website: www.rubylane.com/shop/sarabernsteindolls
E-mail: santiqbebe@aol.com

Sharing My Dolls & Stuff
Helen Welsh
799 Bent Creek Dr.
Lititz, PA 17543
E-mail: helen1005@aol.com
Website: www.rubylane.com/shops/sharingmydollsnstuff

Sidney's Second Childhood
SidneyBennett
1116 Mistletoe Circle
Hermitage, TN 37076
(615) 883-3637
Website:http://www.rubylane.com/shop/
sidneyssecondchildhood

Terri's Treasures From Above
Terri Viola
Website:http://www.rubylane.com/shop/terristreasures

Trish's Treasures Antique Dolls
Website: www.rubylane.com/shops/antiquedolls

DOLL VALUES

The Doll Works
Judith Armitstead
PO Box 195
Lynnfield, MA 01940
Website: www.TheDollWorks.net

Turn of the Century Antiques
1475 South Broadway
Denver. CO 80210
303-702-8700
Website: www.turnofthecenturyantiques.com

Usefulcollectibles
Marsha Anderson
Liberty MO
816-781-5598

Auction Houses

Alderfer Auction Company, Inc.
Website: www.alderferauction.com
501 Fairgrounds Rd.
Hatfield,PA 19440
215-393-3000
Fax 215-368-9055

McMasters Harris Apple Tree Doll Auctions
1625 W. Church Street
Newark, OH 43055
800-842-3526
E-mail: mark@mcmastersharris.com
Website: www.mcmastersharris.com

Morphy Auctions
2000 N. Reading Rd.
Denver, PA 17517
717-335-3435
Website: morphyauctions.com

Skinner, Inc.
274 Cedar Hill Street
Marlborough, MA 01752
508-970-3232
Website: www.skinnerinc.com

Sweetbriar Auctions
PO Box 37, Earleville, MD 21919
Ph. 410-275-2094
Website: www.sweetbriarauctions.com
E-mail: sweetbriar@live.com

Philip Weiss Auctions
74 Merrick Road
Lynbrook, NY 11563
516-594-0731
Website: www.weissauctions.com
E-mail: info@weissauctions.com

Withington Auction Inc.
17 Atwood Road
Hillsborough, NH 03244
603-478-3232
Website: www.withingtonauction.com
E-mail: withington@conknet.com

Collector Clubs & Newsletters

*United Federation of Doll Clubs, Inc.*10900 North Pomona AvenueKansas City,
MO 64153816-891-7040 Fax 816-891-8360E-mail: ufdcinfo@ufdc.org
Website: www.ufdc.org

Preservation

Light Impressions
100 Carlson Rd
Rochester NY 14610
 1-800-975-6429
Website: www.lightimpressionsdirect.com

Publications

Antique Doll Collector
Keith Kaonis, Advertising & Creative Director
Donna Kaonis, Editor-in-Chief
Puffin Company, LLC
PO Box 239
Northport, NY 11768
888-800-2588
631-261-4100
Fax: 631-261-9684
E-mail: Antiquedoll@gmail.com
Website: www.antiquedollcollector.com
Monthly magazine
https://www.facebook.com/pages/Antique-DOLL-Collector-Magazine/124243334413028

Collectors United
Gary Green, Publisher
PO Box 1160
Chatsworth, GA 30705
706-695-8242
Fax: 706-695-0770
E-mail: diang@collectorsunited.com
Website: www.collectorsunited.com
Monthly newspaper

Contemporary Doll Collector
Ruth Keessen, Publisher and Editor
2145 W. Sherman Blvd
Muskegon, MI 49441
231-755-2000
Fax: 231-755-1003
Website:www.scottpublications.com/catalog/
Subscription information: 800-458-8237 Toll and Outside US: (248) 477-6650
Bi-monthly magazine

Doll Castle News
Barry Mueller, Publisher
Dorita M. Mortensen, Editor
PO Box 601
Broadway, NJ 08808
908-689-4236; 800-572-6607
No Fax
E-mail:editor@dollcastlemagazine.com
E-mail:info@dollcastlemagazine.com
Website: www.dollcastlemagazine.com
Bi-monthly magazine

Doll News
UFDC Corporate Office
10900 N. Pomona Avenue
Kansas City, MO 64153
816-891-7040
Fax: 816-891-8360
Website: www.ufdc.org
Official publication of the United Federation of Doll Clubs, Inc.
Quarterly magazine

Dolls
Joe Jones, Publisher
Carie Ferg, Editor
Jones Publishing, Inc.
N7528 Aanstad Rd, P O Box 5000
Iola, WI 54945-5000
715-445-5000; 800-331-0038
Fax: 715-445-4053
E-mail: jonespub@jonespublishing.com
Website: www.jonespublishing.com

Modern Doll Collectors Convention®

Modern Doll, Inc.
Patsy Moyer, President
21 Swains Pond Avenue
Malden, MA 02148
Phone: 763 634-2614
FAX: 866-343-1225
Website:www. moderndollcollectors.com
registrar patsy@moderndollcollectors.com

Museums

Arizona
Arizona Doll and Toy Museum
Inez McCrary, Director & Curator
602 E Adams Street, Phoenix, AZ
602-253-9337
Hours: Tue–Sat 10–4; Sun: 12–4.
Website: www.artcom.com/museums/nv/af/85004-23.htm

Colorado
Denver Museum of Miniatures, Dolls & Toys
Wendy Littlepage, Director
1880 Gaylord St.
Denver, CO 80206
303-322-1053
Fax: 303-322-3407
Hours: Wed.–Sat. 10–4; Sun.: 1–4. Closed Mondays, Tuesdays and holidays.
E-mail: comments@dmmdt.org
Website: www.dmmdt.org

Missouri
U.F.D.C.
10900 N. Pomona Avenue
Kansas City, MO 64153
816-891-7040
Fax: 816-891-8360
Website: www.ufdc.org

New York
Margaret Woodbury Strong Museum
1 Manhattan Square
Rochester, NY 14607
585-263-2700
Website: thestrong.org; museumofplay.org
M–TH 10–5; FR/SA 10–8; SU 12–5

New Jersey
Princeton Doll and Toy Museum
8 Somerset St.
Hopewell, NJ 08525
609-333-8600
Hours: Mon., Fri. & Sat.10–5
Website: www.princetondollandtoy.org
Virginia B. Aris, Director
Telephone: (609) 333–8600
E-mail: virginiaaris@aol.com

Ohio
Mid Ohio Historical Museum Doll & Toy Museum
700 Winchester Pike
Canal Winchester, Ohio 43110
Hours: Wed–Sat 11–4:30
April–Dec.
Website:www.dollmuseumohio.org
614-837-5573

Utah
McCurdy Historical Doll Museum
246 North 100 East
Provo, UT 84606
801-377-9935
Hours: Tue–Sat, 12–6,
winter: 1–5
Website: www.myjoaquin.tripod.com/sites/dollmuseum

Vermont
Shelburne Museum
6000 Shelburne Rd., PO Box 10
Shelburne, Vermont 05482
802-985-3346
Fax: 802-985-2331
E-mail: info@Shelburnemuseum.org
Hours: May–Oct M–SU
Website: www.shelburnemuseum.org

Wisconsin
The Fennimore Doll & Toy Museum and Gift Shoppe
1135 6th St.
Fennimore, WI 53809
608-822-4100
Hours: May–Oct 10-4
Mon–Sat 10–4
Website:www.dollandtoymuseum.com

Doll Artists

NIADA (National Institute of American Doll Artists)
Website: www.niada.org

ODACA (Original Doll Artist Council of America)
Website: www.odaca.org

SYMBOL INDEX

Square with Heubach
.... Heubach, Gebrüder
Star .... C.M. Bergmann, Heinrich
.... Handwerck, Kley & Hahn
Star with G... Metal Head
Star with MOA....................................... Arnold, Max Oscar
Star with S PBH..................................... Schoenau & Hoffmeister
Stork .... Parsons Jackson
Sunburst .... Heubach, Gebrüder
Triangle with eye................................... Ohlhaver
Triangle with Marque Depose
.... Marque, Albert
Triangle, moon .... Handwerck, Max
Turtle Mark.. Rheinsche Gummi und
.... Celluloid Fabrik Co.
Wings of bird, Holz-Masse .... Cuno, Otto & Dressel
A.C. .... American Character
AHW .... Hülss, Adolph
AM.. Marseille, Armand
AMC.. AverillAmerican Character
BL .... Jumeau Schmidt, Bruno
CB .... Bergner, Carl
CH .... Hartmann, Carl
CMB.. Bergmann, C.M.
COD .... Dressel, Cuno & Otto
CP .... Catterfelder Puppenfabrik
CP .... Pannier
CSFJ .... Chambre Syndicale des
.... Fabricants de Jouets
D .... De Fuisseaux
D&K... Dressel & Koch
Deco .... Effanbee
DIP.. Swaine & Co.
EB .... Barrois,
EED .... Denamure, Etienne
ED .... Danel & Cie
EH .... Heubach, Ernst
EIH .... Horsman
EJ... Jumeau
EJ/A .... Jumeau
F .... De Fuisseaux
F&B .... Effanbee
FG.. Gaultier, Francois
Fre A .... Steiner, Jules
Fre C .... Steiner, Jules
FS&C.. Schmidt, Franz
FY .... Yamato
G&S.. Gans & Seyfarth
GB .... Borgfeldt & Co, George
GK .... Kuhnlenz, Gebr‚der
GKN .... Knoch, Gebr‚der

H	Halopeau, A
HG	Henri & Granfe-Guimonneau
HS	Steiner, Herm
JD	J. DuSerre
JDK	Kestner
K&CO	Kley & Hahn
K&H	Kley & Hahn
K&H	Hertel Schwab & Co.
K&W	Koenig & Wernicke
KH	Hartmann, Karl
KPM	Kʼnigliche Porzellanmanufaktur
KW/G	Koenig & Wernicke
LA&S	Amberg, Louis & Sons
Lori	Swaine & Co.
M&S	Muller & Strasburger
MMM	E. Maar & Sohn
MOA	Arnold, Max Oscar
PAN	Delecroix, Henri
PD	Petit, Frederic & Dumontier, Andre
Petite or Petite Sally	American Character
PM	Porzellanfabrik Mengersgereuth
R&B	Arranbee Doll Co.
RA	Recknagel
RC	Radiguet & Cordonnier
RD	Rabery & Delphieu
Revalo	Ohlhaver, Gebrüder
S&C	Schmidt, Franz
S&H	Simon & Halbig
	Schuetzmeister & Quendt
SCH	Schmitt & Fils
SFBJ	SFBJ
SH	Simon & Halbig
SIC	SociÈtÈ de Celluloid
Sie A	Steiner, Jules
Sie C	Steiner, Jules
SNF	SociÈtÈ Nobel Francaise
SPBH	Schoenau & Hoffmeister
SW	Strobel & Wilkin
U	Uneeda
W&S	Walter & Sohn
XI	Kestner, Heubach

MOLD INDEX

101.................Kämmer & Reinhardt
101.................Schoenhut
102.................Unknown
102.................Kämmer & Reinhardt
102.................Schoenhut
102.................Schuetzmeister & Quendt
103.................Kämmer & Reinhardt
103.................Kestner103   Schoenhut
104.................Kämmer & Reinhardt
104.................Schoenhut
105.................Kämmer & Reinhardt
105.................Schoenhut
106.................Kämmer & Reinhardt
106.................Schoenhut
107.................Kämmer & Reinhardt
107.................Schoenhut
107W.............Schoenhut
108.................Kämmer & Reinhardt
108.................Schoenhut
108W.............Schoenhut
109.................H. Handwerck
109.................Kämmer & Reinhardt
109W.............Schoenhut
110.................Wislizenus
110W.............Schoenhut
111.................Unknown
112.................Kämmer & Reinhardt K‰ommer & Reinhardt
114.................Kämmer & Reinhardt
115.................Kämmer & Reinhardt
115a.............Kämmer & Reinhardt
116.................Belton
116.................Kämmer & Reinhardt
116a.............Kämmer & Reinhardt
116a.............Kämmer & Reinhardt
117.................Belton
117.................Kämmer & Reinhardt K‰ommer & Reinhardt
117N.............K‰ommer & Reinhardt K‰ommer & Reinhardt K‰ommer & Reinhardt
118A.............K‰ommer & Reinhardt
119.................H. Handwerck
119.................K‰ommer & Reinhardt
120.................Belton
120.................Goebel
120.................Gans & Seyfarth Puppenfabrik
121.................Kämmer & Reinhardt
121.................Recknagel
122.................Kämmer & Reinhardt
123.................Kämmer & Reinhardt
123.................Kling
124.................Kämmer & Reinhardt Kling
125.................Belton

185..................Kestner
187..................Kestner
188..................Kestner
188..................Kling
189..................Unknown
189..................H. Handwerck
189..................Kestner
189..................Kling
190..................Belton
190..................Kestner
190..................G. Knoch
191..................K‰ommer & Reinhardt
192..................K‰ommer & Reinhardt G. Knoch
193..................G. Knoch
193..................Belton–type
195..................Kestner
196..................Kestner
199..................H. Handwerck
200..................Arnold, Max Oscar
200..................Catterfelder Puppenfabrik
200..................A. Marseille
200..................Schoenhut
201..................Arnold, Max Oscar
201..................Catterfelder Puppenfabrik
201..................G. Knoch
201..................Schoenhut
201..................Schuetzmeister & Quendt
202..................Kling
202..................Schoenhut
203..................Jumeau
203..................Kestner
203..................G. Knoch
203..................Schoenhut
204..................B‰ohr & Pr^schild
204..................G. Knoch
204..................Schoenhut
204..................Schuetzmeister & Quendt
205..................G. Knoch
205..................Schoenhut
206..................Kestner
206..................G. Knoch
206..................Belton–type
206..................Schoenhut
207..................Catterfelder Puppenfabrik
207..................Schoenhut
208..................Kestner
208..................Catterfelder Puppenfabrik
208..................Walter & Sohn
208..................Jumeau
209..................Catterfelder Puppenfabrik
210..................Catterfelder Puppenfabrik

283.................M. Handwerck
285.................Kestner
285.................M. Handwerck
286.................B‰ohr & Pr^schild
286.................M. Handwerck
289.................B‰ohr & Pr^schild
291.................M. Handwerck
291.................G. Heubach
292.................Kley & Hahn
293.................B‰ohr & Pr^schild
293.................F. Schmidt
297.................B‰ohr & Pr^schild
297.................M. Handwerck
300.................E. Heubach
300.................Schoenhut
300.................Schuetzmeister & Quendt
301.................Unis France
301.................Schoenhut
301.................Schuetzmeister & Quendt
301.................SFBJ
301.................Unis France
302.................Schoenhut
302.................E. Heubach
303.................Schoenhut
304.................Schoenhut
305.................Schoenhut
306.................Jumeau
306.................Schoenhut
307.................M. Handwerck
307.................Schoenhut
308.................Schoenhut
309.................B‰ohr & Pr^schild
309.................Schoenhut
310.................A. Marseille
310.................Schoenhut
311.................Schoenhut
312.................Schoenhut
313.................Schoenhut
314.................Schoenhut
315.................Schoenhut
316.................Schoenhut
317.................Schoenhut
318.................E. Heubach
319.................E. Heubach
320.................E. Heubach
320.................A. Marseille
321.................E. Heubach
322.................E. Heubach
322.................A. Marseille
323.................A. Marseille
325.................B‰ohr & Pr^schild

325..................Borgfeldt
325..................A. Marseille
325..................Kley & Hahn
326..................A. Marseille
327..................Borgfeldt
327..................A. Marseille
328..................Borgfeldt
328..................A. Marseille
329..................Borgfeldt
329..................A. Marseille
330..................Unknown
332..................B‰ohr & Pr^schild
338..................E. Heubach
339..................E. Heubach
340..................B‰ohr & Pr^schild
340..................E. Heubach
341..................A. Marseille
342..................E. Heubach
345..................A. Marseille
348..................E. Heubach
349..................E. Heubach
350..................E. Heubach
350..................A. Marseille
351..................A. Marseille
352..................A. Marseille
353..................A. Marseille
360..................A. Marseille
362..................A. Marseille
369..................Unknown
370..................Kling
370..................A. Marseille
371..................Amberg
372..................Unknown
372..................Kling
372..................A. Marseille
373..................Kling
377..................Kling
379..................B‰ohr & Pr^schild
390..................A. Marseille
391..................Unknown
394..................B‰ohr & Pr^schild
399..................E. Heubach
399..................Heubach K^ppelsdorf
400..................A. Marseille
400..................Schoenhut
401..................K‰ommer & Reinhardt
401..................A. Marseille
401..................Schoenhut
401..................H. Steiner
402..................K‰ommer & Reinhardt
402..................Schoenhut

585.................B‰ohr & Pr^schild
586.................B‰ohr & Pr^schild
587.................B‰ohr & Pr^schild
590.................A. Marseille
600.................Marottes
600.................A. Marseille
600.................Simon & Halbig
602.................Bonn or Kestner
602.................B‰ohr & Pr^schild
604.................B‰ohr & Pr^schild
612.................Bergmann
619.................B‰ohr & Pr^schild
620.................B‰ohr & Pr^schild
620.................A. Marseille
624.................B‰ohr & Pr^schild
630.................Alt, Beck & Gottschalck
630.................B‰ohr & Pr^schild
630.................A. Marseille
639.................Alt, Beck & Gottschalck
639.................Simon & Halbig
640.................A. Marseille
641.................B‰ohr & Pr^schild
642.................B‰ohr & Pr^schild
678.................B‰ohr & Pr^schild
680.................Kley & Hahn
686.................B‰ohr & Pr^schild
698.................Alt, Beck & Gottschalck
700.................A. Marseille
700.................K‰ommer & Reinhardt
701.................A. Marseille
701.................K‰ommer & Reinhardt
711.................A. Marseille
715.................K‰ommer & Reinhardt
717.................K‰ommer & Reinhardt
719.................Simon & Halbig
720.................Simon & Halbig
728.................Kämmer & Reinhardt
729.................Simon & Halbig
739.................Simon & Halbig
740.................Simon & Halbig Simon & Halbig A. Marseille
758.................Simon & Halbig Simon & Halbig Simon & Halbig K‰ommer & Reinhardt K‰ommer & Reinhardt
784.................Alt, Beck & Gottschalck
790.................Bonn or Kestner
790.................A. Marseille
791.................Bonn or Kestner
792.................Bonn or Kestner
800.................A. Marseille
830.................Unknown
833.................Unknown
852.................Simon & Halbig

870.................Alt, Beck & Gottschalck
880.................Alt, Beck & Gottschalck
881.................Simon & Halbig
886.................Simon & Halbig
890.................Simon & Halbig Alt, Beck & Gottschalck
900.................A. Marseille
905.................Simon & Halbig Simon & Halbig Alt, Beck & Gottschalck
912.................Alt, Beck & Gottschalck
914.................Schoenau & Hoffmeister
915.................Alt, Beck & Gottschalck
916.................Alt, Beck & Gottschalck
919.................Simon & Halbig
927.................A. Marseille
927.................F. Schmidt
927.................Simon & Halbig Simon & Halbig
938.................Alt, Beck & Gottschalck
939.................Simon & Halbig
940.................Simon & Halbig Simon & Halbig
950.................P.M.
950.................Simon & Halbig
966.................A. Marseille
969.................Simon & Halbig
970.................A. Marseille
971.................A. Marseille
972.................Amberg, Louis & Sons
973.................Amberg, Louis & Sons
974.................Alt, Beck & Gottschalck
975.................A. Marseille
979.................Simon & Halbig
980.................A. Marseille
982.................Amberg, Louis & Sons
983.................Amberg, Louis & Sons
984.................A. Marseille
985.................A. Marseille
990.................Alt, Beck & Gottschalck
990.................A. Marseille
991.................A. Marseille
992.................A. Marseille
995.................A. Marseille
996.................A. Marseille
1000.................Alt, Beck & Gottschalck
1005.................AverillG.
1006.................Amusco Alt, Beck & Gottschalck
1009.................Simon & Halbig
1010.................Simon & Halbig
1019.................Simon & Halbig
1020.................Muller & Strasburger
1028.................Alt, Beck & Gottschalck
1029.................Simon & Halbig
1032.................Alt, Beck & Gottschalck
1039.................Simon & Halbig

1040...............Simon & Halbig
1044...............Alt, Beck & Gottschalck
1046...............Alt, Beck & Gottschalck
1049...............Simon & Halbig
1059...............Simon & Halbig
1064...............Alt, Beck & Gottschalck
1069...............Simon & Halbig
1070...............Koenig & Wernicke
1070...............Kestner
1078...............Simon & Halbig
1079...............Simon & Halbig
1080...............Simon & Halbig
1099...............Simon & Halbig
1100...............Catterfelder Puppenfabrik
1109...............Simon & Halbig Alt, Beck & Gottschalck
1123...............Alt, Beck & Gottschalck
1127...............Alt, Beck & Gottschalck
1129...............Simon & Halbig
1142...............Alt, Beck & Gottschalck
1159...............Simon & Halbig Simon & Halbig
1170...............Simon & Halbig
1180...............F. Schmidt
1199...............Simon & Halbig
1200...............Catterfelder Puppenfabrik
1210...............Alt, Beck & Gottschalck
1222...............Alt, Beck & Gottschalck
1234...............Alt, Beck & Gottschalck
1235...............Alt, Beck & Gottschalck
1246...............Simon & Halbig
1248...............Simon & Halbig
1249...............Simon & Halbig
1250...............Simon & Halbig
1253...............F. Schmidt
1254...............Alt, Beck & Gottschalck
1256...............Alt, Beck & Gottschalck
1259...............F. Schmidt
1260...............Simon & Halbig
1262...............F. Schmidt
1263...............F. Schmidt
1266...............F. Schmidt
1267...............F. Schmidt
1269...............Simon & Halbig
1270...............F. Schmidt
1271...............F. Schmidt
1272...............Simon & Halbig
1272...............F. Schmidt
1279...............imon & Halbig
1288...............Alt, Beck & Gottschalck
1294...............Simon & Halbig
1299...............Simon & Halbig Simon & Halbig
1303...............Simon & Halbig

1304...............Alt, Beck & Gottschalck
1304...............Simon & Halbig
1305...............Simon & Halbig
1308...............Simon & Halbig
1310...............F. Schmidt
1322...............Alt, Beck & Gottschalck
1329...............Simon & Halbig
1339...............Simon & Halbig
1342...............Alt, Beck & Gottschalck
1346...............Alt, Beck & Gottschalck
1348...............Cuno & Otto Dressel
1349...............Cuno & Otto Dressel
1352...............Alt, Beck & Gottschalck
1357...............Alt, Beck & Gottschalck
1357...............Catterfelder Puppenfabrik
1358...............Alt, Beck & Gottschalck
1358...............Simon & Halbig
1361...............Alt, Beck & Gottschalck
1362...............Alt, Beck & Gottschalck
1367...............Alt, Beck & Gottschalck
1368...............Alt, Beck & Gottschalck
1368...............Averill, G.
1368...............Simon & Halbig
1376...............Schuetzmeister & Quendt
1388...............Simon & Halbig
1394...............Unknown
1394...............Borgfeldt
1402...............AverillG.
1428...............Simon & Halbig
1448...............Simon & Halbig
1469...............Simon & Halbig
1478...............Simon & Halbig
1488...............Simon & Halbig
1489...............Simon & Halbig
1498...............Simon & Halbig
1890...............A. Marseille
1892...............A. Marseille
1893...............A. Marseille
1894...............A. Marseille
1897...............A. Marseille
1898...............A. Marseille
1899...............A. Marseille
1900...............E. Heubach
1900...............A. Marseille
1901...............A. Marseille
1902...............A. Marseille
1903...............A. Marseille
1906...............Schoenau & Hoffmeister
1907...............Recknagel
1909...............Schoenau Hoffmeister
1909...............A. Marseille

1909................Recknagel
1909................Schoenau & Hoffmeister
1912................A. Marseille
1912................Cuno & Otto Dressel
1914................A. Marseille
1914................Cuno & Otto Dressel
1914................Recknagel
1916................Simon & Halbig Recknagel
2015................Muller & Strasburger
2020................Muller & Strasburger
2023................B‰ohr & Pr^schild
2023................B. Schmidt
2033................B. Schmidt
2048................B. Schmidt
2052................B. Schmidt
2072................B‰ohr & Pr^schild
2072................B. Schmidt
2092................B. Schmidt
2094................B. Schmidt
2095................B. Schmidt
2096................B. Schmidt
2097................B. Schmidt
2500................Schoenau & Hoffmeister
3200................Marottes
3200................A. Marseille
3841................G. Heubach
4000................Schoenau & Hoffmeister
4515................Muller & Strasburger
4600................Schoenau & Hoffmeister
4700................Marottes
4700................Schoenau & Hoffmeister
4900................Schoenau & Hoffmeister
4900................Schoenau & Hoffmeister
5000................Schoenau & Hoffmeister
5500................Schoenau & Hoffmeister
5636................G. Heubach
5689................G. Heubach
5700................Schoenau & Hoffmeister
5730................G. Heubach
5777................G. Heubach
5800................Schoenau & Hoffmeister
6688................G. Heubach
6692................G. Heubach
6736................G. Heubach
6894................G. Heubach
6897................G. Heubach
6969................G. Heubach
6970................G. Heubach
6971................G. Heubach
7246................G. Heubach
7247................G. Heubach

7248................G. Heubach
7268................G. Heubach
7287................G. Heubach
7345................G. Heubach
7407................G. Heubach
7602................G. Heubach
7603................G. Heubach
7604................G. Heubach
7622................G. Heubach
7623................G. Heubach
7644................G. Heubach
7657................G. Heubach
7658................G. Heubach
7661................G. Heubach
7668................G. Heubach
7671................G. Heubach
7681................G. Heubach
7686................G. Heubach
7711................G. Heubach
7759................G. Heubach
7847................G. Heubach
7850................G. Heubach
7911................G. Heubach
7925................G. Heubach
7926................G. Heubach
7972................G. Heubach
7975................G. Heubach
7977................G. Heubach
8191................G. Heubach
8192................G. Heubach
8221................G. Heubach
8316................G. Heubach
8381................G. Heubach
8413................G. Heubach
8420................G. Heubach
8429................G. Heubach
8552................Unknown
8556................G. Heubach
8661................Limbach
8676................G. Heubach
8682................Limbach
8686................G. Heubach
8723................G. Heubach
8764................G. Heubach
8774................G. Heubach
8819................G. Heubach
8950................G. Heubach
8995................G. Heubach
9027................G. Heubach
9055................G. Heubach
9056................G. Heubach

9355................G. Heubach
9457................G. Heubach
9573................G. Heubach
9578................G. Heubach
9693................G. Heubach
9743................G. Heubach
9746................G. Heubach
10532..............G. Heubach
11010..............G. Heubach
10016..............Unknown
11173..............G. Heubach
15509..............Unknown
22674..............Unknown

MARKS INDEX

Alabama Baby

Alabama Indestructible Dolls Marks:
"MRS. S.S. SMITH//MANUFACTURER AND
DEALER IN//THE ALABAMA
INDESTRUCTIBLE DOLL//ROANOKE, ALA.//
PATENTED//SEPT. 26, 1905."

Henri Alexandre

Alt, Beck, & Gottschalck

Arranbee Doll Company

ARRANBEE//DOLL
Co. or R & B

Max Oscar Arnold

Art Fabric Mills

Art Fabric Mills Marks:
'ART FABRIC MILLS, NY,
PAT. FEB. 13TH, 1900" on
shoe or bottom of foot

Georgene Averill

Tag on original outfit reads:
"BONNIE BABE COPYRIGHTED
BY GEORGENE AVERILL MADE
BY K AND K TOY CO."

COPR GEORGENE AVERILL
1005/3652 GERMANY

Bä hr & Pröschild

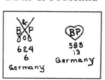

Marks Index

Barbie*

1659 - 1962
BARBIE™
PATS. PEND.
©MCMLVIII
BY//MATTEL, INC.

1963 - 1968
MIDGE™©1962
Barbie/©1958*
BY//MATTEL, INC.

1964 - 1966
©1958//MATTEL, IN.
U.S. PATENTED
U.S. PAT. PEND.

1966 - 1969
©1966//MATTEL, INC.
U.S. PATENTED//
U.S. PAT. PEND//
MADE IN JAPAN

E. Barrois

E 3 B
E. 8 DEPOSE B.

C.M. Bergmann

C. M. B
SIMON & HALBIG
Eleonore

Bru

Fashion-Type Mark:
Marked "A" through "M," "II" to
"28," indicating size numbers only.

Bru Jne Marks:
"BRU JNE." with size number on
head, kid over wood body marked
with rectangular paper label.

Bru Jne R. Marks:
"BRU JNE FL" with size number on
head, body stamped in red, "Bébé
Bru," and size number.

Bebe Brevete Marks:
"Bébé Brevete."
Head marked with size number
only; kid body may have paper
Bébé Brevete label.

Bye-Lo Baby

© 1923 by
Grace S. Putnam
MADE IN GERMANY
7372 145

Marks Index

Catterfelder Puppenfabrik

C. P.
208/34 S
Deponiert

1100
Catterfelder Puppenfabrik
2

Century Doll Company

CENTURY DOLL C°.
Kestner Germany

Chuckles mark on back:
'CHUCKLES//A
CENTURY DOLL"

Chase Doll Company

"CHASE STOCKINET DOLL"
on left leg or under left arm.
Paper label, if there, reads
"CHASE//HOSPITAL DOLL//
TRADE MARK//PAWTUCKET,
RI//MADE IN U.S.A."

M. J. C.
Stockinet Doll
Patent Applied For

Chase doll mark,
1889 - 1894

PAWTUCKET, R.I.

Chase doll mark,
1908 - 1945

Columbian

"COLUMBIAN DOLL,
EMMA E. ADAMS,
OSWEGO, NY"

Marks Index

Danel & Cie

E. (Size number) D. on head,
Eiffel Tower "PARIS BEBE"
on body; shoes with "PARIS
BEBE" in star.

Cuno & Otto Dressel

E.D.

EDEN BEBE
PARIS

Eegee

Trademark, EEGEE,
or circle with the words,
"TRADEMARK//EEGEE//
Dolls//MADE IN USE"

Later changed to just
initials, E.G.

Effanbee

Some marked on shoulder
plate, "EFFANBEE//BABY
DAINTY"
or "EFFANBEE//DOLLS//
WALK, TALK, SLEEP"
in oval

Fulper Pottery Company

Marks Index

Gans & Seyfarth Puppenbabrik

François Gaultier

Gesland

Ruth Gibbs

Gladdie

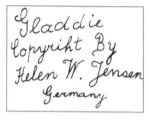

Wm. and F. & W. Goebel

Ludwig Greiner

Marks Index

Gund

"A Gund Product, A Toy of
Quality and Distinction."

From World War II on: Stylized "G"
with rabbit ears and whiskers.

Mid 1960s - 1987: Bear's head
above the letter "U."

From 1987 on: "GUND."

Heinrich Handwerck

HANDWERCK
5
Germany

Max Handwerck

Max Handwerk
Bebe Elite
286/3
Germany

283/28.5
MAJC.
HANDWERCK
GERMANY.
2¼

Carl Hartman

Globe Baby
DEP
Germany
C 3 H

Marks Index

Karl Hartman

Hasbro

1964 - 1965
*Marked on right
lower back:
G.I. Joe TM//COPYRIGHT 1964//
BY HASBRO//PATENT PENDING//
MADE IN U.S.A.//GIJoe"*

1967
*Slight change in marking:
COPYRIGHT 1964//BY HASBRO
//PATENT PENDING//MADE IN
U.S.A.//GIJoe"
This mark appears on all four
armed service branches, excluding
the black action figures.*

Hertel, Schwab & Company

Ernst Heubach

Gebrüder Heubach

E.I. Horsman

*"E.I.H.//CO."
and "CAN'T
BREAK'EM"*

Marks Index

Mary Hoyer Doll Manufacturing Company

"THE MARY HOYER
DOLL" or
'ORIGINAL MARY
HOYER DOLL"

Adolph Hülss

Ideal Novelty
and Toy Company

"IDEAL" (in a diamond), "US
of A; IDEAL NOVELTY," and
"TOY CO. BROOKLYN, NEW
YORK," and others

Jumeau

E.J. Bébé
1881 - 86
6
E.J.

Jumeau, early EJ mark
1881 - 1883

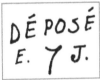

Jumeau, EJ Déposé mark
1883 - 1886

DÉPOSÉ
TETE JUMEAU
B^{TE} SGDG
6

Jumeau, mark used on body
after 1887

JUMEAU
MEDAILLE D'OR
PARIS

Tété Jumeau mark

539

Marks Index

Kamkins

Kämmer & Reinhardt

J.D. Kestner

Kewpie

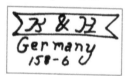

Kley & Hahn

C.F. Kling & Company

Marks Index

Gebrüder Knoch	Lanternier

König & Wernicke	Lenci
Richard Krueger	A.G. Limbach
"KRUEGER NY//REG. U.S. PAT. OFF// MADE IN U.S.A." on body or clothing seam	
Käthe Kruse	
Gebrüder Kuhnlenz	

Marks Index

Armand Marseille

> Armand Marseille
> Germany
> 390
> A. 4. M.

> Queen Louise
> Germany
> 7.

> Made in Germany
> Florodora
> A 5 M

May Freres Cie

On head:
MASCOTTE
On body:
Bebe Mascotte Paris
Child marked:
Mascotte on head

Morimura Brothers

Mark for Morimura Brothers,
Japan 1915 on

Gebrüder Ohlhaver

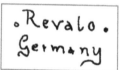

Petite et Dumontier

P 3 D

Rabery & Delphieu

Mark: R. 3. D

Theodor Recknagel

Marks Index

Rohmer

Bruno Schmidt

Franz Schmidt

Schmitt & Fils

Shield on back: "SCH" in
shield on bottom of
flat-cut derriere

Schoenau & Hoffmeister

A. Schoenhut & Company

Marks Index

Schuetzmeister & Quendt

S.F.B.J.

Shirley Temple

Shirley Temple//
IDEAL Nov. & TOY on
back of head and
SHIRLEY TEMPLE on
body. Some marked
only on head and
with a size.

Simon & Halbig

1079
HALBIG
S&H
Germany

S×H. 1249
DEP
Germany
SANTA

Germany
SH 13-1010 DEP.

Margarete Steiff

Button in ear

Hermann Steiner

Made in
Germany
HermSteiner
18
0

Marks Index

Swaine & Company

Unis France

Unis France mark

A. Thuillier

Unis France diamond mark

Louis Wolfe & Company

$$152$$
$$L.W.\&C?$$
$$12$$

INDEX

H

Hagara, Jan 210
Hale, Patti 66
Half Dolls 240
Half Pint 210
Hallmark 228, 270
Halopeau 116
Handwerck, Heinrich 126, 242
Handwerck, Max 140, 233, 243
Hanna 434
Hansel & Gretel 272
Hansen, Cathy 66
Happifats 44, 48
Happinus 51
Happy 22
Happy Birthday Doll 202
Happy Boy 210
Happy Days 376
Happy Hooligan 278
Hard Plastic 244
Hardy Boys 311
Harmonica Joe 201
Harmony 289
Harriet Hubbard Ayer 289
Harry Potter 239
Hartmann, Carl 247
Hartmann, Karl 248
Hartmann, Sonja 69
Hasbro 248
Haut Melton 66
Head Kane, Maggie 67
Heath, Phillip 69
HEbee, SHEbee 44, 268, 272
Heidi 419
Heizer, Dorothy 66
Heller, Karin 69
Hello Dolly 419
Her Highness 416
Herman Munster 369
Hermans Hermits 250
Herm Steiner 133
Hertel & Schwab 255
Hertel &Schwab 231
Hertwig 45, 46, 122, 141, 231
Hertwig & Co 257
Heubach, Ernst 43, 126, 234, 258
Heubach, Gebruder 127, 140, 234, 259
Heubach, Gebrüder 75
Hiawatha 416
Hibel, Edna 210

Highbrow china 169
Hilda 121, 129, 184, 318
Himstedt, Annette 69
Hina Matsuri 78
Historical Dolls 203
Historical Replicas 203
Hitt, Oscar 235
Ho-Ho 154
Hol-Le Toy 174
Holly Hobbie 333
Holz-Masse 191
Honey 197, 203, 210, 227
Honeybun 23
Honeybunch 289
Honeymoon 289
Honey Walker 211
Honey West 225
Hopalong Cassidy 290
Horsman 10, 12, 13, 43, 54, 71, 77, 84,
112, 136, 146, 150
Horsman, E.I. 265
Hotpoint Devil 12
Hottentot 327
Howdy Doody 198, 287, 290
Hoyer, Mary 274
Hug A Bug 419
Hug A Bunch 311
Huggums 23
Hug Me Kids 238
Hulss, Adolph 275
Humpty Dumpty 211
Huret 276

I

Iacono, Maggie 70
Ice Queen 203
Ichimatsu 78
Ideal 11, 13, 111, 112, 136, 138, 213,
279, 294, 388, 417, 446
Ideal Novelty & Toy Co 277
I Love Lucy Baby 56
Ilya Kuryakin 225
Immobiles 46
Imperial Crown Toy Co. 245
International Velvet 311
Irish Mail Kid 201
Izannah Walker 486

T

ABOUT THE AUTHOR

Linda Edward has been collecting and dealing in antique, vintage, and contemporary dolls since 1976. From 1987 to 2005, she exhibited a collection of more than 18,000 dolls at The Doll Museum in Newport, RI, where she lives with her husband, Al. She has mounted numerous special doll exhibits for museums, collector associations, and libraries. she works toady providing collections consultation, appraisal, and doll repair services.

A lover of doll research she has contributed numerous articles to publications including, Doll News, Antique Doll Collector, Doll Reader, Contemporary Doll Collector, Dolls, Nutshell News, and other doll related journals and served as editor of Doll News, the official magazine of The United Federation of Doll clubs, Inc. (UFDC). She is a two time winner of the prestigious UFDC Award of Excellence, is a Past President of the Doll Collectors of America, Inc. (DCA), and a Past President of UFDC.

Author of Cloth Dolls Ancient To Modern, she took over the authorship of Doll Values, previously authored by Patsy Moyer and originally published by Collector Books, with the Ninth Edition, which was published in 2007.

CPSIA information can be obtained
at www.ICGtesting.com
Printed in the USA
LVHW011417030119
602607LV00033B/410/P